"WHO ARE YOU, BOY? WHO ARE YOU?"

Her face was half in light and half in shadow, but her eyes I could see, and they were watching.

"I am a soothsayer," she said. "Now give me your hand." I gave it without resistance. She turned the palm up and rubbed it with her thumb before tracing lines with a fingertip. Her eyebrows rose and creased with puzzlement. She peered closer, spreading my palm wide as if it would open up another chapter to her glance. "You are—you are the eye of the storm. You do not create the storm and yet it swirls about you."

She continued tracing, and then there was surprise in her face. "I see many people, many places. I see high places, and low. I see battle. I see blood. I see—"

She let go of my hand as if it were a rattlesnake, and in the uncertain lamplight her red face paled.

The Chronicles of Scar

RON SARTI

AVON BOOKS • NEW YORK

Dedicated to L. Sprague de Camp, Robert A. Heinlein, and Walter M. Miller, Jr.

And with sincere thanks to Odile, Ken, Eileen, and all who lent encouragement and support

THE CHRONICLES OF SCAR is an original publication of Avon Books. This work has never before appeared in book form. This work is a novel. Any similarity to actual persons or events is purely coincidental.

AVON BOOKS
A division of
The Hearst Corporation
1350 Avenue of the Americas
New York, New York 10019

Copyright © 1996 by Ron Sarti
Front cover art by Greg Call
Published by arrangement with the author
Library of Congress Catalog Card Number: 95-94630
ISBN: 0-380-77939-0

First AvoNova Printing: January 1996

AVONOVA TRADEMARK REG. U.S. PAT. OFF. AND IN OTHER COUNTRIES, MARCA REGISTRADA, HECHO EN U.S.A.

Printed in the U.S.A.

RA   10   9   8   7   6   5   4   3   2   1

Contents

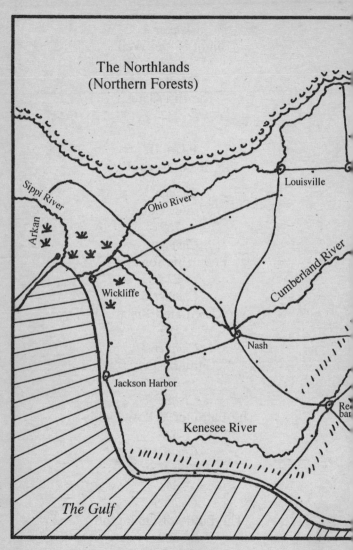

Map of Kenesee
2652 A.D.

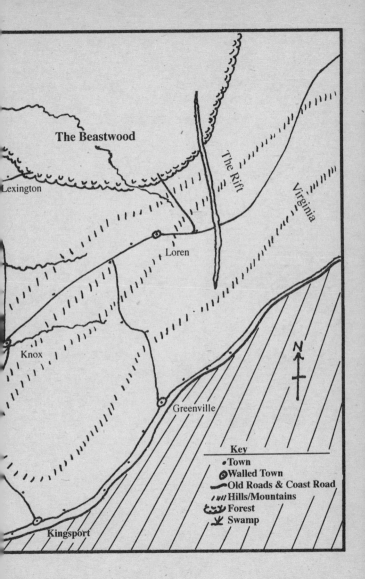

Prologue

Rite of Manhood

"Now, Arn," said King Reuel, putting an arm around my shoulder. "Are you sure you know what to do?"

I nodded. Certainly I knew what to do. I listen very carefully when my life is at stake. Knowing was not a problem.

Doing was the problem.

We moved aside as the wagon driver unhitched his team and led the horses past us, their tails swishing futilely at the flies and gnats. What with the king's advisors, representatives of the noble houses, and a score of royal guards clustered around the wagon, our party filled the available ground. We were on a narrow finger of dry land extending into the Great Swamp that bordered the mouth of the Ohio River just before it emptied into the Gulf.

The coast road was to the west. We had come up it three days before. It was not an Old World road like most of the other main routes in Kenesee, but much of it was paved with flat chunks of white crete salvaged from the ruins. The causeway we were on was little used, an old track that might have had a purpose before the Cataclysm, but now turned off eastward and stretched into the swamp for uncounted miles. I imagine it eventually sank into the heart of the muck.

Our site was carefully selected. The dense foliage fell off on both sides at this point, the grassy causeway running between two wide, shallow pools that burped the occasional bubble of gas from the volcanic depths that warmed the swamps. There should be no surprises—if I stayed reasonably alert—

and I'd have a clear shot with the bow at my trophy. Anything approaching would have to wade across twenty yards of open space to get to me.

I suppose I should have been comforted by the thought.

"Stay near the wagon," the king continued, the rest of the entourage listening respectfully and some nodding in agreement. "Dinosaurs look slow, but they're not. When you spot your trophy, be content with getting one arrow into him. The beast will go for the bait before you, and that will give you time to get your spear and ground it properly. Then be patient. Let the beast impale itself a few times. Wait until it's weakened to bring it down."

"Yes, sir," I reassured him, a headache beginning to pound away inside my skull as my heart thumped in my chest. "I'll be all right."

"And be content with a man-sized creature. If anything larger comes along, just use the cage and wait till it wanders off."

Content? I'd have been content with going home there and then.

My brother Robert looked on from horseback with a smile. "Just watch out for deinonychus," he warned pleasantly, the bandage over his slinged arm giving ample evidence to his words. "They're fast. I was lucky there was only one."

"That is correct," added Professor Wagner, fulfilling his role of Head Instructor. He was an arrogant little man who had accumulated a great deal of knowledge and never done anything with it, except pass on doses of undiluted facts to his students without analysis. And perhaps that was just as well.

"The dromaeosaurids usually hunt in small packs, although members do make excursions of their own, as occurred yesterday. The forelimbs of deinonychus, as you saw on Robert's trophy, are quite formidable, and the long spear is therefore the best weapon against a creature of this sort. Don't hesitate to seek safety in the cage if there are more than one. That will be your only hope against a pack. However, they do like to keep moving, and it's quite likely that they are far from here by now. I doubt that you'll encounter any of them today."

That would be a blessing. The dromaeosaurids were considered some of the most dangerous beasts in the swamp, primarily because they hunted in packs. Deinonychus was the largest of the lot, growing to six feet tall and over three hundred pounds of bone and sinew. Besides a mouthful of inch-long teeth, it boasted an array of claws that worked most convincingly on chain mail, leather, and flesh.

In all honesty, I had no desire to encounter one of these hungry nightmares, and cursed the Old World for resurrecting the whole nasty lot. Obviously, the Cataclysm had not come soon enough. They weren't content with growing mammoths and sabertooths for their zoos. They had to bumble into the Jurassic and Triassic for variety.

Professor Wagner reviewed what he had already drummed into Robert and me with his drawings and charts in our classroom. "Any reasonably man-sized carnivore would be acceptable as a trophy, as well as those herbivores known for their aggressiveness, such as the ceratopids." While Robert had expressed his hopes for a fierce meat-eater with teeth and claws enough to satisfy any trophy hunter, I'd kept my tongue. I couldn't admit aloud that I wanted nothing more than to survive, and would gladly accept a plant-eater, preferably a sick one that would fall dead before it could charge.

Robert had gotten his wish. His vigil had started at dawn the day before, and by late afternoon we'd heard the single blast of his horn signaling that he'd taken his trophy. We rode forward to join him, and true to form there was Robert, standing proudly over the fallen beast. Once mounted, it would be one of the finest heads on the trophy wall.

Everyone expected Robert to do something like that, of course. He would, quite naturally, do all the right things. A well-placed arrow, resolute combat with the beast, and then the finish. Even with an arm broken by the slash of its tail, Robert had cut down the creature. By the time we arrived at the site he'd already hacked the head from its body and held it aloft in his one good hand, receiving a roar of approval from everyone in the party.

And now it was my turn.

A guardsman uncorked a large earthenware jug and, holding it at arm's length, emptied the contents in a glop a dozen paces from the wagon. The fetid smell of the swamp was immediately enhanced with a sickening odor of rotting fish and rancid meat guaranteed to interest any roaming predator or scavenger within a mile. How helpful. I considered putting an arrow through the guardsman.

The king nodded in the direction of the royal herald, who took a scroll out of its case. Voices faded until I was surrounded by a score of silent faces, pale and tan and brown. The herald cleared his throat with a harumpf, opened his mouth to speak, and instead spat out a large fly that had flown in.

He tried again. "To all citizens of Kenesee, and to all friends of the kingdom, let it be known that on this day, June 16 in the year 613 Anno Cataclysmos, or 2649 Anno Domini, that Arn of Kenesee does hereby embark on the Rite of Manhood as established by King Hobart the Just in the year. . . ." He went on like that for a while, explaining the need to test the courage of princes, the honor of the rite, the distinction of the royal line, and other such nonsense. The dutiful silence wasn't broken until the final word was spoken and the scroll was returned to its case.

"Well. It's time to leave you," the king said, lines of concern written on his face. The same lines had appeared the day before when we left Robert, and the dark circles under the king's eyes evidenced sleepless nights. "You'll do fine," he added, perhaps more to himself than to me. He gave me an embrace that I could feel even through the leather and chain mail I wore, and then he mounted.

"Sergeant Black, is all in order?"

The sergeant had been clambering over the wagon, carefully inspecting its equipment. "Yes, sir. All in order."

"Fine. Then we're off." With a last look at me, the king led the party of dignitaries and guards to their horses and set off at a slow trot down the causeway.

Sergeant Black was the last. He swung from the wagon onto his horse, reined in close, and leaned over. "Nervous, son?"

Of course not. I enjoy risking my life before breakfast. "Yes," I admitted.

"Good." Black said grimly. The same lines of concern seemed to be on his face too. "Remember, the odds are in your favor if you stay calm."

That might be so. At the castle, the trophy wall held the heads of thirteen reptiles taken by the various princes of the realm over the last two hundred years, and a greater collection of toothed horrors could not be found. Not bad for a bunch of sixteen-year-old boys. And of the thirteen princes who took their trophies and became men, most were not adversely affected by this rite of manhood, except for Randall One-Eye and Eric the Lame. But the wall also held the portraits of six boys who did not come back from their rite.

"Stay alert," Sergeant Black continued. "That'll be hard to do after a few hours when the day heats up, but do it anyway. They get you when you're not looking."

He pointed at the wagon. "Use the ballista and the cage if you have to. Don't worry about honor if the odds are too high. But don't run away! You'll be easy meat if you do."

I nodded, and the headache burst inside my skull.

"One last thing. See the bait they spilled there to attract the predators? The beast will go for the bait before it goes for you, even if you've already put an arrow into it. You let the reptile have as much of it as it wants."

"Why?" I asked, puzzled.

"Never mind. Just let it eat. After it's done it'll notice you, and then worry about killing the damn thing."

My strategy would have been to get in a few jabs with the spear while the creature was licking the causeway clean for snack time. Maybe not honorable, perhaps, but safer. Still, Black had never given me bad advice.

"I'll remember that. By the way, Sergeant, you didn't happen to bring one of the weapons displayed at the museum, did you?"

"Those are against the Codes, son. Besides, they'd probably kill you instead of the beast. They haven't been fired in centuries."

"Ah, well. Just a little joke," I said regretfully.

"Of course." He looked at me intently, and his hand reached down to grip my shoulder. "You'll do all right. Believe me."

He rode off to catch up to the others.

And I was alone.

Well, not quite alone. I was kept company by swarms of flies and gnats which, deprived of horse flesh, found the glop and my skin reasonable substitutes. The sun rose in the sky, the temperature climbed, and sweat began to drip off my face, irritating the gnats that had been feasting there. Leather and chain mail make the finest steam bath known to man. Actually, we used chain mail only rarely, as most felt leather armor to be the best trade-off in protection and mobility. But the rite had its little traditions that had to be observed. I paced around, staying right next to the wagon, and waited.

And waited. At first I stood at the ready, with bow in hand and an arrow nocked. After perhaps an hour my hand threatened to cramp, so I took the arrow and just held it next to the bow. Another hour and I laid the bow next to me on the wagon and began to stretch and bend to overcome the stiffness in my limbs.

The sun moved across the sky until it was almost overhead, and I took food and drink from a basket in the wagon. I gulped the liquid down but, to my amazement, found I had no appetite for solid food. My stomach, which had already been churning for the last twenty-four hours in anticipation of this glorious event, had gradually tightened into a knot as the hours went by and the inevitable contest was delayed. My head continued to pound and although sweat poured off me freely, my hands were cold.

There are many variations of fear, as I know from personal experience. My fear during this wait was pervasive, but it was not terror. No, terror is an experience of the moment. Fear is the anticipation, terror the reality. But the problem with fear is that it can go on and on and on, like a nagging toothache. And when it ends. . . .

A nosy muskrat emerged from the underbrush and climbed onto the causeway, looked my way, and trotted forward cautiously. It came near, sniffed the dinosaur bait, then took a few tentative licks and gulped a small piece of the glop. Suddenly losing interest, it wandered over to the water's edge, lay down, and died. I walked over for a closer inspection, nudged the muskrat with my toe, and confirmed its status. It was most thoroughly dead.

The knot in my stomach unwound itself, the pounding in my head stopped, and my hands began to warm up. The vague beginning of an appetite stirred.

A good man, Sergeant Black. Practical.

*   *   *

I managed to eat, then stretched my limbs and gave a contented sigh. It was turning out to be a tolerable day after all. I checked the weapons wagon to make sure all was in readiness, examining the devices that had been included to put the odds in my favor. The racks held bows and arrows, spears, swords, and axes all honed to razor sharpness, as well as a shield or two, helmets, and other spare pieces of armor. The rear of the wagon mounted a ballista, really just a giant crossbow that is drawn tight with a winch. The ballista fires an inch-thick, metal-tipped bolt not unlike a giant arrow that could knock a horse flat or skewer a half dozen men. Several are mounted on the parapets of the castle, and it's an effective weapon in the right circumstances. In addition, a sturdy wood-and-metal cage stood man-tall in the front of the wagon just behind the driver's seat, a great horn hanging from a thong inside the bars.

According to tradition, when a suitable dinosaur approached the site the vigilant prince was to engage the beast with an arrow or two from his bow, impale it on a spear, and finish it off with spear or sword. If the beast turned out to be larger than man-sized, or there was more than one, the ballista might be used with honor. Likewise the cage, and from it one could give two blasts of the horn to signal a request for help. However, use of the cage was frowned upon in any other circumstance, except as a last resort.

Well, what they didn't know wouldn't hurt me. My little muskrat friend had shown me the way. When a suitable opponent came along I would retreat to the cage, allow the beast to gorge on the bait, and then, when it was quite dead, I would emerge from safety to give it a few suitable stabs and hacks before blowing the horn.

Good planning is essential to success.

By tradition—a word I tire of very quickly—the royal party could not interfere until the horn was blown once or dusk had fallen. If no trophy had been taken the first day, the vigilant would then be brought back to the encampment for the night to rest before resuming his quest at dawn. The longest vigil had been kept by Prince (later King) Randall Brant, who with unexpected stubbornness refused lesser prey and waited five days before trading his left eye for a nine-foot-tall ceratosaurus.

The afternoon passed slowly, with no more excitement than the morning. Small creatures ventured near, saw me pacing, and disappeared back into the swamp. I didn't allow them to taste the bait, but otherwise was in a generous mood, my spirit much improved over the morning. Perhaps this ridiculous rite of manhood wasn't so bad after all, except for the gnats and flies and mosquitoes. I got up and paced around the wagon a few times until it became boring, examined all the weapons again, tried a few, did a bit of sword play with imaginary opponents, then returned the weapons to their slots in the rack.

Nothing happening.

Nothing at all. With bow and quiver I wandered up a few feet forward of the wagon, and then sauntered to its rear. Back and forth, back and forth, around and around, each time widening the ellipse until I was wandering fifteen or twenty feet from the wagon, as if in my boredom some part of me was tempting the giant reptiles to find me.

And still nothing.

I was starting to feel some pressure to relieve myself, but held off. It was no easy thing in royal battle dress to take care of nature's call. Urinating isn't so bad. Just haul up the chain mail skirt, unbutton the leather pants, find the opening in the underwear, and go to it, hopefully without soaking garments and equipment (no use getting the chain mail rusty). But squatting down with pants around your legs while holding the mail skirt out of the way was a challenge, especially when the mosquitoes are finding delightful new feeding grounds.

There was no other answer, though. It was still hours till dusk, and I had to go. I was not, however, about to dirty my own nest. Taking one of the special heavy spears with me I paced off ten short steps and looked around carefully.

Everything seemed to be fine. Nothing was stirring. The buzzing of the insects was normal. The cawing of the birds was normal. The crackling of branch and bush behind me was—

A great hissing filled the air.

I turned slowly around, keeping control of myself. I am not a complete coward. It was just fear. A few noises are not enough to make me lose control of myself.

It was when I looked up that I lost control, and terror replaced fear.

Thrusting through the leaves and fronds, a head fully three feet long emerged from the undergrowth and hung there amidst the treetops. The mouth opened and its tongue flicked out, as if tasting the air. The head was two-thirds jaws, and the jaws were lined with dagger-sized teeth.

Professor Wagner, doubtless, would have been delighted. *"Oh, my. A carnosaur. Yes, a carnivorous theropod from the late Jurassic, and most likely allosaurus, to be precise. And quite mature. How unusual. We have never found a full-grown specimen before, and by the size of its head, I believe we have underestimated its maximum growth."*

Thank you, professor.

For all its great bulk, the creature was amazingly graceful as it stepped out into the watery clearing, its body sliding through the branches and vines until all but the tip of its massive tail was in the clear. When moving, its head came down and its tail rose to balance its ponderous weight, but still the creature stood at least fifteen feet tall upon hind legs as solid as tree trunks, while its smaller forearms, each revealing three formidable claws, folded and extended in anticipation. The creature lowered its tail and raised itself erect, so that its head loomed twenty-five feet above the earth. Its back was a dark green, while its belly paled to gray. And I hope that is enough detail for you, Professor Wagner. If you want more, I recommend you do your own field research.

Its head twisted to the left, and then to the right, and then its eyes focused upon me as if with a gleam of pleasant surprise.

Ahh. How delightful. Fresh prince for lunch.

The allosaurus let out a hissing roar that reverberated through the swamp, and all else grew silent. There was not a bird chirping, nor a fly buzzing. I looked at the puny spear in my hands, threw it down, and made for the wagon in great, loping strides.

The wagon was less than a dozen paces away from me, and yet the creature closed the distance before I did. It splashed across the open pond in a few strides, and then stopped, its feet in the water while its great head swung like a crane over the causeway. Its tongue flicked out again, the head lowered and with one lick scooped up the bait and gulped it down. For good measure it took my friend the muskrat too.

A tasty appetizer before the main course, or so it might have thought. My confidence returned as I climbed onto the wagon. Oh ho, my fine guest, let's just see what happens now. Choose me for your meal, will you? I stepped behind the crossbow and waited, expecting to see the creature go down in a heap, and ready to jump clear if it should collapse upon the wagon. Any moment now and my troubles would be over. This would be a trophy like no other.

Or so I thought. Perhaps the bait loses its poignancy over time. Or perhaps the beast was just too big for the dosage. For rather than falling dead, the creature smacked its lips appreciatively, and then looked around for the main course.

Whatever the reason, the continued good health of the creature meant I was again in trouble. I had to make a decision. My first option was to run—which is my basic inclination in most situations—and be promptly snapped up.

Or I could dart into the cage. It had been designed to resist large beasts, but not anything like this; those powerful jaws would clamp down and crunch it into toothpicks.

Or I could take my place bravely behind the giant crossbow and discourage the creature with a bolt. Maybe it would slow the beast enough for the bait to start working. Maybe. But there were no other options.

The creature sidled through the pool, still standing in the water while its head and forearms extended over the wagon itself. That massive body actually blocked out the sun, putting me into shade for the first time that day. Its head cocked to the left, and then to the right, turning first one eye and then the other upon me. Perhaps it had never seen a man before, and was curious. Perhaps it was just a giant cat playing with a very feeble mouse. Or perhaps I needed salting.

Whatever the reason, it gave me the moment needed to aim the crossbow. That morning, I had assumed that such a weapon could bring down any creature. Now, even the great bolt looked tiny in comparison to my giant guest. Where to aim on something this big? The chest? I wasn't sure the bolt would penetrate deep enough to reach anything vital. The head? Most of it was bone protecting the tiny brain. Where else?

With trembling hands I fumbled with the crossbow, placed the sight on target, pulled the trigger, and let the bolt fly. The creature had decided I didn't need salt and was rearing back to strike when the missile buried itself in its neck. It took a step back, shook its head, did not like the result, and roared again.

There was no time to crank up the crossbow for a second bolt. I fell to my knees, crawled into the cage, and pulled the bars shut behind me. The horn. Where was the horn? I clawed myself erect, grabbed for the horn, missed it, grabbed again, and let blow the double blast for help. Nothing came out. Perhaps breathing would help. When would the creature start dismantling the cage? I took a great gulp of air, tried again, and blew two quavering notes.

The carnosaur listened to the sound and looked around warily. Blood was beginning to trickle from its mouth into the water. Hmmm. Lunch was fighting back. Nasty stinger on these little humans. And what had that strange noise been? Did it come from this little mammal, or was there another opponent nearby? And could there be a bit of indigestion starting? Must have been the appetizer. Maybe it was time to move on.

The creature gave me one last, suspicious look, snorted regretfully, and waded off into the underbrush, the giant tail disappearing like the end of a serpent as it slithers through the grass, and then all trace of its passage was gone.

I clung to the bars of the cage for a few moments, crawled out, and lowered myself to the ground. I was still alive. I didn't have a trophy, but I was alive. I laughed. Nothing could be as bad as what I had just seen. Nothing could compare with the gut-wrenching terror of that giant monster eyeing me and then splashing across the pool, jaws gaping wide. Nothing.

And then I heard the scrape of pebbles close behind me, and the smile froze on my face. I reached out slowly, closed my fist around the hilt of a sword, and tensed.

"GLEEP."

It was too much. With a scream I twisted around, slashing out with the weapon.

Before me stood a creature less than five feet tall. *"Ahh. A hadrosaur. Corythosaurus. A harmless plant-eater, known to be curious and friendly. And this one is little more than a baby, really. Must have wandered away from its herd. An interesting crest, wouldn't you say? Too bad you killed it."*

My sword had caught it across the throat, which now spurted blood in a pulsing fountain that sprayed over me. The plant-eater looked puzzled, gave out a last, feeble "gleep," and collapsed.

I stumbled backward and fell on my backside against the wagon wheel.

The spurts of blood diminished to a trickle before I felt a drumming in the earth, and then heard the thunder of hooves pounding down the causeway. Ahead of the party rode King Reuel and Sergeant Black, spurring their horses at the gallop and leaping down to assist me.

The king reached me first, looked at the blood covering me, and paused, afraid of causing greater injury. "Arn. Where are you hurt?"

I shook my head. "No. Not hurt."

"Of course you are. Just lie still. The doctor is here."

"What happened?" Sergeant Black asked me as others rode up and dismounted. The guardsmen took up positions around the party while the royal physician knelt beside me and began unlacing the straps of my chain mail.

I clutched the arms of the king and the sergeant while my garments were peeled off.

"Carnosaur," I managed to gasp. "Big one. I shot it."

There were a variety of expressions on the faces around me. And though I finally got the full story out as I regained my wits, the doubt that covered many of the faces did not abate. It was a strange tale, I must admit. A carnosaur? Where was the evidence? Why did I blow the horn if the beast had had enough? The body of the hadrosaur was simply an embarrassment. The king and his advisors examined the place where the bait had lain, the crossbow, and the ground up and down the causeway.

The king pronounced his findings. "The bait is gone. That is enough for me. The prince speaks the truth. Are there any here that doubt?"

None spoke. Wisely.

"Good. Then the Rite of Manhood has been completed."

Professor Wagner cleared his throat reluctantly. "But sir, a trophy has not been taken."

"What about that?" The king pointed at the body of the hadrosaur.

"Well, sir, you see, only a few of the herbivores are aggressive enough to qualify as trophies. The hadrosaur is not—"

"Enough," the king said loudly. "A fierce beast has been defeated. That is enough for me. The Rite has been completed. If a trophy is needed, take what you find. I will not suffer through another day of this."

I gave silent thanks, and allowed them to help me to my feet.

We returned to the castle, and when the heads had been mounted and hung, I snuck into the dining hall and noted mine. It wasn't a bad trophy, after all. A little small, perhaps, but it did have a nice set of molars if you looked far enough back in its mouth. And it fit well in the corner where it was placed. High up, near the top. But I didn't mind.

At least my portrait wasn't hanging in its place.

Other than the addition of the two new heads, the wall was unchanged from the first moment I had seen it. I looked at the other trophies, and the portraits of the unlucky six. There was dust on some of the heads and the picture frames. Two hundred years of history, and it was getting dusty. I turned and studied the room. The same. The same tapestries and paintings on the walls. The same tables and chairs on the center floor. The same cabinets holding the same dinnerware. Unchanged from the first time I had entered it with the unbelieving eyes of a child just eight years before. . . .

PART • ONE

THE LOST
SON

1

Kieno

I was running, and they were gaining upon me.

The half dozen gutter rats of the Greenwood Gang shouted dire warnings of my fate and waved their sticks in anticipation. Several were a year or two older, and had no difficulty keeping up with their prey.

Where were the sheriffs when I needed them?

I raced into a narrow alley, realized my mistake almost instantly, but had no choice in the matter except to continue running. Ahead the way was blocked by an unfortunately high and sturdy wooden gate that left no cracks for even a starving seven year old. Stupid. I knew better than to be trapped in a dead end, and now there was only one chance. Still at a full run I leaped and clawed for the top of the gate. Instead, I hit the wood with a thud, and bounced off.

The first pair following me into the alley whooped with glee as they realized my plight and closed in for the kill. They were dirty and ragged like I, but their faces radiated the joy of the chase and the courage of the mob as they came upon their victim. This was a pleasant diversion for them, a bit of sport to enliven the morning. And now they had me at bay.

I picked up a stick, turned to face them, and—

That sounds nice, but no.

I didn't pick up a stick. There were none to be found (the only clean alley in the whole filthy town), and it would only have made them angry. I didn't challenge my attackers with ringing words of courage. I didn't turn and fight bravely against hopeless odds. I didn't drive them off by my fierce and indomitable will.

Instead I cowered back into a corner, cringing with a style and flair developed from much practice. My arms covered my head protectively, and I pleaded for mercy in the few words I could manage, fat lot of good it did me.

But I didn't cry. A gutter rat never cries.

The boys were quite effective with their sticks. They pummeled me thoroughly about the head and shoulders, but my carefully placed arms absorbed most of the blows. I was experienced in matters of this sort, and patience is critical. Usually they just tire of their sport and leave the victim with the echoes of their laughter and scorn after a good beating. But this time one observant gutter rat with a bright future had an idea, so they dragged me back up the alley and out to the street, where a convenient slops barrel on a cart had just received the contents of the public latrine. With a lusty enthusiasm they upended me into it head first. The worker who had emptied the latrine swore loudly as the Greenwoods fled in laughter. I could hear him as I hauled myself out of the barrel, wiping the stinging liquid from my eyes. Since I was the last available gutter rat, the worker helped me on my way with the toe of his great boot.

I stumbled off, walking a bit oddly for a few steps thanks to his kindness, and tried to sort out what to do next. I needed to get clean; while a gutter rat never smells good, I was a walking cesspool and couldn't beg if I stank to high heaven. More importantly, I needed to dry off. It was early spring, and the weather was not just chill, but cold with the last of winter's breath. If I stayed wet I'd freeze before the night was out. So, what to do? I had to bathe, but where? The river, of course.

My misfortune took place in the middle of town, near the marketplace where I had been begging for pennies and thieving for food. Soaking and filthy, I ran down the streets without pause, earning looks of dismay from respectable townspeople. Even the dogs sniffed and refused to chase me. I exited town through the river gate and onto a wharf that ran along the town wall and extended out over the riverbank. A half-dozen piers jutted out irregularly from the wharf like broken teeth on a comb, most holding a few small rowboats and sailboats, and one or two securing larger craft like the riverboats and coast skimmers that went down to the Gulf. Over the longest pier was a sign in faded red letters welcoming newcomers to LOU-ISVILLE. I couldn't read, of course, but someone had once told me what the sign said. It was a quiet afternoon, most of the docks were empty, and only a few sailors and porters were scattered up and down attending to boats and business.

I turned right to go to the end of the wharf so that I could get down to the water's edge, looked up for no good reason, and stopped. Swinging gently in the breeze was a sign with a great tub and a scrub brush painted on it, as well two words which were read to me later. *Public Bath.*

The bath, which served the docks and the north edge of town, was merely a rude, wood frame building squeezed into the row of warehouses and stores tucked between the town wall and the wharf. A smoking brick chimney poked out of a hole in the roof. The entry door was in the center of the building front, while further down a second door led into an attached woodshed. Tacked on the wall next to the entryway was another unintelligible sign neatly and professionally done in flowing letters:

MEN: M, W, AND F; WOMEN: T, TH, AND S
BATH: NO CHARGE
SOAP & TOWEL: 1 PENNY

And crookedly scrawled in smaller block letters at the bottom:

NO LOITERING; NO BOTHERING OTHER BATHERS
ALSO, NO TOBACCO CHEWING, SPITTING, OR PISSING
AND TAKE OFF YOUR BOOTS ON THE MAT INSIDE

I hadn't thought of the baths before. By royal decree, the public baths, like the public latrines, were established throughout the kingdom and made available to all to promote the health and well being of the people of Kenesee. That was the idea, at least, and the unattended latrines were open to all. I used them regularly myself. But we gutter rats didn't bother trying the baths, since most of the attendants looked on us with suspicion and barred our way, having no desire to see their establishments and bathers robbed blind. Perhaps this was just as well, since many strange adults hang around such places. But as my shivering increased, the bath idea looked better and better. If it didn't work out, I could still wash in the river.

That didn't solve the problem of getting dry, but I could think about that while I washed. I might have to find the solution in the beggars' camp outside town. The camp was much worse than the baths for gutter rats, and not to be entered by a homeless boy or girl without good cause. But a fire always burned in the center of the camp, and if I could get in and out before dark, I might be all right.

On the bench next to the bath's entryway sat a formidable-looking man wearing a loose shirt and leggings, his sleeves rolled up above the elbows and his feet encased in heavy boots greased or waxed for waterproof. While I stood considering my options his nose sniffed and wrinkled in dismay, and he looked up for the first time. He was big, tall and barrel-shaped, muscle now layered with fat. A heavy beard covered his face, and his long hair was fastened into a ponytail. He gave off an aroma of beer, and indeed a large mug waited impatiently beside him. The chill air seemed to affect the man not at all, as if he were sitting in the warmth of a sunny summer afternoon. He leaned forward with his elbows on his knees, and I had a brief glimpse of thick fingers holding a large, shiny knife. He was whittling a block of wood that was taking on the undeniable form of an unclad woman. Quickly the carving disappeared into a pocket and he sheathed his knife.

Even seated he was big enough to have to squint down at me, doubtful eyes set above a bulbous red nose lined with veins. He sniffed again and rolled his eyes. "Whew. Just my luck," he said resentfully. "All right. Stop right where you are. There. That's right. By the edge of the wharf. Now, you just wait there." The man disappeared inside.

Perhaps this wasn't a waiting bather, as I had supposed, but the attendant. Well, so far so good. He hadn't driven me off with a curse and a kick, as so many might have done. Or was he having a good joke, leaving me to stand and freeze while he toasted himself at the fire? Thoroughly chilled by now, I tried to control my shivering and occupied myself with fantasies of revenge upon the gang that had done this. I could turn them in for murder, and they would all be hanged. Or better, I would discover their lair, lock the door, and burn down the building with them inside. Now that seemed to hold promise, except they might discover me. That was the problem with revenge. There was always some risk. I wanted revenge without risk.

The attendant reappeared with two full buckets, and a cascade of cold water poured over my head, stopping my heart and lungs but washing the majority of the filth off. At least I would die clean, or as clean as a gutter rat ever gets.

The man stepped back and surveyed his handiwork. He frowned. "Well, guess that'll have to do. Now, get outta those things. Quick like. What's the matter, can't you even undo a few buttons?" My heart decided to resume beating, and so, with numb fingers, I worked at my clothes while he went inside and came out again. At least no one else was near to observe my public display. I stood naked on the dock, my hands clutched protectively in front of my privates, while he poured another bucketful over me.

"Well, that's better," the man grunted. "Now. Inside with you."

I left my rags on the wharf and stepped within the building. The warm air was a blessed relief from the chill of the day.

"Get in a tub." The tubs were recessed into the floor so I stepped down, and he poured a kettle of water from the stove into a funnel, which carried it down a trough to a sieved bucket overhead. Chilled as I was, I luxuriated in the water. Blessed warmth! My shivering lessened, and the numbness in my fingers began to fade.

A piece of soap and washrag bounced off my chest into the tub. "You'll warm up soon enough. Start scrubbin' head to toe. I'll be back in a few minutes. Be done." He went outside and left me in peace. I forgot to scrub as the water rolled over my body and left me glowing. What more could one need besides food and warmth to be happy?

His head popped back through the door. "Start washin'!"

I grabbed the washrag but dropped the soap. Once I'd found a piece of soap on the street, but it didn't taste good so I threw it away. I hadn't known the properties changed when it was wet, becoming an unclutchable hunk of slippery softness. I finally got the soap by wrapping the washrag around it, then began to clean myself. It was really quite enjoyable, and not at all the unpleasant sensation I had expected. Too soon the bucket emptied and I stood waiting. The man came back, and to my surprise began wringing out my clothes from a bucket of soapy water and draping them over the sides of the stove.

He gave a glance and tossed me a towel. "All washed? Good."

I dried, wrapped it around my waist, and stepped out.

"Stand over here by the stove," he ordered gruffly. I stepped up and he tossed in several more chunks of wood, stirred the fire with a poker, and then shut its door.

He looked at me closely, his eyes going to my shoulders and arms, which were even now turning a most decorative shade of black and blue. "Who did this?"

"Gang," I answered.

"A gang?" he asked. "Not a grown up?"

I shook my head no.

"Well, then I can't do anything about it. But I did wash your clothes. I don't get paid for washin', let me tell you. Been on the job for a week, and everybody's got problems. Everybody needs help. Don't suppose you got any money, do you?"

"No."

"No, SIR!" he corrected.

"No . . . sir," I said slowly.

"I didn't think so. Well, you owe me. In this life, there's a price. You got to pay for what you get. The towels are a penny each to use. And the King pays me to keep the baths, not wash clothes!" And the pay must have been little enough, for his clothes, while clean, were well worn.

"I'll . . . pay you," I croaked, afraid he might hit me, and still harboring lingering suspicions that he might be hoping for different sorts of payment. Yet without clothes in this weather, there was no hope for escape. And the big, shiny knife was still sheathed at his belt, easily accessible if he should decide to pin a convenient gutter rat to the wall.

"I . . . promise," I added, hoping to placate him. A gutter rat doesn't survive without lying.

His eyes narrowed into a frown. "Promise? You promise? Be careful, boy. Lyin' is one thing, and bad enough. Breakin' a promise is quite another. A promise can't be taken back. It's a man's word. His oath. Never, ever promise unless you mean to keep it. You understand?"

"Yes, sir."

The frown faded. "All right, then. We'll find a way for you to pay me back. Just don't expect me to wash those rags again, understand? The law says you get a free bath, and that's it."

A last shiver took me, and then was gone.

He noticed. "No meat on your bones. That's the problem. Hungry?"

I nodded. It was best not to say too much. Once in a while I got lucky.

A cloth sack appeared from behind a stack of wood, and in it was a smaller sack into which he peered, as if surprised at what it held. "Don't suppose you like sausage. You do?" He took his knife and cut it in two. "Here. It's too much for me to eat all by myself."

Too much? With his belly, a cartload wouldn't be too much.

I stretched and took it from him at arm's length, wary of any attempt to grab me. But he didn't even notice.

"Let's see, got to have bread with it." He tore off a hunk for me. "Can't eat sausage without bread. And what's this? A piece of cheese. Hmmm. Half for you, half for me. Fair?"

Bread, sausage, cheese. Any one would have been a meal for me. Two was a rare stroke of good fortune. All three made a feast. With the decorum of a starving child—which I was, after all—I gobbled down the food.

"Slow down," he warned. "Slow down. Nobody'll take it away from you."

I ignored him. He was wrong. The first lesson of the streets is to eat whatever you get. Immediately. Or it will be taken away.

He was only half through with his when I gulped down the last morsel and burped contentedly. I eyed what he had left, but decided not to grab the food out of his hands. Discretion is important.

He finished his meal as my clothes began to steam, and he pulled each piece off the stove with a shake. "There. All dry now, and clean too. How's the shoes?"

I put on the battered lumps of leather. They flopped on my feet—holed, soggy, and too large.

"Still pretty damp, heh? Well, here. He ripped an old towel into two pieces. "Wrap these around your feet. They'll help." He was right, they did feel better. My feet actually felt halfway warm. So that was why people wore socks.

"You could say 'thank you,'" he muttered.

"Thank you."

"Now, don't go gettin' any ideas, boy. You need a shower, you're entitled. I cleaned your clothes, but that's it. End of good deed."

I sat and watched him, more confident now. I could flee if I had to. He frowned and looked away. "See that pile of wood? Bring me a piece."

I grabbed the topmost slab and heaved. It heaved back and I flopped onto the stack. I tried again, clutched it with both arms, and staggered over.

"Now, open the stove and throw it in," he ordered. I set down the slab, opened the door, and heaved the piece of wood in with the last of my strength. There. Any gutter rat could have done it. "What's your name?" he asked.

"Arn."

"Mine's Kieno. You a robber?"

"Yes . . . sir." "Robber" is a nice term for gutter rat.

"Interested in work?"

I was immediately on my guard again, but answered, "Yes, sir."

"All right. Here's the deal. I can use some help 'round here. But it comes out of my pocket, see? I don't get rich in this job. So, all I can do is give you food. You come each mornin' and help pump water and feed the stove and such, I'll split lunch with you. And you don't have to worry about any funny stuff from anybody. I don't allow that 'round here, no matter what they do elsewhere. Agreed?"

A meal each day? A chance to work inside where it was warm? No one to bother me? And a good chance to steal? "Yes, sir!"

"But no stealin'. You steal from me or the bathers, or take somethin' belongs here, and I'll track you down and break your arms. Understand?"

Most clearly. Threats I always understood.

But three out of four wasn't bad.

I arrived for work at dawn, and Kieno was as good as his word. We cleaned out the ashes, fired up the stove, pumped water for the kettles, and folded towels that had hung on the line overnight. The bath house was not a large place. Towards the back on a high stone base was a flat brick stove holding large kettles of steaming water, and next to it was a water pump. Stairs led up to a platform serving these. The big kettles he handled himself. I tried lifting one, but even empty I could barely move it. Towards the front, round tubs were recessed into the wooden floor with sieved buckets hung above them. The tubs had plugs and drains which, I was to discover later, carried the dirty water in wooden piping under the wharf and into the river. The sieved buckets were fed by elevated troughs, each emerging from a funnel next to the stove. An open doorway on the side led directly into the woodshed. Kieno swept and mopped vigorously, and kept the bath spotless. He enforced the rules on chewing, and made sure bathers left their muddy shoes just inside the door.

Bathers trickled in throughout the day, but especially after the church bells sounded noon, and late in the day after their own workday was over. They each took a quick shower in a tub, and Kieno or I were there to hand out a towel as the allotted kettle of water ran out. Kieno did not allow lingering, nor undue socializing inside the bath with each other or with us. Most of the bathers—sailors, fishermen, dock workers and the like—were rough sorts, like Kieno, but happy to get clean, and not about to get into an argument with the giant attendant. Only a few seemed to have unusual interests but it got so we could recognize them, most times. Kieno kept his eye out, and made sure they didn't bother anyone, or else he got them out fast, sometimes with a poke of one meaty finger and a few menacing words.

We had fewer problems with the women who lived in the dock area. A few actually worked on the boats or docks, but most were wives, tavern and household maids and cooks, seamstresses, and various other types of "working girls." For them Kieno would string a line and hang a couple of sheets, separating the platform from the tubs so the ladies could have their privacy, a courtesy earning shrill jokes from some of the ten-penny girls who used the baths, especially two or three that Kieno seemed to know.

I can still remember the lunch of that first workday, for it seemed even more wonderful than that of the day before. After we'd worked through the noon rush he took out his sack and brought out its treasures. There was bread, smoked fish, soft cheese, an apple for each of us, and nuts that he cracked smartly with a hammer. He also cracked one open with his bare hand, just to show me it could be done, and I'm sure he was gratified to see my eyes widen into saucers. Afterwards, I sat next to the stove and watched while Kieno quietly sipped his beer and whittled his wood. There was also a large tin he'd brought for me that I gulped from before looking. I gagged.

Kieno watched me.

"What . . . is this?" I asked.

"Milk," he said. Don't tell me you never—" The rest of his face turned the color of his nose. He got up from his stool and paced back and forth angrily, cursing.

I wondered what I had done wrong, but knew better than to draw his attention directly to me. If he was getting ready to swing a blow, I certainly wouldn't remind him of my convenience as a target. He didn't get violent, though, and sat down after a while and gulped down his beer. I forced down the milk, and am happy to say that I did come to enjoy it after a few weeks.

When it slowed we'd sit outside on the bench while he whittled and drank, and this became more and more pleasant as spring turned into summer. Kieno would hone his knife on a stone and then take a piece of pine or aspen or poplar or basswood and start rounding it out. In his large, callused hands the wood gradually took on the raw dimensions of shape and proportion, and that seemed appropriate. What produced a sense of awe was what he did with the wood thereafter. From rough proportions emerged figures of grace and delicacy, lines flowing smoothly into each other, detail and expression emerging surely and quietly. Almost all of his figures were people, statues perhaps eight or ten inches tall. I saw him complete figures of a wizard and a sailor, as well as the bust of a soldier. More often he did women, and many of them were at least partially unclad, the curves and lines endowing them with a grace and beauty that did not end with their figure but were enhanced by the joy and sadness caught in the detail of their faces.

I became a trusted confidant of his work. "What you think, Arn?" he would ask. "Is she real for you? Come on now, let me know. There's no one else I can show them to." And he didn't, keeping several dozens of them safely collected in a sack that he carried in with him each morning and out each evening, as if unwilling to leave it anywhere. During the day he hid the sack behind the woodpile in the bath house. He never showed his work to anyone. When someone passed by he would put his hand over the carving or tuck it into a pocket. "Don't want to be embarrassed by people laughin' at me," he'd joke when hiding his art, and perhaps that was the truth of it.

The unaccustomed richness of a steady diet helped me in my work as I slowly gained strength and endurance. At dawn every other day a wagon load of firewood arrived and had to be brought in to replenish the shed. Slab by slab, we piled the wood along the wall. Kieno was a stickler for neatness and insisted the wood be placed in straight rows. Then there was sweeping the floor and collecting the dirty towels. Nothing odious or beyond the capability of a child, but Kieno was a hard worker, and he made me work hard too. I didn't mind because for the first time I was confident that nothing else was expected of me. Kieno had no ulterior motives, no hidden purposes, no intent to gain my trust for his own plans. Give him his beer and he was happy—more or less.

There was only one time that I was worried, needlessly. Kieno insisted that I take a bath every week too, and I did, quite willingly. Normally he ignored me in the process, discreetly averting his eyes as he did for any bather. This time, something caught his attention, for he stared at my privates.

"What's wrong?" I asked, concerned.

He looked up and smiled reassuringly. "Nothin'. Nothin' at all. You've just got a birthmark there. I hadn't noticed it before." He grew thoughtful. "Reminds me of a story used to be told . . . but don't matter none. Just a strange place for a mark. Anyway, don't worry, the girls won't mind."

After that, sometimes, when we sat outside I would catch Kieno watching me, a speculative look on his face. "Just watchin' you grow up and puttin' on the inches," he'd explain when I caught him at it. "You know, I wasn't much bigger than you were when I went to work. Forty years slavin' away, and I don't have nothin' to show for it. Nothin' but a big gut." And then he'd laugh and so would I, and he'd look out at the river and watch the boats. Sometimes a coast skimmer would push off and raise its sails.

"Look, Arn. That's what we need to do. Get aboard a coastal and head south. Louisville ain't got nothin' to stay for. Most of these go down river to Wickliffe. That's by the Gulf. And some of them keep goin' along the coast to Kingsport. You know what we're goin' to do one day, Arn? We're goin' to go to Kingsport. That's right, Kingsport. That's the biggest town in the kingdom, Arn, sittin' there right off the Gulf and gettin' the fresh sea breeze. I tell you, Kingsport is the place to be. Ships like you ain't seen; not just riverboats or coast skimmers, but ships to challenge the oceans. Inns and shops all over, and pretty ladies everywhere. I knew a woman there once. Named Angie. . . ."

He was silent a moment, then continued. "And the castle. Arn, you got to see the castle. It's not just a tower or keep, like we've got here, but the biggest and strongest castle in the kingdom, because that's where the King lives. It's a sight. I tell you, a man can make a fortune in Kingsport. That's where your fortune lies. We'll go one day, you and me. How would you like that?"

It was fine by me. Long as Kieno provided food and warmth, I would follow him with utmost loyalty. But the spring faded into summer and we stayed as we were, content with a quiet routine broken only by the vagaries of the town as it went about the calendar of its business.

In June, stonemasons began to work on the town wall directly behind us, erecting scaffolding, hauling up stone and mortar, and repairing cracks. Kieno allowed me to earn an occasional penny by fetching beer for the masons when I went to get his. They were not a bad bunch, and Kieno would go out the back door to chat with them, leaning against the scaffolding while they worked ten or twenty feet above him. While they were happy with the work on the wall, there were doubts about what it all meant.

"How's it comin', Amos?" asked Kieno one day.

"Well as can be expected. It's getting damned hot in the sun, though."

"Try workin' next to my stove all day. This job goin' to last long?"

"Through next spring, I'd imagine," the mason commented

knowingly. "The guild got a good contract. Haven't had one like this for awhile."

"Looks like it's about time," said Kieno. "These walls haven't had any attention for years."

"You're right there," Amos agreed. "You know, my brother in Nash says they're getting contracts to repair their walls, too. Now, that's a lot of work contracted all at once. Maybe the King's got something on his mind for us. What do you think?"

"Could be," Kieno admitted. "There's always the beast-men to worry about. We gotta do somethin' about them some day. Heard they got a family out past Benton way."

"I heard about that. Beastmen killed them all. No respect for the Codes or anything decent."

"Course too, there's always the Virginians to worry about."

"You're right there. Can't trust those Easterners."

And then they got into a discussion of the Pirate War, discovered they were both veterans, and had a good time swapping stories and lies before getting back to work. The conversation must have stirred memories, for Kieno was more talkative than I could remember. When it slowed that afternoon and he had his beer close at hand, we sat together while he whittled. I stared at the piece of wood, fascinated by the shape which was forming. Could it be a boat? That would be different.

"What do you think, Arn?" he asked. "Does it look like a ship much? It's goin' to be a trading schooner. You know, I used to sail on a ship like this. Then after that on the *Greenville* in the King's Navy. Spent five years cruisin' the Gulf. I was even in a battle one day, all our ships against the pirates. That's what they called themselves, but damned if they weren't mostly Islanders and Texans. The catapults were slinging oil pots, and their ships seemed to go up like kindlin'. We burned most of them, and captured the rest.

"Remember we had these two characters aboard ship—wizards, they told us, an old guy going bald, and another one, younger than I was, dark-skinned, and always grinnin' friendly-like. Old guy was often seasick. Anyway, the captain didn't want them on board; felt they were in cahoots with the devil, you know? He didn't think they could do nothin' but get in the way, and I guess I got to agree with him.

"Their magic ain't nothin' but hocus-pocus, you ask me. One of 'em did a magic act for the crew, and it was mostly makin' puffs of smoke and things catch on fire, tricks with cards, stuff disappearin' in boxes, and scarves comin' out of his mouth. I figured most of them out. The neatest thing was when he twirled some feathers in the air without touchin' them. I couldn't figure out how he did that. But that was about all the magic I ever saw them do. I don't see as how they did very much in the battle, nor why they should be there, although the young one was a fighter, I'll give him that.

"When the battle started the wizards were right there, on deck, watchin' what happened until we got boarded and had a fight on our hands. The young one had his hands full with one, and I bashed two more who were tryin' to get to the old man.

"You know, Arn, one good thing about you is you don't talk much. You know when to keep your mouth shut. In those days I always had a mouth on me. I was too dumb just to say 'Yes, sir,' and get along. Always acted like I knew better than everybody else, when I didn't know nothin'. So if anybody noticed what I did, they didn't care. Need to have an officer see you being a hero, otherwise it don't count.

"Anyway, I guess it didn't matter much. But I've seen a lot. Wouldn't trade that for nothin'. Saw Virginia, and Arkan. Even visited the Isles, and slept on the beach there once, with no blanket or nothin'. Didn't need it. Saw lots of Kenesee, too. Used to make runs from Jackson Harbor to Kingsport."

One of the girls who worked the area sauntered by. I recognized her as one who used the bath each week. She looked better with her clothes on. "Hello, gentlemen," she said pertly.

"Hello, Maggie," Kieno answered attentively.

"Interested today?"

"Interested, but short on money."

"It's always that way at the end of the month. Haven't had a customer all afternoon. How about the little guy? I'll give you a two for one special."

"In seven or eight years."

"In seven or eight years I'll be an honest woman."

"Maggie, you're already an honest woman."

She laughed. "Glad somebody realizes it. Tell that to my boyfriend." She had never stopped strolling as she tossed out the banter, and gave us a little wave as she continued down the wharf.

Kieno stroked his beard. "You know the difference between dogs and cats? Well, that's the difference between men and women."

I must have looked puzzled.

"Think about it."

In his water-roughened hands the carving slowly took shape, a hull emerging curved and smooth, with a flat deck broken by a low cabin and storage well. A small hole for a mast was carved out of the center. He held it up. "Pretty neat, huh?"

I nodded vigorously. Could it be for me?

"Course, it needs a lot more work. Think a kid would like it?"

I nodded again.

He grinned. "Good. I know a boy who I want to give it to for Christmas."

I didn't nod. Of course. How silly to hope it might have been for me. How stupid. Perhaps I could steal it from the boy.

Time passed happily enough. I had two decent meals each day once Kieno started bringing extra food for the evening, and it got to the point where my ribs didn't show. I was gainfully employed, fed, and warm. Kieno even started letting me sleep in the bath house after I showed up for work at dawn following a cold night in a doorway kicking away rats of the four-legged kind. Kieno looked at me close. "How come you got those dark circles under your eyes?" In truth, bleary eyes were common among those who lived in the streets, and I explained why my sleep had been less than restful. He got a chamber pot and let me stay at night when he padlocked the door. I would sleep on the hard wooden floor next to the warm stove and thought it the next best thing to heaven.

My only payment was having to listen to Kieno mumble his little tokens of wisdom while he drank and whittled and got feeling sorry for himself. One day it was "Don't listen to others. You do what you want to. That's all. Just what you want to." Another time it was "Arn, if a man could know he'd done just one good thing in his life, made a difference somewhere, it would help. Just one good thing. . . ."

Except for these pearls, it was a fine life, especially through the summer. I don't mean to make light of poor old Kieno's words, but at the age of seven I had little use for such advice and philosophy. Life was a struggle for food and warmth. Beyond that I had no experience.

I should have known things were too good to last, however. One morning in the fall I awoke at sunrise, rekindled the fire from the banked coals, and built it high. I waited and listened for the sound of the key in the padlock, but there was none. The sun was above the horizon. I folded the towels hung to dry the previous night and filled the oil lamps. No Kieno. A disappointed bather shook the padlock, then wandered away. I swept the wood plank floor. Still no Kieno.

I tossed another log into the stove, removed my apron, and wriggled out through the back window, hanging by my fingers and then dropping to the ground while the window swung down and shut firmly behind me. It was too high to reach from outside in any case. Then I turned and ran into town through the river gate, the sole of one broken shoe flapping noisily on the paving stones. I had walked Kieno back to his room several times before I started sleeping at the bath. Two blocks down, one block up, and I paused breathless in front of the doorway to Sailor's Rest, a tavern and inn serving the docks. A two-wheel cart pulled by an ill-fed horse filled most of the narrow street, and the rest was taken up by a small crowd that clustered around the doorway.

"They're comin' out," said a voice. "Make way." At which, of course, the fools crowded in even more. "Make way, make way!" the refrain was heard, and the crowd parted slightly to allow two struggling, bent figures to back out of the doorway, followed in turn by two others. They held the corners of a large burlap sack that stretched and sagged in the middle. The men maneuvered the sack next to the cart, set it on the ground, and paused to get their breath.

"Thanks for your help, good men. He's a big 'un," said one, mopping his brow with a dirty sleeve. "Must weigh over two fifty, easy."

"What happened?" came a voice from the crowd. "Who is it?"

The sweaty carrier leaned an arm on the cart, happy to take a few moments to chat. "What happened? Don't know, exactly. Sheriff's been and gone. Someone found this one in bed this morning. Not a mark on him. Just didn't wake up. Sheriff thinks maybe he just tipped one too many. Had a nose like a beet."

Another carrier rubbed his bulbous nose thoughtfully, then shrugged. "C'mon, Joe, we got to get going."

His companion regretfully ended his soliloquy. "Not a thing to his name except a bunch of wood carvings, I understand. Sheriff took a sack of them. Well, let's get him aboard, Jamie. We've got to get going, folks. Give us room now. You two want to help again? Thanks."

The four men braced themselves, grabbed hold of the sack from either end, and lifted. The body went into the cart with a dull thump.

Two of the townspeople passed. "Who was it?" whispered one.

"I don't know," said the other. "Does it matter?"

The cart took the road out of the west gate and up to a low rise a few hundred yards from the town wall. Stone tablets and wooden crosses dotted the rise, surrounded by a badly tended picket fence. Outside the fence was a large pit with piles of lime and dirt next to it. I followed the cart at a distance, though I could have sat on the tailgate without being noticed. Joe rambled on about weather, war, and women, and Jamie grunted in response.

They backed the cart up to the pit, and then without ceremony tumbled the sack off so that it rolled into the pit and came to rest against one of the suspicious mounds of soft dirt at the bottom. Grabbing shovels, the men deposited a few shovels of lime and followed this with earth until the sack was covered. Their work done, they leaned on their tools and rested a moment, basking in the fullness of the morning sun. Joe noticed me for the first time and nudged the other. "Look at the boy."

Jamie did. "Gutter rat."

"Hey, robber," beckoned Joe. "Come over here."

I stayed my distance. I didn't want to talk to them.

"Wonder why he's here?" Joe scratched his head. "Relative, do you think?"

Jamie cleared his passages and spat into the pit. "Stealin', more likely."

"What can he take out here? There's nothing we'll leave around except our shovels."

"Take them with us," the other said, solving their problem. And so they did, tossing them in the back of the cart, clambering aboard, and going back into the town for their next task.

When they were near the main road and no longer bothered to glance back, I crept forward to the rim of the pit, ignoring the sour smell that rose from below. All was still, except for the buzzing of numerous flies. It was a big pit. There were many small mounds of dirt at the bottom, and the sack was just one more, identifiable by the darkness of the newly shoveled soil.

I sat on the edge of the pit throughout the morning, and then into the afternoon, and finally into the evening. Jamie and Joe never came back, leaving me alone with the buzzing of the flies and the smell of decay. I watched carefully, but there was no change in the earth, no movement of the freshly turned soil, no stirring in the quiet mound. And so that was the end of Kieno, a burlap sack tossed into a pit, a few shovels of dirt, a lonely burial in a pauper's grave, a final repose sharing the earth with a dozen other nameless and forgotten wretches. He was gone. My companion was gone, and with him went my livelihood. And if others were to ask me what I felt at that moment, I could not tell them. There was only a numbness.

At last the dusk rose around me and the stars began to appear. The gate guard blew final warning before nightlock and I went back into the town to find a place to sleep.

Tomorrow I would leave for Kingsport.

2

Kingsport

The next morning I went to the docks and found a ship heading all the way to Kingsport. The couple who owned the coast skimmer, Nora and Simon Waters, eyed me closely. I think they were more afraid of what vermin I might have brought aboard than anything else, but my temporary cleanliness spoke in my favor. My clothes were ragged but clean, and my face did not have the layers of grime typical of a gutter rat. They let me earn passage by working as cabin boy with a warning from Nora. Steal, and they would break my arms.

The trip down river was pleasant. Forests covered hill and plain, crowding down toward the riverbank on both sides. Cultivated fields could be seen through the screen of foliage when we neared habitations, usually followed by the appearance of a landing which marked a village or small town huddled close to the bank. At one spot a pair of mules walked along a path on the bank, pulling a riverboat upstream.

Nora pointed out the ruins of Old World cities, isolated bits of wall and girder still sticking skyward, but most of the debris was covered by undergrowth and trees. Nora liked to talk, and she went on about how the old cities supplied most of the crete used in constructing our own buildings and walls and towns. Still, a variety of beasties used the ruins as lairs, and workers had best go armed when searching through the rubble.

The hazards of the Old World were not limited to land. Nora indicated the ruined stone abutments on either side of the river that marked where the great arches of bridges had once spanned the water. Their broken remains still lingered on the river bottom, thrusting up sharp girders that waited to snag unwary ships. "See that, Arn?" she asked, pointing out the abutments. "Six hundred years and they're still standing. The quakes couldn't knock down everything. Watch for the abutments, and steer clear of danger." When we got further south, where the banks turn into swamp, Simon and Nora became even more careful, taking a course down center stream and carefully watching the surface of the water.

I noticed their caution. "I don't . . . see any abutments."

Simon untied a long, heavy pole with a wicked metal point on one end. "Not worried about bridges, boy. Watching for beasties—the swimming kind. I've never had to use this thing, and pray I never will. Course, we don't take chances like some fools sailing close to the banks. Beasties like the shallows. Doesn't happen often, but sometimes a man will be snatched right off the deck."

Simon explained to me that great creatures lived deep in the swamp, and that smaller ones roamed the edges to snatch the unwary man or child who might venture too near. Occasionally beasts that liked the water even left the channels of the swamps and entered the river to prey on swimmers and small boats. If he was trying to frighten me with these tales, he succeeded quite well. Nothing, I was sure, could ever get me to enter the swamp. I found excuse to go below.

No creature disturbed us, and in fact our voyage was quite peaceful. Except for necessary cautions, life on the river was quite enjoyable. The work was hard, but nothing I wasn't used to. And they were treating me fairly. I thought this might not be such a bad life. But when we got to the open water of the Gulf I turned green and became seasick. The rest of the voyage was spent in my bunk, wanting to die. It was to my great relief that I awoke one morning and found myself feeling reasonably decent. I thought I was finally adjusting to sea travel until I realized we were docked.

Simon and Nora saw me off, and Nora even gave me a tenpenny piece. Two or three days of fine eating! I waved goodbye, and then walked away as calmly as I could. My pockets were empty, except for the coin. But they didn't notice I still had on the old sweater and waterproof jacket they'd given me to wear. I almost felt bad about taking the items, then came to my senses and began to hum a tune.

A man was selling bread on the pier, so I bought a loaf for

morning meal. It was a tradition, or so he told me, for new arrivals to break bread on the pier before they got into town. I tore off huge chunks with my teeth and gobbled them down while wandering up and down the wharves. The south face of the town fronted upon the Gulf, but here its west face was bordered by the sheltered waters of the King's River, along which the docks had been built. The docks were a forest of masts and spars and rigging from deep water cargo schooners, a fleet of fishing boats, river craft, coastals, and a half-dozen ships of the Royal Navy. All about were sailors, porters, fishermen, workers, and craftsmen. Kieno had been right. The docks did seem to go on forever.

It was as I emerged from the forest of ships that I looked up and had my first clear view of Kingsport. At that time the town had a population of only thirteen thousand, and yet it was the largest town in Kenesee and boasted a level of commerce, trade, and activity unmatched by any other. Lining the waterfront were warehouses, storage sheds, and shops devoted to shipfitting. Behind these structures a high wall with battlements and towers encircled the old town, although on its landward side much new construction had already taken place outside the wall. On a bluff immediately adjacent to the town, and smiling down upon it protectively, sat the king's castle. It was moated and walled, towered and turreted, colorful banners unfurled from the battlements and pennants flying from the rooftops, a solid edifice of stone and mortar that had stood for almost two hundred years against siege and storm.

The sight took my breath away, but there was a living to make. Hitching up my tattered pants, I strode through the river gate and entered Kingsport.

Some of us stumble upon our fortune in good time. Others need a bit longer. I, apparently, could number myself among the latter. The largest town of the kingdom was no more friendly to a gutter rat than the poorest backwater. The sneers were the same, the curses were the same, and the kicks were the same. There were just more of them.

Such is opportunity.

I had arrived in the late fall. With winter coming, my survival was complicated by the need to learn my way around a new town. I needed to know the layout of the markets and shops, the streets and alleys, the gates and walls. I needed to determine the best spots to beg money or steal food, where to shelter during the cold nights, what dangers there were from sheriffs, lowlifes, and other gutter rats, and what escape routes and hiding places existed for a poor robber. At night I slept in doorways with one eye open for two-legged predators. During the day I spent virtually every hour walking the length and breadth of the town and beyond, begging where I dared, grabbing food from busy market stalls, and learning my way around.

Within the west wall of the city, a variety of inns, taverns, and other commercial establishments crowded near the two gates leading to the docks. Also in this area were stables, squatters' alleys, and the Street of Pleasure. Craftsmen and artisans tended their homes and shops in the northeastern part of the town, while the wealthier merchants lived in the shadow of the southern wall. There were two market squares to serve the residents, one close to the castle in the south, and the other further north. Work on an uncompleted cathedral went on next to the southern market, and apparently had for generations. The town had outgrown the original plan, so that homes and shops clustered thickly outside the east gate, while army barracks and parade grounds were located outside the northern portal. Beyond these spread pastures and cultivated fields, eventually giving way in a few miles to the mountains and valleys of the Smokies.

Next to the merchant homes was the outer wall of the king's castle. The castle lay behind a dry, grassed moat, accessed only by a drawbridge and single large gate that was always flanked by two watchful guardsmen. A glance inside showed a large courtyard surrounded by stables, barracks, and the king's house itself. I noted it just once, then forgot about it. Since it was off limits, it could make no contribution to my existence.

The royal presence did have some positive impact upon my activities. On most days, squads of guardsmen would pass the marketplace on their way to the parade grounds outside of town. Often they accompanied royal persons such as the king or his son. I saw the royalty from afar, but never bothered watching closely because I always took advantage of the moment. The daily event was an excellent distraction, as many of the market sellers took their eyes off their stalls and watched for a glimpse of the king.

"There they are," said a seller of vegetables to another selling cheeses. They stood next to their carts and watched the procession with interest. "Looks like King Reuel and Queen Jessica, both! And there's Prince Robert, too."

The other nodded. "The Brants have been good for this country. The Kingsport Journal prints freely, and he doesn't interfere. How many other nations allow that, eh?"

While they talked I slipped nearer, behind a wide-hipped woman craning to see. I reached out a hand and grabbed a large potato from the nearest corner of the pile. Just one, of course, for greed has been the downfall of many a grab. I shoved the potato under my coat, turned, and walked away to find a quiet alley. Yes, the king was quite popular with the people, and he was quite popular with me, too.

There was the usual variety of lowlifes wandering the streets, and a fair collection of gutter rats. Happily, the organized gangs that had bedeviled the town of Louisville seemed to be absent, possibly due to the larger number of sheriffs in Kingsport. The lawmen might turn a blind eye to a robber or two discreetly begging on a street corner, but they responded vigorously to anything resembling gang activity. Certainly, there were always two or three rats who might band together and watch for an easy victim, but the spy system, the sense of territory, and the organized viciousness were absent.

Still, there were dangers. There were always dangers.

In my years on the streets I observed most forms of degradation and abuse that one human can perpetrate upon another, and neither sex nor age made any difference. I heard every profanity, saw every form of coupling. That I avoided the worst was due to an innate caution, distrust of others, and fast legs. To speak of it further would serve no purpose.

Yet I did not escape it all, suffering minor forms of abuse that could in themselves be threatening to life. Older gutter rats had stolen food from me with regularity. Adults had propositioned me frequently. Occasionally gangs had beaten me or tried to steal my very clothing. I lost my waterproof jacket to a father and his son, who took it from me, both smiling and showing their crooked teeth as they did so.

Not all the street people I met were necessarily dangerous, for there were always the harmless characters who roamed about, strange in body or mind, though lacking the vicious cruelty of their saner cousins. And there was one whom I could not quite place so easily.

On a darkening evening soon after my arrival I was scouting out an empty, narrow alleyway behind the Street of Pleasure. A thick figure emerged from the shadows. The figure resolved itself into a short, stocky woman shrouded in a colorful shirt and long, loose skirt cinched up with a wide belt. A blanket roll hung on her back, and a wide-brimmed felt hat sporting two eagle feathers was jammed firmly atop her head. Straight black hair emerged from beneath the hat and flowed down to her shoulders. The woman's face was round, with a thick, prominent nose jutting out at an imposing angle. Her squinting eyes were surrounded by reddish skin that had been weather-beaten into a thousand tiny lines and wrinkles. I could not tell her age.

She looked at me and seemed surprised. "Boy!"

I backed up a step.

"Boy. This is no place for a little one to be. Don't come here again." She studied me for a moment. "Humph. Come along. I'm going to the wharves. Follow me." And with that she turned and walked away. She didn't seem to pose any threat. Maybe a meal waited on the docks. As long as I was careful, there should be no harm following the woman. And so I did.

She threaded her way through the town, unknown and un-noticed by the other pedestrians on the streets. At the docks, she got a wave from one woman closing up a ledger book outside a warehouse, and a nod from a sailor coiling his ropes.

She sat down on the end of a pier in the twilight, and watched the sun disappear in the West. There was no one else around, and no places where strangers might lurk in hiding. I sat down but kept my legs beneath me, a good arm's length between us. We were settled at last, but the big woman remained silent.

"Who . . . are you?" I ventured at last.

She gave a grunt. "They call me Crazy Mary, they who

cannot see beyond their nose. I am a soothsayer.''

"Sooth . . . sayer?"

"Fortune-teller.''

Oh, one of those. Fortune-telling could be quite a good profession. I'd watched a lady working the crowds on the edge of the marketplace using a deck of cards. Another time she'd come back and used bones. The fortunes always seemed to be the same.

Crazy Mary read the expression on my face. "No," she said with bitter pride. "I'm not one of those. I won't tell you what you want to hear. I have foresight. The true power. There are few in Kenesee with foresight, and none as clear as mine.''

She waited, as if for acknowledgment, but I simply sat and stared.

She grunted again and went on. "I pass a thousand each day and the future is only a flicker. This woman will burn her hand at the stove. That man will marry soon. That other will lose his purse. Just flickers. But you walk by, and I am lit with sight.''

Night had come, and a lantern hung on a pole overhanging the water. Her face was half in light and half in shadow, but her eyes I could see, and they were watching me. Ignoring the moths that buzzed about the light, she offered me a canteen.

I took it and drank a large gulp before realizing it wasn't water. It burned like whiskey, and yet I couldn't say what it was. My eyes watered and my nose began to run. I congratulated her. "Good stuff.''

She took a long swig from the canteen and then put it away.

The night must have warmed considerably in the next few minutes, because the sweat began to pour from me. I sat in contemplation, listening to the noises of the evening. Water lapped against the pilings in reassuring monotony. The moths buzzed in frustration as they sought entry to the flame of the lamp, and their end. The last crickets of the fall still chirruped from the shore, and an owl hooted as it waited for its mate. On the far bank a fox yapped after missing a squirrel, and far off to the north something roared with the pleasure of the kill.

Crazy Mary was silent for a long time, staring across the water until suddenly her eyes caught mine and held them— held them until the light and the moths receded into a vast distance and all was seriousness and purpose. She moved closer. Her hand reached out and a finger gently traced a path down my cheek, leaving an invisible trail of burning pain. "There," she said as she traced. "It will be there."

I tried not to flinch.

"Now, give me your hand." I gave it without resistance. She turned the palm up and rubbed it with her thumb before tracing lines with a fingertip. Her eyebrows rose and creased in puzzlement. "Who are you, boy? Who are you?" She peered closer, spreading my palm wide as if it would open up another chapter to her glance. "I see something. You are— you are the eye of a storm. You do not create the storm and yet it swirls about you."

She continued tracing, and I wondered when she would run out of lines. Then there was surprise in her face. "I see many people, many places. I see high places, and low. I see battle. I see blood. I see—"

She let go of my hand as if it were a rattlesnake, and in the uncertain lamplight her red face, glistening with sweat, paled. Turning, she crawled up to the very edge of the pier and sat beneath the lantern facing the river.

I followed and shook her. "What did you see?" I whispered. "What did you see?"

She looked at me one last time, her eyes filling with tears. And then she began to chant, low and sonorous, intricate yet unvaried, over and over. A chant mournful, and sad, and full of fear.

The days were growing colder as winter approached. While the temperature was warmer than up north in Louisville, there was more rain here, and often my breath clouded in the open air. I found various corners and doorways to sleep in, but knew that I must soon find better shelter.

The waterproof jacket was a real loss, although the sweater helped. Already I awoke shivering in the mornings, and only an hour's brisk walk would gradually restore warmth to my limbs. A night of frost and I would be in trouble.

I found my winter lodging while strolling down a narrow alley behind a row of tradesmen's houses. The buildings fronted onto a wider street, each containing a shop of one sort or another, behind and above which lived the shopkeepers and their families, diligently plying their trades during the day.

Back doors led onto the alley for the delivery of goods to the shops and wood for the fires.

Many of the buildings on this block had small wooden shutters near the ground leading into cellars. In the darkness of the night I tried each in turn, until one loose latch provided the solution. I found a stick, stuck it in between the frame and the edge, and knocked the clasp loose. The shutter swung inward to reveal undisturbed darkness. I waited for my eyes to adjust, and then, every sense ready to give warning, crawled through and lowered myself to the dirt floor.

It was not a large space. An adult could not stand erect. A set of narrow stairs—almost a ladder—led up to the trapdoor in the floor of the house. There were various boxes and crates neatly piled in the corners, some open and others sealed. Several of the crates were stacked on simple brick-and-board shelves. The open ones were filled with plain earthenware, each piece carefully cushioned in straw. A few boxes were empty, but one contained rags and scraps of cloth, while another held a stack of old copies of the town journal.

I climbed the first three steps slowly, and nearly screamed when one creaked beneath my shoe. I listened at the crack, and heard a woman singing to herself. Quietly, I backed down the steps. So far, so good. Two adjacent boxes provided a hidden corner that I could curl up in. I found another empty crate and placed it below the shutter opening as a step. Then I exited the way I'd come, closing the shutter behind me but leaving the clasp undone so that I could open it again without difficulty. I took position at the end of the alley and watched for any evidence of discovery, but there was none. Then I headed off in a last effort to secure something to eat.

It was too dangerous to use the cellar before the people above were asleep. Later that night, when most of the windows in town were dark, I returned to the alley and dropped into the cellar, closing and latching the shutter behind me—wouldn't want some thieving gutter rat to find my hideyhole and interrupt my sleep. I lay down behind the crates and covered myself with the rags from the box. I had done all I could to ensure my safety.

Finally out of the wind and rain I slept, and was pleased to find myself tolerably warm during the night. I woke without the usual chill in my bones, quickly replaced the rags as I'd found them, and left as the sky began to glow orange above the rooftops.

The trick to such living arrangements is preventing discovery. That's why I never touched any items in the cellar, nor tried to go upstairs. Missing items would arouse suspicions. Suspicions would trigger a search. A search would reveal the unlatched shutter. Thus, for weeks I was able to sneak into the cellar late at night and leave before any awakened in the morning.

This schedule worked while the weather held, but after the cold rolled in for good one clear January night, it was not so easy to keep. I wandered about during the day, scrounging what food I could, and occasionally winning a penny from my beggarly efforts. But when the sun went down the cold penetrated, and I was shivering by the time it was dark.

Earlier than before I found my way to the alley, and noted that the small windows were lit on the main and upper floors. They were still awake, but I was cold. Giving in to my own weakness, I slowly and carefully undid the clasp and entered the cellar. I lay down and covered myself with the rags, but the cellar too was chill, and I knew from experience that my nights of comfortable sleep were over.

Above I could hear the voices of children, the scraping of chairs, footsteps, and—intolerable to one from the streets— the pleasant odor of food being served. My own stomach, being empty as usual, began to growl loudly and I considered whether they could hear it above. I dozed, woke chilled, and dozed again. And so it went, waking a dozen times during the night, curling myself into an ever tighter ball and burrowing deeper under the inadequate rags.

Then, perhaps a week after the winter cold had arrived, I dropped silently into the cellar, closed the shutter, and allowed my eyes to adjust to the darkness. There was a shadow—a dark thing—crouching on the bottom-most step of the stairs. I jammed myself back against the wall, ready to flee, and hardly daring to breath. The shape did not stir, and shrank from an immense and terrible form to a rather small and inoffensive one.

I approached slowly, reached out a hand, and touched it. The surface was round and hard beneath a soft covering, and slightly warm to the touch. A covered bowl wrapped in a towel. I unwrapped the towel, raised the lid, and there before me in the bowl lay a piece of cheese and a hunk of bread.

Except for the months with Kieno, my life had been, as long as I could remember, a constant quest for food. This day had not been a particularly successful one. Many beggars were out, but moneyed walkers were in short supply. I'd noted a prosperous-looking couple and approached them respectfully, sticking out my hand and putting on a forlorn look of misery. I was watching for a kick or blow from the man, and was therefore unprepared when the gentle beauty at his side cursed and lashed out with her boot. I limped away from them quickly. Life is full of such surprises.

Now, the smell of food that permeated the cellar from the open bowl made my lack of success no easier to take. I was hungry, very hungry, and the aroma of strong cheese and fresh bread filled me with desire. Yet I hesitated to eat. Either the food was left there by mistake, or it was for me. If left by mistake, its disappearance would betray the presence of an intruder. The shutter would be inspected and fastened tight. I would lose my sanctuary and freeze the next night. End of problem. End of all problems.

If the bowl was for me, someone already knew and tolerated my presence. They were extending a bit of charity to the poor little robber with nowhere to go and nothing to eat. If that was the case, I was certainly grateful. It wouldn't stop me from stealing them blind given the opportunity, but I was grateful.

I covered the bowl and left it in place, resolved not to risk what I had. I arranged myself in my corner and shut my eyes, squeezing them tight. Unfortunately nothing could squeeze out the heavenly smell. My stomach began to play tricks with my backbone, and without food for the day my own body heat was at a low ebb. Shivering, I moved over to the step of the stair. I reviewed the situation from all perspectives and concluded that it would be extremely foolish and shortsighted to succumb to temptation.

Then I gobbled down every crumb. The deed done, I lay contentedly, a soft burp escaping as I curled up amidst my rags. Ah, well, perhaps I would be caught. Perhaps I would freeze tomorrow night. At least my last meal had been pleasant.

I left the cellar the next morning before dawn, spent the day with some small success among the artisans, and came back after dark with one meal in me from lunch, courtesy of a kindhearted street cleaner. The day had been cold, bitterly so, and that evening I waited for darkness anxiously. My approach to the cellar window was uneventful, and the latch was as I had left it, so I peered in and listened. Only the cold wind whistling past the buildings was heard. My eyes adjusted to the darkness, but there was nothing.

No, not nothing. There was something on the lowest step. Two things, in fact. One was the same covered bowl. The other was a mug filled with a liquid that turned out to be warm milk. Inside the bowl was a thick bean stew and bread. Miracle of miracles. I sat on the step and supped in fine fashion, listening to the family take its dinner above me. The voices of four or five children chattered happily as they ate with the adults. I imagined a table filled with bowls and plates of food. That came readily enough; but when I tried to imagine people at the table, I could not.

After a month I had grown accustomed to finding some morsel of food on the step each night, and looked forward to discovering what delicacies were waiting. Usually it was bread with a bit of cheese, or beans, or fish, and once or twice a bit of meat. Sometimes the bowl held thick soup or a stew. One evening I also found an old blanket folded and placed upon a crate. Such riches to be discarded! The blanket wrapped around me, and covered with a layer of rags, for the first time I was almost warm in the winter's night. Perhaps I would not steal them blind after all.

I pulled the blanket up to my chin and went to sleep.

It was a hard winter for Kingsport, as happened every nine or ten years. Icicles formed on the eaves of houses, and the snows that blanketed the town piled up rather than melt. The occasional thaw was immediately followed by a freeze and more snow. And always the wind blew in from the north, numbing the face and hands and piercing thin coats and ragged shoes.

The icy weather held late, but gave way to a spring eager to catch up with itself. One day there was ice and snow everywhere, the next day the temperature soared and all melted away in the heat of the sun. It was after the thaw that I returned to my cellar quarters one evening.

And found the shutter barred against me.

I pried sticks into the cracks, shook it, and forgetting caution, pounded on it with hands and feet, but it held closed as securely as any fortress gate. So the man and his wife had finally got around to fixing the clasp. For lack of anything better to do I went around to the front of the house. The area behind the shop window was dark. On the door was a notice, and beneath it a chain and lock securing the shop against any entry. Inside, all was empty. The woman was gone. The man was gone. The children were gone. And so were my rags, my dinners, my blanket, and my refuge.

3

Chance Encounter

There has been a great deal of misunderstanding about the next part of my tale, and several versions have been quite entertaining to hear and read. The real story is much simpler, and yet no less important to me.

It was a warm, sunny day perhaps a month after I had lost my cellar refuge, and I had no idea that anything momentous was going to happen. In fact, the day had been notably unsuccessful, and I had not yet eaten. My struggle for survival continued. The afternoon found me working the streets of the merchants in the general direction of the castle, with one eye out for sheriffs and the other for a likely pedestrian with a kind face. I had worked the area a dozen times before, and was familiar with the streets and crossings. But there was no specific purpose in my wanderings. Quite by chance, I found myself in front of the stables of the royal guards, located outside the castle moat on the King's Way North.

The guardsmen caring for their mounts would sometimes drop a penny for a boy to shovel out a stall or comb a horse. The older gutter rats tended to get this work. Other times, the guardsmen would wager a race or other contest between two or more of us and reward the winner with an extra coin. I had never succeeded in being chosen for either of these honors.

While the merchant district had a fair level of traffic, the stable area was quiet. Few people were about, and I saw no gutter rats. This chance lack of competition was encouraging, and might offer some opportunities. A stable hand with a bad limp slowly shoveled manure from a pile next to the stable door onto a waiting cart.

He shut me off before I could speak. "Sorry, boy, nobody's here, and I don't have no money." I looked around, but other than fourscore of horse, the stables were empty. The stable hand stopped shoveling and shook his head as I peered around. "They're over at the Silver Spur." The Silver Spur was located up the street, the sign over the door showing the image of its name. "But the guards don't like to be bothered when they're restin'. And you get some rough characters from the First Regiment there too."

He gave good advice. Still, I really didn't want to go to bed without eating that day. I ambled along the street until I was in front of the tavern and studied the entrance carefully. Two stone steps, a single door with a handle and latch, and stained glass in the small windows to either side of the entrance. All I had to do was walk through the door and try my luck.

No, not today. Outside I could run, inside I was trapped. Too many bad things could happen. What a shame. With my eyes still on the entrance I started to walk away, and promptly bumped into someone who smelled almost as bad as I did. I looked up and gasped.

Crazy Mary stood above me, her felt hat with the two eagle feathers pulled securely down to her ears. Where she had come from, I had no idea. But she did not look happy. Not happy at all.

"You want to go in there?" she asked, gesturing towards the Silver Spur.

"No . . . no, ma'am," I answered. Not since she'd shown up. I just wanted to get away from her.

"I could kill you," she stated in a flat tone that nonetheless carried her anger. She lifted her shirttail, and hidden at the waist was a large sheath from which protruded the handle of a knife. "I'm good with it. I can hit a rabbit when I want." She let her shirttail fall. "I could use my knife. Or better, I could just let you walk away. That would change things. You just walk away from here, and everything would be different."

"Yes, ma'am. I can . . . walk." I took a step. No use wasting the opportunity, now that I knew why they called her crazy. I resolved to stay away from fortune-tellers from now on.

"NO!" she said as I stepped away, and I froze. She sighed, her shoulders slumped, and her face fell. "No. I can't interfere."

That sounded more promising.

She looked at me again. "You have to go in there. In the tavern."

I shook my head. "No. Thank you. I . . . have to go—"

"You have to go in," she persisted, and her voice firmed. "Now. Go in now. Do not make me angry again." She put her hands on her hips. They were uncomfortably near the knife.

If I had to go in to get away from this crazy woman, I would. A drubbing from the innkeeper was better than a knife in the back. I stopped outside the door, looked back, and saw her standing there still. She made shooing motions with her hands. Taking a deep breath I lifted the latch and pushed against the solid oaken door. Nothing happened. Bracing myself, I put my shoulder against the door and shoved. The door swung open, I slipped through, and the spring mounted at the top closed it behind, leaving me inside a short arched way with another door leading into the main hall.

There would be no fast getaways through that springed door, and so no stealing here, for sure. But as long as I had come this far, why not try for a handout? My stomach growled in agreement. I certainly couldn't go outside with the crazy woman waiting with her dinosaur slicer. The inner door opened easily, and I stepped into the tavern.

The Silver Spur was not greatly different from a hundred others in Kenesee. The room was smoky and dark, except where the gloom was banished by the glow of the fireplace and two oil lamps. The smell of beer, tobacco, and food tickled

the nose in a pleasant mixture of aromas. The high ceiling
beams were festooned with clumps of dried spice, cuts of
smoked meat and fish, sausages, and round cheeses collected
in nets. On the floor sawdust had been thickly spread, and was
dotted with the tobacco juice of chewers who had expressed
themselves most freely. At the back of the room was a short
serving bar with shelves of mugs and tapped kegs, with an
open doorway leading out into the kitchen.

Clustered at two long tables that got the most light were a
dozen men taking their rest. Those at one table were black-
uniformed guardsmen, while those at the other wore the brown
tunics of the Army of Kenesee. Their caps and coats hung
from pegs on the thick uprights supporting the roof beams.
Most were drinking and talking, while a few played cards. One
pipe-smoking guardsman was writing in a book. To a boy of
eight they seemed very old, but most were young men barely
in their twenties.

There was nary a tavern keeper or barmaid in sight, which
was encouraging, for they guarded their taverns jealously. Soldiers can be a rough lot, especially when in a group. A good
jest is one thing, and they will not miss a chance for it. However, most will not do anything to lower their standing in the
eyes of their fellows, and picking on a gutter rat does not stand
high in the list of martial feats. Therefore, I should be all
right—unless one was in a particularly bad mood and wanted
some sport.

I put on a sad face, went into my best poor-little-beggar
role, and stuck out my hand to the nearest guardsman. His
face registered mild surprise, then he shook his head and went
back to the cards in his hand. I went to the next guardsman
and tried again. The man looked at me and sighed. "Not here
too. Can't we ever get away from you little beggars? No. Go
away."

The third guardsman was the one writing in a book, a lank,
hard-featured man with three stripes on his sleeve. He took
the pipe from his mouth and tapped the bowl out into an ash-
tray. His voice was clear and sure. "There's rules, son. The
stables are fair, the tavern isn't. Better get going."

Warning enough. Perhaps I could slip out the back way. I
accepted defeat gracefully and turned away to leave. It was
then that someone from the second table grabbed me by the

collar and lifted me until my feet swung well free of the floor. My captor was a big man with bristly hair and a nose that had been broken and set askew. He looked mean, and I had little doubt that he could have hurled me against the wall rather as one might bounce a ball. I knew I wouldn't bounce very well.

He spat a wad of tobacco juice on the floor. "So," the soldier sneered for the benefit of the others. "Now the little thieves are coming in here to do their dirty work. Maybe you're the one who stole my wallet last week, heh?" He shook me as he finished, and I gave a good imitation of a rag doll.

Another soldier at the same table spoke deferentially. "Maybe you should let him down, Sergeant Petty."

"Is that so? Why?"

"Because he can't breathe and he's starting to turn blue."

"Oh," said my captor. He lowered me to the floor and loosened his grip.

Breathing is a wonderful thing, a fact we become aware of when not permitted to do it for a minute or two. Quite important to one's well-being.

Another man with a sly-looking face snickered and elbowed my captor. "Maybe he's not a thief, Sergeant Petty. Let's see. Hey, rat. Maybe you were selling something. How old is she?" General laughter from the table greeted the jest. I swallowed and opened my mouth, but no words came, and so I shook my head, waiting desperately for an opportunity to escape.

Obviously my captor had had a bad day. His sneer increased. "This place is off limits, and it's time you gutter rats learned it. Here, Murphy, move the mugs and hold him."

The sly-looking man, a helpful sort, took my arms and pinned them so that I was stretched face down on the table, with my legs dangling to the floor. Then I felt my coat being pushed up and my pants down, so that bare buttocks smiled out.

I released gas, and drew cheers and laughter from my audience. The big sergeant was not amused, and removed his heavy leather belt.

A voice at the next table whispered. "Sergeant Black?"

"It isn't our affair, Jenkins," answered the voice of the pipe smoker.

The big man swung, the belt cracked across my bottom, and

I responded with a scream. The belt cracked again. It's amazing how much pain a simple leather belt wielded by a healthy man can cause. I screamed again, and then began to whimper. I was extremely good at whimpering.

There was laughter following the first blow, but it diminished and finally died, so that after the fifth there was only the sound of the belt striking, followed by my mewing.

And then the pipe smoker spoke up. "All right, Petty, that's enough. You've made your point."

The belt cracked again and the big man spoke. "Listen, Black, when I'm finished, I'm finished."

He swung the belt three more times to show he wasn't scared of the other man, and then he laughed. "All right. Let him up. He's learned his lesson."

My hands were released and I stood sore and shaken, glancing around furtively for possible escape. The pipe smoker glanced at me, did a double take, and put down his book. I felt behind me and was surprised to find my rear dry, the blood I had felt being totally imaginary. I slowly pulled up my pants over the sore flesh, while in the doorway to the kitchen a man with a stained leather apron, the tavern keeper, looked on disapprovingly.

My torturer waved to him. "Well, it's about time. Look, Miguel, we did your job for you. How about a free round for my table?"

The tavern keeper wiped his hands on a towel and shrugged. The price of doing business and keeping the customers satisfied. "All right, Sergeant Petty. One free round for table. Beer, not booze."

There were cheers while the tavern keeper came forward and dragged me into the kitchen and through the back door. He stopped outside in an alley. I covered my face with my free hand and braced for the blow.

"You all right, little guy?"

I peeped out from between my fingers and nodded.

"Good. You don't come in here no more, understand? You do, and I give you same the sergeant did. Now, you sit down on step and I get you something to eat. First time, last time, that's it. Understand?" With that, he scooted back and carefully closed the door behind him.

The door opened again immediately, and another face

peered down. The pipe smoker. Black. Sergeant Black. I tried to bolt, and found I could not. My backside was too sore. He caught me without effort and stood me on the step.

His face was intent, his eyes hard, his grip strong. I tried to twist myself free, but could not. "Drop your pants." Oh oh. One of those. And he hadn't seemed a bad sort. Well, you just never knew.

"Drop them." The tone in his voice left no room for argument, or even discussion. I would not like what would happen if I disobeyed. Reluctantly, I pushed my pants down around my knees and prepared to scream if he touched me. The sergeant stared intently at my groin for a moment, then shook his head in disbelief. "All right. I've seen enough. Pull up your pants and sit down."

I did so without further encouragement.

"Your mother," he said sternly. "Where is she?"

My mother? This man was crazy too! A nod or the shake of the head was not going to suffice in this exchange. My throat constricted, but I tried to calm myself.

"No . . . mother," I managed to croak out.

He shook me. "No lies. Where is she?"

"No . . . mother."

"Is she dead?" His hands clenched.

I winced. "Sir. No mother. Never had . . . a mother."

The fire in his eyes blazed for a moment, and then burned down. He frowned, let go, and sat down on the step beside me. He was silent for a long moment, then rubbed a hand across his brow.

The tavern keeper came out with a hard roll sandwich and a broken-handled mug.

He looked at us suspiciously. "Everything all right, John?"

"No. But don't worry about it."

"I be inside. Let me know you need anything." He gave us a last glance. "I want the mug back, robber, you understand? Leave it on step." The door closed.

The crazy sergeant made no move, so I began stuffing the sandwich into my mouth. Good food, I had to admit. The sandwich was gone in about three seconds, washed down with beer.

One beating, one meal. Some pay more. Much more.

Then again, I still had the crazy sergeant to contend with.

He looked at me again. "What's your name?"

"Arn."

He repeated it silently. "Of course. Her father's name. Where do you come from?"

I thought about it. No harm in telling the truth. "Louisville."

"And before that? What do you remember first?"

"I . . . don't remember," I said, honestly. "I worked . . . for a man. Public Bath."

"Do you remember your mother?"

I shook my head no, and he began to pace before me, his hands clasped behind his back. He was silent for a long time, striding up and down in the alley until I wondered whether he had forgotten me. "Ahh, Nancy. What would you have me do?" he muttered to himself, then looked at me again and shrugged. He held out his hand. "Come along, son."

I glanced around, estimating my chances. It was still quite light out, and we were alone. I had little doubt he would have me within three paces if I tried to run. And he hadn't done anything to me when my pants were down. Best just to go along with him until I saw my opportunity for escape. I stood up carefully, hitched my pants into place, and took his hand. It was dry and strong, closing around mine in a firm grip that would not easily be broken.

"Where are . . . we going?" I asked, fear gripping me as firmly as Sergeant Black.

He nodded towards the castle.

"Up there. To see the King."

4

The First Days

The two guards at the drawbridge looked oddly at us, but nodded respectfully as Sergeant Black led me through the outer gates. We passed under a raised portcullis and then through a short tunnel. A pair of inner gates framed the stone courtyard where several trees had been allowed to grow.

On the left was a stable with wide double doors that had been swung back to reveal a line of stalls, each holding a horse that was magnificent in line and limb. On the right was a two-story stone barracks. An off-duty guardsman leaned in the doorway and flirted with an attentive laundress holding a basket of clothes.

Directly in front was the king's house, a huge, stone edifice with its own battlements overlooking the outer walls. These battlements were topped by towers and turrets which stretched yet higher above us. Three wide steps led to massive oaken doors reinforced with metal strips and bolts. A guard stood duty on either side.

I was craning my neck, awestruck, until I tripped on a paving stone and almost went down. The sergeant shook his head in exasperation and tugged me up the three steps. The guards looked at each other but didn't say a word as we went through the doors. We were in a long, wide corridor with passages, stairs, and doorways on both sides. At the end was a set of finely carved doors.

Sergeant Black led me down a passageway to an unpretentious door and knocked. A muffled voice responded. The sergeant removed his cap, opened the door, and pushed me through in front of him. The room was barely adequate for a bed, desk, shelf, and washstand, its main light coming from an oil lamp upon the desk. Behind the desk sat a small, balding man in the same uniform as Black, but with four wide slash marks adorning each sleeve. He looked up from papers and ledgers, smiling when he saw the sergeant but giving me a puzzled stare.

Sergeant Black came to attention next to me. "Good afternoon, Sergeant Major Nakasone."

The sergeant major raised his eyebrows in faint surprise. "Official business, John?"

"Sorry to bother you, Sergeant Major."

Nakasone sighed and then spoke. "Haven't had a problem for the last hour except these supply inventories, so I guess I was due. Well, how can I help?"

The sergeant stood at ease. "Sergeant Major, I'd like permission to see the King."

Leaning back till his chair balanced on the rear two legs, the sergeant major clasped his hands behind his head. "Well, I can see his Secretary. Maybe fit you in next week."

"I'll have to see the King now, Sergeant Major."

The man shook his head. "Let's have it, John. What is this all about?"

The sergeant gestured at me. "This boy is the son of Nancy Brown."

The chair came down onto all four legs with a thunk. The sergeant major stared at me as if I'd turned into a fire-breathing dragon. "Nancy Brown? Good Lord, John. Are you sure?"

"I've questioned him. I've seen the mark. It's him."

"All right. Tell me the story."

Sergeant Black related what had happened at the Silver Spur. I couldn't fault his version, but didn't like being described as a "smelly little robber." Sergeant Major Nakasone considered me again, shook his head in disbelief, and stood up. "Wait here," he ordered, and went out.

The sergeant paced slowly up and down the confines of the room. He was silent for a long moment. "You'd better not be a mistake, son."

"No . . . sir." I had no idea what he was talking about.

"The Sergeant Major will get Graven. He's High Wizard and Secretary to the King. Graven will scoff but—"

The door opened with a bang and the sergeant came to attention as the high wizard entered. He was a tall, thin man with gray hair who wore a richly textured robe sashed at the waist. His hands were mottled with spots and patches of red and purple.

"Is this the boy?"

"That's him," said the sergeant major, following the wizard in.

"Have the boy show me the mark."

Sergeant Black put a hand on my shoulder. "Drop your pants, Arn."

Again? Reluctantly, I untied the rope and let my pants fall.

"Turn to the side," ordered the high wizard. "I don't see anything."

I turned. Sergeant Black rapped his knuckles on my head impatiently. "The other way."

I turned around. With a scowl, the wizard swept out of the room.

"He's his usual cheery self," cracked the sergeant major. "Uh, you can pull up your pants."

After a while the door opened and another man strode in, followed by Graven and a half dozen official-looking dignitaries. The man was handsomely built, with an expansive chest, broad shoulders and neck, and a square face framed with a red beard and red hair. He seemed to emote confidence and energy. His clothes were rich and embroidered with threads of gold, but upon his head he wore the simplest metal crown.

The guardsmen sprang to their feet. I stood up too, eyeing the man suspiciously. I am not such a fool that I could not guess who had entered.

The man immediately looked for me. "I am the King. What is your name?"

He stared at me. Graven stared at me. The guardsmen stared at me. The dignitaries stared at me. I felt my heart pounding and the room grow warm. I opened my mouth to speak, but only a croak came out.

The king frowned. "What's wrong with him?"

"He can speak, sir," explained Sergeant Black. "But is very reluctant to. I suspect the circumstances may be leaving him tongue-tied. His name is Arn."

"Arnold?"

"Possibly, sir. He gave the name Arn."

"Humph. Arn. And the proof?" asked the king, doubtfully.

Someone tapped my shoulder. I was getting the idea by now. I dropped my pants and turned so they could see the mark. I even thrust out my hips to give them a better view. There were gasps and murmurs from the newcomers.

"Where is my physician?" asked the king, never taking his eyes off me.

Another man pushed forward through the crowded room, leaned over, and examined the mark closely with probing fingers. A lamp was held close for extra light while he scraped and scratched at the mark with various materials. I was sore for a week.

"Well?" demanded the king, impatiently.

"It appears to be a natural birthmark, sir. And his size and development do seem to indicate the appropriate chronological age. . . ."

"Does the mark match the birth records?" asked Graven.

"I'll have to look. It's been a long time."

A leather envelope was produced and the physician took out documents and selected a page. He looked at it closely, then at the mark, and then back again, and after a long glance handed the page to the king and cleared his throat. "In regard to the shape, there can be no doubt. The mark is exactly the same, sir."

The king's voice quivered as he put a hand on either of my shoulders and looked at me intently. "Then this is my son?"

"Unless this is a clever ruse—the evidence seems to indicate that this is the offspring of Nancy Brown. Your son."

The king's eyes moistened. He looked at the page and my mark, and then studied my face closely. "He has brown hair. And gray eyes. She had both, I remember. Yes, this is her child."

There was no space left to move in the room, and yet the others drew back respectfully as a woman entered. She was tall and stately, blessed with an hourglass figure and a perfect face framed by a glorious mass of black hair. On her head rested a bejeweled crown. Her dress was cut tightly from the waist up, accentuating her femininity. Even though only a child, I could recognize the exceptional beauty of the woman. She swept the room with a cool glance, her eyes briefly catching those of Graven. "What is this all about? My maid informs me of a matter of importance. Why wasn't I called?"

The king sniffed back a tear. "Jessica. We've found my son."

"What?" She looked at me for the first time. "How can you be sure?" she asked.

Graven spoke up. "We may devise other tests, my Queen, but it appears there can be little doubt." He looked at her intently. "We all share the joy of our King."

"Of course. Yes. This is . . . wonderful. I am very happy for you, Reuel. Now you have our Robert—and this one too."

The king released me and wiped his nose with a royal sleeve. "Well. Well!" He turned and took the woman's hand, kissed it, then smiled all around. He reached out his other hand and took mine. "There is so much to do. But first things first. Prepare the royal bath for the Prince."

Prince?

Graven nodded without expression. "And check him for lice."

The royal bath was nothing more than a large tub of steaming water in a bare room. I sat in the tub and staff stood around and questioned me without pause about my past. I grunted out a yes or no where appropriate, but just stared when a more complicated answer was required. Given the constantly changing audience, my unfamiliarity with any of them, and my own wish to concentrate on the pleasures of the water, I could manage no more. Yet even these responses were dutifully scribbled in ledgers.

The servants despaired of getting me out of the water (which I refused to leave) until their pleas turned to warnings that I would miss supper. But it was a trick, because then my hair was cut and I was turned over to the royal physician, whom I was not happy to see again. His name turned out to be Amani, and he wasn't a bad sort as doctors go, quite proud when he took me into his clinic—a single room filled with gleaming instruments of torture—for an examination in which I was thoroughly pinched, poked, and prodded, as well as weighed and measured in every direction, each fact duly recorded in yet another ledger. The doctor pronounced me malnourished but free of vermin and disease, which, by his expression, he somehow felt was a miracle.

Colorful garments of rich cloth were brought. "For . . . me?" I asked.

The woman and man who helped me dress were named Marta and Walter, an old couple on the domestic staff. "Well, they belonged to Prince Robert before," said Marta, "but he's outgrown them, so I think we can say that they're yours now, Prince Arn."

Prince Arn. It was the first time I had heard the title put with my name. If being a prince meant hot baths and fine clothes, then I was all for it. A prince I would be.

Dressed and combed, I was led down a passageway to a large dining hall. I came to an abrupt halt in the entryway, trying to take everything in. The room was high vaulted, with tapestries and curtains lending warmth and color. On the far wall were portraits and a number of stuffed trophies of nightmarish proportion: large heads of reptilian beasts sporting evil teeth, sinister horns, and snakelike eyes that seemed to follow wherever you went in the room. I looked away from the deadly sight. There was a massive fireplace at one end which remained unlit this evening, while a dozen lamps provided light. The hall was able to seat a hundred quite comfortably, but for this meal it was no more than a third full. The diners were clustered at several long tables near the fireplace and waited upon by a half dozen young men and women.

Silence fell among the diners, and every eye swung upon me. I didn't really see them. A delicious aroma assailed me, and my attention focused upon the tables loaded down with food. Each table held one platter with thick, juicy slices of roast beef and a second platter offering large roast chickens baked golden brown. These centerpieces were framed by steaming bowls of boiled potatoes soaked in butter, carrots covered with melted cheese, and beets. Pots of thick vegetable soup and loaves of crusty bread filled the little space remaining. The servers waited with more platters bearing cheeses, fruit, and nuts. It was not a banquet, but merely—as I found out later—an ordinary dinner, standard fare for the table of the king and his court. There had been no time to organize any celebration in my honor. Yet the display of prepared food on each table was greater than any I'd ever seen, and I was struck with wonder.

Marta and Walter stood at the doorway and pushed me forward. "Over there, Prince Arn. See the King's table? You go in by yourself, and we'll see you after the meal. Go on now, the King is waiting for you."

I tore my gaze from the food and spotted him at the head table, beckoning me forward. All watched me closely, some with smiles of welcome, some with curiosity, and some, perhaps, with other thoughts. I stopped before the king, who smiled his approval at my appearance. Then, barely restraining his joy and to the applause of all, he announced that I was found and would now join the royal family as his second son, with all the duties(?) and privileges(!) of that position.

A boy of self-assured dignity stepped forward. He was two inches taller than I, well-formed and solidly built, with a smiling face and the red hair of the king. "I'm Robert. I have wanted a brother for a long time, and now I have one. Welcome, Arn." And then he threw his arms around me, and hugged tightly.

I stood in his embrace with my hands at my sides. I didn't know what to do. Robert backed off then, his hands still resting upon my shoulders, looking a bit puzzled—and disappointed. He lowered his arms, shrugged, and the smile returned to his face.

The king gazed down fondly upon both of us. "It has been a bit lonely for Robert, you see, since there are no other boys of his age among the noble families. But Robert is only six months older than you, so I think that problem has been solved." He grinned at the diners. "Now, since Arn is eyeing the food, let us begin. There will be time later for him to meet everyone."

Robert and I sat down next to each other and across from the king and queen, and for some time my attention did not go beyond the bounty on the table. The food tasted even better than it looked. I noticed others watching me silently.

"Something . . . wrong?" I asked Robert.

"No. I just never saw anyone eat the bones too."

A good point. Why bother with bones when so much else was available? I took another chicken leg.

"Well," said the king, watching as I cleared the table. "Remind me to raise taxes."

There was laughter and then people were chattering in conversation. Robert rambled on about how much fun we would have, to which I listened with one ear. The High Wizard Graven sat opposite me next to Queen Jessica, listening to her while she talked, but glancing too often at me. She spoke softly, so that Graven had to lean towards her to catch her words. Perhaps others could not or did not hear, but I had no trouble listening to the two while cleaning my plate.

"How could this happen?" she asked, nodding pleasantly to another table.

The high wizard tore a piece of bread in two. "I think this is not the place to speak of such matters."

"You said everything was taken care of. What went wrong?"

"I don't know. I saw them board the ship myself, and watched it sail for Texan. I have sent your money to the man faithfully each year since. Obviously, there has been treachery."

"Treachery. Yes. And what shall we call our deed?"

The high wizard looked at her. "My Queen, it was you who came to me for help."

"I know. I know. But what do we do now?"

"That we must think about."

The king turned to them and put an arm around the tiny waist of the queen. "Well, has my High Wizard figured out how Arn could have lived for so long inside Kenesee without being detected by our magicians?" The king's tone was lighthearted, yet beneath it was a hard edge.

Graven shrugged. "I have no answer for you, my King. For two years after his disappearance our best magicians searched the kingdom in vain. He must have returned after we stopped looking. I was remiss."

"And I did not think to tell you to continue the search. Well, it is over, and all has turned out well in the end. That's all that matters." The king smiled across at me. "Had enough to eat, Arn?" he inquired hopefully.

Not quite, but since I had been slyly stuffing my pockets, I nodded yes anyway and with that the king rose, signaling the meal's end. He took me around to each person in turn, faces looming up before me. I would come to know them all well, but for now names and titles blended in a long roll call of confusion. The ordeal ended at last, after which Marta and Walter took me to a room which they assured me was now my own.

"This is the bachelor quarters," Walter explained. "Prince Robert's room is right next to yours, and across the way is High Wizard Graven's room, and next to it Mr. Kendall's. That alcove on the end is used by the High Wizard's Apprentice. He gets a new apprentice every nine or ten years. And here you are. This room is yours."

A fire had been lit in the hearth. It was quite cozy, except for the cold stone walls. It held a comfortable reading couch, desk and chair, dresser, shelves, and a soft bed with lots of blankets. I had never slept in such a bed before but, inviting as it looked, I would not let Marta and Walter undress me. When they finally left I reached into my pockets, removed the food I had stolen and hid it all under the bed. For the first time, I could eat my fill and still have food left over. By the end of the week I had a sizable horde, but Walter discovered the hiding place and assured me I could have whatever I wanted from the kitchen merely by asking. I asked, and a large tray of fruit, cheese, and bread was set before me. I allowed him to clean under the bed then, and perhaps it was a good thing, for the meat had turned a most interesting shade of green.

On the morning after my arrival a tailor came, measured every limb twice, had me try on a closet full of Robert's outgrown clothes, and left with an effusion of wishes for my continued health and good fortune, due no doubt to the promise of rich fees for his work. Within days my closet filled with an array of clothes which I could not believe, and most of which I didn't know how to put on. One outfit had thirty-two buttons. I counted them, once I'd learned how to count. There were clothes for daily wear, for court activities, for ceremonies, for celebrations, for traveling, for hunting, and even uniforms in black akin to those of the royal guards which were worn during military training.

Little was expected of me the first few days, and I was allowed to roam the castle and grounds until I became familiar with every building, every hall and chamber, and every tower and battlement. I've already mentioned that inside the castle wall were several stone buildings, the principal ones being the king's house, the barracks, and the stables. Behind these were several grassed and flowered terraces arranged in staggered tiers. The walls of the terraces could serve as secondary barriers should the outer wall be breached. Although all the buildings were stoutly built and could be defended if need be, the king's house was intended as the final stronghold against any assault. Its walls were thick, with shuttered arrow slits rather than windows. Only the highest towers had actual window openings, so that most chambers were quite dark and had to be lit by oil lamps and torches.

I found the thick stone walls . . . comforting.

It was dry inside, pleasantly cool in summer, but drafty and cold in winter except in front of the fireplaces. The king had considered putting stoves in for greater efficiency, but the high wizard was shocked at the suggestion, and asked him to consider the history and tradition of the castle which we were upholding. Reluctantly the king agreed. Thus I learned the power, and folly, of tradition.

The house was even larger than it appeared from the outside, since two levels were below ground. In its cellar were an armory, larders, cistern, and a well. On the floors above were the great hall (which held the throne), dining hall, second hall, council room, library, royal quarters, ladies' quarters, bachelor quarters, guest quarters, servant quarters, kitchen, pantry, and a few chambers tucked in odd corners such as the sergeant major's room.

Robert was my constant companion and guide during this time, and he seemed quite proud to introduce me to the household. I met—and began to remember—the advisors in the king's council, the members of his royal staff, and the soldiers of the royal guard. There were only a few dozen who actually resided within the walls of the castle, excluding the hundred men of the guard. The staff was quite small, and any special services or needs were contracted out to the guilds and merchants of the town. In fact, after visiting the houses of the other four noble families I noted that life in the king's castle was relatively austere in comparison.

All of the household were properly respectful to Robert and me, but forms of deference were limited. Everyone stood when the king or queen entered, and remained standing while they did. No one stood for princes. We came and went without note, and the staff might greet us with a good day or a nod of the head as they would anyone, or even ignore us if they preferred. We were just playful boys roaming through the castle while others did more meaningful tasks. We were free to interact with all, from the lowest dishwasher to the high wizard, but Robert made clear to me that there were definite expectations in regard to our behavior and the rights of citizens. Thus, I could go into the kitchen to watch the cook work and listen to him chat—which I enjoyed doing—but to bother him when he was busy, to enter his quarters without his permission, to disobey, to cause a mess, or to otherwise treat him with less than full respect would earn me a floured slap across the face from the cook and a verbal reprimand from the king. Any member of the staff or guard could give us fair punishment without hesitation. It had not always been so with each generation that had grown up in the stone walls of the king's castle, but in the reign of King Reuel Brant, as he told us, it would be, by God. The king wanted princes, not spoiled brats.

This back-to-basics, commonsense attitude extended to almost everything the king did. For example, he had abolished saluting in the army and for the guards. For ceremonies a salute of honor could still be rendered, or as a special token of respect for heroes. But the king felt the men had better things to do than worry about saluting, especially when burdened with spear and shield. The castle guards were the same. When standing watch, guards were expected to be alert and watchful, not acting like statues while someone snuck up on them. Most of the nobles emulated the king's example with their own household troops.

None of this hurt his standing in the kingdom. The king's respect and appreciation of the common man had made him, by the tenth year of his reign, one of the most popular kings in the line of Brant. He had been saddened when his father King Richard had died, but he knew himself to be ready to assume the duties of the kingdom. Administration was not his greatest strength, as he himself recognized, but he was decisive, and a good judge of ability; he surrounded himself with advisors and experts who more than compensated for his own weakness. He was strong-willed and proud, but also fair and just, honestly wanting the best for the kingdom and its people. And he was an excellent warrior, strong and skilled in weapons, and all too ready to defend his borders should they be threatened.

Unfortunately for his martial dreams, the only threats to the kingdom at this time came from the counties in the northeast, where travelers and the occasional farmhold were being assaulted three or four times a year. Those assaulted were always killed. The matter was discussed at meetings of the king's council of advisors.

Most meetings were open to Robert and me, although our own schedules later would preclude sitting in on many. I considered the sessions downright boring. The council consisted of the king and his four advisors. Just a few weeks after my arrival the king asked that we sit in on one morning session. Under discussion as we arrived was a most recent tragedy. A party of travelers had been found—all dead—on a road bordering the Northern Forests. It was the work either of highwaymen or beastmen. The king pointed to a map on the wall, giving the background to Robert and me, although perhaps Robert already knew all this, and it was for my benefit alone.

"In the northwest, the Ohio River separates us from the forest tribes of men on the northern bank. In the east, that whole part of the forest is called the Beastwood, and a goodly portion of it extends south of the river. The beastmen live there."

Beastmen. I had heard the term before, and had once seen a drawing in the window of a print shop. The beastmen had fur over their bodies and pig noses and fangs and wicked eyes. Or so the drawing had shown them.

"They were created by the devil to challenge man's possession of the world," intoned Bishop Jebediah Thomas. The head of the Church of Kenesee was a distinguished-looking man of moderate learning and little thought. But he was an effective preacher who tempered the brimstone of his churchmen and bent to the will of the king as needed.

"Perhaps," said Paul Kendall. "Or perhaps the beastmen are just men like ourselves, and only differ on the outside, with as little meaning as the shade of our skins." Paul Kendall, a homely, deceptively quiet young man originally from the far off nation of Pacifica, spoke with a faint, though not unpleasant, accent. He was the king's science and foreign affairs expert.

"Even if they were men at one time, Mr. Kendall," the bishop retorted, "they are no longer. Now, they bear the mark of the beast. And though all fall within God's Plan, the beast that offends shall not be suffered to live. That is what the testament says, and that is what I believe."

"The Catholics believe the beastmen have souls," offered Sir Meredith.

"Yes, but the Papists have many strange beliefs," the Bishop responded.

Souls? The king had talked to me about souls, and religion, and God. The bishop had talked to me about sin, and punishment, and hell. I knew heaven was impossible for me, and I was scared of hell, so I ignored the whole lot and was much happier for it.

"We must leave the discussion of theological issues for another time," the king reminded them. "I'm interested in the security of our people. Graven, has your intelligence service been able to find out who is behind these attacks?"

"No, sir. A few of them, doubtless, are just common high-waymen and bandits. But it is thought that the beastmen are responsible for most, and are trying to make it look like the work of men. It is rumored that some of the women even had tufts of fur in their hands which they tore from the beastmen in their struggles before they were killed. None of the fur has come to us, unfortunately."

"The sheriffs will have to do a better job of this," said the king. "And the men-at-arms of the nobles, too. Valuable evidence has been overlooked."

"Yes, my King," said Sir Meredith. The popular Sir Meredith Sims—son of the aged Duke Gregory of the House of Sims—was a modest, friendly, and capable man representing the five noble families. His quiet dignity and ability made him the most respected of the nobility, though not the most senior by age or succession. He was not always as quick as others in thought and decision, but given time he would see more clearly to the bottom of matters than any other. "I will look into it," he continued. "But some say the fur was actually horse hair."

"We cannot know," admitted Graven. "But who can say

beast fur and horse hair are not similar? What is definite is that nowhere else in the kingdom is the banditry as vicious in its attacks. It is only in the northeast, where the Beastwood lies, that we suffer.'' The High Wizard David Graven was the senior advisor, his mottled hands gesturing freely. He had a frown for every topic, and did not look happy even when his advice was followed.

The king sat back. ''So. What do my advisors recommend?''

Graven spoke up first. ''Perhaps a punitive expedition up to the Ohio River would remove the threat, and teach them a lesson. If we were to occupy the area, it would also allow us to anchor our border on the river, rather than at the forest edge. Certainly, our town defenses are now in better shape than they have been for decades, and most of the troops are better equipped than ever before. We have spent much in the last few years to make them so.''

''Force is in order,'' said the bishop. ''The beastmen have an animal cunning, but lack any kind of organization. They exist in mere tribes, and should be easily defeated by our army.''

''Bishop Thomas, we can't be sure of that,'' Kendall responded. ''None of our spies has ever penetrated their territory successfully, nor has any military unit. They may be better organized than we think. If so, any venture against them could be hazardous. Remember they don't follow the Codes, and can't be depended upon to fight according to the rules of battle.''

The king turned to the nobleman. ''Sir Meredith?''

''I'm still not sure. We really don't know much about the beastmen, do we? And we don't know who is doing all this. The High Wizard says that the beastmen are making it look like men are responsible. Perhaps men are making it look like the beastmen are responsible.''

''Sir Meredith has a good point, sir,'' Kendall agreed. ''The House of Sims has responsibility for that region. Perhaps Duke Sims might increase patrols in the area. And sending a few spies to the border would give us more information to make a decision.''

Sir Meredith drummed his fingers on the desk. ''We could do that. Perhaps we could also build a small keep on the border and run patrols from it, though it wouldn't be completed until next year, at best. I'll have a word with my father, the Duke. He's getting on in years, and is a bit forgetful now. But we'll do as suggested.''

"A keep would be helpful," the king agreed. "I presume the House of Sims can afford to undertake its construction? Good.'' The king wrote a note to himself. "We have discussed this before, and always come to the same impasse. The High Wizard and Bishop have made their point. We've tolerated these attacks for several years, and they have only grown worse. As you admit, Kendall, our spies cannot penetrate their borders, and there is no greater likelihood for success now. But I tire of these attacks. If they continue I will respond.''

"God's Will be done," the bishop intoned.

Kendall opened his mouth as if to speak, then closed it. It was useless to argue with the king once he had declared a course of action.

"And now, what is the next item on the agenda?''

Graven checked his notes. "Care for the orphans of the kingdom, sir.''

"Yes, the orphans. Arn, you have told us there are no orphanages?''

"Just the . . . Catholic one. The Shelter. It was full." I was learning to speak to friendly individuals with less difficulty, and was working on small groups. I could almost get out a short sentence without pause. This was progress. But the council of advisors was intimidating.

"And they had no room, you say? Are there many 'robbers'—that is the term, I believe—on the streets?''

"Many," I answered.

"All over?" asked Sir Meredith.

"Maybe. In Kingsport. In Louisville, too. I don't know . . . where else.''

"Our population is growing," Kendall observed. "With the new health measures the King has implemented during his reign, more children survive. The existence of these children is a measure of our success, but it has also created new demands. I had not realized the extent of the problem until the discovery of Prince Arn called it to our attention.''

"That means there must be hundreds all over the kingdom," the king said sadly. He looked at the bishop. "Only one orphanage. Can't we do something?"

Bishop Thomas looked uncomfortable. "The congregations undertake numerous charitable ventures, my King. The people contribute to the basket every Sunday. However, the cathedral is still not completed, and labor costs go up every year. We have very little money, and very many demands. Perhaps if the kingdom could grant financial support, we could open a home in each major town."

The king shook his head. "All of the taxes are committed. Once this matter with the beastmen is cleaned up, perhaps we can use some of the defense moneys. Could not the towns do something?"

"The towns are in a similar strait," Sir Meredith cautioned. "The public latrines, baths, and other health measures you ordered each town to pay for have gradually gained favor with the people, and the town officials no longer begrudge the money spent for these. However, little is left over."

The king frowned, and then brightened. "Graven, when will the masonry work on the walled towns be completed?"

"By this fall at the latest, sir."

"Then we'll use those funds. Bishop Thomas, may I ask you to research this matter? Good. I'd like a report on your findings by our meeting next week. Now, let's move on to the next item."

After the meeting the king motioned for Robert and me to stay when the advisors departed. He pulled his chair back and stretched out.

"Ahh, that's better. These meetings aren't always the easiest, but they are necessary." He thought for a moment before going on. "Let me tell you a few things about the council. I have chosen these four men for several reasons. First, they are all good administrators and good managers who develop plans and make them reality. Second, they are very influential with powerful groups that are important to the stability of the kingdom. Third, I believe they are all loyal to the throne. Each has his own ideas about how to achieve success, yet I believe they are united in wanting what is best for the kingdom. Otherwise, I would not have them here. I listen to all they have to tell me. Every fact, every opinion has value. But in the end, only the King can make the decision. And once the decision is made, it should not be altered. Can you remember all that?''

Robert and I looked at each other and nodded.

''Each man has his own beliefs, ideas, and ambitions. Know them so that you can use them. That is the duty of a King, to use those men for the good of all. I tell you this because I want you both to know how to be King in a world of men. Robert, you will become King upon my death. If you die, Arn would become King unless the Queen has another male child. Dr. Amani has cautioned us not to have more children, so I don't think that will occur. I want you both prepared, both ready in case anything should ever happen. No, Robert, I don't anticipate my early demise. But there are accidents, and illness, and if we go into the Beastwood, as I'm afraid we'll have to, then a sword can cut down a King as well as a private.

''Now, the subject matter of our little chats is only between the three of us. Do not discuss it, do not repeat it. Otherwise, you'll find out what it's like being dropped from the battlements. If you have questions, hold them. You'll learn more when you need it. For now, watch, listen, and learn.''

The king paused, thoughtful, and then concluded the discussion. ''That's enough for now. Robert, I'd like to talk a moment with your brother.''

''Of course, sir,'' he answered without concern, and left us.

The king sat up, put his elbows on his knees and folded his hands. He hesitated, searching for words. ''I've wanted to talk to you in private, Arn. We'll have many talks in the future, and there is much for you to learn. But I did want to tell you the story of your mother and me. Have you heard anything of that?''

''No, sir,'' I lied.

''Good. Good. Have you wondered about your mother?''

''No, sir,'' I lied again. There is value in consistency.

''Do you remember anything about her?''

I thought back. Was there a shimmering image of a face, a woman's face, smiling down upon me? Yes, but it was faint. I concentrated. Her hair was dark, and framed large eyes and a tired smile. But that's all I could recall; everything else was clouded and obscure. Who was to say it was my mother, and not some other woman? I could remember the last two or three years of my life, alone, on the streets. The rest was gone, or at least buried somewhere. Perhaps this void of memory should have disturbed me; but forgetting, too, can be a means of survival.

"No, sir," I answered a third time.

"Well, I remember her. You know about the king's servers? Each year a half dozen sons and daughters of prominent citizens are chosen to live at the castle. During meals they wait upon the king's tables, and during the day they are tutored by the faculty of the university. It is quite an honor for the families to have their offspring chosen, and a privilege for the server to receive a year of the finest education available in Kenesee.

"Nancy Brown was the daughter of Arnold Brown, who at that time was mayor of Jackson Harbor. Your grandfather was a decent and honorable man, and he wasn't a bad mayor, either. He was heartbroken when she didn't return, and his health had been bad anyway . . . but first things first. Nancy was a pretty girl, pert and happy, and she couldn't have been more than seventeen or eighteen when she came to the castle. She had a subtle presence I felt most attractive. While I often joke with the servers, I found myself enjoying the exchanges with her more than the others. Apparently, she enjoyed them too. We began to meet in off moments, and matters developed from there. Several months later I was notified that Nancy was pregnant. She hadn't mentioned the father, but it is hard to hide anything in the castle, and soon word spread that I had fathered the child.

"It was my fault, really. You'll find when you get older that royalty offers opportunities not accorded to others. The worth of a man holding the title does not matter. Position alone is enough to gain benefit. This is true in all realms of endeavor, including romance. Many will be attracted to you not because of what you are, but because of who you are. Sometimes they will have their own motives, and care must be taken in such matters. In this case, Nancy was quite innocent in her own way, and I should have been more careful. I was not, and she became pregnant.

"Several heirs to the throne have come from unions without benefit of marriage. While it provides a feast for the scandal mongers, and the church frowns upon such behavior, the people grudgingly accept such on the part of their king if it is kept within bounds. I think some rather expect it, and are disappointed if we are too virtuous. . . ."

He paused, considered his theory, then shrugged and went on.

"Nancy was removed to a religious house of the Catholics. They seem to handle such matters with less fuss than we do. Two weeks early, she gave birth; and because it was known by then that you were my offspring, the Royal Physician was in attendance and complete records were made. Everything seemed to be well. I visited you both, as did others. Even Queen Jessica went to see Nancy, and I was pleased to see that Jessica had accepted the situation so well. Jessica had tolerated my occasional, uh, 'lapses', but I had never fathered other children. I expected to move Nancy back to the castle or her father's home, as she preferred, when she recovered. Eventually, you would be brought to the castle and raised with Robert, who had been born several months before.

"Unfortunately, that did not happen.

"A day or two after your birth the doctors visited the religious house and found Nancy had taken you and disappeared into the night. The nuns had no idea how or why she did this. No one could discover where Nancy and you had gone. I had both formal and private searches conducted, and news of your disappearance spread throughout the kingdom, but it did no good. You both seemed to have vanished. Why Nancy went away still remains a mystery. I have some ideas, but—well, no need to go into that. Nothing can be done about it. We must come to terms with the past, and go forward. Where Nancy took you, I can only guess. I do not think you remained within the kingdom. And when you returned must remain a mystery, unless you discover that memory within you.

"Where Nancy is now, who can say. We can only assume she is dead. I don't think she would have left you while there was breath in her body. Remember that. Your mother came from a good family of noted citizens, and she was worthy of respect. I remember her fondly, and none dare speak ill of her in my castle.

"But you're home again, at last. I have thought of you often through the years, and prayed for your safety and return. Now, my prayers have been answered, and for that we must be thankful." The king gave me a hug and cleared his throat.

"Well. Enough of this for today. Now you know. Do you have any questions?"

What was there to say? I had been given a history, but that's all it was to me. My mother, whether the woman of the shimmering image or not, was gone forever. About the past I felt nothing, and it meant little in any case. It was the present that mattered. I was well fed and warm, and I didn't wish to do anything to disturb that situation. Yes, I had my own suspicions after overhearing Queen Jessica and Graven, but what if I did tell the king? Would he believe me? And if he did, what could he do?

"No, sir. No . . . questions."

He brightened and smiled. "Enough of the past. We must think of the future. You've been with us three weeks now. It's time you begin to learn all you need to know. Get a good night's sleep tonight. Tomorrow you begin your instruction."

5

Instruction

Our course of instruction comprised a steady routine for the next ten years. Unless we were invited to the council of advisors, or the king's court of appeals was in session, or we traveled, weekday mornings were devoted to academic study and afternoons to military training.

One hour after sunrise, Robert and I took our seats for the morning in a round tower chamber—one of those with actual window openings rather than just arrow slits—while our tutors came and went on the hour as we changed subjects. The person responsible for our instruction, a little man named Henry Wagner, was the foremost scholar of the university as well as the royal professor and head instructor. He provided the daily lectures that started each morning, while under his guidance other noted scholars tutored elementary mathematics, reading, writing, language, history, geography, and science.

I required the most basic education in these areas, while Robert received more advanced instruction in accord with the years of previous learning he had enjoyed. In a matter of weeks I had learned the alphabet and was reading simple passages. Likewise I quickly reached such elevated levels of mathematics as addition and subtraction. I must grant Professor Wagner his due. The course of study was effective. We learned, and we learned well. He was arrogant, pedantic, and impatient when questioned, but the professor knew how to teach. He was a gifted speaker who excelled at the broad sweep of summary, and could deliver great masses of undigested facts and data in a clear and interesting manner.

I can still remember his lectures dealing with the Old World, and I believe that Professor Wagner was deeply moved when recalling the tragedy of its demise. I was impressed with his performance, which inspired me to later read the original, dust-laden journals and diaries from the Cataclysm. He kindled in me an abiding interest in history. It helped me to understand the world in which I lived and to realize the unchanging weakness and stupidity of human nature as each generation seemed to repeat the mistakes of its ancestors. It also gave meaning to the evidence of that ancient civilization still dotting the landscape, poking out from beneath grass and behind bush. The story was a sad one.

Over six hundred years before, on the morning of May 22nd in the year 2036 A.D., a geologic upheaval of unparalleled magnitude in recorded history had shaken the earth, seriously rending the complex web of Old World civilization. The books say there were billions—not millions, but billions—of people living at that time, though it is hardly possible to conceive of such numbers. In contrast, Kingsport, the largest town in Kenesee, had a population of only thirteen thousand the year I arrived at the castle, and the total for the kingdom was estimated at less than one hundred and forty thousand. The other nations were of similar size.

Unfortunately, along with the great achievements of the Old World there were a few dubious accomplishments. From destroyed laboratories escaped diseases that not only killed outright but also may have affected the genetic makeup of future generations. Perhaps the beastmen sprang from this cause, though we can never be sure. At any rate, one-quarter to one-third of the global population died in the quake or during the three months following.

And then, on September 5th of the same year, the second and greater quake hit, destroying the advanced society of the Old World and shattering the technological web of civilization. New volcanoes appeared, rifts and chasms were torn in the earth. The west coast sank into the Pacific, while the Atlantic and Gulf rushed in to submerge the eastern coastal lowlands beneath hundreds of feet of water. The Cataclysm was complete. Not one in ten survived. And these remnants were further decimated by starvation, disease, and conflict, so that their numbers continued to decline for another four hundred years.

During those years, new generations scraped what they could from the ruins, but most of the relics simply rusted and rotted away. Complex devices quickly became nonfunctional. Simpler items were useful, but then these too wore out over the centuries. No one made them anew, for they did not know how. Knowledge was in the books, but the tools to make such devices no longer existed, and people were too busy plowing the earth in the struggle to survive.

Like Professor Wagner, I always felt a great regret for the demise of the Old World. To have such luxury and wealth! Homes warm in winter and cool in summer; automobiles to speed along the roads; countless items for convenience and comfort; food of every variety from every part of the world, and fresh fruit and vegetables throughout the year. The people of that age must have spent every waking moment thanking God.

But my regrets for the Old World soon turned back to my own situation, and I wondered if their children had an easier way to finish school lessons. Basic skills I learned quickly, and I could recognize the concepts that lay behind pronouncement of "facts" and "truth." But I never could trust the spoken or written word as some people do, to their credit or foolishness. I had learned the lessons of the street well—and found, to my disappointment, that the same lessons could be had in the castle.

One morning only a few weeks after my arrival, Professor

Wagner sent me back to my room to fetch a forgotten assignment. As I retrieved the paper, I could hear voices across the hall.

Graven was direct. "Have you found out anything from the boy?"

Marta's motherly voice was soft and conspiratorial. "Yes, sir, I have. I talk with him each day, just like you asked me to. He doesn't say much, that one, nor show much either, but I'm able to get him to share."

"What does he think of Kendall?" Graven asked.

"Oh, he likes Mr. Kendall," responded Marta. "All the children do. Mr. Kendall tells them stories, plays ball with them, and the like. I'm surprised he doesn't have a family, but what with his coming and going all the time, I'd feel sorry for the poor woman."

"Does the boy say anything about me?"

"No, sir," she assured him. "He doesn't have a word to say when your name is brought up."

"Humph. Go on."

The rest of the conversation consisted mostly of lies as Marta reported conversations which had never taken place. Otherwise, she would have had little to report. Most were minor items about my preferences among the court, tutors, and staff, and were of little concern. One entirely fictional conversation implied that I was jealous of Robert and would "bring him down a notch or two," to which Graven responded with an "Ahhh!" of satisfaction. Actually, she was quite good at her fabrications, and at the end Graven counted out several coins from a purse and dropped them one by one into her hands. Not quite forty pieces of silver perhaps, but she seemed pleased.

I slipped out without being seen and returned to the tower classroom, where I was chastised for taking so long. Concentration was difficult. So Marta couldn't be trusted. I'll admit I was disappointed in the sweet old lady, but at least her husband Walter wasn't involved. Why was Graven interested in what I thought of him, and what was he hoping to hear from his spy? My distrust of the scowling magician, raised at that very first meal in the castle, was increased. I could only keep my mouth shut, watch, and listen.

This listen-and-learn attitude carried over into the classroom. I accepted information but waited for proof before taking it as fact, and silently pondered theories which had no definite answers. I volunteered little. I was still reluctant to speak unless absolutely necessary, and I was not about to call attention to myself by asking questions on every conceivable topic.

Not so, Robert. We were different in that way. I was intelligent enough in my studies, although nothing exceptional. Robert was the quick one, absorbing facts and mastering concepts and ideas with a hungry fervor. But even more, he was inquisitive, analyzing each subject, pulling it apart, finding the flaws and deriving new approaches. For example, Professor Wagner spent many hours lecturing about dinosaurs, but covered Old World electricity in one hour. When he announced we would move on to the next topic, Robert's hand shot up.

"Sir? I appreciate all the information we have about dinosaurs, especially the success of the Old World in cloning these through the DNA, whatever that was. But, if I understand you correctly, that involved a level of science and technology we will not reach for generations, if ever. Therefore, the information is of no practical use to us today. In contrast, you have implied that electricity was used throughout the land, as commonly as we light an oil lamp. Yet electricity, which was commonly used and is of great practicality, has been covered only briefly. How can we know so much about dinosaurs and so little about electricity?"

Professor Wagner drew himself up before Robert. "Young man, the amount of information conveyed within this chamber on any topic does not necessarily reflect the body of knowledge which we have available to us. Nor does Old World use correlate to current applicability. Dinosaurs exist. Have you not looked at the trophy wall in the dining hall? In a few years your knowledge of dinosaurs is going to come in quite handy to you and your brother, and before that time we will spend many hours studying them, for which you will eventually thank me."

"Yes, but in regard to elec—"

"At some point," interrupted the professor, "it may be appropriate for us to attempt to regain the use of electricity. Currently, the Codes do not allow room for this area of investigation."

I had heard reference to this before, but knew little more. I raised my hand.

"Codes?"

Professor Wagner buried his face in his hands, muttered to himself, and then peeped out from between his fingers. "We will cover that at a different time."

Eventually the whole matter of the Codes was explained to me. The Codes were promulgated two hundred years before when the nations were formed. Pacifica, already a nation on the new western coast of the continent, sent representatives who toured all the tiny zones, wards, districts, territories, landholds, fiefdoms, provinces, islands, and whatever else the local independent governments called themselves in those days. It was an incredible feat, but the Pacifican representatives were able to unify all these minor principalities into the six nations under six rulers.

Not all events of the period were documented, and many details were lost to historians. What persuasion the Pacificans used on the petty and tyrannical leaders of that time is uncertain, but the common people were happy to see larger governing bodies replacing the chaotic and despotic rule under which they toiled. Many felt a debt of gratitude toward the Pacificans, and each of the nations has had a Pacifican representative ever since serving as advisor and friend.

A kingship was established for each nation, though it took a different title in each land. The mountainous Isles, made up of the islands of Nicaragua, Costa Rica, Cuba, Dominica, Puerto Rico, Jamaica, and a dozen smaller land masses, called their king "prime minister." Distant Mexico named theirs "patron." The great nation of Virginia made their leader a "governor"—though to us he was just one more "Easterner," as we called the Virginians. And cruel Texan had a "president." Only Arkan and Kenesee kept the title of "king," though why they did, given the fabled tradition of democracy in America, none can remember. Less hypocritical, perhaps. Still, beneath the king and the nobles, Kenesee adopted an elective, representative form of government for towns and villages which worked about as well—and as badly—as any other system.

The Pacificans made a second major contribution to the founding of the nations when they promulgated the Codes and persuaded the new kings to adopt their strictures. Formally called the Codes of Progress, the Codes were basically a series of laws and directives which regulated warfare, scientific research, and technological implementation. For example, the Codes prohibited research or development of explosive, combustive, or compressive devices unless all the nations agreed on their appropriate return to Man's service. Quickly the Codes went beyond mere legal and political jurisdiction. They became moral sanctions, blessed by church leaders and carefully observed by worshippers. For many, questioning the Codes was akin to questioning the Gospels.

It was a confusing time back then, with many changes and much turmoil. From the disorder had come stability, and most saw an improvement in their condition. If war had not been eliminated, it had been regulated. If tyranny had not been abolished, it had been moderated. Times were not as bad as they had been. Yet in two hundred years rulership can evolve, for better or worse, and not all nations were as benevolent as Kenesee. Nor were all individuals as devoted to the Codes.

Which brings us back to Robert and Professor Wagner. Robert was still not to be deterred. "But in regard to electricity, doesn't it seem strange that—"

"Prince Robert," the professor interrupted sternly, "much was lost during the Cataclysm, and much was lost during the Dark Centuries afterwards. We are fortunate to have what knowledge we do. We work with what we have, observe the Codes, and try to avoid the mistakes of the past. When you are older, you will learn more. Until then, I recommend you apply yourself to learning the material we give you."

"I still think we could do more," Robert persisted.

"Some have tried," Professor Wagner sniffed, but a touch of caution and sadness came into his tone. "It is not wise to dabble in the wrong areas. Those who do come to a bad end."

Robert slumped back in his desk until the end of the lecture, after which Professor Jameson sat down to tutor him in science. Jameson was a likable man, younger than Professor Wagner, but both curious and ambitious. "Don't worry about it yet, my boy," he whispered. "Things are not as bad as Professor Wagner thinks. Perhaps it is time to achieve more."

Robert brightened. "Do you think so?"

"Yes. Why, I'm working on something myself," he admitted indiscreetly, assuming a careful pose of modesty. "I'm researching an Old World device called a steam engine. I think we could build one, if we tried." He went on to explain what a steam engine was.

"That would be wonderful," Robert exclaimed. "Don't you think so, Arn?"

"Hmm? Yes." Actually, I had my doubts. What was this "bad end" that Wagner had mentioned?

Professor Jameson was gratified by Robert's enthusiasm for the project, but cautioned him. "This must be our little secret, all right? Only a few of my most trusted colleagues know about my research. You must not share it with others quite yet. Do I have your promise? Good. Now, let's move on to our regular lesson."

I wondered if too many people might already know his "little secret."

Apparently too many did. One evening a few weeks later I was in my room, struggling through a reading lesson in Old World English when I heard a knock at Graven's door. I recognized the voice of Professor Jameson, who was ushered in with a grunt. "I'm sorry I couldn't come earlier," said the scholar, a chair creaking as he took a seat. "I had classes this afternoon with the king's servers."

"You have come, and that is the important thing," Graven stated. I could hear him pacing up and down in his room, and could imagine him gesturing with his mottled hands as he spoke. "You are one of the finest scholars and teachers in the kingdom, and your work is well respected by your students and colleagues. Likewise, the King and his court think highly of you."

"Why, thank you, Wizard Graven. Your kind words are appreciated."

"There is one area of your work which has given us concern. You are engaged in study of Old World technology, I believe?"

Jameson's voice grew cautious. "Yes, that is correct."

"And your research includes the operation and use of the 'steam engine,' does it not?"

"Yes, it does. The knowledge is not hidden. There are numerous references to compressive engines in the library, and several even describe their operation. A pity so many of the pictures in the books have faded out.''

"I understand that. However, it has come to the attention of the King's Council that you have started building this device.''

"Oh. Well, no, not really. I've been experimenting with the quality of our metals and casting. But the pieces I've assembled are tiny. The engine would be no more than a small model which could be put upon the corner of your desk. A toy. It would have no practical use.''

Graven sounded tired. "The immediate practicality of the engine is not the issue. Our concern is with the Codes. You are treading dangerously near the edge of the directives.''

Jameson's chair creaked. "But what harm can come of this?''

"The harm is precedent. If you are allowed your little project, then the next man will want to build a larger model. And the next will want to put it to use.''

"Is that so bad?'' Jameson responded. "Isn't it time we started introducing one or two devices of the old technology, if we can? Just one or two, mind you, simple engines that will help us advance our society. Perhaps it's time to try.''

"Perhaps,'' said Graven, forcing himself to be patient. "Or perhaps not. In any case, such innovation is not for any one country to decide. It would take a meeting of the nations to discuss such a thing, and all would have to agree. At this time, most would disagree. Our societies are already advancing. We are making strides in agriculture, medicine, and health. That is enough progress.''

"Is it?'' Jameson persisted stubbornly. "Our population is rising, and I assume it is rising in all the nations. How large can it get before we need the old technology again?''

"That is not our concern. For two hundred years the Codes have served us well. If we do not have engines and electric lights and communications devices, we also have no cannons, no fire weapons, no bombs. The council discussed all this, and we see no immediate need to change the Codes. In ten or twenty years, perhaps the matter will be reconsidered. The Council has decided you must stop your construction of this 'toy.'''

Jameson sighed. "All right.''

"The Council also recommends that you halt your research into this area and turn your efforts to other areas of study."

"I will consider it."

Graven's voice turned surprisingly soft. "After a time, people forget things that happened in the past. You are probably too young to remember the last young man interested in resurrecting the Old World."

"Who was he?"

"*Who* does not really matter. What matters is that he died soon after declaring his purpose. And he was not the only one."

"Are you threatening me?" Jameson asked in disbelief.

"No," said Graven. "I do not threaten. I'm giving you warning. For many, the Codes are sacred."

Then the professor got angry. "I see. I SEE." Jameson stomped out, and Graven continued to pace, muttering to himself.

"Young fool. He won't stop, and then it will be too late. Young fool."

Barely a month after his meeting with Graven, Professor Jameson was found in his workshop. Quite dead. Officially, he died of a heart attack. Many reacted with sadness but without surprise, as if hearing expected news of the passing of a friend who had been terminally ill. At the next council meeting there was a moment of silent prayer for the professor, and then the king ordered the model engine destroyed. For the rest of the week, Professor Wagner's lectures were very subdued.

But lectures were not all I had to endure. Lunch was a welcome respite from the hours of concentration, though even here my instruction did not stop. Manners, customs, and routines had to be learned, as well as people's faces, names, and places in the hierarchy of the court. I sat with a different person each day, and listened as they told me everything they thought appropriate about themselves, the kingdom, themselves, the court, themselves, and the weather, not necessarily in that order. I was taught to eat without using both hands as shovels, and the quantity I consumed actually began to decrease as my body became used to a dependable flow of sustenance. All in all, in spite of the social demands, noon meal remained one of the three favorite times of the day for me.

After lunch we would change into our uniforms, and military training filled the afternoon. We went to an area that was tucked between the barracks and the outer curtain wall. Here, while squads of guardsmen practiced in the background, we would learn the glorious art of killing under the instruction of Sergeant Major Nakasone. We started with warm-up exercises, ran endless laps around the outer wall, and continued with sit-ups, pull-ups, knee bends, and other forms of slow torture. I was only half-dead by the end of the exercise sessions. Then the training in arms began. The first half hour was taken swinging a heavy but dull sword at a wooden upright, a task which Robert found quite easy but which made first my left arm and then my right akin to an overcooked noodle.

While I might almost hold my own in the classroom with Robert, there was never any hope of this happening on the training grounds. With bow, sword, and spear, Robert was the epitome of the warrior. With maturity he could be expected to surpass all but the masters in his skill at arms. During practice Nakasone smiled with satisfaction, easily turning aside the hacks and thrusts of his pupil, but nodding encouragingly at the quickness of each blow and the promise held by the boy's steady eye and strong arm.

With me, Nakasone nodded blandly and mumbled. "Much improved." An old woman who teeters out of bed might be much improved, too. I readily admitted to Robert that I could never match him in sports or arms. I was slim, he was sturdy. I was quick, he was faster. I developed endurance, but his was greater. Most telling, Robert enjoyed such activity. He reveled in the physical exertion and competition, while I regarded it all as an unpleasant necessity to satisfy the king.

After such practice we would get our horses, join up with the guards by their stables on King's Way North, and ride with them to the parade grounds outside the city. Here we learned to walk, trot, canter, and gallop individually and in formation, progressing gradually to the use of lance, sword, and bow from the saddle.

My first occasion upon a horse was less than spectacular. Upon the sergeant major's selection, the stable hand brought me Runner. The name should have given me warning. Runner was a young, sleek-coated mare who looked me in the eye and immediately declared victory. After teaching me how to mount, the sergeant major led us around the courtyard a few times and gave me specific instructions for controlling the animal.

"Are you ready?" Nakasone asked. He handed me the reins. "Don't worry, this is the gentlest horse we have in the stable." With that, Runner immediately bolted through the castle gates and galloped down the street past the stables and the waiting squad of surprised guardsmen. Townspeople scattered before the horse while I hung on to the saddle horn with a death grip, my rear end rising a foot in the air and slamming painfully into the saddle with every stride. Clattering along thirty yards behind me in a desperate effort to catch up came the sergeant major, then Robert, and finally the guards. We raced through the north gate, past a marching company of the First Infantry Regiment, and turned off the road into the parade ground. Runner slowed, stopped, and began munching the grass. I slid off and stood shakily, wondering whether it was possible to execute a horse.

Robert and the sergeant major reined in beside me. "Good Lord, are you all right? Runner's never done that before." Of course not. The horse had never had a fearful amateur on its back before. I refrained from telling the sergeant major what I thought of his choice. His face was pale with fright, no doubt wondering during our wild ride when I would be thrown from the animal and his career ended in one mistaken choice of horse. "Ahh yes," they would say. Poor Nakasone. Twenty years of loyal and efficient service wiped out when the prince was thrown. Terrible mess in the street, the way the boy landed on his head and all. And just when the poor lad was learning his table manners.

The worried look on Nakasone's face changed to relief when he saw me stand unaided, then became stern as he heard the arrival of the guards behind him. "Prince Arn," he said severely, "galloping in the town is forbidden. You could have injured the townspeople or your horse. Please do not show off."

"I . . . won't." Quite cynically, my first assumption was that he was trying to cover up his mistake, but I was wrong. He immediately reported the incident to the king when we returned to the castle later, and accepted any blame for the affair. He wasn't trying to avoid responsibility, he was just trying to help me save face. I always remembered that.

That evening, the king congratulated me on my perseverance during the afternoon, even after the uncontrolled gallop through town. Of course I had persevered. The sergeant major had forced me. The king smiled broadly and gave me a squeeze. "Good boy. We don't run away from challenges. We face them."

That was fine for him to say. I was the one whose brains could have been splattered on the cobblestones. Fortunately, Runner and I somehow arrived at a conditional truce. She would not endanger my life, and I would not poison her oats. Eventually I would become a competent rider, but never a true horseman. I didn't trust horses.

Even after rigorous practice sessions, our instruction was still not done. Late every afternoon, we followed Nakasone back up to our classroom in the tower. There stood another guardsman, Sergeant John Black, calmly waiting for our arrival.

While attention might wander during Professor Wagner's lectures without undue penalty, Sergeant Black would allow no such occurrence. When it did occasionally happen, he would fall silent in front of the daydreamer, clasp his hands behind him, and wait. Within seconds the miscreant would awaken to find a punishment bestowed.

"Excuse me, Sergeant."

"You are excused, sir. We have been discussing the Battle of Westport. Please submit a five-page summary of this battle by tomorrow. Now, can you tell me which principles of war were violated by the Arkans in this battle?"

And so it went. Black had much to teach, and no time to waste. There was little humor to his classes, although a certain dry wit could be noticed in his phrasing. It was as instructive to watch him with his men as it was in the classroom. His squad was perhaps the best in the royal guards. He demanded excellence from his men, and received it. They seemed to like to be around him, though he really said little and left the banter to them, his stoic features admitting the whisper of a grin at a particularly good joke. At a word the men would fall silent, waiting for his directions. He was calm and patient, but still not a man to cross.

Black's instruction covered military history, strategy and tactics, the principles of war, command and control, maneuver, logistics, and—most elementary and yet most difficult of all—leadership. "The essence of leadership," he would say, "is to inspire men to do the right thing at the right time. There is room for neither pride nor fear nor arrogance nor timidity. Leadership is decisive, and decisions must be made upon a cold analysis of information—facts, not hopes. The failure of leadership has lost more battles and more wars than all other circumstances."

In particular, Black emphasized three principles over and over throughout the years: "Speed. Surprise. Security. An army must move quickly, do the unexpected, and make sure it is not surprised in turn. And just because wizards march with an army doesn't eliminate surprise." He used both the great and small of military history to illustrate his points, citing campaigns and battles in detail without ever using a reference book.

Black was not always so direct, sometimes leaving us to ponder a concept or situation before clarifying the lesson he wished to teach. For example, he gave us puzzles that he would repeat from time to time, even after we knew the answers. "When is an army not an army? And when is an army most vulnerable?" he asked the first time, watching our faces crease in confusion.

Even Robert could not figure out the answer. We tried to cajole Sergeant Major Nakasone, but he only laughed. "So, John's got you stumped, does he? Well, you keep thinking about it. But remember, an army doesn't exist only on the battlefield."

Finally Black gave us the answer. "When is an army not an army? When it sleeps, of course. And when is an army most vulnerable? After victory. Now think about why."

Nor were our military studies limited to the classroom. Black, and the king too, often led us around the castle and town defenses, and we ranged as far afield as needed to illustrate each lesson. We toured the battlements, studied fortifications, examined gates and moats, and computed angles of fire on ballista and stone throwers. In all kinds of weather we rode out into the countryside, Black pointing out the effects of terrain and the elements on the employment of men, horses, wagons, and weapons.

I can't condense years of instruction into a few pages, but perhaps this has given some flavor of our military training. Robert, of course, delighted in it all, while I dutifully paid attention and learned what I could in order to avoid Black's unwelcome writing assignments. Robert had the feel for military matters, a sense that he and Black and the king shared, a sense which I did not, and never would, have. Answers that came naturally to them required calculation and study on my part. If we passed meadowed fields, they saw defensive positions and lines of maneuver. I saw grass and flowers.

And so I learned to be a prince and a warrior, though the education exacted its price. By the end of each day my head had been stuffed with facts and figures, my body ached from falls and blows, and I waited with anticipation for the dinner bell to ring. When this happened, Black dismissed us with a wave of his pipe, and we were free to attend supper.

Fortunately, my appetite needed no training.

Nor did I need coaching in listening. I had quickly realized the value of eavesdropping and took to leaving my door open while I studied in the evenings, tuning one ear to conversation. It wasn't difficult for me, as I had already realized my hearing was exceptionally good. The explanation for this unique and unusual ability I would not discover until many years later.

Since my first evening at the castle I had paid particular attention to Graven's discourse for my own protection. One evening perhaps six months after my arrival, a maid came to Graven's room to say the queen was expecting him. I interrupted my studies and found reason to head in that direction soon after the high wizard. The guard at the entrance of the passage to the royal quarters smiled at me. No need to stop a prince of the realm from visiting.

The door of the queen's chamber, according to propriety, was left open. This made it laughably easy to accomplish my purpose, for though they sat at a table far from the door and spoke in whispers I could hear them clearly. I simply leaned against the wall of the passageway and pretended to wait, absorbed in a book and seemingly oblivious of any who might pass by. And to those who might, I would be just one of the princes waiting to speak to the queen.

The two were already deep into their whispered discussion when I placed myself along the wall outside the queen's door and heard Graven's voice. "—And that, Jessica, explains part of the mystery of his return. The rest, we may never know for sure."

"I see," said the queen.

"The information does not change our current situation, of course. The boy is with us now. Reuel is happy. The son he mourned has been found."

Did I hear a bit of relief, perhaps, in his tone? It couldn't be.

The queen spoke with a distant scorn. "And how is our newest prince doing?"

"His performance has been adequate in the classroom and in the field, but he is no match for Robert," Graven reported truthfully enough, though with rather more satisfaction than necessary. "Arn has neither the intellect, nor the spirit, nor the skill." Again, true enough. "He grows jealous of Robert and may seek ways to elevate himself in the eyes of the king." This was false. I wasn't jealous of Robert. Envious, perhaps, but not jealous. Though I knew now who was responsible for putting such nonsense in his head—if indeed he needed anyone to provide him with nonsense.

"Kendall is attempting to win over the boy with stories and attention, as he does with Robert," Graven mused. "I have succeeded in countering Kendall's influence with Robert, but am not inclined to do so with Arn. In fact, it may be beneficial to have Kendall enjoy some success with Arn, and so concentrate his attentions upon the boy. Then he'll have less time to sway Robert to his purposes."

"You're sure Paul Kendall wants to control Arn?" the queen asked. "Reuel feels he is devoted to the well-being of Kenesee and the observance of the Codes."

"Jessica, I do not trust Kendall. I did not trust his father. I do not trust any Pacifican. They have their own ends. Can we believe what Kendall tells us of his homeland, little enough as he shares? Is Kendall's loyalty to Kenesee, or to Pacifica? The Pacificans have their own goals, and want to control the rulers of the six nations. Why else would the Codes state that each nation must host a representative from

Pacifica? I think . . . never mind. I will keep watch, even if no one else does.''

"Poor David. So many burdens. I hope my news is not another.''

"News?''

"I have decided to have another child.''

Graven was surprised. "My Queen, is this wise? Dr. Amani expressed concerns after Robert was born. He feels you shouldn't bear any more children.''

"I know.''

"Then why risk your health?''

"By the rules of succession, my sons are the legitimate heirs to the throne before any other offspring of the King. If I am to guarantee the continuity of my line, then I need another son.'' Graven sighed. "My mind is made up,'' she continued. "Do not attempt to dissuade me. I disagree with Dr. Amani. Second pregnancies are easier than the first, and I have never felt better. It may take some time, I fear, for Reuel is so cautious in such matters now.''

"But Dr. Amani—''

"When the boy first appeared, I admit I was shaken by doubts. About him, about our actions. Now, sometimes, in the darkness of the night I lie awake and think how much simpler it all might be if the boy were not here. Things would be as they were. I would not have to endure another pregnancy. If he suddenly disappeared. . . .''

"My Queen, do you know what you're saying? Are you asking this of me?''

"Such a look on your face, my dear David. No. Certainly not. Certainly not . . .'' The room was silent for a moment, except for another deep sigh from Graven. A sigh of relief.

"And yet,'' the queen continued with slow words, "you would do it if I asked you, wouldn't you? Yes, I can see that you would.'' She paused, but Graven made no denial. "Of course,'' she went on, "it would be no different than those others, like Jameson—the violators of the Codes—who seem to perish with such unfortunate dependability.''

"You think I am responsible for that?'' Graven retorted. "Even you?''

"My dear David—High Wizard of Kenesee—who else might it be?''

A chair scraped on the floor, and there was the sound of his boots as he paced the floor. "My Queen, I . . . I . . ."

"Goodness, the High Wizard at a loss for words. You are upset. Never fear, David. I will bide my time. There is the baby to come, first. We shall see how that turns out. If it's a boy, I may be content. My new son would be the second heir, and the throne would be secure. If it's a girl, perhaps we shall have another discussion on this subject. We will worry about it then. Everything will work out."

"Is the King aware of your decision?"

"About having another child? There is no need. He would only object because of what the physician said. But when I'm pregnant he will be pleased."

"I advise against this course. I fear for your well-being."

"Thank you, David. That is quite touching. You have been one of my closest friends since I became Queen, and I will always remember your loyalty and help."

"Such as it is," he said. "Such as it is."

"David, don't be so modest. If I were not a loving and faithful wife, I know who would be more than a friend."

"My Queen," the high wizard said, with shy delight. "It is my pleasure to serve. Not since Princess Irene has the castle seen such a beautiful or charming lady living within its walls."

I left when it was clear that their meeting was over, my head down, deep in thought. If the queen wanted another son, well and good. I did not want to be in line for the throne. I had no desire for power, no jealousy of Robert or anyone else. To be left alone was as much as I asked. I could be unobtrusive, inoffensive, and innocent (or as innocent as my nature allows). Unfortunately, my very being seemed to generate feelings and attitudes towards me which I could neither understand nor alter.

I did not sleep very well that night, nor for many nights after.

6

Street Visit

Robert and I told each other as much about our past lives as we could remember. His stories revolved around life in the castle, and mine around life in the streets. We each heard the other's tales with skepticism, although I was quickly finding out by observation and experience that all he spoke was the truth. My own tales filled Robert with awe and disbelief. He longed to go into town and see life as it was.

And then one day he declared his intention. "We must go into the streets."

I looked at him in shock. For over a year I had enjoyed the security of the castle. Now he wanted me to leave it and return to the town? "It's forbidden," I argued, thanking God for rules. "And besides we couldn't get past the guards. There's only the main gate and that's always watched. They wouldn't let us out."

Robert just smiled. "We must find a way."

I tried to put the matter off for a time, but he kept coming back to the subject and finally pressed me for a solution. For all of his accomplishments in the classroom and on the training ground, simple matters such as deceit and bribery were beyond him. I considered the situation and then laid out a basic plan that unfortunately had a very good chance of succeeding.

Although our schedule during the week was full, weekends were our own—except for church on Sunday and the occasional ceremony. We took advantage of these times. The arrow slits of our rooms overlooked the courtyard and the gate, so each Saturday morning we watched the comings and goings of the castle folk and prepared for the next step.

The stable boy Moses stopped sweeping and stood respectfully when we approached. He was only a few years older than us, but seemed suitably awed at our presence, though I suspected even then that his awe was more calculated than we thought. Robert is the one with the words, and I let him do the talking. Besides, it was good training for him. I had drilled Robert well, for with just the few simple arguments to overcome Moses' reluctance, the transaction was completed. Moses smiled broadly when the coins were in his hand.

The next Saturday we went up to the hayloft and found a sack hidden exactly where it should be. Robert untied the string and dumped the contents upon the straw. The revealed treasure elicited a sigh of satisfaction from him. We had obtained the stable boy's outgrown castoffs. Two faded shirts. Two pairs of trousers worn thin in the seat and knees. Holed socks. Worn shoes. And two soft visored caps. Only a year before I would have regarded it as a wardrobe fine and luxurious. Now, I was not inspired by the thought of putting on the clothes of a stable boy. The rags I had been discovered in had been taken from me to be thrown away. Or so I thought, for later I was to find they had been put in the town's Royal Museum and become one of the most popular items on display.

At least Moses' castoffs were clean, thank goodness. I was the only one in the castle who insisted on a daily bath, and the thought of being dirty again held no allure.

The clothes fit us quite well—one more piece of the plan falling into place too easily. We bundled our own garments into the sack and hid it beneath the straw. Robert made sure our caps were pulled down over our foreheads, and then, watching for a quiet moment, we picked up a basket of manure ready for hauling, strolled out of the stable with it, and across the courtyard to the gate. The two guards on duty eyed the basket for a moment, glanced at us, and then resumed their impassive stance. Just two boys doing their normal morning chores, we went through the gates.

Like it nor not, I was in the streets again.

We emptied and hid the basket at a convenient manure pile, and then began strolling along. Robert's head swiveled left and right in delight, like the merest country bumpkin come to gawk at the sights of the town. It was as if he had never seen the streets before, and in a sense, he hadn't. We reached the market square and stood watching the normal activity of a Saturday morning, the busiest day of the market. There were scores of booths and carts arranged in neat rows selling their wares while hundreds of women and men, children in tow, browsed and made their purchases. The sounds of friendly haggling drifted across the square, while our noses were teased with the smell of onions cooking and chickens roasting and rare coffee brewing.

Robert was aglow, his face bright with joy and anticipation. I was feeling ill thinking of all the things that could happen to us.

"This is wonderful," Robert said in awe.

"You've never been to the market?"

"Never like this. We ride through and it's just a blur of people and stalls. It looks different from here."

An older lad pushed by hauling a load of firewood on his shoulder. "Out of the way, boys. Coming through."

People are much less polite when you don't have a squad of guards behind you.

Robert strode on, and I followed in his wake.

If this was a totally new experience for Robert, in a way it was quite new for me, too. There was a difference in the way people perceived me from my previous existence in the streets. I was not wearing rags, and I was not filthy. I was no longer a gutter rat and potential thief. Humble as they were, Moses' clean and neat clothes denoted a respectable lower-class worker rather than homeless poverty. I was no longer looked upon suspiciously, and the sheriffs didn't watch me in anticipation of thievery. I didn't have to worry about being treated as a gutter rat. Who I was did not matter. It was only my clothes and manner that counted. With a feeling of relief, I moved up beside Robert and even managed a smile.

"I want to buy something," he said with certainty.

"What do you want to buy?"

"I don't know. I just want to buy something. I've never bought anything before."

"Oh. Well, go ahead. Buy something."

Robert looked uncomfortable. "How do I do that?"

"You took money like I told you? Good. Pick out what you'd like. Give the sellers money and they'll give you change."

"Of course," said Robert. "How simple." He stepped up to a fruit stall and took in the array, each mound neatly adorned with a small white card announcing the price.

The seller smiled at us. "Good morning, young men. How can I help you today? Apples, perhaps? Cold cellar stored from the fall. A few wrinkles don't change their taste. The best you'll find this time of year. I take care they don't get bruised."

Robert nodded. "Yes. Apples would be fine."

"Good. How many would you like?"

"How many?"

"It's cheaper by the half-dozen and dozen, just like the sign says."

"In that case, we'll take them all."

The seller cocked his head forward. "Huh?"

I grabbed Robert by the arm. "I think it would be better, uh, if we just took a dozen."

Robert looked disappointed. "But I thought we might take some back to the—"

"Robert, a dozen."

"Perhaps you're right. We will take a dozen."

The seller grunted. "Got a sack? No? Well, here, let's use this old one. I was going to toss it out 'cause it's giving way, but it should hold a dozen with no problem. Here you are. Twelve even."

"Thank you, sir," said Robert, turning to go.

"Uh, young man, I will need to ask that you pay before you go."

"What? Oh, my apologies." Robert held out a ten-dollar piece.

The seller's eyes widened.

I slapped Robert's hand down. "Always joking, hah-hah. It's a fake. Robert, give him . . . a penny."

Robert dug into a pocket and gave the man a tenpenny piece. He received his change and looked at the coins with delight. "Look, Arn, I've received nine in exchange."

I put a finger to my head, made a circling motion and whispered to the seller. "We take him out . . . once in a while. Mother thinks the sun . . . will do him good."

The seller nodded in commiseration. "Poor lad. Had a cousin like that once, till he decided to ride the miller's waterwheel. Well, take care of him and God bless you both."

I dragged Robert away from the stall, and made a decision. Before, I had been anxious to return to the castle. Now, I would try to keep Robert out as long as possible so that his curiosity would be satisfied once and for all.

I noticed several people pointing and directed Robert's attention. We were going to have the well-timed opportunity of hearing a royal pronouncement from the view of the common citizen. Robert wanted to push to the front, but I held him near the back of the crowd where we couldn't be recognized. A street preacher reluctantly gave up his place on the Speaker's Stone. The royal herald mounted and, after trumpets were sounded, cleared his throat and began to speak.

"On this happy day of July 9th in the Year of our Lord 2642, King Reuel Brant announces to all citizens and friends of Kenesee that his beloved wife, Queen Jessica, is with child."

There were oohs and aahs and heartfelt applause from the crowd, and then the herald continued. "According to the Royal Physician, the baby is due in February. Queen Jessica is in good health and thanks all for their prayers and support. Journalists may pick up this announcement at the castle gates, and I have a few copies with me now. Sorry, journalists only, thank you. This Royal Announcement is now concluded."

Queen Jessica had finally succeeded in becoming pregnant. Why it took so long, I had no idea. Perhaps the king was cautious, and she had to catch him in a weak moment. Whatever the case, the public announcement was no surprise to us, since we'd been informed the week before. But it was news for the townspeople. Robert watched them with pleasure. "Arn, do you see how they reacted to the news? They actually seem happier now."

"That's because they have something new to gossip about. They were getting tired of talking about Deacon Jones and the chicken."

We strolled up and down the market and Robert, still infused with the glories of commerce, bought some cheese and bread with his pennies. He'd started to get the hang of it. We sat down on a bench which encircled a large old oak in the middle of the square and had a midmorning snack. Robert thought our excursion the most exciting thing that had happened since my discovery. He watched and listened with delight to the friendly greetings and cheery voices as citizens of every class rubbed elbows around the stalls and booths. And his eyes widened in horror at the diversity of popular expression.

A jug of milk tipped over and the seller expressed his feelings with an impressive variety of curses. A little girl holding onto her mother's hand listened with amazement. Nor was she the only one.

"Did you hear that?" asked Robert. "I have never heard such language in my life." This was probably true. Even the guards, who can be as rowdy and bawdy off duty as any, know that there are strict limits on such language within the castle. "And little children heard too. I think that man needs correction."

He stood up.

"Robert. You want to be discovered?"

"But shall we do nothing?"

"This is not the castle. What you hear is normal. I have heard much worse."

"You have?"

I nodded. He thought about it and then sat down. Robert always was a fast learner.

We had to be back at the castle for the noon meal or our absence would trigger a search. But there was still a good bit of time left, and so after our snack an idea came into my mind and I took Robert up several streets and stopped in front of a row of shops. A tailor had set up business in one shop I knew, although in a corner there was an unused kiln. A sheriff stood on the corner, and I went up to him warily. But he merely nodded at me, and I was emboldened to speak. "That shop," I said, pointing.

"Uh huh. What about it?"

"Sir, who . . . lived there?"

The man was briefly puzzled. "You mean before the tailor moved in? Family by the name of Johnson. Norman Johnson, he was. Potters by trade. Nice people. They went back to Westport, I hear, when they couldn't make a go of it. Their work wasn't bad, it's just you need a good stake to get going in Kingsport. People don't change who they do business with that quick.''

''Thank you.''

''You're welcome, young man.'' Civility. From a sheriff.

We wandered a bit towards the docks and, when the church bell sounded eleven o'clock, headed back south in the direction of the castle. We took a narrow street that angled back toward the main way, and then I stopped and pointed. ''There. See that boy? The one carrying the loaves of bread. Let's follow him.''

''Why?''

''I'll tell you later. Come on.'' I dogged the steps of the boy ahead. We followed casually until he turned a corner into another empty street. We were now only a few paces behind him. Vengeance is nice, but I had rarely indulged myself in this pleasure. It was too dangerous. But Robert was tall and strong. With him beside me, I had little to fear.

I hurried up behind the boy, swung the sack of apples and smacked it into the side of his head. He stumbled, turned, and sat down in a daze, the loaves of bread spilling out onto the bricks. His mouth hung open, revealing a set of crooked teeth.

''Why did you do that?'' Robert exclaimed at the turn of events.

I grinned with a rare satisfaction. ''He stole an oil jacket from me. And then he beat me up while his father held me by the arms.''

''That was dishonorable.''

''Yes.'' I agreed. ''These swine need—''

''No. What you did.''

I had been ready to give the boy another taste of apples. I stopped at Robert's words. ''But he deserved it.''

''Then you should have challenged him to a bout of fists.''

This didn't make any sense to me. The boy was big and husky and would have beaten me into a bloody mess. ''He's bigger than I am,'' I protested. ''He'd win if I fight him that way. Why fight when you know who'll win?''

''It is the way to resolve disputes,'' Robert said, as if intoning a line he had heard elsewhere. He picked up the boy by the armpits, set him on his feet, then collected the spilled loaves and put them into the boy's hands. Still dazed, and perhaps recognizing the strength of his rescuer, the boy merely sneered and walked away muttering. Robert turned to me, disappointment written on his face. "Arn, I want you to promise you'll never do such a thing again."

"All right. I won't hit him again."

"No. Promise me you will forsake revenge, and only challenge wrongdoers in an honorable way."

"I don't know. Can I think about it?"

"Otherwise, I shall have to tell Father."

Would the king put me back on the streets again for a dishonorable act? Probably not. Then again, they did take that silly code of honor seriously. So why take chances? Still, a promise was not lightly given. Robert noticed my hesitation. "Arn, if you give me your promise, I pledge that you shall have your own castle when we are grown."

Now, that was more like it. "With guards and servants and all the rest?"

"Of course."

Well, then. "Yes, Robert. I promise."

I was to regret this oath many times in my life.

Pleased, he threw his arm around my shoulder and we continued on our way. We retrieved the empty manure basket and carried it back to the castle, the gate guards looking at us suspiciously. "What? Gone all morning just to empty one basket? You lazy good-for-nothings. Somebody should tell the stable master. Now get to work."

We went into the hayloft and changed clothes.

I would like to say that we never went out into the streets again and that Robert's interest in the common life had been answered—but I cannot. All too often Robert would want to play the commoner, and out we'd go to rub elbows with the citizens. After a while he became quite familiar with town life, and learned much about the people he would someday lead. "One cannot solve problems without understanding what those problems are," he would say. "That was a deficiency with leaders of old. The rich wished to lead the poor. Those 'with' made the laws for those 'without.' I will know the people I lead."

Since he really didn't need me anymore, I tried to let him go alone, but he wouldn't hear of it. My previous experience was to be enriched by more lessons of life, for I needed to be prepared too. And so, out the gate we would go.

Moses enjoyed a most lucrative trade in castoffs.

7

Play Time

"Can we have a story, Mr. Kendall?" Megan Sims pleaded. Megan, daughter of Sir Meredith, was a pretty, blond-haired girl a month younger than Robert who did not let being a lady interfere with challenging the princes in sports and games.

Sir Meredith grinned knowingly at Paul Kendall, who nodded. The chess game Megan and Robert had been engaged in was immediately abandoned. We sprawled on the grass in front of the two men, who had just come out and seated themselves in shaded lawn chairs beneath the white birch trees of the terrace.

Our excursions into town on Saturday mornings—begun only the week before—were not our only weekend activities. If the castle walls were the limit of our playground, the tiered garden terraces were our favorite location during the gentler months. Sports, games, adventures, shows, and stories were all played out in the sun and shade, flower beds and trellises thick with ivy providing circles of color around us.

Kendall stared off, pursed his lips in thought, brushed thinning hair back from his forehead, and began a story. Kendall seemed to have an endless supply of such tales. This particular one was about a farmer going to market with his donkey, and the people he tried to satisfy along the way. The farmer ended up carrying the donkey at the end, which pleased no one and earned him the laughter of the town.

The little tale done, Robert asked Kendall to tell us about the Old World, after which we all chimed in with the same plea. The advisor threw up his hands in surrender. "One at a time. What do you want to hear about this time?"

"Tell us more about Donald the Duck," begged Megan.

"And Epcot World," added Robert.

"Again? All right. Hmm, let me think. Now, Donald was quite a fellow, you know, and he lived in Epcot with his nephews Hubert, Dewert, and Louis. One day he decided to visit. . . ." Kendall had an informal way with words akin in effect to Professor Wagner's formal lectures. While Wagner was able to paint vast landscapes of drama and grandeur, Kendall created intimate portraits rife with living detail. I don't know if my own face showed anything, but Robert wore a happy smile and Megan's eyes glowed as she listened, spellbound. For a few moments we could almost imagine ourselves amidst those children of the past, watching their entertainments and walking with them through the streets of fantasy now buried far beneath the waves of the Gulf.

But too soon the story was finished.

Kendall reached behind Megan's ear. "What's this, here? Why, it's a tenpenny piece. Is that where you keep your money, girl? Oh, where did it go now?" The coin was gone from his hand, and he reached behind her other ear and found it again. He gave her the coin, and then reached into Robert's shirt pocket and under my cap in turn. By the end of any session with Kendall, each of us always had a couple of tenpenny pieces to keep.

"All right, ladies and gentlemen. Remember, this is just sleight of hand, a trick, and not magic by any means. Magic requires wizardry, and I'm not a wizard. If you want magic, you must go to the High Wizard. Now, that's enough stories for today and I'm all talked out. Go and play. How about showing us what you can do at catch-ball?"

Robert and I drew off to the center of the terrace and began throwing while Megan lingered behind with Kendall and her father. We threw the ball back and forth with vigor, but I kept one ear tuned to the men sitting beneath the trees.

Megan stood before Sir Meredith, her face serious. "Father, I have something to tell you."

"You do?"

"I'm going to marry Mr. Kendall when I grow up."

Kendall paused with his mouth open. "What?"

Sir Meredith gave a hearty chuckle, which did not seem to disturb Megan's quiet certainty. "That's quite an announcement to make, daughter. But you know, it isn't just one person who chooses marriage. Both must decide. Have you spoken to Mr. Kendall about this? Has he agreed? Perhaps Paul has already chosen a woman."

Megan addressed Kendall, but a bit of doubt had crept into her voice. "Mr. Kendall, have you already chosen someone to be your wife?"

The homely advisor's face was turning red. "Ummm, no Megan. I haven't."

"Do you have a woman friend?"

Kendall smiled in embarrassment. "No, I don't."

The doubt had left her voice. "Then you'll marry me when I grow up?"

He smiled weakly. "Megan, there are many handsome boys your own age who will be most interested in you. Why, you have the qualities of a queen. It all depends on who you choose."

"I have already chosen. Now you must choose."

Wordless for once, Kendall looked at Sir Meredith with a silent plea for rescue. Sir Meredith, ever interested in the beauties of nature, studied the tree branches above with a broad smirk and began whistling tunelessly.

Kendall thought for a moment, and then responded. "My lady, if you feel the same way ten years from now, I will be most happy to marry you." He smiled with relief, pleased that he had cleverly slipped out of the situation without offending anyone.

Megan, however, was not one to be put off so easily.

She stared at him intently. "Do you promise? A real promise, not just pretend?"

Oh oh. I could tell Kendall about the danger of promises.

He looked at Sir Meredith for help, and then gave up. "Yes, Megan. I promise."

Now she smiled. "Father, I'm going to marry Mr. Kendall when I grow up."

The nobleman continued to stare at the branches. "So I've heard. Well, let's see what the future brings. I'm sure you will do whatever you wish, just as your mother would. And I will give my blessing."

Satisfied at last, she joined us at catch while the two men

still reclined in their chairs. Kendall shook his head. ''Well, friend, you were a big help.''

''Paul, who am I to involve myself in affairs of the heart?'' Sir Meredith responded innocently. ''You see, I told you to settle down, or at least find some steady companionship. Some at the court wonder what your preferences are. Why, if we hadn't visited the Street of Pleasure together, I'd wonder myself. You should have a woman friend.''

''I have never been very—successful—with the ladies.''

''Bah! Women would welcome your attentions. Your position alone now would bring you success. Then you wouldn't have to pay for it—though there are fewer entanglements visiting the Street of Pleasure, especially for an available widower like myself. Come to think of it, you have to worry too. You're promised now, so you'd better hope you don't meet the woman of your dreams. I wonder what it will be like having an outlander in the family. At the least we can continue to visit the Street together, father and son-in-law.''

And with that Sir Meredith burst into laughter.

No sooner had his laughter subsided than Queen Jessica and her ladies-in-waiting arrived with the high wizard. The queen and Graven joined Sir Meredith and Kendall beneath the trees, while the two ladies discreetly retired across the terrace to await any summons. The queen got out her knitting and settled in comfortably while Graven watched us with a hawklike gaze.

The queen's remarkable figure was covered now in a loose garment that only partially hid the first swelling of her breasts and belly. If anything, she was even more sensuous in her condition. Her pregnancy had been greeted joyfully by the kingdom, but doubtfully by the king. And she had scolded Dr. Amani for the worried look on his face during the announcement to the court.

Now she smiled at Sir Meredith. ''You seem most amused.''

He nodded and smiled back. ''Yes, I was. Just a bit of humor at Mr. Kendall's expense.''

Graven took his eyes off of us and focused upon the adults. ''A courier arrived with news. Another border incident, I'm afraid. Four dead.''

Sir Meredith shook his head. ''In spite of increased security. Well, the new border keep will be finished in a few months, though some of the locals say the beastmen won't take kindly to its presence. A patrol will operate out of it, which should help. But that's the third incident this year. The king is running out of patience.''

''And well he should,'' the high wizard stated. ''Think back, Sir Meredith. You, at least, are not too young to remember the pirate wars. Their threat began the same way. First, fishing boats were missing. Then, a merchant ship disappeared. And another. And another. Finally, we endured raids on coastal settlements, with the taking of captives and their sale to the Texan slave markets. Don't you see the pattern? The pirates first tested our resolve with pinpricks. King Richard, God bless his soul, was too patient, thinking reason and good will would solve the problem. Instead, the pirates were emboldened by their initial success and grew strong, until Richard realized his mistake and committed the entire fleet in open battle to defeat them. Now, the beastmen test our resolve by ambushing the defenseless. How soon before they are emboldened to attack a village or town?''

''If it is the beastmen conducting these acts,'' Kendall responded.

''Yes, IF,'' the high wizard said. ''But have you been able to prove otherwise? Has Sir Meredith?''

''No,'' Sir Meredith admitted. ''We have not.''

''Show me evidence, and I will gladly change my view. Until then, I will continue to advise the King to act. The lesson of the pirate wars should not be lost. Don't you agree, my Queen?''

She smiled demurely. ''Of course, High Wizard. Though I really am unschooled in such matters.'' Not likely. The queen had a mind as sharp as a rapier, knew everything going on both political and personal, and didn't hesitate to persuade the king when she wanted. Fortunately, he was not a man easily persuaded.

We took a break from catch-ball that I gratefully welcomed. Robert and Megan had kept me sprinting after pop-ups, and I was tired. We trotted over to the adults and the waiting lemonade.

''Robert is doing very well,'' Graven said benevolently. ''Soon he will be as strong as his father.''

''Yes, he will,'' the queen approved.

"But mother, what about Arn?" my loyal brother asked. "Don't you think he's getting stronger too?"

I knew what she would say, of course. A cool nod of agreement, and then a quick change of subject. This had been her attitude throughout the year that I'd been at the castle. But I was surprised. Perhaps pregnancy had mellowed her. Slowly her eyes shifted to me, and for once, just once, it seemed as if the ice in her eyes was beginning to melt. There was an unexpected acceptance in her glance, as if she thought that, yes, this boy might remain with her own and be their lesser companion and possibly even serve them well. She put out a hand, touched my hair, and seemed about to speak. The breeze stilled, and for a moment it seemed that even the birds had turned silent, all listening for her answer.

"My Queen. . . ." Graven whispered in surprise rather than objection, yet it caused her to pause, hung for a timeless moment of indecision. Then the hand was withdrawn, the eyes turned cold, and the moment was gone forever.

Sir Meredith glanced at Kendall and, almost imperceptibly, shook his head sadly. Robert and Megan looked from the queen to the wizard to me, sensing that something had happened, but uncertain what.

"You are all growing up," the queen said to us politely. Shaking off their doubts, my playmates enjoyed the forgetfulness of childhood as she offered us our drinks.

King Reuel came out, breathed deeply of the air, and grinned broadly. "Thank God for the terraces. What a delightful day." He joined us, settling into his chair with a sigh. "The High Wizard has informed you of the news?"

Sir Meredith and Kendall nodded.

"We'll talk of it later in a council meeting. For now, let's not spoil such a day."

The adults chatted for awhile about this and that, though nothing important.

Robert waited for a quiet moment and then presented a question to the king.

"Father, may I ask the High Wizard a question?"

"What? You're asking my permission for a question? Get the doctor." All laughed at the joke, and even Robert smiled at his own expense.

"Aye," said the king. "You may ask."

Graven folded his mottled hands together. "Yes, Prince Robert. What is your question?"

"What is magic?"

Graven looked at the king.

The king nodded. "I think they're old enough now to be told. They can keep a secret."

He caught the queen's eye.

"Megan," the queen said, standing carefully. "I feel like a bit of exercise. A nice walk around the terraces would be good. Will you accompany me?"

"Oh, Queen Jessica. I want to hear what the High Wizard will say."

"But I would enjoy some company," the queen stated more firmly. "Come along."

Megan recognized the inevitable. "Yes, my Queen. I will come." She leaned towards Robert and me, whispering loudly as she followed the queen away. "But it's not fair."

Sir Meredith and Kendall rose. "We will excuse ourselves, too."

"You are welcome to stay," Graven offered. "I can say nothing that you don't already know."

"And that is why we're going," Sir Meredith responded with a good-natured grin, to which Graven nodded in agreement.

Robert and I were now alone with the king and the high wizard. "Yes, my King, they are old enough," Graven said, looking doubtful. "But I must have their pledge. Robert and Arn, do you swear to keep silent about what I tell you?"

"Yes, I swear," Robert pledged.

"Fly sweat," I mumbled faintly.

"What was that, Prince Arn?" Graven asked suspiciously.

"I—uh—swear." Another oath. Drat.

"So be it. Then I will tell you. There are two kinds of magic. You have seen magic acts. I have performed them myself. I don't think you could find a wizard who hasn't done a few, especially in youth while trying to make a living. There are traveling magicians who do little else, or so it would appear.

"All wizards are trained for such public displays. Most of the tricks, I regret to say, are simply that—illusions which can be duplicated by anyone with practice. Some involve material devices such as a box with a false bottom. Others require sleight of hand such as Mr. Kendall practices when he pulls coins from behind your ear, like this.''

He reached behind Robert's ear and pulled out a ten-penny piece. ''And now it is gone again.'' The coin disappeared. Then he turned his hand over. ''But see, it is there, tucked between my fingers. You think the coin vanishes, but it is merely a trick of perception, an illusion. The coin is still in my hand.'' Then he dropped the coin safely back into his own pocket. He was careful with his pennies.

''Still other tricks require distraction to work, such as motions, or noises, or props, or smoke and flame, or even a pretty girl. Colored smoke and other effects can also enhance the mystery of the magic show. The result is an audience entertained and intrigued, many believing the illusions are in truth magical. Those of my profession have found it better not to dissuade the believers. Others who are wiser are still left puzzling over how a trick was done, and that means they have enjoyed the show too.''

The king listened to the explanation with amused tolerance.

Graven leaned closer, and his voice fell to a whisper. ''But there is another type of magic, more powerful, more important, and more difficult. It is the magic of the mind.'' He tapped his head with a finger. ''The Old World referred to this magic as extra-sensory perception. Psychic power. Those who had this gift—this talent—were rare, and there was no formal training in the discipline. Few knew they had any power, and those few had no one to teach them to best use their talents.

''Psychic powers became more prominent after the Cataclysm, though we do not know why. We've learned to use this power of the mind to accomplish certain ends for the good of the kingdom. The power has manifested itself in several talents. Telepathy. Telekinesis. Precognition. The ability to communicate with, and yes, possibly influence, other minds and thoughts. The ability to move or affect physical objects. And the ability to foresee future events, to foretell, however clearly or dimly.

''It might seem that a man with these gifts would be all-powerful. And he would be, if he had all these talents in all their forms, had strength in all, and had total control of them. Fortunately or unfortunately, this individual does not exist, nor is anyone even close. Most magicians have only one or two talents. The strength of each talent varies by individual but is most often low, and it takes a lifetime of practice to use them consistently and effectively.

"In addition, almost all human beings give off a psychic presence that deters the magician. This presence serves as a psychic interference or static that might be likened to the sound of water in the background. A few men nearby seems like the bubbling of a brook. A village of people is a drumming rainstorm. A town is the roaring cataract of a mountain stream. Nor is that all that interferes with the use of magic. Many wizards can put out an intentional mental static to block another magician's efforts."

Robert listened intently, and then spoke. "Can you read minds?"

Graven shook his head. "Not thoughts alone. The talent can take many forms, but I know of no wizard who can do that directly. But we can often sense emotions of individuals and groups, if we try."

Robert continued his inquiry. "Can you throw rocks? Can you shake apart a castle wall? Can you fly me across the terrace?"

"No, nor can we fly to the moon," Graven said sharply, and then caught himself. "But some of us can turn an arrow in flight so that it misses its target, and some can ignite flammable materials. Some can calm animals. Some can nudge another's thinking, making him more favorably disposed, for example. Some of us can detect the presence of an enemy from afar. And a few of us can even anticipate events, on occasion. No, Robert. Don't ask. We can't tell the exact future—though I did meet a woman long ago who claimed she could. It's more a feeling we get, an impression of something that might happen, good or evil. As often as not, the feeling is wrong. Precognition—foretelling—is perhaps the most valued and most difficult of the gifts.

"So, that is magic, Robert. It's not the magic of the stage, and yet, miracle of God, it is real." Graven tossed three coins into the air and they hung there, suspended while the high wizard watched our faces. "This is true magic."

My mouth hung open waiting for the next fly to buzz in, mollifying Graven somewhat. I had seen such a feat only from a distance, and had assumed it was a trick. Now I knew it was not. I was impressed.

Robert, however, was unaffected.

"Is that it?" he asked. "No fireballs? No lightning bolts?"

"Is that it?" Graven sputtered, and went speechless.

Robert continued resignedly, already knowing the answer. "And the Silver Sword of Detroit? The Death Spear of Pittsburgh?"

The king answered for Graven. "No more real than Excalibur and Glamdring and the Singing Sword of Valiant. Myth, all myth. Would that they were real."

"Still," Robert mused, "I suppose magic might be of some use. . . ."

The king laughed. "Don't be disappointed. And don't underestimate magic. The High Wizard is one of the greatest magicians in the kingdom, and has earned his position in service of Kenesee. His premonitions have served this country well. You will better appreciate such powers when you have need of magic."

Unfortunately, the king was right.

8

The Battle of the Beastwood

It was only a few days after our pleasant afternoon on the terrace that the matter of the Beastwood finally came to a head. Word came that a full company of beastmen had attacked the almost completed border keep, overwhelmed the patrol, slaughtered the workers, and destroyed the construction. There was no doubt this time, for the body of a beastman had been inadvertently left behind. His fur did not resemble horsehair in the slightest, but the attack upon the keep was decisive. And so the

King's Call went out to the forces of Kenesee. There was much eager speculation that this would be a chance to push the Beast-wood back to the Ohio River which, the oh-so-wise declared, was our proper border.

God, of course, gave his sanction and blessing through his earthly representative, Bishop Thomas, whose fiery sermons on behalf of chastising the beastmen were printed throughout the kingdom. Nothing like Holy Approval for a good bloodletting.

By August the level of court activity had grown to a peak, with daily council meetings, conferences, and messengers coming and going all day. Throughout the kingdom supplies were collected, preparations made, and men assembled. A thousand men of infantry and five hundred of cavalry at last came together at each of the ten walled towns of the kingdom, pitching tents in the fields outside. They organized and drilled and waited for the order that would put them on the road and begin the last step in the assembly of the Army of Kenesee. In Kingsport, the First Infantry Regiment of active duty mercenaries continued to drill. The royal guard reserves trickled in from across Kenesee, swelling the ten-man squads into fifty-man squadrons until over five hundred horsemen in black uniforms performed their maneuvers on the parade ground.

By the end of August all was ready, and the king marched forth. Behind him came Robert and I, followed by advisors, staff, messengers, and most of the men of the court. Before and behind us came the guards, all of them present except for the Queen's Second Squadron, left to guard her and the castle until the king's return. Then followed the long columns of cavalry and infantry which would stretch longer yet as we marched north and other units joined us.

From Kingsport we passed quickly out of the coastal lowlands and into the mountains, moving slowly and steadily northward. The road followed the highway of the Old World, rolling through clefts in the hillsides and along the sides of mountains. The fields and woods had encroached upon the remains of the Old World, so that the great smooth highway of the past had narrowed in spots to where no more than four men or two horses could march abreast. Yet, these old roads were still the best paths in Kenesee.

At various locations the geologic upheaval had split the road, moving the broken ends horizontally or vertically until they were separated by a dozen feet. Professor Wagner took great delight in pointing out spots where the quakes had broken the road, and the engineering employed to fill in narrow chasms or smooth vertical gaps. At these places earth had been piled to smooth the difference, and chunks of flat crete laid to provide a continuous, hard surface across the breaks. At rivers the abutments left intact by the quakes had been used to build bridges of wood, mortar, and crete.

Professor Wagner took advantage of the travel to continue our education even as we marched, his horse between ours. "And what road do we march upon? Prince Robert? Prince Arn?"

"We march north upon the Kingsport-Redbank Road," Robert replied with assurance.

"And what was the name of this road before the Cataclysm?"

Robert and I exchanged glances. Before the Cataclysm?

The king looked on, amused.

Professor Wagner pointed. "There. Read that." We passed a small wooded knoll upon which had been set a square stone monument perhaps five feet tall. In its side was an inscription. It was too far away to read, and so we rode over and let our horses pick their way through the trees. Letters had been carved into the stone itself, still waiting to be read, the first line of text contained in an impression shaped like a shield. The letters were in Old World English, but by now I was familiar with the basics of the old tongue. It wasn't too hard, once I'd learned how to read and write common English.

US ROUTE 75
RECONSTRUCTION PROJECT PLAN A
BEGUN 2008, COMPLETED 2018
ON JUNE 30, 2018, THIS FINAL STRETCH OF I-75 WAS COMPLETED AND ALL LANES WERE REOPENED TO TRAFFIC. I-75 WAS ONE OF THE FIRST INTERSTATE HIGHWAYS CHOSEN FOR RECONSTRUCTION UNDER THE TRANSPORTATION AND EMPLOYMENT ACT, C06.107.372.42, PASSED BY THE UNITED STATES CONGRESS AND SIGNED INTO LAW BY PRESIDENT KENNEDY IN 2006 A.D. LANDSCAPING WAS PARTIALLY PAID FOR BY THE CHILDREN OF THE UNITED STATES THROUGH DONATIONS TO THE NATIONAL BEAUTIFICATION AND PRESERVATION PROGRAM OF AMERICA.

The professor gave us a minute to read the text, and then repeated his question. "And what was the name of this road?"

Robert looked puzzled. "Numbers? They numbered their roads?"

Professor Wagner nodded his head smugly. "That is correct. This was Road Seventy-five. I know it isn't sensible, but the Old World seemed to enjoy numbering everything."

I raised my hand. "What is landscaping?"

The days passed as we marched through Laketown and Lafayette to reach the walled town of Redbank, where we added more regiments to our column. From Redbank we headed northeast for Knox. By day we could track our progress by looking north-eastwards and following the column of white smoke from Kelley's Inferno, the largest volcano in the kingdom. Nor was it forgotten at night, when a faint glow came from within its cone as it brooded in the dark, waiting for a proper time to terrorize the villagers in the valley below. Gradually it fell away to the southeast, and was behind us as we reached Knox. Eight regiments of foot and horse were encamped around that town and fell in on the march northwards to Lexington.

The mountains gave way to hills and then leveled out somewhat, making travel easier on the legs of both men and horses. Our pace was a moderate fifteen miles a day, for the king wanted to keep straggling to a minimum. We passed Corban and London on our way, the people coming out to cheer our column, partaking in the excitement and glory of the quest. It had been that way at each town and village, and would be until the army reached the Beastwood. Beyond Richmond the cultivated fields grew larger while the number of individual farmsteads declined in favor of small villages surrounded by palisades. Lone farm houses were built with strong outer walls and gated inner courtyards, and all in the villages had stout shutters and doors. While the big raids from the Northern Forests had ended generations ago, habit died hard, and even I had to admit the wisdom of some customs.

As we neared Lexington the hillsides were more often dotted with vineyards. The hills formed a shallow valley through which the road ran into town and then northward to the Ohio. Lexington was a prosperous town, well tended and picturesque, with impressive battlements backing up to a steep hill covered with vineyards. The town was noted for its vintage grape. Famous wineries resided within the walls, and their vaulted cellars held casks and kegs of all sizes.

Around the town were encamped another six regiments, and at last the muster of the Army of Kenesee was complete. Ten regiments of infantry and ten of cavalry were ready and strengthened by the Nobles Regiment and the Royal Guards Regiment. Over sixteen thousand men waited to do their king's will. The soldiers set up camp for the night while the king's party rode into the town and to the Castle of Sims. Rooms had been prepared for us, and after a good meal we settled in for the night in real beds, of which I heartily approved. Camping is fine as long as I am not the one doing it.

The time of parting had come. Robert and I and other noncombatants would be left behind—watched over by a squadron of royal guards—while the soldiers marched east to the Beastwood. Robert was none too happy about this, while I found the news most welcome. Robert expressed his displeasure in a meeting with the king, who listened sympathetically, shook his head in a final no, and then turned to me as if waiting for my objections. I told him that I would obey his orders, which pleased him. It pleased me, too.

The next morning the king was to take the army and march off to the east. Sir Meredith and his household troops had joined the king, so we were hosted by Megan and her grandfather, the aged Duke Gregory. The duke seemed immensely old to my young eyes, a stoop-shouldered man who limped along with a cane, muttering to himself in an intermittent grumble. Duke Gregory, Megan, Robert, and I stood together upon the battlements, enjoying a gentle breeze and watching the army move off. Horsed messengers galloped back and forth, horns and bugles and drums were sounded, banners and flags flew above the dust, and thousands of men burst into song as they moved out.

Robert pounded his fist on the stone. "We should be marching with them."

The old duke shook his head. "No, sonny, I'm afraid not. You're still too young, and you couldn't stand against the enemy. Your guards would have to die protecting you. Do you want to be responsible for someone's death because you're on the battlefield before your time?"

"No," said Robert, thinking about it. Then he pounded his

fist on the stone again. "You're right, but I still don't like it."

"You boys will get your chance, most likely. Just wait a few years. Besides, fighting in woods isn't the way to do it. Men should fight in the open fields, like God intended. No telling what could happen in that forest."

Robert picked up on the comment. "Do you think the army will have any problems?"

The duke gestured angrily with his cane. "Some are going into this thinking all they've got to do is beat up on a few disorganized tribes of beastmen. I don't buy that. Sure, some people venture a mile or two into the edge of the Beastwood. But no one who went deeper ever came out. Now, if the beastmen are just so many disorganized tribes, how come their border security is so good? Nope, I figure they've got a pretty efficient watch on the forest, and that takes organization and manpower. And are they going to follow the rules of warfare laid out in the Codes? Hah! I mentioned it to the King. But does anybody listen to an old man? Well, they'll find out, one way or another."

Megan looked concerned for the first time. "Are they in danger?"

The duke at last seemed to realize the implications of what he was saying, and his tone softened. "What? Danger? Did I say that? No, I didn't. The King's no slackard. He'll take every precaution," the old man reassured us. "It might just be a little harder than they thought it was going to be. That's all. Now, don't you go getting upset because of what some old blabbermouth says who likes to hear himself talk. Come on, let's go to morning meal."

We got to know the layout of Castle Sims quite well over the days we were there, as we had free run and Megan had given us a tour, playing lady of the castle with great pleasure. Megan was especially pleased that old Duke Gregory followed along behind, catering to her airs of dignity. In the entry hall she stopped next to a glass-enclosed display cabinet.

"And this is Grandfather and Father's collection of art works," she announced with a flourish. "Some are quite old, and some quite new. Aren't they beautiful?"

I pressed my nose up against the glass and stared.

The duke came up behind me. "So, Arn, you like my collection, eh?" he chuckled. "What are you looking at? The carvings?" On one shelf were wood carvings. One was a woman in a flowing gown with arms outstretched, waiting to be filled. And next to it was another piece.

"The boat," I stated softly.

"What? The boat? Oh, yes. Nice, isn't it? Look at those lines. The detail. It was done by the same carver who did the woman there next to it. Look at her expression, the sadness. The man was a genius at his art. No one knows who he is, really, though one story says he lived in Louisville. His pieces are becoming quite popular now. I was lucky to get these two."

"Come along," said Megan. "I have to show you the paintings in the great hall."

I gave a last glance at the display, and then gave up the thought.

The cabinet was securely locked.

And so we waited at the castle, exercising for most of each morning, but playing during the afternoons and eating well throughout. I congratulated the beaming cook and got two recipes to pass on to the kitchen staff in Kingsport. The days passed pleasantly enough. We did whatever eight and nine year olds do when left to themselves. The three of us knew it could be many days before our men returned, but worried little about them, for who could harm the mighty Army of Kenesee? Still, when we could not find Megan elsewhere, we knew that she had ascended the battlements and was watching eastward.

After noon meal of the eighth day we were in the courtyard of the castle, covered bows in hand, quivers of arrows on our backs, Duke Gregory seated in the warm sun watching the children under his care. Megan had challenged us to an archery contest, and a target had been set up against the outer curtain wall. For the contest she had pulled back her golden hair into a tail and secured it with a light blue ribbon. A squad of royal guards were on duty and watched attentively, armed and ready to defend our lives. Others lounged about and followed the match as a form of entertainment.

Robert and I took the covers off our bows. Megan took out hers. We looked at her bow. We looked again.

Some of the onlooking guardsmen developed coughs.

Robert made a face. "*What*," he asked, "is *that*?"

"This is my bow," she said with complete assurance. And then her voice took on a dangerous note. "Don't you *like* it?"

Robert swallowed. "Like it? Why, it's quite—unique. I've never seen a bow painted, uh—"

"Powder blue. I knew you'd approve. And you, Arn? What do you think?"

I was no fool. "The ribbons at each end, uh, match very nicely."

She nodded in satisfaction. "I'm glad you both like it. Now, shall we begin?"

An ill-perceived idea began to form in my mind that Megan's entire reason for this contest was to show off her bow. How someone as sensible as Megan could do such a thing, I didn't know. But then again, I wasn't a girl.

"Ladies first," Robert bowed his head to Megan.

"Royalty before all," Megan responded, bowing her head in return.

Courtesies fulfilled, but still eyeing the fluttering ribbons on Megan's weapon, Robert stepped up to the line chalked on the cobblestones. He placed one end of the bow against his instep and with effort bent the wood and strung his bow. He pulled an arrow from his quiver, eyed the target carefully, pulled back, and let fly. The arrow hit the second circle from the bull's-eye and buried itself to midshaft in the straw backing. A spate of applause and cheers greeted this feat. Robert fired two more, one again in the second circle and one in the first. More applause and cheers.

I took my place at the line, struggled to string my bow, and finally let loose three careful shots. The first two were in the outer circle, earning a few polite claps. The last missed and hit the wall, shattering.

There was another spate of coughing and the clearing of throats.

"Oh, Arn," Robert sighed in embarrassment.

I would be in for it when Sergeant Major Nakasone returned. "Prince Arn, what's this I hear about you missing at twenty yards? Isn't the target large enough? Shall we find a convenient barn to paint bigger circles on? Hmmm?" And then he would have me fire two or three hundred arrows after dinner. My fingers ached with unhappy anticipation.

Now it was Megan's turn. She wrapped a leg around the lower half of the bow, placed her back within the arc of the wood, and pulled down on the upper end while pressing her back against the arc of the bow. It took all her strength, but using the leverage of her entire body, she managed to bend it far enough to slip the string over the end. The intelligent application of force instead of brute strength.

Megan took out an arrow. It was painted blue. Robert rolled his eyes.

Megan nocked the arrow, took a breath, and pulled back hard, realizing she could not hold the tension for long. She hit the second circle, the point burying itself deep in the straw. A quick pull, and the next blue arrow likewise found the second circle. She took out a third blue shaft, nocked it, and then looked at Robert with a smirk. "I have a new friend in the town. Her father will be the next mayor. She says that if you don't let the man win, he will hate you." Megan's glance took in both of us. "Will you hate me?"

"It has never made a difference before. It would be dishonorable to hate someone just for beating me," Robert stated thoughtfully. "But you haven't won yet."

She nodded, took a deep breath, and brought up her bow. Before she could release the arrow, there was a call from the battlements.

"MEN ON THE ROAD!"

All eyes turned to the lookout. "MEN ON THE ROAD!"

Megan dropped her bow and streaked up the steps. We followed on her heels, the guards trying to keep up with us.

"Grandfather! There *are* men coming up the road. Soldiers!"

The duke followed behind more slowly, placing his cane on each step before ascending. We were silent until he arrived.

"Well, what's happening?"

One of the guards shook his head. "This doesn't look good, Duke Gregory."

Down the road a squadron of our cavalry approached in good order, although without any great spirit. But behind them came the infantry companies of a regiment. It had departed with neat ranks and voices raised in song, but now the ranks were sloppy and the men silent. As they came nearer we could see more. Uniforms were dirty, weapons trailed in the dust, and there was much straggling. Many wore bandages, and it was evident that there were fewer in the regiment than had left a week before.

The first troops reached their old encampments and threw themselves down, exhausted and sullen.

The regiment behind was no better.

"As I feared," sighed the old duke. "Send word to the mayor to open all inns and houses to the wounded. Any with medical knowledge should report to the town hall."

And thus the infantry and cavalry trailed in throughout the morning. Near the end of the procession came the king and his party, followed by the nobles unit and, last of all, the royal guards. Surprisingly, most of the guards marched on foot, their horses gone. One of those on horseback was Sergeant Major Nakasone, his shirt off and bandages covering his chest. He was swaying in the saddle and propped into place by a guardsman on either side. Behind him was Sergeant Black, striding indomitably up and down the short column of dusty black uniforms, and calling out to the unit to look sharp for the town.

Back in camp, the king and his commanders were busy organizing and reorganizing, caring for the men and posting security and preparing defenses in case the beastmen were to follow. But the conflict was over. The Battle of the Beastwood had been fought, and the beastmen had won.

We heard many bits and pieces from people who spared us a moment, but most were too tired or too busy to talk. It was evening before Duke Gregory was able to latch onto Mr. Kendall and get the full story. I saw them head up to the duke's room, and I followed discreetly. The old duke let Kendall in, then spoke to the shadows where I hid. "All right, Arn, if you want to join us, come now or I'm shutting the door." Age had not totally affected his vision or hearing. He closed the door behind me and I took a seat on the clothes chest.

Kendall sat in a chair with a mug of beer in his hands and leaned back with a sigh of relief. "I'm tired."

"Wait until you're seventy, and then you'll see what tired is. Now, tell me what happened, beginning to end."

Kendall took a sip of beer and began to relate the story.

In three marches the army had reached the edge of the Beastwood. A camp was established in the last open fields and meadows before the forest closed in on the road. All the wagons and other impediments were left there, along with four cavalry regiments to guard the camp. The next morning the rest of the army marched into the forest and followed the old road eastward, dropping off cavalry squadrons as they went to secure their line of supply.

The only enemy spotted were a few beastman scouts skirmishing with our own. Overall, the army made good progress. That evening the men camped along the road and the next morning took their breakfast. It was as the morning light sifted through the trees that the beastmen sprang their trap, and at that moment an important discovery was made. The beastmen were somehow not attuned to "hairless" magic, and psychic talents were not effective against them. The magicians with the army had been unable to detect the beastmen—to Graven's humiliation. And so, without benefit of warning from the wizards, the beastmen fell upon the Army of Kenesee.

A surprise attack designed to strike the front and flank of the column was launched by the enemy. Fortunately, the king had not relied only upon magic. Scouts and flankers prevented complete surprise in the tangled forest, and there was enough warning to deploy before the beastmen struck. Swarms of well-disciplined bowmen pinned down the newly formed Kenesee battle line, while aggressive units armed with sword and shield closed at key points. The beastmen threw themselves upon the infantry with all the ferocity of those fighting on their own soil. The shock of seeing the vaunted "beastmen" in the flesh was too much for some men, and a few ran from the battlefield. The king put himself in the places of greatest danger, shouting encouragement at threatened spots, charging in with a yell when needed and inspiring the men to hold against the assault. To the credit of the regiments, most of the infantry held their place, loyal to country and comrades. Only the First Infantry Regiment, upon whose mercenary ranks so much money and equipment had been lavished, broke before their childhood nightmare. A gap was opened for the beastmen.

Sergeant Major Nakasone fell wounded by an arrow and Sergeant Black took over command of the royal guards. Dismounting the men, he attacked into the gap and his tough fighters held the beastmen. Other companies were given to Black as they became available, and the situation was stabilized. Still, something would have to be done, for the enemy was already attempting to maneuver around the new battle line. Reluctantly, the king ordered a withdrawal, chastened by the success of a force he suspected was numerically inferior to his own.

If the conduct of a retreat in the face of the enemy is the most difficult military maneuver, then the army and its commanders performed very well, indeed. Through the day and then through the night, the battle went on. Regiments leapfrogged each other backwards as the army slowly withdrew along the road, sometimes having to clear enemy skirmishers from their path. By the next morning the forest thinned and the open fields of Kenesee were reached. The beastmen did not follow, but watched from the edge of the wood before fading back into the forest, unwilling to leave its protection in the face of our cavalry.

The fighting was resolute, intense, vicious, even fanatical at points. Our men seemed to have given as good as they'd got, but most of those who fell wounded had to be left behind, and the beastmen were neither giving nor asking for quarter. Losses had been heavy. One in five never returned from the Beastwood. Of the royal guards, only half ever made it out.

And that was the end of the Beastwood Campaign. We waited for several days at Lexington, but the beastmen never left their forest. Reports indicated that their force had withdrawn into the interior of the Beastwood. So the royal party returned to Kingsport while the units of the army marched back to their homes and stood down.

But matters did not end there. A meeting was called with the advisors, nobles, army commanders, and guard leaders in attendance. The group was so large that the council room would not serve, and we had to meet in the second hall.

Bishop Thomas began the meeting with a prayer, and then the king stood and addressed the group.

"The Beastwood Campaign has failed," King Reuel began, and there was silence. No one could deny this truth. "I accept full responsibility for the defeat—and for the many who died," he stated, and to shouts of protest held up his hand. "You saved the army from disaster, and I thank you. But if there was any fault, if there is to be any blame, it is mine. I do not want anyone pointing at another.

"But that is not my purpose for calling you together. Rather, I want us to learn from this campaign and use those lessons to the benefit of the kingdom. How can we improve our forces?

What changes in the army should we make? This is your job, and I await your recommendations. Now, Sir Meredith will conduct the proceedings for us.''

The meeting went on for almost a week. From this came several reforms in the forces of Kenesee. Since the mercenaries had done so badly, the First Infantry Regiment was made a reserve unit manned by volunteers, just like the other regiments, and its pay the same as the others. This change was popular, as the elimination of the mercenaries returned a goodly chunk of pay to the treasury. Thus, the only active duty forces would be the navy, royal guards, and a few special units such as the garrison of the Rift Gates.

Each infantry regiment would now have eight companies of long spears, one company of archers, and another of axemen, except for the Fourth Infantry Regiment, which would have eight companies of archers and two of spearmen. A revised manual of arms, developed by Sergeant Black, was also adopted. I understood now what he had been doing writing in that notebook in his spare moments. Though he wore only the three stripes of a sergeant, the salvation of the army was due as much to his efforts as to any man's, except the king. His suggestions were listened to seriously.

The overall result would prove to be an army that was more efficient, more flexible, and less costly. I would not have expected such positive results from any meeting of so many disparate individuals. I suppose a military defeat provides great motivation. That, and not allowing anyone to leave the castle until the deed was accomplished.

After it was all over, the king met with Robert and me in his council room for another of his ''listen and learn'' sessions. He pushed back his chair and slouched down with his legs thrust out before him. ''Well, that puts one mess behind us. Who knows, perhaps some good might come from it after all. The whole thing *was* my fault. The army was lucky to escape destruction.''

''No, father,'' objected Robert. ''You did everything you could.''

The king shook his head sadly. ''I did not. I'm fortunate God doesn't strike me down for my sin. I was willful instead of wise, and I ruled in accord with my desires and dreams, rather than with reason and reality. Because of my pride, many good men have died—men of Kenesee and, yes, of the Beastwood too. They *are* men, I think, after all. Only men could fight so hard and so well.''

He was silent a long moment, his eyes unseeing until his thoughts at last returned to the room. ''Enough brooding upon the past. We must go forward. It's time for a change in priorities. I'm sending a messenger to the Beastwood bearing a request for negotiations. We'll do what we should have done in the first place.''

The king was as good as his word. Escorted by two guards, a messenger left within the week, and the court waited expectantly for an answer.

But no answer came, for the messenger never returned.

9

Birth and Death

The months went by filled with instruction and activity but without undue incident. The leaves changed color and fell. The days shortened and turned gray. The temperature cooled, and then grew cold as winter approached. In December I enjoyed my second Christmas in the castle, with a Yule tree and decorations and new clothes and toys and similar items of interest to a nine year old. The Christmas dinner was exceptional, and I made a special visit to the kitchen to congratulate the staff.

The winter was another bad one, the second in three years. The castle grew amazingly chill. The thick walls which had helped cool us during the summer now seemed to radiate cold. Some grumbled about their discomfort, which provided me with amusement since we all enjoyed heavy clothes and warm socks and dry shoes and burning logs in every fireplace. It occurred to me that somewhere out in the streets below us, huddling in doorways and cellars, gutter rats shivered in their rags. The thought was disturbing, but I was kept sufficiently busy that I could dismiss it from my mind just as the others seemed to do. Besides, something was being done. There were orphanages now and there would be a bed for every gutter rat. Eventually.

It was in January that the queen came due. Her condition had become more prominent with every week, and one evening the summons came to us amidst a flurry of activity not unlike that of a nest of ants that has been turned up with a spade. There was a steady flow of people into the queen's chamber, including the king, his advisors, the court, and the royal physician with four other medical doctors assisting, as well as pharmacists, nurses, attendants, and two almost forgotten princes. The crowd fluttering around the queen's bed varied in number from twenty to forty as various personages and attendants scurried in and out. All of these were apparently essential, being needed to witness, verify, sanctify, or otherwise assist in the royal birth. I was wondering when they would call in the cooks and guards.

Comments were many. "Her color looks good," said one. "She'll certainly have enough milk if she wishes to nurse," whispered another. "You're stepping on my foot," moaned a third. "We need more light," commanded one of the physicians.

"Contractions are closer now," noted Dr. Amani.

The queen gave her first cry of pain, and Robert was startled by the sound. Then she screamed and we were hustled out of the room, the heavy wooden door closing behind us. Benches were brought and we plopped down outside the room and played chess. I could tell by the game how seriously distracted Robert was by the situation. Within fifteen or twenty moves he would usually have me beaten. We were up to our twenty-fifth and it was still anyone's game.

Perhaps my face reflected my feelings as well. Robert and I were both worried, but each for our own reasons. He feared for his mother. I feared for my life. A far larger game was being played out, and I realized the weakness of my position. What if the child was a girl? Would the queen suffer me to stay at the castle, or even to live? What order would she give

Graven? I had no friends near. Kendall was gone on another of his mysterious journeys, his whereabouts and return completely unknown. Robert was still only a boy, powerless. And the king? Would he dare suspect his queen should I fall sick and die? With two children by his queen to care for and their mother doting on him, how long would he lament the tragedy of the poor gutter rat's sudden disappearance? Even as I moved a piece on the chessboard I went over my plan for a hasty departure. From the streets I had come, and to the streets I could return, if need be—and with a goodly number of coins in my pockets. I was ready, if necessary. But we would see what the future had in store.

We waited perhaps an hour, hearing moans, muffled cries of pain, and the whispered muttering of the queen's audience. We had glimpses of the room as the door was opened for attendants bringing towels, or pots of steaming water, or armfuls of wood for the room's roaring fireplace. The backs of those crowded around the bed blocked any further view.

Impatiently, Robert finally stopped a nurse as she hurried in. "What's going on now? Why is it taking so long?"

"Ah, poor children. Havin' to wait. Now don't worry, Prince Robert. The Queen's doin' fine." She hurried in, but must have mentioned to the king that we were still waiting. A moment later he came out, carefully closing the door behind him. We stood in greeting and he gave us a warm grin and dropped his arms across our shoulders.

"Getting impatient, my young princes? Everything is perfectly normal so far. It takes a while. Why, Jessica was in labor for a day and a night with you, Robert. The doctors say that the baby will be born within the hour. It's just a matter of waiting."

The attendant we had talked to stuck her head out the door. "Sir, it's coming."

The king's face lit up. "Aha! Back in I go. It's almost over now."

"Sir!" I blurted out.

He stopped with his hand on the latch. "What, Arn? Quickly, now."

"Don't forget me, sir."

He looked puzzled for a moment, and then—was there a flicker of understanding somewhere deep within him? Or was it nothing? "Forget? How can I forget one of my sons? Enough gibberish. Don't worry. It will be soon now."

The door closed behind him with an anxious grate of wood against stone.

And so we waited some more. But now Robert paced up and down the cold hall, while I sat quietly musing upon the content of the king's words, trying to squeeze the last drop of reassurance from them.

Noises came from the bedchamber. Voices. Exclamations. The cry of a newborn. And yes, sobbing. The attendant we had talked to and another came out carrying baskets of soiled sheets and towels. They talked in hushed voices as they hurried down the passageway. "Heaven protect us," said the one, struggling with the basket. "The mark of the beast."

"A beastchild," agreed the other. "Who would have thought it."

"What will they do?" asked the first.

"What can they do? The law's the law."

A beastchild.

The king came out of the room then, closely followed by the high wizard and the bishop. He walked slowly, his shoulders slumped and his face filled with disbelief.

Robert saw this and ran up to him in fright. "Mother? How is mother?"

Graven intercepted Robert and calmed him. "Your mother is fine. She's asked for you. Go in now and comfort her."

Robert looked doubtful, then went in to join the queen.

The king rubbed his forehead. "The incidence of such births has been declining over the past few generations. Why has God done this to me?"

The bishop had guided the king a few yards down the hall and assumed I was out of earshot. But the sounds carried clearly to my seat on the bench.

Graven seemed as if he wanted to reach out, to touch, to comfort his king, but after a feeble gesture folded his mottled hands within his robe. "It's not your fault, nor the Queen's. It may happen anywhere, to anyone."

"It is His Will," the bishop said softly.

Still befuddled, the king looked from one to another as if

looking for an answer to a mystery he could not fathom. "I can't believe it. My child. . . . My son. . . ."

"You must not think of it as your child!" Graven spoke sternly. "It has the mark of the beast."

The bishop crossed himself. "The High Wizard is right, sir. It is the devil's spawn."

"What can I do?" the king asked weakly.

Both advisors were silent.

"Perhaps we could steal it away," ventured the king, speaking more to himself than the others. "Like the common women do near the forest. Leave it there and—"

Graven shook his head. "My King, it could not be. This is not a farmer's cabin removed from curious eyes. Too many know. The law must be followed."

Bleakly, the king nodded. "Yes, you're right, of course. And yet I feel dread at what must be done. . . ." He hesitated, and then took a deep breath. His features hardened and resolution flowed into his voice. "But the laws must be obeyed, in spite of all. Have the child brought to me."

"Sir, we can take care of this matter for you if you wish. There is no need—"

The king cut off the wizard. "No, it is my responsibility. I must do it. Somehow."

Ever helpful, Graven offered a suggestion. "My King, it is very cold outside. . . ."

A swaddled bundle was brought by the nurse. Her eyes were wet with tears but she carried the bundle warily, as if it might bite her. The king took the child and lifted the flap covering its face. I caught one brief glimpse of a tiny face covered with dark hair that was still sleek with wetness.

The king looked down at the face, then lowered the covering. "We will go to the battlements. My advisors will accompany me to bear witness."

"Sir," objected the bishop, "there is no need to bear witness to you."

"You will come," he repeated sternly, and strode off. They followed slowly behind the king, and I followed them, unnoticed. I could not quite fully understand what was going on, but I wanted to find out.

We entered a tower, climbed its steps, and exited onto the

battlements that topped the king's house. Small drifts of snow were piled into corners, to be whipped and swirled about by the brisk wind which whistled as it found its way around corners and eaves. A guard huddled in the lee of the tower against the biting wind, his coat and helmet flecked with the white of snow. He challenged us, then fell silent when he saw who approached. The king dismissed him from duty. With several backward glances, the guard took his weapons and left the wall.

Enfolded in the bitter cold of the winter's night, the battlements were feebly lit by lanterns that flickered with the shifting winds. The lights of the town far below were hidden by the hard stone of the battlements, and for us the whole earth was dark, and the clouded sky black and forbidding.

I pulled up the hood of my coat and stood with the others just outside the tower door. The king took a lantern from the wall. "Wait here," he commanded, and walked off, the bundle cradled carefully in one arm. He faded quickly into the darkness. Only his light was seen, growing smaller until it held steady at a point that must have been halfway down the length of the battlements. And then, carried by the wind, came the cry of the baby. The crying continued even while the lantern light grew again until we could see the features of the king as he returned. His arm was empty.

"Now we will wait," the king gasped, breathing heavily, as if he had just fought a great battle.

"Did you remove the wrapping?" asked Graven.

The king gave a single nod.

"It will be quicker that way," Graven stated. "Kinder."

The bishop began to mumble prayers.

The wail of the infant continued.

The king noticed me. "Arn," he exclaimed tiredly. "What are you doing here?"

The others turned and saw me for the first time.

"I came . . . to see," I admitted. "I don't understand."

"Don't try to understand," he said harshly. "It doesn't do any good." The iron went out of his voice. "But I'm glad you've come. Here, stand by me." I did so and he put an arm around me, enfolding us in his cloak. "Wait with me, Arn. Wait with me." And then he fell silent, and we listened to the sounds of new life brought by the wind. The cries of the infant rose and fell faintly, objecting to the coldness and cruelty of the world into which it had been born. The minutes passed slowly, and the cries grew yet fainter as the tiny voice weakened.

"This does not feel right," the king mumbled, perhaps to me, perhaps to himself. "I am being punished, and that is just. But this . . . this is not right. We must not do this thing." He tightened his grip upon me. Though he spoke, he made no other move, and stood either lost in thought or listening.

I understood now what was happening to the child. This was no second son of the queen, to assure her line of succession and thus remove her threat to me. Male or not, it was a beastchild, and so useless to my hopes. I should have hated it. Yet I did not. Listening to it wailing was disturbing. It had done me no harm, nor could it. Whether the beastchild possessed a soul or not, it was an innocent creature being condemned to freeze to death. It too would soon be wrapped in a sack and buried in the frozen ground and forgotten.

Yet I could do nothing. This was a matter beyond me, a thing of adult law and religion and belief which I was only beginning to learn. And so the wind blew and the baby cried on. And I pondered how soon I should flee the castle.

The high wizard and bishop kept vigil with us, and then Sergeant Major Nakasone mounted the battlements and stood at a discreet distance. He seemed about to speak, then he too held his words. Perhaps he understood these things as little as I.

In spite of my coat and the king's cloak, I began to feel cold. Eventually I was shivering, although the king seemed not to notice. The crying of the baby became fainter and then fainter still, until only an occasional wail could be heard. It was an hour, perhaps more, before it was over and the wind bore no sound but its own.

Still the king stood unmoving.

Graven approached. "My King, I think it is over."

The king sighed then. His face was pulled into a deep-lined grimace. "It took so long. I never imagined it would take so long."

"We will take care of the remains," Graven told him. "Please go down now and try to rest."

"Make sure—"

"Never fear, my King. We will. We will."

The king gave a last look down the length of the battlements. Then he rested his hand upon my shoulder as we went down the steps of the tower, as if I were a crutch upon which to lean. At the bottom we met Dr. Amani.

The royal physician's face was grim too. "I'm sorry, my King. I have bad news." He explained about the queen, about the bleeding that had started and couldn't be stopped, about her last moment of life.

The king's face was blank. "Why was I not called?"

"My King," the distraught doctor responded, "things seemed well until just a short time ago. She started bleeding very suddenly, and it was too quick. Just minutes, and she was gone. We did not know where you were."

The king was still for a long moment while we waited. Suddenly his features contorted and tears welled up in his eyes. "Now my punishment is complete," he said, and loosing his grip upon me, collapsed to the floor in a heap.

PART • TWO

THE
DUTIES
OF MEN

1

The School of Magic

The trumpeter blew the wake up call, and I opened a bleary eye to confirm the unfortunate truth. Yes, it was time to get up. The September sun was still just a glow peeking over the hills, but since High Wizard Graven wanted us in the saddle at dawn, we enjoyed the trumpet's music at first light.

Sergeant Black stood next to the trumpeter in the middle of the camp, his arms folded across his chest, looking well-rested and ready. Over the years his dark hair had turned salt and pepper at the temples, and the lines around his eyes had deepened. Otherwise, he was as lean and hard as the day he'd brought me to the castle more than a decade before, his craggy features unchanged, his straight face revealing as little as ever.

"Good morning, men," he called out, and the fifty guardsmen around us returned his greeting as they sprang out of their blankets.

"Today," the sergeant announced, "is Prince Robert's twentieth birthday. Congratulations, sir."

"Three cheers for Prince Robert," shouted another guardsman, and the cheers were sincerely given. The guards folded their bedrolls and began to eat their morning meal.

"Thank you," Robert said, and bounced up as energetically as the guardsmen. He had grown into a handsome, charming young man, strong and virile. Robert had kept his intellectual vigor and curiosity, and to it had been added a somber dignity and presence beyond his age.

Graven too roused himself, although I noticed the grimace on his face as he stretched upward. Good. Let him feel the result of sleeping on the ground, since he was the cause of it.

Bishop Thomas, Professor Wagner, and I were a bit slower rising. The bishop's dark hair was rapidly turning gray, but it merely made him more distinguished than before. Professor Wagner wore spectacles and was now almost bald, although his last fringes of hair were still dark.

"Happy birthday, Robert," said the high wizard. The years had told on Graven. The lines in his face had grown deeper, his hair was rapidly going from gray to white, and his thin frame had become gaunt. He was still a man to regard warily, even if no longer under the spell of a queen. "I'm sorry we won't be able to take time to celebrate today," he continued, "but the tour is almost over. Another ten days and we'll be back at Kingsport, as long as we push on."

Push on.

Those had been Graven's favorite words since King Reuel left us a few weeks ago with half the royal party, interrupting the tour and starting the precipitous rush in which we found ourselves.

Part of King Reuel's success as a ruler had been the royal tour, which he had instituted after the Beastwood Campaign and conducted each year since to keep in touch with his subjects. The royal party on the tour included the king, Robert and me, the advisors, a visiting noble or two, various assistants and messengers, and the royal guards. Normally, traveling in early fall and experiencing all the best of the harvest in fruit and vegetables, the tour would include much visiting, celebrating, and renewing of loyalties. But the travel was more than just a pleasure trip. Reports were made, investigations conducted, judgments pronounced, and corrections made. Problems were brought forth and solved. Troubles were dealt with while small. Although not every major town and county could be visited each time, a fairly thorough coverage of the kingdom was achieved over several years.

This tour began pleasantly enough, the weather holding fine with sunny days and balmy breezes. And then one afternoon only a few weeks into our travels, a messenger from Kingsport caught up with our party on the road northward. The horseman sped past our ranks to the head of the column. He was a young man, covered with dust and tired from his ride. The column came to a halt and we reined in around the king as the messenger reported.

"King Reuel, the Mayor of Kingsport sends his greetings and reports that emissaries have arrived from five nations. They came aboard a single ship."

"A single ship?" Graven asked in surprise.

The emissary drank from a water skin we gave him and then replied. "Yes, High Wizard. The ship is supposed to have sailed from New Richmond. The five emissaries represent Virginia, Arkan, Texan, Mexico, and the Isles."

"But that's impossible," Kendall objected. "I have no information of any plans to send emissaries." Kendall's appearance had changed little over the years, his homely features still holding a boyish quality when he smiled, though his hair had thinned in front to a mere wisp.

"They demand audience with the King," the messenger continued. "The Mayor has put them up in the guest quarters of the town hall, and is keeping them entertained and watched. He was able to learn nothing more in the brief time before I was sent to find you. I've been riding for five days."

The king nodded and had a fresh horse brought for the man. "Well done. Return to the Mayor and tell him that I am following. Safe journey."

The messenger rode off and the king pondered the news in silence.

Graven spoke up. "I have never heard of such a thing happening before. One emissary, or even two would not be untoward. But five? We have always had cordial relations with Arkan, and King Herrick recognizes our friendship. Why would his emissary come with the others? Mr. Kendall, you have your countrymen in all of these foreign lands. Why didn't you warn us of this occurrence?"

Kendall looked embarrassed. "I have no answer. This bodes ill. We must assume the visit is not friendly. Yet I don't see how it could happen without my receiving word. Perhaps something happened to my countrymen. You had no premonition of these events, High Wizard? You, nor your wizards?"

It was Graven's turn to be embarrassed. "Uhhmmm . . . no."

The king waved his hand to diffuse the situation. "So. For once our information services fail us. My concern now is how best to handle this matter. I will return to Kingsport immediately with Sir Meredith, Mr. Kendall, and half the guards—''

''Sir,'' Graven interrupted, ''I feel it would be best if I also accompanied you—''

''No, my friend. I need you to lead the tour and ensure that it is successfully completed. Besides, you still have to visit the School of Magic to choose your new apprentice. You will take Robert and Arn, Bishop Thomas, Professor Wagner, and the remainder of the guards.''

''But my King—''

''High Wizard, do you accept this duty?''

''Uhh—yes, my King.''

''Good. The success of the tour and the safety of the princes are in your hands.''

The king headed back to Kingsport soon after with those designated. The rest of us continued on our way at our normal pace. But the next morning the high wizard told us what to expect. ''My sleep has been troubled. I sense that we must complete the tour quickly, and return to Kingsport as soon as possible.''

''A premonition?'' Robert asked, unable to mask a bit of doubt in his voice.

''Yes. I believe it to be so.''

Robert was thoughtful. ''Is it you who must return quickly, or all of us?''

''All of us. I cannot tell you why. It's only a feeling, but very strong.''

Robert and I exchanged a glance. Unspoken was the thought that the king was alone with Kendall for delicate matters of state. Was Graven experiencing true foresight, or was he just worried about that situation? The high wizard was beside himself after that, snapping at guards, impatient with everyone and frustrated beyond all solution, knowing that we needed to complete the tour as rapidly as possible. I derived much amusement watching him fume each morning beside the horses as the party doted on details of cinches and saddle bags while he was anxious to be off.

Never could the horses put enough miles beneath their hooves. We rose before daylight and rode until we reached our next destination. We conducted whirlwind inspections and ceremonies, and were on our way again before the afternoon was over. Nobles, officials, and innkeepers were shocked as they found our party pounding on their doors and gates far ahead of schedule, and then disappointed as we clattered out of their courtyards after the briefest of visits. The pace eased somewhat only when Sergeant Black informed the high wizard that we would soon ruin the horses. Still, often we passed a last inn at dusk just to put a few more miles behind us, and slept wrapped in blankets beneath the trees, far from the nearest shelter. And that was why, even on the eve of Robert's birthday, we had slept in a meadow instead of under a roof.

The rest of the party greeted Robert as they roused themselves, and wished him well. Twenty years old. Already, Robert was twenty. I would be too in six months and the thought of reaching such an advanced age gave me pause. The time had gone by so quickly.

During those years my education and training had continued throughout, and I grew taller and stronger, becoming a reasonably healthy and able young prince of the realm. I was not bad-looking, if not particularly handsome. While I was neither a born scholar nor a natural warrior, the intensity of my training made me more than competent in both endeavors. And outwardly, the crude manners of the gutter rat had been replaced by the polite behaviors and social graces of the court. I had been readied for leadership in the realm, but prayed I would never have to lead. I was content to fulfill ceremonial duties (no speeches, thank you) and enjoy life. And yes, my interests in life had expanded beyond food and warmth to include the fair sex.

A god who created women could be forgiven much.

"Congratulations, Robert," I greeted him. "Tell the High Wizard that you'd like a hot bath for a birthday present." We would have to settle for a splash of cold water from the stream that ran nearby.

He glanced at the watercourse. "Yes. That would be nice. . . ."

My relationship with Robert had always been satisfactory for me, but seemed less so for him. As a boy, he had shared expressions of brotherly affection, but received none in return. To this disappointment was added my lack of enthusiasm and ability for his favorite pursuits. Still, we had gotten along, and provided a level of companionship for each other that was much needed. And perhaps that was enough. Any true feelings Robert may have had he now kept to himself. There were no more brotherly hugs, no more long chats together in his room or mine. Credit it to the normal course of growing up, or to the queen's death, or to Graven's influence. One reason was as good as another.

We ate the smoked meat and bread left over from supper, and then were on our way. I did not enjoy the riding, but supposed I shouldn't complain too much since I could take the pace somewhat better than others. Robert and I normally spent an hour or two in the saddle each day throughout the year for training. It was the bishop and the professor who had pained looks upon their faces as they bounced up and down at the trot.

We were surprised one cool, overcast morning when Graven led us off the hard-surfaced Louisville-Nash road onto a dirt road leading east.

"Where are we going?" Robert asked.

"A stop that must be made," Graven responded grudgingly. "I rue the delay, and yet it has its purpose." After a mile or two we ascended a wooded, flat-topped hill. In a clearing stood an unpretentious building surrounded by a low wall. Around the building a small village of a half-dozen homes had sprung up.

"Behold the School of Magic," Graven announced as we approached.

Robert looked around. "As you say. But I don't remember ever coming here before."

"We did not stop here on other tours," Graven agreed. "This is the year of my choosing."

"Your choosing?" Robert asked. We were all listening now.

"My old apprentice, Garth, has grown to manhood and power. He is his own magician now. I have let him go, and he serves the House of Trudeau in Wickliffe. So the High Wizard of the realm needs a new apprentice. Today I will choose one. And see an old friend."

The school was an unimposing stone and wood structure of two stories, with two narrower wings enclosing a tiled courtyard. A well and benches occupied one corner of the courtyard, while two great oak trees provided shade. The gate stood open and inside a brown-skinned figure stood awaiting us in short robe and pants, his crossed arms tucked into the loose folds of his sleeves.

We dismounted, whereupon the figure bowed deeply to us, stepped forward, and threw his arms around Graven. "Greetings, old grumbler. Greetings. Ahh, yes, as stern as ever, harsh even to your old companion. You rascal. Taking the matters of court too seriously, I can see, and living up to your name.'' The man paused for breath, and smiled anew. ''It's good to see you.''

I was amazed to see—yes, it was, a smile! A smile on the face of Graven. His scowl lines did not know where to go. I nudged Robert. ''I didn't know he could do that.''

''It has been rumored,'' Robert grinned. ''Wonder of wonders. My dear High Wizard, the court would gaze in awe.''

''Enough,'' said Graven. ''You see why my scowl is set, Murdock. Impudent princes to teach, and they make fun of a defenseless old man. Better I was the Schoolmaster, and you the High Wizard. Prince Robert, Prince Arn, this is the Wizard Desjardins Murdock, also known as Murdock the Magician, Murdock the Magnificent, Murdock the Mysterious, and a half dozen other names he calls himself depending on the story he is telling.''

''Alas, not all the names are quite so complimentary,'' said Murdock. ''But I've forgotten my manners for such exalted guests. My pardon, gentlemen. I should have introduced myself. We met briefly when you were boys, but you probably don't remember. I haven't visited the court for years.'' He grinned at us in turn and shook hands. ''Prince Robert, I take it, grown to manhood. You look like your father. And Prince Arn, the lost who was found. Strange ways in a strange world. Bishop Thomas, always good to see you. Professor Wagner, my pleasure again. And this is Sergeant Black, if memory serves me, and the honored members of the royal guards. Welcome. Welcome to you all. But enough chatter. I could keep you all talking for a month, but you're hungry, there is much to do, and you wish to be on your way, if rumor is correct?''

''You are correct,'' Graven confirmed, his face once again relaxed into his familiar scowl. ''I wish to return to Kingsport within the fortnight.''

Murdock raised his eyebrows. ''The King has already returned there, I've heard. Is there a tale to tell in this change of schedule?''

''There may be, but we won't know more until we join the King. We can talk of it over refreshment.''

''Of course,'' Murdock agreed. ''Sergeant Black, your men

may tether their horses along the wall over there. Wizard O'Dowd predicted you would arrive today, so noon meal is waiting for you and your men inside. First door on the left of the entry hall. We'll be in the room on the right. Plenty for all, but none to serve you, I fear. Class is in session. Oh, they know you're coming. Couldn't keep that from them. But I try not to break routine, even for special occasions. Discipline, you know. Do you agree, High Wizard?''

Graven snorted. ''I would, in the name of discipline. But your violations of discipline are as well known as your irreverence for rank, Schoolmaster Murdock. Beware, Robert, he would have the royal family travel like pilgrims if he could, and eating out of the common pot and sleeping in the public hall. Yet, he is loyal to the kingdom beyond all doubt, and were I to—but never mind. To table, Schoolmaster. Let's hope you've prepared more than gruel.''

Murdock was an amazing fellow. It normally takes me a goodly while to begin liking someone, and longer still to trust him. Yet I took immediately to this wizard. He seemed perhaps the most charming and friendly man I had ever known. Apparently this sentiment was shared by others, for Robert whispered as much to Graven as we followed the schoolmaster to the dining room. ''He seems to have a permanent charm spell,'' Robert laughed.

The high wizard nodded. ''Perhaps that is not far from the truth.''

Murdock led us into a low hallway and through a door into a long room set with table and chairs before a large fireplace. The table was already laden with bread, cheese, ham, and milk.

We took our seats. Bishop Thomas cleared his throat, gave Robert and me a disapproving look till our reaching forks retreated from the ham, and began grace. ''Lord, we thank You for bringing us safely to this place of Your special children. Bless us and all who dwell here with Your Grace. Especially, guide the High Wizard in his choice today for Your greater Glory and the service of Your appointed one, King Reuel. And thank You for the virtue of patience, which even princes must learn. Thy Will be done. Amen.''

The food was good, and quickly disappeared. We listened while Graven told Murdock of the arrival of the five emissaries and the king's return to Kingsport. Graven feared the worst, and the schoolmaster digested the information with numerous comments.

"Quite frankly," mused the schoolmaster, "I can't figure out why the five nations would come to us like this. Do they come with requests—or demands? Are they seeking our help, or have we offended them in some way? If they plan war, what motivates their rulers?"

"We would all like answers to those questions," Graven admitted.

"Why did we not have warning of this?" Murdock continued. "What about Mr. Kendall? Why didn't the other Pacifican advisors notify him?"

Graven shook his head. "Those mysteries I cannot yet solve."

There was silence while the wizards pondered the future. I took another piece of bread and cheese. Murdock noted it and beamed at us, seeking to lift our mood. "Ahh such hearty young men. Prince Robert, so healthy and strong, and a fine warrior I hear. And Prince Arn is a bit of the historian and writer, I am to understand. What I wouldn't give to be your age again, with the vigor of youth and the challenge of adventure. Graven, do you ever tell them of our deeds? Our journey through the Great Swamp, the voyage across the Gulf, the Battle of the Plains? It seems like yesterday."

Graven swallowed a piece of cheese and shook his head. "That was long, long ago, and young men do not want to hear the boasts of tired old men."

"Ha. Always the modest one. If he did not tell you, it was because he was the hero of our stories, and of a courage matched only by your grandfather. Have any of you ever seen his back? I thought not. He bears scars from the slave pens of Texan, just as I do. The same whip administered to both of us, and how we escaped is a tale for a long night with plenty of drink. If you were staying, I would tell tales that you would scarcely believe."

"We cannot stay," Graven repeated. "But do not mislead them so. My princes, if there were any heroes in those days, it was Desjardins Murdock. He was apprenticed to the great Speros, the wizard who set the pirate fleet afire long ago. I have heard the tale. Their ship was boarded during the battle, and were it not for Murdock, the pirates would have struck down

Speros. Murdock held off the pirates single-handedly.''

"That's not true," corrected Murdock. "A crewman was our defender."

"As you wish," Graven conceded. "But if all are finished, perhaps we might complete the purpose of my visit?"

The class continued working dutifully at their books as we entered, twenty boys and young men arranged at benches behind long tables, few older than Robert and me. Their heads remained bent over their work, but some peeked slyly when their teacher turned to greet us.

The teacher was introduced to us as Wizard O'Dowd, one of the most accomplished magicians in Kenesee. O'Dowd seemed embarrassed by the praise but smiled with a shy pleasure at the words. He turned to his students and cleared his throat with a sharp harumph. "Class, all stand." They popped to their feet, viewing us with open curiosity and wonder. "We are honored today beyond all expectation. We have long anticipated a visit by the High Wizard Graven. He is here for the Test." He paused while the students exchanged nervous glances with each other, and then went on. "We are doubly honored, however, to have members of the royal family observe this moment." He looked inquiringly at Murdock, who took over introductions.

"It is my pleasure to introduce Prince Robert, Prince Arn, Bishop Thomas, and Professor Wagner. You have heard their names, I am sure, and now for the first time you meet them. This is a high honor."

Murdock nodded to the teacher, who gestured to the students. "Now be seated, and do your best, my boys. That's all anyone can ask of you."

Graven stepped forward. Was it my imagination, or were some of the students actually trembling behind their desks?

"I am here to choose an apprentice," he scowled. His glance went around the room. "Look at me and do not avert your eyes," he commanded, and twenty pairs of eyes locked upon his gaze. Slow and intent, he stared at each in turn, his face impassive. As he took each under attention, the victim stiffened and then relaxed. One row, then two, three, and then the fourth underwent the ordeal.

He completed the process and nodded. "You. The one on the end, third row. Yes, you. Come up here."

Teacher O'Dowd's eyes darted to the boy. "Oh no, High Wizard. I'm sure—"

Graven was impassive. "Yes?"

"The boy is malformed," O'Dowd whispered. "A cripple."

"He has power."

"Yes, High Wizard. That is true. Telepathic and kinetic. But he would be most . . . unsuitable . . . for the court."

"Nevertheless, I will see him." Graven's voice hardened with impatience. "Boy, come up here."

The student rose and straightened. Or, at least he straightened as much as he might. And then he came forward. He was perhaps two or three years younger than I. His sandy hair was thin and cut short. His face was ungainly, a large nose poking out from a narrow face, ears protruding outward from the sides of his head, a parody of a chin receding into a birdlike neck. One shoulder lifted higher than the other, adorned by a hump, while his arms seemed to stretch almost to his knees. He limped only slightly, but the misbalance of his form enhanced the movement. His appearance was not so much ugly as humorous.

The boy stood silent before Graven. There was fear in his eyes.

"Stand up as tall as you might. Turn around. Now, look at me."

The boy did so, meeting the wizard's eyes.

Graven scratched his chin in contemplation. "What is your name?"

"Lorich." The boy's voice trembled.

"Very well, Lorich. Do you see that feather pen on your teacher's desk? I am going to raise it. Stop me."

"Sir?"

"Are you deaf, too? Stop me."

"Yes, sir," Lorich said despairingly.

Lorich stared at the desk, a look of intense concentration besetting his brow. Graven never took his eyes from the boy. Yet the feather pen lifted effortlessly off the desk, and hung suspended. There were murmurs from the others in the class. Lorich watched the pen in dismay.

"Sir, I cannot."

"Of course not," Graven responded. The pen descended to the desktop and was still. "If I ask you to be my apprentice, will you accept? It's your decision. One must choose this road of his own will.''

"You want me, sir?'' Lorich said in disbelief.

Graven was impassive. "I don't have all day, boy.''

Lorich looked doubtful, and then straightened as well as he might. His voice still trembled. "If you want me, sir, I will go with you.''

The high wizard grunted. "My good Schoolmaster, I have chosen. Prepare him to join me.''

Murdock's features were troubled. "As you wish, High Wizard. Teacher O'Dowd, please see to it. They leave shortly.''

The teacher swallowed his concern and nodded. "It will be done.''

We left the classroom with Graven and Murdock. In the hallway Robert walked beside Graven. "A strange choice, High Wizard.''

Graven shook his head. "No, my prince. You don't see all that transpires, or know all that is real. The boy did not fail. His raw strength is already as great as mine. But do not expect a schoolboy to defeat a wizard in magic.'' He turned to Murdock. "You don't think the choice is wise, my friend.''

Murdock shrugged. "I fear for the boy.''

"How so?''

"We are the lad's family, and this is his home. He's accepted for what he is. He has his place. Our training is hard, but Lorich has prospered here. The world may not be so kind.''

"Nor will it be,'' retorted Graven. "The world is harsh. There is no room for weaklings. One must endure or die. I think he will find the strength.''

"I hope so.''

"Anything I should know of Lorich?''

"The boy is naive, and ignorant of the world. He will have to be guided carefully, or his power could be misused by others.''

Graven snorted. "And so it is with all of us. Don't you agree, Prince Arn?''

He never missed a chance to drive in his little barbs. The best way to handle his continual prodding was to defer to him. "Most certainly, High Wizard.''

Graven turned back to the schoolmaster. "It has been a productive visit, my friend. I thank you for your hospitality.''

"The pleasure has been mine. But must you leave so soon?

Please reconsider. There is much to learn here that would be of value to a prince of the realm. Won't you stay a little while. Just for the night?''

"No," said Graven solemnly. "Critical matters are at hand, and the King will need our counsel. Yet we still have many towns to visit."

A few more minutes of chatter, and the visit was done. Sergeant Black summoned the guards to attention as we stepped into the courtyard. Standing warily next to a sorry-looking mare was Lorich, holding the reins as if they were snakes. Sergeant Black reported. "The men have eaten and the horses are fed and watered. Is the boy coming with us? His horse may be a problem if we keep the pace we have."

Murdock looked at the animal. "My apologies, Sergeant. It's the best we have in the stable. We aren't given to much traveling."

"It will do," stated Graven as he mounted. We swung up into saddle. The boy stood unmoving. "Well, my new apprentice. Are you waiting for an invitation?"

Lorich gulped. "I'm sorry, master. I don't know how."

There were smirks from the guardsmen. Graven rubbed his forehead in exasperation. "Schoolmaster?"

A marvelous thing happened. The schoolmaster's brown cheeks turned red. "Perhaps we have been remiss in areas of training," he admitted. "Most of the boys can ride before they come to us. But—"

"Enough," fumed Graven. "Get on the horse, boy."

Lorich eyed the animal, then the wizard, and determined which was the greater threat. He swung a foot into the stirrup. The horse shied, and the boy gained intimate acquaintance with the tiles of the courtyard.

The guardsmen broke into a roar.

"Silence!" commanded Graven, and the yard was still.

The schoolmaster rushed over and lifted the boy. "That's all right. My fault. You should have been instructed. Let me help."

Tears were welling up in the boy's eyes.

"He must do it himself," said Graven. "Try again, boy."

Murdock nodded in obedience and stepped back, but put a steadying hand on the horse's bridle. Lorich clenched his teeth, grabbed the pommel and hauled himself up, hung awkwardly in the air for a moment, then somehow found himself in the saddle, holding on tightly with both hands.

Murdock handed him the reins. "Gently does it. She'll follow the others. Just give her some rein. That's it. Feel all right?"

"Yes, Schoolmaster. I wish to—that is, I. . . ."

Murdock cleared his throat. "I know. I know. We expect to hear great things of you. You've been chosen for high honor. Listen well to your master. Study hard. Obey him as you've obeyed us. We'll miss you."

Sergeant Black barked a command, and fifty guardsmen mounted as one.

Graven extended his arm and took the hand of the schoolmaster. "And so we part. Teach them well, for I fear we shall soon have need of them."

"Yes. How much time do we have?"

"That depends upon our fellow nations. Too little, I fear. Many things must be—" Graven stopped, stared at the schoolmaster, and then up at the sky, as if reading the clouds. He gazed again at Murdock, a look of surprise on his face. "We shall have need of you. Put the school in order and come to Kingsport. Arrive within the fortnight."

Murdock read the other's face. "A premonition?"

"Yes. And I've had others. Why do you think I hurry?"

The schoolmaster covered Graven's mottled hand with his own. "I will come. Take care of yourself, old friend. Remember that we are getting old. Don't take your duties too seriously. There is other wisdom besides ours." He stepped back. "Our thoughts will be with you. With you all."

Graven nodded. "And with you." He eyed the boy. "Sergeant Black, we march at the walk for one hour. Who is your best horseman?"

"Corporal Jenkins!" Black ordered without hesitation. "Front and center."

Jenkins spurred forward. "Yes, Sergeant." Corporal Jenkins was a cocky little rooster of a man, a proud hothead whose face turned various shades of red, warning of the level of his temper. But for all that he was a good trooper, second in command of Black's Fourth Squad, and temporarily in charge of it while Black commanded the five squads of guards during the tour. Sergeant Black thought highly of him.

Graven pointed the boy out to Corporal Jenkins. "This is Lorich. We march at the walk. You have one hour to make him a horseman."

Jenkins looked at the boy and made a face not unlike that of a condemned man. "I'm a guardsman, sir. Not a miracle worker." Black cast a look at him and the corporal sighed. "Yes, High Wizard. I'll do my best."

Graven ignored him.

The guardsmen sandwiched us in the middle of the column, while two galloped ahead to scout the way. Graven and my brother rode in front, I plodded next to Bishop Thomas, and Professor Wagner followed. Bringing up the rear were Corporal Jenkins and Lorich.

The bishop was already into his prayers and mumbling his chants. Were prayer alone the key to heaven, the bishop had already collected a jingling ring full. I myself think many will find a different kind of lock.

Behind us, the voice of Corporal Jenkins was rising in exasperation. His face had turned a nice shade of crimson. "Lolich—"

"Lorich, sir."

"All right, Lolich. Now try the left rein. No, don't stick your arm out to pull. Just pull straight back. Steady pressure."

"I'm trying, sir."

"The left rein, Mr. Lolich. The LEFT rein!"

We rode on in silence, the day quiet except for the clop of hoofs and the little drama in educational frustration being played out behind us. Around us the hills were low, the area not as scenic as the mountainous areas to the south. But the countryside was prosperous. There were many woods, but each human habitation was surrounded by fields of vegetables and grains, fruit orchards, and pastures holding cows, sheep, or sleek horses. The soil was good, the contours of the land gentle, brooks and streams and wells providing ample water.

For an hour we kept to the walk, and it was pleasant to do so. This was how the tour should have been conducted.

Robert finally spoke, his tone serious. "This is quite a change."

Graven was roused from his musings. "Hmm. What? Well, it's only for an hour."

"Do you think an hour is enough?"

"The boy must keep up or catch up. I will not coddle him, deformities or not."

Robert turned in his saddle. "I was not talking about the boy."

"Yes. I know."

"Our pace is too great," Robert stated, considering his words. "We're leaving problems behind us. In Louisville, the Eighth regiment was ill-trained, their parade a farce. At Bowling Green, security was lax. The Mayor of Portland is corrupt. And Duke Collins's roads need repair."

"Agreed."

"If father were here, each of these would have been addressed."

"But he is not here," countered the high wizard.

"We go too fast. We need more time."

"Why? You recognized our problems. That is the purpose of our journey."

"But we haven't corrected these things. They will haunt us later."

Graven shook his head. "Ever since the King left us, I've known that speed was imperative. I have done my best to follow the King's order and still respond to that need. Never fear. Our report will be made to the King. He will see to the remedy, as he has always done."

Robert scoffed. "More may remain hidden. We have made no reprimands, no punishments, no fines. Wrongdoers and slackards will be encouraged, and the problems will grow. Were it my choice, I would retrace all our steps and administer justice."

Graven shook his head. "The king has vested authority in me, and we will proceed as I deem wise."

"Your fear of Kendall is warping your judgment. My father is not one to be twisted about his advisor's finger just because you're not there. He has given you a trust. Your duty—"

"DUTY? Indeed." The high wizard gestured emphatically with one mottled hand clenched tightly into a veined fist. "When you have shed blood and health and youth for your kingdom, then may you speak of duty to ME."

Robert did not often become angry, but this time the muscles bunched across his shoulders. He spoke slowly and carefully. "I will ride ahead to check on the scouts." He spurred his horse and galloped off. Sergeant Black made ready to send a squad after him, but Graven signaled the guardsman to do nothing. The wizard sighed, then turned and looked back at us. Professor Wagner looked at his hands; Bishop Thomas shrugged.

I smiled.

"Do not gloat," Graven said resignedly. "Our disagreement is temporary. The prince is as quick to cool as he is slow to anger."

"I'm not gloating."

"He will see soon enough. As I see. As you should."

"My brother is right," I said. "We go too fast."

2

Homecoming

In the first week of October—and three weeks early—we entered Kingsport by the north gate just before nightlock. The days since the School of Magic had passed uneventfully, with stops at the larger towns on the way for briefings and reports by mayors and military commanders. Nothing new, nothing significant. A general picture of efficiency and effort with a smattering of incompetence, injustice, stupidity, and greed. We kept to the maximum pace that the horses could take without ruining them, and Corporal Jenkins was at last successful in teaching Apprentice Lorich how to ride a horse. We all looked forward to getting out of the saddle and sleeping in our own beds.

It was already dusk when we came to Kingsport, and we trotted along beneath the glow of the street lamps along the King's Way. There was a single, belated trumpet blown from the town's gate watch, and then another from the castle guard. We dropped off Bishop Thomas at his church house and then clattered over the drawbridge and into the courtyard. By the time we drew up before the king's house, stable boys and servants were already assembled.

"Tell the King that we have arrived," Graven directed one servant. "By his leave, I will see him within the hour to give a brief report on our journey. You may go."

Sergeant Black took his squads to the stables while Graven, Robert, and I went into the castle. Thirsty, I went first to the dining hall for a mug of beer, where a servant popped in, looked around, and hurried over to me before I could tap the keg.

"Prince Arn, there is a young man at the door."

"Hmmm?"

"He appears rather . . . odd," the servant stated in a tone mixed with pity and distaste.

"Oh." I went back and found Lorich waiting shyly in the courtyard, his horse beside him and his saddlebags at his feet. In his haste, Graven had even forgotten about his new apprentice. "What are you doing out here?" I asked.

He looked relieved and gestured up at the battlements. "Is this—?"

"This is it, Wizard Lorich."

"I had not imagined—does Master Graven live here?"

"Along with the King, the royal family and the guards, among others. And the High Wizard's Apprentice too, if he ever comes in. This is your home now."

There wasn't a separate room for apprentices, but a curtained alcove at the end of the bachelor's wing had served well in the past. Walter and Marta, still tottering around despite their age, quickly prepared it for him, dusting off the wooden cot, chair, and chest that had been Apprentice Garth's and a dozen more before him. Lorich seemed quite content with the curtained space, exclaiming that he had never had such privacy before.

I pulled Marta aside where the boy could not hear. "Make it clear to all that Graven has a charitable concern for the boy. He is quite fond of Lorich, in spite of the boy's appearance. Anyone showing disrespect can expect the attentions of the High Wizard himself."

"Oh yes, sir," she agreed quickly, and went back to her preparations. "Here, Mr. Lorich, you let me know if you want us to move the furniture around to be more convenient for you. We'll have clean linen on the bed in just a minute. And how many blankets do you think you'll need?''

The castle was in a dither, with servants going to and fro. A meal was being prepared, but we had time to wash. The beginning of a warm fire was already crackling on the hearth, and Walter poured hot water into my wash bowl. ''Prince Arn! Welcome back, sir, welcome back. It's good to see you again after these long weeks.''

''And how have you been, Walter?''

''A new ache here, a new ache there. These old bones keep moving, though, which is better than the alternative, if you get my meaning. But it's been a strange time during your absence.''

''How so?'' I asked in response to his expectant look.

He beamed. ''Well, sir, the King has been in a solemn mood since those ambassadors left, though 'emissaries' is the more proper term, they tell me. Five of them. Proper gentlemen, though a bit curt with the servants at the town hall, I heard. And always whispering among themselves. Why they came when the King had already left on the tour is a puzzle. They must have known they'd cool their heels till he came back to Kingsport—''

''Unless they wanted to disrupt the tour,'' I ventured.

''That could be,'' Walter admitted. ''They were here for over two weeks before the King returned, and then the meetings started. Every day for a week the King would meet with the ambassadors, and every night he and Sir Meredith and Mr. Kendall would get together in the council chamber till all hours talking and calling the archivist for maps or books. The room is in disarray, but the King won't let us touch it.''

I sat down on a chair and pulled off my muddy boots. ''And when did the emissaries leave?''

He poured a drink for me. I gestured, and he poured one for himself.

''Well, long as the missus doesn't find out. Ahh, that's good. Warms the old bones. Now, let's see. It's been two weeks at least, since they left. Got aboard five ships and sailed away in as many directions. Yet they arrived together, supposedly on the same ship. Now, what does that mean? It means they came together from somewhere after hatching their own plans for us, and now they're going to tell their Kings it didn't work.

"Ha! I don't know what they thought they'd accomplish. Did they think Kenesee was going to go along with whatever they had in mind? They've always been jealous of us, those other countries, and found excuses to invade us. I was just a boy during the last big war, but I remember. Kenesee has never attacked anyone that didn't attack us first, you know—except maybe the Beastwood. We can be proud of that record. Kenesee, Gem of Nations—we've earned that title, I tell you.

"Why, we—oops, here I go twisting your ear off when you're just back from a hard journey. Well, I won't say no more, except there is one thing. I suspect Mr. Kendall may be leaving soon. Had his traveling bags out again. I can always tell when he's getting set to go off like he does."

"Please let Mr. Kendall know I'd like to see him as soon as possible."

"Of course, sir. I know he'll be happy to see you. Thank you for the drink. I'll go now." And so he did.

I had just finished washing when Kendall stuck his face in the door. "Welcome back, my fair young prince. No maiden in your bed yet?" He managed a smile, but lines of worry marked his face. The lines had not been there before.

"You look tired," I noted.

He sat down near the fire, which was beginning to burn quite brightly. "I am, and so are we all. Walter told you what's been going on, I presume? You must be wondering what will happen."

"You could say that."

"The tour is important, and this last most of all. You're back too soon. Graven hurried the party, I presume?"

"He led us at a pace that even had the guards grumbling. I thought he'd weary, but he didn't."

"Don't underestimate him. He didn't become High Wizard without reason. Yet, I think he has done a disservice to the kingdom for which he toils so faithfully."

"Robert would agree with you," I added. "Graven had a premonition that we had to hurry back. We slowed a bit this last week, but he begrudged every moment we were away from here. He'll hold that against you."

Kendall shrugged his shoulders. "Only one more thing in

a long list—some real, some imagined. But this was none of my doing. Your father decided who should return with him. He felt the High Wizard would have more weight with the nobility and mayors, and the rest of you had your duties too. Who knows? You and Robert may be leading armies over the same ground.''

His last words stopped me. "Are things as bad as that?"

"I'm afraid so. The other nations have formed an alliance against us. The emissaries made several demands. Basically, they wanted us to tear down our walls, limit our armies to a few regiments, and surrender several key border counties, including the valley to the Rift Gates. Oh, and one more item. They asked for hostages to guarantee peace. You and Robert were their prime choices.''

"Hostages?"

"These gentlemen did not expect defiance. Only an alliance of overwhelming strength could make such unreasonable demands.''

I considered his words. "Is there any hope, then?"

"Not much," he said regretfully. "Any one enemy would have a difficult time inside Kenesee. Any two we could probably match on our own ground. Three would be a struggle. Four, an exceedingly difficult and dangerous situation with the odds steeped against us. With all five . . .'' His words tapered off into silence.

"So. But how could this come about? Why are they doing it?"

He frowned and threw a chip of wood into the fire, where it quickly took flame and was consumed. "That I don't understand," he said, puzzled. "In two hundred years, never have more than two nations allied for any conflict. And an alliance should not have been formed without my knowledge. The other nations have long envied Kenesee's central position and advantages. We dominate the sea lanes and control the best waterways. Our agricultural yield is higher and more varied than the other nations. And before the Beastwood Campaign, we won every war in which we fought. All of these are cause for resentment. But to form such an alliance just for the purpose of destroying Kenesee is unlikely, and to do so in utter secrecy is unheard of. My countrymen would have advised against it. Unless . . .''

"Unless?"

"Never mind. There is more to this than we know."

"And so you are going to find out what," I added.

"How did you—oh, Walter. Well, yes. I was going to tell you. Tomorrow morning I leave. We must know what's going on. Every nation has one of my countrymen serving its ruler. There may be treachery against my colleagues in those lands. I need to find out. With a great deal of luck I might even upset whatever plans are in store."

"It sounds dangerous."

"It may be. I should be back by January . . . if at all. You have a task to fulfill too, Arn. There is a mission the King has decided upon for you."

"Oh?"

"I think it is for him to tell you. But be prepared for what you hear. Your task will be dangerous too."

I could have done without that last piece of information.

On the way down to the dining hall I crossed over to the king's quarters to greet the king before supper, but his door was closed and the sound of angry voices came from within. I leaned against the door frame, made as if I had just knocked, and then listened.

"—and I felt that we were needed here!" exclaimed a voice belonging to Graven.

The king's voice was severe. "To whom did I entrust command of the tour?"

"Sir, these are grave times which—"

"High Wizard Graven, to *whom* did I entrust command of the tour?"

"To me, sir," he stated resentfully.

"And was not your mission to complete the tour?"

Graven's voice grew quieter. "Yes, my King."

"And is not the purpose of the tour to see to the well-being of the kingdom?"

"Yes, my King."

"And was it not your duty to accomplish this task?"

"Yes, my King."

"And did you accomplish this duty with the care and attention it deserved?"

"No, my King." The voice was subdued.

"Now, of all times, it is essential that the kingdom be put in order. You know what happens in the countryside if we do not follow matters closely. Things go astray. Training gets put aside. Mistakes multiply. Injustices are done. Corruption breeds corruption. The tour has worked well these last ten years. I esteem it the most important method we possess for ensuring the well-being of the kingdom. Had I known what you would do, the emissaries would have cooled their heels until I had completed it. I thought I could trust you with this duty."

"Yes, my King. I have failed you."

"Need I ask the reason for your return so soon?"

"I had a premonition after you left us, my King. I sensed that we had to return to Kingsport as quickly as possible. There was something that had to be done, and we needed to be here for it."

"What had to be done?"

"That I don't know."

"I see. Well, your foresight is explanation enough. And yet—were there any other reasons? Perhaps you thought I would be swayed by another's counsel."

"My lord, I do not deny that I mistrust Kendall. He has other loyalties besides the kingdom."

"Yet has he ever disobeyed my orders or failed in his duties? You and Kendall and the Bishop and Sir Meredith are my advisors—advisors, not guides. I am subject to no man, nor do I follow any advice that I deem counter to my own judgment. Do you trust me so little? Have I governed so ill that only you can protect the kingdom from my decisions?"

There was a moment of silence, and then a faint voice. "Forgive me, my King. I have become too old for my duties. My pride grows greater as I grow more weary. I would have no other King in this time of need, nor serve any other man while you live. If you would prefer another for my place, I will understand."

Yes, I gloated from behind the door. Now is our chance. Get rid of the old buzzard!

The king's tone became conciliatory. "No, old friend. The responsibility has been heavy on us all these last few weeks, and I am out of sorts. I can ill afford to lose the talents of my High Wizard. Now more than ever, you will be needed at my side. Enough of this. Tell me what you have done these last weeks.''

Disappointed, I consoled myself with the wizard's private humiliation and hurried on to the dining hall.

Dinner that evening was both a festive and solemn affair, lightened by our return and weighted with uncertainty about the future. The king entered and threw his arms about Robert and me in turn, a smile of welcome upon his face. King Reuel had changed little in ten years. His red hair had thinned a bit, but he was still in early middle age and in good health. His exuberance was now tempered by experience, but he was no less optimistic than before. He remained a dedicated and effective leader. His reign had been peaceful and benign, with many good works to his credit and a generally steady economy to ensure the welfare of the citizens. Social ills had been addressed, and towns and villages had become better places to live. Commoner and noble alike realized how much they enjoyed as citizens of Kenesee, and they were proud of their citizenship. King Reuel loved his people, and they in turn were devoted to him.

The latter was especially true of the fair sex. The king still enjoyed a friendly dalliance or two, but had so far refrained—to the bitter disappointment of half the eligible women, and the sweet hope of the rest—from choosing permanent companionship.

He greeted the diners, took his place, and the rest of the court sat down.

Lorich stuck his head into the hall, wondering if he should be there. Since the high wizard had not yet entered, I waved him over to the long king's table, had him sit beside me, and introduced him to those seated around us. He looked about wide-eyed, his gaze coming to rest on the trophy heads that adorned the wall. A shudder went through him. ''Prince Arn, what a collection of horrors.'' I explained to him what they were. ''Killed by princes my age? They're all so formidable! Except maybe for that small one, up in the corner. Which one is yours, Prince Arn?''

I shoved a loaf of bread at him. ''We'll discuss such things later.''

Shortly thereafter Graven slipped in and took his seat after we had begun eating. The room was filled with talk of the past few weeks, what might happen, and the preparedness of the kingdom, but the high wizard had little to say.

Kendall's words had had their effect upon me too, and I pondered the future during the meal. Could the tranquillity of the last decade really be changing? Were there actually forces stirring across our borders that could threaten the life I had enjoyed for so long? Were we ourselves in physical danger? Could it all end?

I remembered a miserable gutter rat huddling in the wintry doorways of the town.

Yes, it could end quite easily.

The court musicians began playing old songs, ancient songs, ballads slow and soft and melodic. I became aware of the dinner as one brief moment in time, here and then forever gone. The flickering light of lamps and hearth, the tapestries, the mounted heads on the trophy wall, the sounds and laughter, the smell of meat and fruit and oily smoke, the taste of cool beer, the feel of a soft chair, the voices of those who had populated my world for so long. I opened myself to it and drank it all in, so that when the reality faded, at least I might have the memory.

"Prince Arn," a clear, bright voice spoke. "Are your thoughts far away?"

Megan Sims smiled at me from several places down the table, her golden waves of hair shimmering in the light. Sir Meredith's daughter had blossomed into a beautiful young woman, long-limbed and well-formed, charming and confident and unmarried.

"My thoughts?" I responded. "Not far away. Not far away at all."

"That's good. I've missed my two old friends."

"Have you now?" Robert asked from her other side. "We would never have known it." In the past, Robert and I had each tried dallying with Megan. I, certainly, had gotten nowhere, curse the luck. She had taken my romantic forays with humorous good nature, deftly turning such matters aside while maintaining a spirit of friendly camaraderie. I had long since given up the effort, and found another who held my attentions. Robert was not so easily discouraged, though he took it all quite casually. As with me, a matter of lust rather than love,

I would imagine. Whether he had been more successful than I was doubtful, though who could say for sure?

Megan laughed. "Not every woman will fall to your charms, Prince Robert, no matter how tempting."

He perked up. "Ah. So you are tempted."

She smiled wryly. "I did not say that. You did."

"Ah, well. I keep up hope. All good things in time."

"One should never give up hope," she bantered. "Just don't expect fulfillment. And now. Why did our two dutiful princes not send any letters during their absence? I received nary a one from either of you. My friend Angela received none from Arn. Have you learned such manners from Mr. Kendall, perhaps?" Megan nodded at the king's advisor, who was seated with his back to us at the next table.

Patiently explaining some point about the Codes, Paul Kendall lifted his head and turned at the mention of his name. He saw us looking at him. "Yes?"

We laughed.

"You don't send letters either, do you Mr. Kendall?" Megan taunted. "Just official dispatches to the King. But nothing to your friends. You sail away and return months later, with nary a word."

He looked embarrassed. "Perhaps I have been remiss."

"Perhaps," echoed Megan.

Kendall grinned shyly, and turned back to his own table.

"He is always so busy," she said, smiling pleasantly and staring at his back. "Busy with the King. Busy with plans. Busy. Busy. Busy."

The meal drew to a close and the king rose, putting out his hands and gesturing for the rest of us to remain seated. There is not usually a scribe present at meals, but tonight there was. He took up his pen and waited. The room fell silent except for the sound of the servers.

One picked up a plate of bones and the king nodded at him. "You. Stop. All of you, stop and listen. These words are for you, too."

Around the hall, the servers froze and waited. The king not only had their polite silence, but also their rapt attention. A cook or two peeked out of the kitchen and watched in wonder.

"My loyal subjects, my fellow countrymen, my friends. The last ten years have been a time of peace and the kingdom has prospered. In that time, we threatened no war, we claimed no land, we offended no people. Yet, unbidden, the specter of war has arisen. Five emissaries came to us, five lands threaten war. From the East, and the West, and the South have come demands we cannot and shall not meet.

"We have fought some of these nations in the past. We have lost battles. Never have we lost a war. Now we face an alliance more powerful than any before. Perhaps they will think better of their plans, and the spring will bring continued peace. More likely, it will bring fleets and armies to breach our shores and invade our land. The struggle will be more fierce than any we have faced, more difficult than any our ancestors faced.

"With the cloud of war looming over us, we must prepare for the storm. We have only a few months. We must use them wisely. All must work and prepare. With your help, your loyalty, your courage, we will preserve this kingdom and this land for our children and our children's children. With God's blessing, we shall be victorious."

There were cheers and applause. Men leaped to their feet and thrust up their arms in salute. The king always could get an audience going when he wanted to.

"There will be great labor," he continued. "Some of us will soon be making journeys for the kingdom, and it may be long before all of us are gathered together again, if ever. I have cherished your counsel, your loyalty, your friendship. Though we may have quarrels, though I may chastise and correct you—" He looked around the room taking everyone in, but perhaps lingering just a moment longer at Graven, Robert, and me. "—I love you and need you all. I know you will not fail the kingdom in the hour of need."

More applause.

"My council will meet with me tomorrow after breakfast. God be with you all." He left, and the scribe followed him out as the room broke into excited chatter.

One of the king's servers carried a wooden bowl of fruit and offered it to those still seated who might wish a bit more to conclude their meal. She looked demurely my way. I raised an eyebrow and with a swish of her skirt she ambled over, a healthy girl in the best sense of the word. "Good evening,

Prince Arn. Welcome back from your journey. We have missed you.''

I looked up nonchalantly, as if I had not a thought in the world of grabbing her into my arms. ''Hello, Angela. It's good to see you again.''

She glanced at Lorich.

''Angela, this is Wizard Lorich, the new apprentice to High Wizard Graven. Lorich, this is Angela. She's spending a year at the castle as a King's server. Her father is the Mayor of Lexington.''

Angela took in Lorich's appearance. She did not stare, like so many. Nor was it a look of curiosity and fascination, but simply one of acceptance. The lad was misshapen. The lad also had blond hair. And was a human being. That was the way it was. Next subject.

She gave him a smile, her bright-eyed face framed in a mass of auburn hair that trailed down to her shoulders. The sight would have melted the heart of any man.

''Hello, Wizard Lorich.''

The apprentice stared at Angela as if he were a starving man gazing upon a loaf of bread. He nodded and tried to speak. ''Arrgk.''

Angela nodded back. ''And welcome to the castle, Mr. Lorich. I'm sure we will see each other around. Well, I must be about my duties. Would you like a piece of fruit?''

He shook his head. ''Arrgk grrrg.''

''No? There's always some in the kitchen if you're hungry later.'' She flashed him another smile like a ray of sunshine, and then turned her attention to me. Her eyes twinkled. ''And you, Prince Arn?'' She leaned forward and held the bowl just below her bosom, a sly smile on her lips. ''Would you like some?''

I let my eyes travel downward and spoke softly. ''What beautiful fruit. So round and firm. What man could resist.'' I reached out for an apple and whispered. ''The second hall after dinner?''

''Yes, sir,'' she said coyly, and moved on. She presented almost as pleasant a view going as she did coming.

Lorich sighed.

''How do you like Angela?'' I asked.

"She—she's wonderful," he gasped.

"I'll tell her you said so. She'll be pleased."

His face lit up. "She will?"

"Of course. Women like to hear such things."

"Really? She was so nice to me—" His face grew red. "Uh, Prince Arn, I don't have much experience with women."

"Neither did I at your age. Not until after the Rite of Manhood. And then when we got back to the castle. . . ." I fell silent in the midst of pleasant memories.

"Prince Arn?"

"Hmmm? Oh, yes. Lorich."

"Sir, Angela did not seem to mind my . . . appearance."

"She liked you," I reassured him.

"She liked me?" He beamed, and then grew thoughtful. "Sir, may I ask you a question?"

"You may ask."

"Prince Arn, do you think she and I could—"

"What?" I asked abruptly, wondering what he was proposing.

"Do you think she'd be willing to—that is, uh—"

I sat up. "Do I think she'd be willing to do what?"

He took a deep breath. "Do you think she'd be willing to—to talk to me?"

My mouth fell open. "Huh?"

"You see, I've never talked to a woman before. Not really. Not that I can remember. There aren't any at the School of Magic, and the girls in the village would just giggle when they saw me. I don't know what to say."

I closed my mouth. "I see. Well. Yes. Yes, I think she'd be willing to do that."

"Do you think so? Angela would talk to me?"

"Yes, she will."

A look of delightful anticipation settled upon his features.

"But one thing, Lorich."

"Sir?"

"Not tonight."

3

Companionship

Although there were always the restless wanderers, the castle tended to quiet after dinner and entertainment, many taking a cordial in their rooms and in cooler weather toasting themselves in front of their fires before retiring. The second hall was silent except for the crackle of the hearth, where blazing logs extended a greeting. It was only half the size of the dining hall, with a single fireplace and walls decorated with portraits of the past kings of Kenesee hung between tapestries depicting their greatest feats. These were in darkness, for the only light in the room was provided by the fire. The floor was open except for a few high-backed benches arranged around the hearth and in alcoves to either side.

I sat on one of the benches in front of the fire, grew too warm, and soon had to retreat to an alcove seat. I still had the apple in my hand, now carved into fine slices. I took a slice and found it was as fresh and ripe and tasty as it looked. It was quite pleasant to relax so, and I stretched out on the high-backed bench. I took another slice of the fruit while meditating upon Angela's charms.

Thoughts of Angela had come to me at the strangest times during the tour, and I would often imagine her bright face smiling knowingly at me. No other woman had affected me this way, and I must confess to surprise at the way she lingered in my thoughts. I really was getting much too fond of this girl.

My reverie was broken by the measured click of boots on the floor stones. I peeped over the bench and saw Kendall plop himself in front of the fire, his wide forehead reflecting the light. His brow was furrowed into a worried frown. Behind him, finally catching up, an unnoticed figure paused, watching. Since I was in the darkness and hidden by the bench, they were both unaware of my presence.

Kendall was startled as the figure slid onto the bench beside him. "Megan!" he exclaimed.

"Yes, Paul," she said softly. "May I join you?"

"Of course. Certainly," Kendall answered, shifting nervously in his seat. The bench was long, yet Megan sat near to him. They both stared into the fire.

"You are going away again," stated Megan. "Tomorrow."

"It's hard to keep a secret in this castle."

"I decided to see you before you left. You've been very busy."

Kendall nodded. "I have been."

She glanced at him. "One would think you were avoiding me."

"No man would do that, unless. . . ." Kendall searched for words uselessly, and lapsed into silence. Neither spoke until he broke the quiet in a hoarse voice. "Umm, I hope you enjoyed supper."

"You did not sit by me."

"There are so many who wish to sit at your table."

She was staring at him openly now. "You need only ask."

"Yes. Well. . . ." Silence stretched on again before Kendall ventured to try again. "I'm happy to see Robert and Arn back. They've grown into fine young men. And you—uh—you too."

"I have grown into a young man?"

I stifled a laugh, and almost choked on a mouthful of apple. Ahh, Kendall, silver-tongued Kendall! Bereft of wit and wisdom, a schoolboy next to a beautiful maiden. Thinking that she was alone with him, Megan did not need to hide her glances. She was looking at him as if he were the only man in the world. Things became clear for me at last, and I remembered a day on the terrace of the castle long ago when three children had listened to a man weave tales of the Old World. Yet, Kendall seemed reluctant to accept the truth. Or perhaps, he just did not dare to hope.

He grinned. "You have definitely not become a man."

"I was afraid you hadn't noticed, Paul," she said, shaking

her head so that her blond hair rolled freely on her shoulders. The sight was a feast for the eyes.

Kendall had not missed the gesture, and a look of denied longing flitted across his features. "No man could fail to notice. You are fit to be a queen."

"I don't want to be a queen," she answered, meeting his look with a steady eye.

He was sweating, but I don't think it was from the fire.

"Oh?" His voice was hoarse. "What—what do you want?"

"Do you remember your promise to me? Beneath the birches on the terrace, with my father there enjoying your embarrassment?" She laughed gently. "The romantic dreams of a little girl."

Kendall crossed his arms over his chest. "Yes, I remember. It was long ago. And yet, like yesterday." There was a sadness in his voice. "As you say. The romantic dreams of a little girl."

"I free you of your promise. It was unfair of me to ask it."

His shoulders slumped and he nodded as if hearing bad news he had been expecting. "You've changed your mind," he said, and then smiled bravely. "I knew you would."

"No, I have not."

"You haven't?"

"Never."

Kendall swallowed, and his voice was a pale croak. "It wouldn't work. I have travels to make. I'm in my thirties already. Your position—"

Megan's hand reached out and caressed his cheek. "Enough. All you need do is say that you don't want me."

"I—I can't say that."

Megan's face blazed in triumph. She stared deeply into his eyes.

He hesitated, then extended a hand and placed it over hers. "Are you sure? I'm not handsome like others."

She took the hand in both of hers. "That is true. But to me, you are beautiful." I almost choked again. "I have waited long to be loved," she continued. "I will not wait another night. But I have taken the lead in courtship. Would you have me lead with the lovemaking too?"

For a moment I thought Kendall was going to object. If he

did, I swore I would rush out and beat him over the head with the poker. But he didn't say a word. He took his ring off and looked at her. She nodded, and he slipped it over her finger. There was no time for other ceremony, and perhaps none was needed. He pulled her close and they became much better acquainted. Soon thereafter, he led her off, and I was alone in the hall.

Needless to say, I was burning with desire from this little display of affection, and was happy to see Angela when she finally came. She looked about the hall, but couldn't detect me in the shadows until I called out to her and waved a hand. That glorious smile burst forth again, and she rushed to my side. I enclosed her in my arms, and for a long moment we too became better acquainted. She came up for air and took a deep breath. "Forgive me for taking so long in the kitchen. Many lingered at the tables to discuss the events of the day."

My hand crept to her bodice. "Forgiveness is granted."

"Arn!" she objected.

"No one can see us."

"I know. But you know I'm not comfortable in public."

Another quirk of the female species. "All right," I acceded. "Let's go, then."

She looked across the room, and her voice fell to a whisper. "Look."

It was Lorich, standing in the entrance to the hall and backlit by the lamp in the corridor, his hump pushing up from his back, his hands dangling long at his sides.

"He thinks you're wonderful," I whispered.

"How sweet of him," she whispered back. "How perceptive."

"He has a problem. Maybe you can help him with it. He's never—that is . . ."

Angela's eyes widened, and I refrained from bursting out into laughter.

"He's never talked to a girl. At least, that's what he told me. But I tend to believe him. He was wondering if you'd talk to him sometime."

"Oh, Arn. Of course I'll talk to him."

Lorich overcame his timidity and decided it was all right to enter the empty hall. He clumped into the room with flat-footed steps and sat down in the very spot lately occupied by

Kendall. Settling himself, he proceeded to polish and buff a pair of Graven's boots that he carried with him. His pale skin seemed to glow red in the light of the great fire.

"How old is he?" Angela whispered softly.

"Sixteen, perhaps seventeen. I don't know."

"Poor thing," she murmured.

"Poor thing? One day he may be the most powerful wizard in the land."

"But he looks so lonely."

I had to admit the lad did appear a bit forlorn rubbing the boot leather before the fire. I guess he didn't really have that many things to be happy about. After all, it couldn't be any fun working with cheery Graven. Lorich was still polishing when two female voices could be heard approaching from a corridor. He looked around, then quickly put his eyes to his work. But he sat stiffly now, and when the two servers came in he gave one quick glance and then concentrated on the boots as if they had been made of gold.

The maids sat on another bench in front of the hearth. They were quiet at first, perhaps hoping he would go so they could continue their gossip. Then, seeing that he did not mean to leave, the buxom one pointed at Lorich and made a remark. The other giggled cruelly. Lorich's hand stopped polishing. He collected the boots and shambled out into the hall, more giggles and remarks sending him on his way. When he had gone, Angela bore down on the two startled servers and proceeded to give them a tongue-lashing that would have impressed any guardsman. One of the girls called Angela a name and in return Angela administered a slap that echoed across the room. The two servers retreated from the hall.

I reminded myself never to make her angry.

She returned to me, her cheeks aglow with victory and brimming with indignation. "I can never understand how some women can be so selfish and cruel. Why did they do it?"

"I guess you have to be selfish and cruel to understand," I said placatingly.

"I wish there was something we could do for him."

"What? Who?"

"The boy. Lorich."

"Unfortunately, there is nothing. Come. Let's go to bed."

We went out into the passageway, climbed steps, and entered the corridor of the bachelor quarters. We reached the door of my room before Angela heard the sound. Behind the thin pull-cloth that served as a door to Lorich's alcove there came sobs not entirely muffled. A candle burned on a nightstand, and we could actually see through the thin cloth and observe the form sprawled on the cot. Angela listened and then looked at me. I nodded glumly. "That's where the boy sleeps."

She fell into my arms. "Oh, Arn, it's so sad. I feel we have to do something. I'll talk to him. Cheer him up. Would that be all right?"

I looked at the huddled form on the cot. Oh, well. It had been so long, perhaps a few more minutes wouldn't hurt—too much. "All right. Go talk to him."

She put her hands on my face, pulled me lower, and kissed both cheeks gently. "You are more worthy than any in the land."

"Yes, I must admit you're right," I said, pulling her close. Perhaps I could get in a few squeezes before she left me. She slid out of my arms and padded over to the alcove on slippered feet. "Wizard Lorich?" she called.

The form on the bed sat up and wiped teary eyes. Angela pushed up the curtain and let it fall back into place behind her as she entered Lorich's quarters. She sat down on the bed next to him. And then she started to talk.

I listened briefly before stomping down to the guards' barracks. A job needed doing, and I knew just the man to do it. I waited at the entrance while the watch sergeant got him for me. "Corporal Jenkins reporting for duty, sir," the feisty corporal yawned, still buttoning up his shirt.

"Sorry to interrupt your sleep, Corporal."

"Just resting, sir. A royal guard never sleeps. How can I help you?"

An hour later there was a knock on the door of my room. I got up from my desk and was greeted by the grinning face of Corporal Jenkins.

"Mission completed, sir."

"Shhh!" I warned, and beckoned him into the room.

He put a hand to his mouth. "Oops. Sorry, Prince Arn."

He entered, followed by another figure wearing a dark blue cloak fastened modestly at the neck and buttoned down to the ankle. When the door was shut behind them the figure in the cloak tossed back her hood, revealing a handsome woman with rich black hair falling to her shoulders and disappearing beneath the cloak.

I nodded. "You chose Beth. Perfect."

The corporal winked and handed me back my coin purse. It was lighter than it had been. "Get the finest lady on the Street of Pleasure, you said, and so I did. I've explained the situation and described Apprentice Lorich. He almost drove me crazy learning how to ride a horse. Hopefully, some other rides come more naturally. And we know Beth can be discreet, don't we, sir?"

She began to unbutton her cloak. "Good evening, Prince Arn. You're looking well, as always. I will be kind to the young man. The first time is very important, you know." She undid the last button and took off the cloak. I looked at what she was wearing and gulped.

"Quite a dress, isn't it, sir?" Jenkins approved. "Suggests without showing, so to speak. What a figure she has." His tone grew speculative. "You know, Beth and I had a nice talk on the way over. She's really quite a girl."

Beth smiled gratefully. "It's the man who brings out the best in a woman, Corporal Jenkins."

The fiery little guardsman grinned proudly. "Aye, a good man can do that. Say, what do you like to do when you're not working? Maybe we—"

"Let's move along," I interrupted, picking up the cloak and putting it back over her shoulders. "Keep it on for now. His bed is in the alcove."

Corporal Jenkins looked askance. "The alcove, sir? That's a little public for this sort of thing, don't you think? The lad won't be able to relax for fear of being overheard or interrupted."

"You're right, Corporal," Beth agreed. "I don't mind, but from what you've told me. . . ."

"All right, all right," I grumbled. "Uh—he can use my room, and I'll sleep on his cot. Corporal Jenkins, thank you for your help. You're dismissed. Beth, wait here while I get the lad."

* * *

I pushed aside the pull-cloth and stepped into the alcove. The two were still seated on the cot, Angela chattering away about her life in Lexington. Lorich stood up, a smile stretching across his face from ear to ear. "Prince Arn!"

"Did you have a nice talk?"

"Oh, yes, sir. Talking to girls is—interesting. I like it. Angela is very kind. She asked me all about myself, and I told her. It wasn't hard at all."

"Excellent!"

Angela stood up. "We're just starting to get to know each other, but Lorich is quite an interesting young man. A very nice person."

The young wizard beamed.

"I'm glad you both enjoyed your talk. But I'm afraid it's time for bed. Lorich, come with me, there's someone I want you to meet." I took him down the hall. "Do you feel comfortable talking to women now?"

"Quite comfortable. Oh, sir, it's so good to be close to them and listen to them talk. I even made Angela laugh once. At a joke."

"Good. Then it's time to proceed to step two."

"Step two?"

I pushed him into my room. "Apprentice Lorich, this is Beth. She wants to talk to you too."

Beth had removed her cloak again. Lorich's eyes were bulging when I closed the door on my way out. I tiptoed back to the alcove and explained the situation to Angela.

"That was very kind of you, Arn."

"Well, it does free us to—"

"But Arn, I can't. This place is so open."

"What? We have the curtain."

"Arn!"

"Well, then. Perhaps we can use your room."

"My roommates sleep soundly, but not that soundly."

"Wench, you try my patience."

"Yes, Arn. I'm sorry. If I stay longer, it will only be worse. Tomorrow night." She kissed me one last time and left.

Oh, well. Lorich seemed to be very happy.

And Kendall was happy and Megan was happy and everyone in the whole cursed castle was happy. Except me. I was far from happy. I went back down to the kitchen, but it was empty, as were the halls. I was alone. I walked back to Lorich's little alcove, laid down on his cot, and mused. I closed my eyes and tried to sleep, but without success.

During the summer I'd had Walter buy me a corncob pipe and some tobacco, but had used them only once or twice before departure on the tour. They'd sat on the mantle during that time, but on impulse I'd slipped them into my pocket before dinner. I got out the pipe and tried to light a bowlful of tobacco. It kept going out.

Somehow that seemed appropriate.

I awoke the next morning to a gruff voice bellowing threats in the corridor. "Lorich, where are my boots? Lorich! Wake up, you lazy excuse for an apprentice."

I opened one eye.

The curtain was pushed aside and Graven's face thrust in. "Wake—"

I opened the other eye. "Not so loud, High Wizard."

Graven's mouth hung open. He closed it so fiercely that his teeth clicked. "What are you doing here?"

"Sleeping." I really was getting quite good at repartee.

"Where's the boy?"

"Lorich? In my chambers, I presume."

Graven's eyebrows twitched. "In your room? Has the world gone crazy?" His eyes resumed their familiar glare. "What is he doing in your room?"

"Sleeping. Among other things."

Graven stuck his head back into the corridor. "LORICH!"

A door opened behind Graven and from Robert's chamber came an attractive woman who nodded to us and trotted briskly down the steps. Immediately thereafter, Kendall's door opened and Megan stepped into the corridor. She smiled in embarrassment as her cheeks turned red. She put her finger to her lips in a request for discretion and followed the other woman down the stairs. Like clockwork, Beth emerged from my room buttoned securely into her cloak, and gave us both a dignified greeting. She stopped opposite Graven and bowed. "Lorich will be coming in a moment, gentlemen." She looked past Graven's shoulder, gave me a wink, and then was gone.

Graven's face was a mask of dismay. "Doesn't anyone get married any more?"

Lorich emerged from my chamber in pants and shoes, hastily pulling his shirt back on. The boy's face radiated a magnificent daze which stopped Graven before he could say a word.

The high wizard picked up his half-finished boots, looked at them silently, and then quietly ordered the boy down to breakfast. Grinning foolishly, Lorich nodded and left us. We could hear him whistling a sprightly tune as he went down the steps.

Graven watched him go and then turned to me. "This is your doing?"

"Did you know Lorich had never talked to a woman before?"

His brow creased, but his voice was uncertain. "Perhaps the boy was not ready to become a man."

"You brought him to learn. He's learning."

Graven pondered this a moment, turned to go, and hesitated. "Why did you do this? If I thought it were out of kindness alone, I would give you my thanks."

I pondered the question, considered lying, and then gave an honest reply. "I don't know. It needed doing. It's done."

He thought about my words, shrugged, and left.

After breakfast I went to the council chamber with Robert. Its appearance was changed from the austere, neat room I remembered. On easels and hanging from the wall were maps and charts of this continent and the seas surrounding. Maps for each nation in the Alliance were hung along one wall. On another had been painted a detailed map of Kenesee; it covered almost the entire wall. Shelves had been set up, and were now filled with reference books. Extra lamps had been placed and hung about so that work could proceed in good light throughout the hours of darkness. Stacks of paper, notebooks, and journals were clustered on a small table at one end of the room. The castle was normally kept spotless, but crumbs left from hastily snatched meals spotted the floor. Servants had been forbidden to enter.

All the advisors were there. Graven shifted through a stack of paper, our conversation of the morning dismissed from his

mind by greater concerns. Kendall, already dressed in traveling clothes, was lost in thought, while Sir Meredith and Bishop
Thomas studied the mural of Kenesee.

Three other men had joined us for the meeting. The first
two were Sergeant Major Nakasone and Sergeant Black, and
their presence might not be totally unexpected. The third was
Wizard Desjardins Murdock, the master of the School of
Magic, and he was a surprise. I knew Graven had asked him
to come to Kingsport when we visited the School of Magic.
But why would he be at this meeting?

The formal proceedings began as soon as we arrived.

The king tapped on the table for attention. "Thank you all
for attending. I believe everyone knows what we're facing. I
have already discussed the situation with most of you individually. The Alliance, as they call themselves, made demands
upon Kenesee which would leave us defenseless. They believed the strength of their combined might would intimidate
us into accepting their terms. In this, they have miscalculated.
Certainly the emissaries have reported our defiance to the leaders of their nations by now. Since it is late in the year, it's
doubtful that any coordinated campaign will be launched before the spring, although there may be some preliminary
moves to gain positional advantage during the winter. Does
anyone disagree with that assessment?"

There was no disagreement.

"I have refrained from issuing the King's Call to the regiments, and will not do so until the course of events becomes
clearer. Our economy will have to produce quantities of supplies and weapons before the spring. We cannot put the army
on active duty this early without crippling that effort. Does
anyone disagree?"

Again, there was accord.

"There are steps we can and should take, however, and that
is the purpose of this meeting. First, I have asked Sergeant
Major Nakasone and Sergeant Black to report to us on several
matters."

The sergeant major delivered a report on security, noting
that with the royal guards now reassembled in Kingsport, he
was doubling sentries and instituting a number of other measures for the safety of the castle and its royal occupants. He
was also issuing a set of security guidelines for all towns and

villages to follow, and recommended that the messenger service be put on a war footing. He concluded his presentation by requesting that the royal guard reserves be activated as early as possible.

Sergeant Black delivered a lengthier report on the status of the military regiments, noting that the manual at arms and tables of organization adopted by the army seemed to have worked well over the past ten years. Given the new threat to the kingdom, he recommended expanding the field army by drafting and reorganizing the town and local defense companies into field regiments, thereby doubling the number of maneuver units. Those too old or too young for active campaigning would fill the ranks of a new militia. He provided a copy of training schedules and equipment requirements needed to make these units an effective force.

When he'd had time to work on these, I didn't know. While the rest of us slept the nights away in field and inn, he was probably scribbling in his notebook next to the fires.

The king nodded in satisfaction. "I share the ideas of you both, and I am pleased by your anticipation of our needs. The Council will read your reports and advise me as appropriate. My thanks."

The two took this as their dismissal and rose.

"No, please remain. We may require your expertise later." They sat back down.

Graven checked his schedule. "The next item is . . . the beastmen."

The king picked up a report. "There are rumors Virginia has sent an emissary to the Beastwood. We don't know if the emissary has enjoyed any success, or even returned yet. But the Easterners cannot be allowed to conduct unchallenged diplomacy with the beastmen. It is necessary to contact the beastmen and gain their . . . cooperation. Or more realistically, perhaps it is their neutrality in the coming war which is the prize. If the Beastwood were to join the Alliance as an active member, then every border would be open to invasion and there would be no hope.

"We have decided that extraordinary times require extraordinary measures. Therefore, an emissary will be sent from Kenesee to the Beastwood. He will travel in secret and disguise."

Sergeant Major Nakasone responded to the news with an audible grunt of surprise.

The king seemed not to hear. "Wizard Murdock of the School of Magic has been asked, and has agreed, to be that emissary."

Murdock smiled slyly. "The High Wizard can be most persuasive."

There was general laughter.

The king shook his head. "Consistent with his past record of accomplishment and courage, Wizard Murdock volunteered as soon as the idea was presented to him. The High Wizard and I had hoped he would, for no man in the kingdom is as well-suited for this mission, and none has a greater chance of success. We are fortunate that he was in Kingsport."

I sighed with relief, thankful that it was Murdock who had been chosen. I could think of no better way to assure an early end to my short life than going into the darkness of the Beastwood. I wondered what *my* mission would be.

"When much is at stake," the king continued, "much has to be risked. The beastmen must realize our sincerity and good will. Therefore, Wizard Murdock will not go alone."

Uh-oh. I didn't like the way this was going.

The king looked at me. "As a token of our good faith, I will send a member of the royal family to accompany the emissary."

No. No. No.

Sergeant Black spoke up. "King Reuel, do you think this is wise? Perhaps one of the nobles would serve as well."

"No, I fear that will not do. I have weighed this a hundred times in my head since their return last night, and the answer is always the same. It must be a prince. Perhaps that is the cause of your premonition, High Wizard. Your early return may be right after all. Yet I'm reluctant to order anyone into such danger. Prince Robert will be needed here as a military commander. Prince Arn, will you go with Wizard Murdock to the Beastwood?"

The king looked at me. Robert looked at me. Everyone else looked at me. What was I to say? If the king had come to me alone and asked, I might have told him no in one clear little word. But in front of the leaders of the kingdom I was supposed to turn him down? It's one thing to know you're a coward; it's another to announce it in public.

I couldn't speak. I just nodded.

The king smiled grimly. "I knew you had the courage. Still, a part of me wishes you had declined this task for my own peace of mind." Now he told me. "I will not sleep easy until word that your mission is concluded."

"Sir, may I make a request?" Sergeant Black asked. "There are still dangers for travelers on the northern roads, and another companion would at least help get to the Beast-wood safely. I'd like to go with them."

There were nods of agreement from around the table.

The king pondered his words. "Sergeant Black, I had thought to use your expertise here in the coming months. Yet I cannot deny what you say, nor that you are one of the best fighters in the royal guard. It would be a comfort knowing you were with them. Wizard Murdock, would you accept Sergeant Black's offer, or would you prefer another to accompany you?"

"He is an excellent addition to the party, and I'm grateful for his offer."

"Arn?"

"Sergeant Black is most welcome," I agreed. Most welcome.

"All right. The three of you shall go, and a fourth will join you on the road. In accord with the importance of this mission, I hereby retire Sergeant Black from the guards and appoint him Temporary Colonel in the Army of Kenesee. Wizard Murdock, do you still intend to leave at dusk?"

Dusk? Tonight?

"Yes, my King. The sky looks to be clear and the road, moonlit. I realize the travelers are still fatigued from the tour. I've only come in two days ago myself, and would like nothing better than to enjoy the comforts of the town. But if we are to forestall the Virginian diplomatic initiative, we must offer the beastmen an alternative before they commit themselves. I presume that is agreeable to Prince Arn."

Agreeable? Not in the least. But I had already agreed to go, and could not disobey the first directive from the leader of the party. Again I could see that plans had been made for me to which I could only comply. "Yes," I submitted glumly.

"Good," the king affirmed. "Then you travelers have much to prepare. I will see you before you leave." And with that we were dismissed.

We did have much to prepare. We would be traveling as less than prosperous merchants. The royal tailor was busy much of the morning fitting us with suitably humble and worn clothing, and my long hair was cut short. Murdock and Black might be anonymous, but my face was better known. The haircut did change my looks drastically, and in that sense was a success, but I was not really happy with the result. It would be interesting to see how the fair sex responded to me without benefit of royal stature and styled locks.

Later that morning there was a knock, and standing in the open doorway was Black. "May I come in, sir?"

"Certainly, Ser—uh, Colonel. Please have a seat."

He came in but remained standing. "I'll only be a moment, if you don't mind." And then he closed the door behind him. "I wanted to give you a few items before we go. Gifts, if you will."

"Gifts? Why, you shouldn't have spent money on me, Colonel Black."

"The first gift is a bit of advice."

"Oh. I see."

"We are facing perilous times, and you'll be coming into your own now, a leader of Kenesee. Lives may depend on you. The blood and wealth of a nation can be squandered in minutes by the mistakes of its leaders. Neither pride nor fear nor hate nor desire have any place in leadership. Will you remember that?"

I nodded. "Yes, Colonel. I will."

He seemed satisfied. "Now, we'll be leaving the safety of the castle and guards behind us. We'll be just a few men traveling into danger. Much can happen, and it's best to be prepared. That's the reason for the next gift. It's not your birthday yet, but I wanted you to have this now." From under his arm he removed a package and unwrapped a sheathed knife. The slim sheath was attached to a soft leather harness.

"My gift?" I asked.

"Yes." He took the knife out. The blade gleamed even in

THE CHRONICLES OF SCAR 177

the dull light that came through the arrow slit. It was flat, well-balanced, and very, very sharp.

Black threw and the blade stuck into a ceiling timber. He pulled it out. "It's a fine weapon, held or thrown. Now, take off your shirt."

"My shirt?" What did he have in mind?

"Come on. We have to get this thing on you."

I removed the shirt and he slipped the harness over my shoulders, tightening the straps as necessary. The knife and sheath were positioned comfortably between my shoulder blades.

Black nodded in satisfaction. "A little surprise for anyone with the wrong intentions. Now, put your shirt back on. There. Can't tell you've got it on. Practice with the knife when you're alone until you can get it out in one smooth motion and hit an apple at ten feet."

The gift was not quite what I had expected. But then, what had I expected?

"You think that I need this?"

Black looked me squarely in the eye. "Not while I have a sword in my hand, son. I promise you that." And then, as if embarrassed, he turned away.

"Thank you, Colonel. I'll practice with it just as you say." And I would. If Black thought I might need it on this trip, then I was darn well going to learn how to use it. Besides, I knew he wouldn't let me get away with not practicing.

"By the way, there's one more thing." He pointed at the corncob pipe I'd stuck back on the mantelpiece. "I'd noticed you had that before we left on tour. Ever use it?"

"Last night. It didn't work too well." Not my fault, of course.

"Try this instead." He handed me a new tobacco pipe, curved and polished, and a full tobacco pouch. "Just in case you're interested in having a bowlful now and then."

"Thank you, Colonel Black. Your concern is . . . is greatly appreciated."

"There's a trick to packing the tobacco so that it draws well. Let me know if you need help with it."

I nodded. What more could I say to the man? He drew himself up, opened the door, and strode out.

Later still that morning Lorich came by and admired the

pipe as I transferred it to a jacket pocket while organizing my traveling clothes. I explained that Black had given it to me as a gift, and the young wizard's expression was one of awe. "You are well loved, sir."

"Uh-huh," I said, never at a loss for words. "It doesn't hurt to humor them. Good for morale."

"Yes, sir. I see. I hadn't thought of that."

I looked for Angela at lunch, but found that she had left the castle for the day, blissfully unaware of my mission and departure. She had gone early to visit a sick friend in the city, and would not be back until after dinner. I was not in the best of moods that afternoon as we looked at maps, discussed items we might need on the journey, and put together our saddlebags. The king and Robert came to see us too. We discussed policy and diplomacy, and then they bid us farewell, for they would remain in the dining hall after dinner to divert attention from our clandestine departure.

Robert gave me a manful handshake. "I envy you your mission."

I brightened. "Well, if you really want to go instead . . ."

"I tried to get Father to send me, but his mind is made up. I'll be sitting in garrison on the coast watching the Easterners and waiting for spring, while you go into danger. But duty requires we serve as needed. Be aware that Father will worry during your absence. Conduct yourself with honor, and return safely. I wish you all success."

The king had been listening. He looked me in the eye, and then wrapped his arms around me, a tear trickling down his cheek. "Don't worry, Arn. I wouldn't send you if there was no hope of your return. And that hope will sustain me. Do you have everything you'll need?"

"Yes, sir."

"Good. Good. Kendall's left already, you know. He departed after our Council meeting today. Without fuss, as he always does. He bid you safe journey. Megan was there to see him off. So he's gone. And now you leave. And then Robert tomorrow. The pieces are being placed on the board as they must be." He looked sad, as if wondering what pieces would still remain by the end of the game. "Well. All's said, then. God speed, Arn. Stay well, and show courage."

The meal bell rang a bit early, but other than that dinner was uneventful. I sat with Murdock, but watched every person walking through the archways. Angela was nowhere to be seen. A circus of jugglers and animals came out to entertain us at the end of the meal. Most of the diners stayed for it, as normally occurred, although a few slipped away as duty required. Murdock and I were among these. In my room I slipped on coarser garments of merchant quality: sturdy boots, brown pants, a green flannel shirt and sweater, a fur hat, and over everything a long, all-weather riding coat, hooded and cloaked to the waist. A sword and knife were fixed at my waist in plain scabbards in the manner of merchant travelers, and Black's gift rested hidden between my shoulder blades.

I adjusted my cap at a jaunty angle. On to adventure. On to glory. On to my death if I wasn't careful. I looked around my room for anything I might have missed. My room. Eleven years of my life. I realized I might never see it again. My stomach twisted in response, and I tried with little success to put such thoughts out of my mind. With full saddlebags and a thick blanket roll over my shoulder, I locked the door to my room, avoided the main corridor, and took a side passage to the entrance of the house. The guard at the door nodded to me. "Good luck, sir."

Good luck? How much did he know about the mission?

Murdock and Black were already attaching saddlebags to their mounts, reasonable horseflesh no different from any merchant's. They were warmly attired in clothes not far different from mine, and carried the same weapons at their belts.

Corporal Jenkins waited helpfully nearby, holding the reins of a horse for me. "Everything went fine last night, sir," he mumbled under his breath. "I saw Miss Beth this morning and escorted her back to her house."

The evening was clear and cool, and the walls of the castle stood out sharply in the last light. From somewhere a dog barked, and a timesman could be heard on the street. "Seven o'clock. All's well. . . ."

"Greetings," Murdock said when he noticed me, and he smiled enthusiastically. His heartiness seeped into me and cheered me out of my despondency. He did have the most peculiar effects on people. "You have everything? A full purse? Good." He gave us each a flat leather pouch. "Inside there are instruments of credit, and in case of need, royal passes signed and sealed. I hope we won't have to use them. Now, if Prince Arn will secure his things, we can be off. I want to clear the town gates before nightlock. The less commotion, the better."

I eyed my horse suspiciously, then tied on the saddlebags and bedroll while Murdock and Black waited. A slender figure emerged from the castle door. Megan descended the steps with quiet dignity. "You're going away. The boy has become a man."

"So much for secrecy," said Black.

I bowed to her. "And the girl has become a woman." A nice response. Not bad for me, although I always did communicate better with women.

Were the light better, it might have shone a blush on her cheeks. "Paul—I mean Mr. Kendall—has left already. And now you leave too. I wanted you to know. You and Robert are my friends, and always will be. I wish you well." She kissed me daintily on the cheek, and was gone.

I watched the door close behind her. Beautiful Megan. If only Angela had been with her.

Murdock squirmed in his saddle. "Prince Arn, we really must be—"

The door opened again and Angela came to me, breathless, a shawl thrown hastily over her shoulders. Her face was distraught. "Arn. I returned late and just heard the news. You're going away."

I looked around me in a frown. "Whatever gave you that idea?"

"I'm sorry I was away all day," she whispered. "I thought last night wouldn't matter. I didn't know you were leaving. I didn't know we wouldn't have time." She came close. "I will await your return," she promised, and touched her lips to mine. Tears brimming in her eyes, she bounced up the steps and fled through the door.

The blood pounded within me. If only I had a night. Or an hour. Or—

"Is it always like this, Colonel?" Murdock lamented. "I have been too long away from Kingsport."

"Another typical departure," said Black.

"Ah, well. As long as they are women. And now, Prince Arn, if we may—"

The door opened a third time and Lorich limped down the steps.

"Spoke too soon," Murdock groaned.

Black shook his head. "Corporal Jenkins, is there anyone in the castle who is not aware of our departure?"

The corporal looked thoughtful. "I don't think the cook knows."

Murdock reached out his hand and grasped Lorich's. They spoke briefly, and then Lorich came to me. "I haven't thanked you, sir."

"Ahem. Yes, well, we'll discuss it sometime."

"Angela is wonderful."

"Yes she is."

"Beth is wonderful too."

I sighed. "Lorich, all women are wonderful. But a word of advice. You know the difference between dogs and cats? Well, that's the difference between men and women."

"Really?" he asked with puzzled frown.

"Think about it."

"Yes, Prince Arn. I will give it thought. And I'll never forget you, sir."

"I *do* intend to come back, Lorich."

"Yes, sir. If ever I can help you, I will. You are my friend, and I will be yours."

When you're a prince, everyone wants to be your friend. An impulse took me. I removed the key from my pocket. "Here. It's to my room. In case you need to go somewhere private to—uh—talk. Until my return."

I turned away before he could burst into tears. Why was everyone else crying? I was the one who should be crying. I summoned Corporal Jenkins. Lorich would be madly in love with Angela or Beth or both if his passion wasn't tempered with a little variety. "Take the boy up to the Street of Pleasure for more lessons," I whispered. "Different ladies. You can indulge too. At my expense."

Corporal Jenkins accepted the task with stalwart courage. "Well, if you insist."

Murdock watched Lorich as he returned to the house. "I looked in on the young apprentice today, and he never looked as happy. A great relief. He has grown much in just a few weeks." Murdock winked. "Surely he has had many new and interesting experiences."

"Uh, yes." I mounted and patted the animal gently. Nice horsy. A gelding. Good. "At your pleasure, Wizard Murdock."

"Finally? I have not seen such a send-off since, well, it was before your time. But enough of titles. We are Mr. Murdock, Mr. Black, and Mr. Brant to others, now. And to each other we are Desjardins—no, that sounds strange. Make it Murdock, John, and Arn. And so we shall be until we return. I wonder if we can still make nightlock?"

We took the King's Way at a trot and reached the north gate just as the keepers were about to close the portals. They waited for us as we increased our pace. It was then that I noticed the woman standing in the shadows beside the gates, watching us as we trotted up. She stepped forward into the lamplight, a squat figure wearing a large felt hat with two eagle feathers in its brim. I stared at her as we went by and her eyes followed me. I recognized her, but made no sign. In response, she drew her finger across her cheek.

Silently, Crazy Mary watched us leave Kingsport on our mission.

4

Secret Mission

I was back in the saddle, retracing much of the course I'd taken during the tour. We rode through the community of Laketown that night, making good time out of the lowlands as we headed north. It was late, and there were few people about to mark our passage. In the town, one or two second-floor windows shed light upon the darkness and showed where some lonely souls still toiled, while lamps hung outside taverns and inns, beckoning to us. I picked out the taverns with interest, and eyed Murdock questioningly.

The wizard noticed my glances, but was anxious to put miles between us and Kingsport. "When you're traveling covertly," he said, "always get a good jump away from your starting point in the first day or two. Throws off anybody following." So we kept traveling throughout the night, the roadway stretching before us in the moonlight. In the morning we dismounted and walked our horses another ten miles.

A tender spot on each heel wore into a blister from the unfamiliar pair of boots. I found it hard to limp on both sides and complained to Murdock.

He was quite unsympathetic. "Blisters are wondrous things. God's warning, they are. God's telling you to exercise more. Every morning I walk from the school to a distant farmhouse and back again, and my feet don't hurt. In fact, I feel better on the way back than the way out. But suffering is good for the soul, Arn."

"I don't mind my soul suffering. It's my feet that I mind. These boots are doing it, not lack of exercise. And I'm tired."

"It's a beautiful day for a walk. We shouldn't waste it."
Murdock beamed with happiness. "Ahh, to be adventuring
again. A few less teeth, a few more pounds, but old Murdock
can still keep up with the young ones."

I sought help from Black. "What do you say, Colonel—
uh, John?"

He had already considered it. "Murdock's idea to get us
away from Kingsport is a good one. We should make haste
these first two days. But the horses will need feed and rest."

Murdock's ears perked up. "Good point. We don't want to
wear them out. All right, my dear Arn. The next inn should
be coming up in a few hours. We'll stay there and leave tomorrow morning."

We continued walking. Freed of the responsibility for his
squadron of guardsmen, Black was still silent and impenetra-
ble, granting the merest hint of a smile or a raised eyebrow to
indicate his appreciation of Murdock's jokes. But his eyes
were ever alert, watching the road, eyeing the trees and bushes,
glancing behind at regular intervals, and listening to more than
just our conversation.

"Look!" exclaimed Murdock.

Black's hand darted to his sword.

"What is it?" I asked.

"A red breast. Up in the tree. There. Isn't it beautiful? I
love birds. They're so care free. Their minds can't hold fear
longer than the fact of it. That one is late heading south.
Should have gone by now. A sign, perhaps? Some say it
means God is smiling on the watcher. By the way, John, you
can relax. There's nothing up ahead in those bushes except a
squirrel. I know."

Black let go of the weapon. "You know? A talent?"

"One of them. I hope I don't have cause to use the others,
but we shall see."

Black nodded in appreciation. "You make a good companion."

"Why, thank you, John. What a nice compliment. Especially from a man of few words. I'm most reassured by your
presence, too. We make a fine party. Almost complete."

"I have heard," said Black, "that you've been on many
adventures of one sort or another."

"In my experience, I've roamed from the Northern Forests

to the Isles of the South, and from the coasts of Virginia to the plains of Texan.''

I was about to speak but Black signaled me to hold my tongue. We walked on in silence.

Murdock looked at us. "Well? Aren't you going to ask me about them?''

"About what?" Black responded in a puzzled tone.

"About my adventures.''

"Adventures?'' The wisp of a smile began to emerge upon Black's features.

Murdock burst into laughter. "Teasing me, I see. So, you're not as grim as you appear. Well, hopefully you'll be laughing with me and not at me. Life is full of sadness. If I act the buffoon to make people laugh, is that so bad? I guess by nature I'm a bit of a Falstaff. Do you like Shakespeare, John?''

"In Old World English. The translations are weak.''

"We're in agreement. Any favorites?''

"I like the tragedies. Macbeth. Hamlet.''

"For me, it's the comedies. I love them all. They remove the heartache from the things I've seen. On my travels.''

No one spoke for a while.

Murdock broke down first. "I take it you would like to hear of my . . . travels?''

"We would be honored," Black stated with dignity.

Murdock grinned broadly. "Yes, a most excellent companion.''

We traveled for the next week through Redbank and Knox, and thence north on the Lexington road. After the first march we traveled during the day, and to save the horses put thirty miles behind us by dusk, resting each evening at inns or homes with rooms and stables. There was little time to dally with the young ladies we encountered each evening, and if truth be told, in my new guise there was little interest in my compliments. My transformation from honored prince to unnoticed merchant had worked too well. Not only did the ladies not recognize me, they ignored me. Yet all Murdock had to do was smile sideways at a woman and she blushed prettily and hummed with pleasure for the rest of the night. I credited my lack of success to Murdock's magic. It was quite unfair.

North of Knox and halfway between the towns of London

and Richmond we came into sight of the village of Stockton, a cluster of a dozen homes with barns, a mill, and general store to mark it as the point of commerce for the farmsteads surrounding it.

Murdock pointed ahead. "The village has an inn. The Green Oak."

"And whom shall we meet there?" Black asked pointedly. "Perhaps the owner of the wagon?"

Murdock chuckled. "You do have sharp eyes, my friend. Yes, it's time for the last of our party to join us. Without him, there'd be little chance of success."

As we drew closer I noticed what Black had already seen. Next to the inn's stable sat an unhitched wagon in need of a new coat of paint, an arched red roof covering the enclosed green wagon box. Faded yellow letters across each side proclaimed its owner: JASON THE HEALER. Painted scroll-like beneath the name were various specialties:

DISEASES AND INFECTIONS CURED
SURGERY PERFORMED
DENTAL WORK DONE
REASONABLE RATES
PAYMENT IN TRADE CONSIDERED

"Yes, that's it," proclaimed Murdock.

We entered the yard just as a yell came from the other side of the wagon.

"Aarrgghhh!"

"I told you not to move," a voice said. "And if you'd taken that pain killer I gave you instead of rum, it wouldn't hurt as much."

We came around the wagon and saw a heavyset man in an apron sitting with his mouth open, gripping the seat of his chair with white knuckles. Over him worked a man holding a silver instrument. The man with the instrument was of average appearance except for a handsome head of wavy gray hair and spectacles which had slid down near the end of his nose. Something about him seemed familiar, or perhaps he reminded me of someone. He pushed his spectacles back up his nose and straightened.

"There. That should do it. Don't chew on that side for a few hours."

The man in the apron spat into a pan, drank from a mug, and then rubbed his jaw in resignation. "All right, next time I'll take your damn pain killers. But they taste bad."

"Brush your teeth like I told you and you won't have as many problems."

The man in the chair noted us. He stood up, wiped his mouth in embarrassment, and came forward.

"Afternoon, gentlemen. May I help you? A bit of lunch?"

Murdock grinned. "Yes. And if you'll protect us from your torturer, we'll take a room for the night."

"Very good, sir. Your horses will be seen to. Please have a seat in the dining hall and we'll serve you immediately." The innkeeper was off to his business.

The healer was cleaning his instruments and did not look up. "It seems our misfortune to journey together again." He turned around. "Torturer, indeed. Any bones you need reset?"

"Murdock the Magnificent is well, you scoundrel. Here, come meet my companions. This is Arn, and John Black. My friends, this is Jason Kendall. He claims the humble title of healer instead of physician out of orneriness, claiming he has not graduated from our renowned medical school. Yet he has taught there, and is the finest doctor to be found in the kingdom."

Jason shook hands but eyed us with detachment as he put his instruments into a black satchel and stored it away. "Mr. Black, do you remember me?"

"Yes, sir."

"You were just a fresh-faced private back then. You've done quite well, I understand."

Murdock caught the expression on my face. "Until Jason retired, he was a King's Advisor. His son took over the job."

The resemblance. Jason was Paul Kendall's father.

"Aye, an advisor I was," Jason said, allowing the Pacifican accent to ring clear in his voice. Then he slipped back into a perfect Kenesee lilt. "But sometimes a man needs a change. Enough about me. Time is moving along, and we have matters to discuss. Go on in and I'll join you in a moment."

*   *   *

The inn was small, but had an adequate common room in which we found a quiet corner. We were the only travelers, the few others being locals enjoying a late noon beer. None gave us more than passing attention, and they soon left to return to their work. A young serving maid took our order. She was scarcely more than a girl in years, but her form showed she was already a woman. Murdock's eyes caressed her lovingly as she went for our beer. I couldn't blame him. I had been following her movements with great interest too. "Lovely," he sighed. "Just lovely. Remind me to tell you of my times amidst the girls of the Isles."

"Murdock," I said, "one thing surprises me about you. At the school I saw a practitioner of discipline and denial. Here, I see a man of pleasure."

"And you see a contradiction? Oh ho! One must do without to appreciate having. My predecessor, dear old Speros, encouraged the austerity of the school and I thought it appropriate to continue that tradition. It's good to endure discipline and self-denial at some point. The joys of life are that much richer. God has been good to us in this world. Too often we forget how much we have. Hopefully, those who attend the school learn the lesson of appreciation. Still, denial need not go on forever. Actually, my morning walks from the school are for more exercise than just walking, but enough said lest a woman's virtue be cast in doubt." He laughed. "Believe only half what I say, and this too may be only half true."

The girl brought our drinks, and the healer joined us soon after.

Murdock raised his pint. "Gentlemen, to our success." The beer was not as good as might be hoped for. Then again, we were thirsty. Black filled his pipe, so I took out mine and did the same. I was getting better. I kept the bowl burning for a full minute before it went out.

The healer sniffed the air. "A fine aroma, Mr. Black. Different from my tobacco. May I try a bowl?" Jason expertly filled his pipe, a large one with a carved bowl and a stem of white stone.

Murdock watched. "An interesting pipe, wouldn't you say, John? There's quite a story behind it."

The healer snorted. "Same as ever, eh, Murdock? There's

time enough for stories in the days ahead. Perhaps we should discuss the reason we're here first.''

Lunch was brought, and over bread and stew and boiled eggs the plan was quietly laid out by the healer. A small map of the northern kingdom appeared on the table. Jason's finger tapped the map. ''Here we are now, and four days away by horseback—probably ten with my wagon, at best—the edge of the Beastwood. I'll have to make stops on the way to treat some cases, too, so don't get impatient. Not stopping would attract attention. We'll take the east road out of Lexington and enter the forest here, beyond the town of Benton. I would have gone there first and prepared your way, but there was no time after receiving the message from Murdock. This was all done in a rush, and I think such haste is wrong. The Alliance won't attack before spring. Their leaders are logical and cautious men, and that is both their strength and weakness.''

Black stared thoughtfully at the map while puffing in long, slow draws. ''You're probably right. But some of our enemies could make a preliminary move before then. Now, you say it could take ten days with your wagon. Why not ride horseback with us and leave the wagon?''

The healer lit his pipe and exhumed a mouthful of smoke which curled up to join Black's. ''Good tobacco. I like it. Now, to your question. First, I might not be recognized without the wagon until too late. I have no desire for an arrow in my back. They know my wagon. It's a symbol of my friendship and service to them.''

That put things in a different light for me. ''Well, it certainly is a very nice wagon. I guess we can wait for it.''

''The beastmen tolerate and trust me—up to a point,'' the healer continued. ''But many of them have no great love for us, I'll tell you, thanks to your king's little expedition. I'll probably survive this journey, though one never knows. For the three of you, it's a different matter.''

I tried not to choke on a gulp of beer. ''What do you mean?''

''Without me, you have one chance in three. With me, you have two chances in three.''

''How is it,'' asked Black after a puff, ''that you can enter the Beastwood?''

''Fair question,'' the healer answered. ''A bit of Androcles and the Lion, if you know that ancient tale. Six or seven years ago, some villagers found an injured beastman just on the edge of the Beastwood. It had never happened before. The beastmen make every effort to take their dead and wounded with them. He was lying helpless and alone, hurt in a fall from an embankment the night before. I was in a nearby village, and so the summons came to me. I set his limbs, put him in my wagon, and drove him back into the forest.

"Eventually we ran into their border watch. They debated killing me, but given the circumstances decided to keep me captive until a decision could be made about my disposal. I offered them a new drug they could produce, as well as other useful information. The matter went all the way up to their ruling council, and I had to meet with them. I was released, and eventually permitted to enter and leave the Beastwood as I wanted, on my word that I would keep silent about what I knew. I can travel only in certain areas near the border, and think I'm the only person ever granted the privilege. Now, taking you all in with me will be risky. I'm not authorized to bring anyone else into the forest. They may decide to shoot first."

Nothing like an honest man to make you feel bad.

We were up at dawn, the air cool but still. Another pleasant fall morning. Jason hitched a pair of matched grays to the wagon and set off, Murdock seated beside him while his mare followed, tied securely to the rear stoop of the wagon. Black and I rode at the head of our little caravan. I was silent for awhile, listening to the wagon creak and groan over the roadway, the horses snorting into the air.

Black was not quite relaxed, for his vigilance was unremitting. He seemed rather—content. Yes, content might be the word. I decided to break the silence. "John."

"Yes, Arn?" he responded promptly.

"I wanted . . . to thank you for coming along."

He adjusted the reins in his hands. "No thanks necessary. I've been watching over you for eleven years, now. Didn't want to lose my investment." Black cast a glance my way. "You tossed and turned last night."

"Do you think we'll come out of this?"

"Jason gave us two chances out of three. That's not bad

odds. We've done everything we could. Now we've got to play out the cards. If things start looking bad we'll do what we have to. Of course, fighting our way through a thousand beastmen is a tall order.'' He cocked an eyebrow. ''Now, if we had Corporal Jenkins with us. . . .''

I laughed, and he seemed pleased.

We rolled on north past the town of Richmond, going through villages where Jason was well known. We stopped at several in spite of the press of time. He would set up clinic just outside the village proper, an awning lowered from the side of the wagon, a chair and table laid out beneath, and a sheet strung for privacy. At one a woman brought in a sick child, and he gave her a powder. At the next, a man suffered an infection from an ax cut, and Jason drained the wound. An old woman at the third had belly pains, and he comforted her with words and pain killers. She would die soon.

He commented upon it, his tone philosophical, but unable to hide a note of bitterness in his voice. ''All the miseries of mankind, and they find their way to my door. Not very pleasant, is it? A long way from the castle and those healthy men and women of the court. Well, that's the last one today. We can go now.''

We passed pretty Lexington and turned east. The villages and farms became fewer as we drew near the Beastwood. Even the smaller villages had at least one stout common building suitable for defense. Lonely farmhouses were solidly built, with heavy oak doors and thick shutters.

''There are still one or two gangs of thieves about,'' advised Jason. ''The thieves are just villagers by day, and they leave me alone because I help them and carry nothing of value. Having you with me changes the equation. We'll travel at night now, and pass the villages in the dark.'' It was a wise precaution, but did not save us.

The last evening before we reached the Beastwood was dark and gloomy, clouds covering the sky and pouring a steady rain on us as we splashed through the puddles on the roadway. Two lanterns hung from the roof of the wagon provided the only light, except for the flashes of lightning that lit up the surrounding woods.

It was at a long curve in the road as it wound around a hill that the wagon came to a halt and Murdock gestured to us. A long peal of thunder sounded above, and lightning flashed through the clouds. He pointed around the curve and spoke a few words to Black, who slipped from his horse and disappeared into the underbrush that bordered the road. We waited for what seemed a long time, but was probably less than a half hour. Then Black emerged and joined us at the wagon.

"You were right, Murdock," Black confirmed. "There's a small tree cut down and blocking the road around the bend. I saw three men waiting in ambush. They had swords rather than bows. There are probably at least four or five more in hiding. They knew we'd be coming."

"So what do we do?" I asked, fearing the worst.

Murdock shook his head. "We'll lose a day or two going back to take a different road. And there's no guarantee they wouldn't just follow."

"This is the road I normally take," said Jason. "The Border Watch knows me. On other routes, they don't."

"That decides it," Murdock sighed.

"You have your sword?" Black asked the wizard.

Murdock grinned. "Yes. I'm always armed."

"All right. Jason?"

The healer had a sword beside him and put a hand into his coat. "I'm ready."

"Good. Arn and I will hold back. Stay in the wagon if you can. Make them come to you, and we'll hit them from the rear. Jason, keep to one side of the road or the other so that we can gallop past, and stop at least a dozen yards away from the fallen tree. We'll need room to wheel the horses and charge back. Is that agreeable with you, Murdock?"

"John, in these matters I have complete trust in your judgment."

In the glow of the lanterns I noted a particular thing. The faces of the three men were severe, and yet at the same time they shared something else, a particular mood, an expectation, or perhaps an anticipation. Yes, that was it! Anticipation. They were looking forward to the encounter. They were warriors before the enemy, and the lust of battle was upon them. I didn't know if this pleased or frightened me more.

Black mounted his horse and waited with me while the wagon continued on its way. It rounded the bend, and was lost from sight behind the trees. Black drew his sword and I followed his example.

"Ready, son? They'll try to swarm the wagon. Follow me and stay close. Protect my rear. Use your horse as a weapon. Scatter them with the charge and the battle is half won."

My heart was thudding in my chest and I had difficulty breathing. What was I doing here? I was not made for this. My place was in the bedroom, or the library, or the dining hall. I barely restrained the urge to wheel about and gallop away.

A horse neighed from ahead and there were shouts. We spurred our mounts and galloped around the bend as thunder pealed above us and the rain poured down. The wagon had stopped at a spot in the road where it widened, so that there was ample room on either side for our charge. In the glow of the lanterns, shadowy figures clustered about the wagon, climbing the wheels and thrusting with swords at our unseen companions. Black charged along the left side of the wagon and straight into them, bowling over two of the thieves. He swung his sword and a third went down. My horse jumped over the prone figures, its hooves spraying water in all directions, and followed Black. The colonel reined to a halt next to the downed tree in the road.

"Again!" he commanded, and spurred back down the right side of the wagon. The thieves scattered before him, but then a dark shape launched itself from the roof, landed on top of the colonel and carried him off his horse. The two splashed into the road in a jumble of limbs. My horse leaped over the bodies. Though I can scarcely believe I did it, I reined in, turned, and charged a third time. Perhaps I was more afraid of the darkness than I was of the thieves.

Black was rolling on the ground with his opponent while another thief stood over them with upraised sword. The man did not even realize I was coming, which satisfied me no end. I extended my own blade straight before me and felt it pierce the man, thrusting him aside as it tore from my hand. The force almost knocked me from the saddle as well. I reined in and turned around for another charge, but already the thieves were running into the woods, disappearing into the night.

My stomach churned, and then steadied. It was over.

Black stood with one hand on the wagon wheel, coughing,

while a still figure lay between his feet. Two more sprawled where they had fallen. I dismounted clumsily, my legs quivering beneath me. "John!"

He waved me away. "Got the wind knocked out," he gasped. "That's all. Are you all right? Good." He coughed again, picked up his sword, and then straightened. "Murdock? Jason?"

Murdock was already climbing down from the wagon. "Oh ho! That was good. A bit too brief, but enough to send the blood racing. We're fine. Jason is a perilous foe, he is. As you are, my fine horsemen. Excellent charges. Excellent."

Jason stepped down into the roadway and looked around. "There are three more on the other side. Two will be waking up soon. What do you want to do with them?"

Murdock hesitated. "The penalty is hanging. Of course, we need royal approval for the death sentence. Or we could just—" He reached inside his coat, felt his side, and swore. "Wounded. Again! Ah, me, this poor body of mine."

The healer took one of the lanterns from the wagon. "Off with your coat and shirt. Black, are we safe here?"

"We've cut their numbers by half," said Black. "I don't think they'll be back. Do your work, Jason. Come with me, Arn."

"They're scared," Murdock confirmed, "and moving further away every minute."

On the other side of the wagon three bodies were piled. The top one was alive, but blood pumped from the neck wound that Black had inflicted in our first charge. "Almost gone," he said, and moved the body aside. The other two lay twitching feebly. Black looked closely and grunted. "The healer must have gotten these. Strange. No wounds that I can see." He called out. "Jason, do you have any rope?"

"In the wagon," came the reply.

We tied the two and then came around and checked the other bodies. All three were dead. Black's knife still stuck out of the throat of the man who had knocked him from his horse. The second thief had a deep slice in his skull. Murdock's doing. The third was mine. Black turned him over and pulled my sword out of his chest. It made a sucking noise. "Take a look," he commanded.

I did. The man's face was lit by the lantern. He was older, perhaps in his forties, with a beard and close-cropped hair. He had a surprised look on his face.

"Your first kill, son. How do you feel?"

I probed. "I don't know. I don't . . . feel anything."

"You won't, yet. Later you'll feel quite the giant slayer. Later still, the bad dreams will start. Those will pass too. He might have a wife, children, a home where he'll never return. But he would have killed you if given the chance. He didn't have to be out here. He chose this. Remember that."

I nodded dumbly.

"You did well."

Yes, I did, didn't I? If one considers not running away as doing well.

"But next time, hold onto your sword."

The rain slackened and then stopped, although the trees continued to drip wetly. Murdock was seated on the edge of the wagon step while the healer worked at the wound. Under the lamp light, a variety of battle scars dotted the magician's torso, and his back showed the permanent welts of the lash. Murdock had not told us of all his adventures, it appeared. His most recent wound was a sword thrust which had scraped along the rib cage and left a three-inch gash in the skin. The healer finished stitching the cut, wrapped a bandage around the wizard's ribs, and finally pulled Murdock's shirt down gently.

"I suppose it will be sore for only a week or so," Murdock said hopefully.

"Longer," said Jason. "You know that. You're not young anymore."

"Ahh. For that wisdom I had to travel across half the kingdom. Anything else?"

"Drink this. Try to avoid mortal combat for a day or two." Jason wiped his hands clean. "And now, what do we do with the prisoners?"

The three men looked at each other, then at me. No one had to say anything. We couldn't let them go, and yet there was no one to turn them over to. Only one alternative remained. For anything else, the decision would have been Murdock's. But only the king—or, in need, a member of the royal family—could approve the execution of a citizen.

The choice was mine. What a privilege. What an opportunity. Oh, yes.

"The men weren't masked," stated Black calmly. "They didn't intend to leave witnesses. They aren't starving peasants trying to feed their families. They rob and kill and blame others. I searched them and found a pouch full of human hair."

Hair was still occasionally found in victim's hands—human hair, now that we knew that an adult beastman's hair was like ours—as if it were torn from beastmen during a death struggle. Most now recognized it for the trick it was, but that didn't stop the bandits from trying.

"Make your choice," advised Murdock, "but do it for the right reasons."

I thought about their intent to kill us. And I thought of the Beastwood Campaign inspired by such tricks. I tried to remember the words, as I had heard the king say them.

"Their guilt is proven. Let . . . the law be carried out."

The voice did not sound like my own.

Black prepared the ropes while Murdock and Jason were silent. "You disapprove," I stated. I felt very weary.

The wizard shook his head. "There is no right choice in these matters. Justice and mercy are sides of the same coin. Only God can judge such things."

"What would you have done?"

Murdock shrugged, and then winced in pain. "I don't know. But don't make decisions and *then* ask for advice."

The prisoners' hands were tied behind their backs, and they were gagged. Two ropes were thrown over a tree limb. One of the thieves began to sob. The other struggled. They were both young men in their twenties. We placed them on our horses, secured the nooses, and Black led the horses away. They swung for a goodly while, kicking and jerking, and then they were still.

We cleared the tree from the road, mounted, and rode on.

There was little more said that night.

5

Torture

We camped the latter half of the night just inside the edge of the Beastwood. It had stopped raining but the ground was soaked, so pine boughs were cut and laid beneath the wagon. Black took the first watch while Jason joined me under the wagon, giving up his bed inside to the wizard. The healer wrapped himself in a blanket. "The watch posts are deeper in the forest. This is no-man's-land; only the odd patrol of beastmen comes this far, unless they have reason."

We slept late, made a cold meal, and pushed on along the old road, which quickly shrank to an overgrown track barely large enough for the wagon. Only a few lesser paths crossed the track, meandering back into the trees and quickly lost to view even though most of the leaves had fallen from tree and bush. The paths were the only alternative to the track. Traveling cross-country would involve a continuous challenge of fallen trees, stumps, and thorny underbrush. Progress would be tortuous. I understood how King Reuel's expedition—which had followed this very route—could so easily be turned back by the beastmen. Closely formed troops would be in disarray with long spears tangled in the branches, and cavalry useless.

Yet the Beastwood was little worse than other forests in which we had trained, neither darker nor more formidable. The ghastly place of horror I had imagined since childhood did not exist. It was a place of tree and branch, earth and sky, bird and mammal. That didn't make it any more appealing to me, because forests in general were not my favorite places. I wondered if the beastmen had inns.

"John," Murdock called from the wagon seat. The wizard was up and about, but moving gingerly this morning. "Do you remember this road?"

"Very well," Black responded soberly. "To my regret."

"And mine," the wizard added. Black held up his hand and we halted. In the silence he listened. Murdock listened too. "I don't sense anything, John. But we found that magic can't detect the beastmen. Do you hear anything?"

"No. I've just got a feeling of being watched."

Jason snorted. "Of course they're watching. We already passed their first outpost, you know. They'll be ahead, and not too much farther. As I've said—when you see them, make no move toward your weapons. Beastmen will be watching with bows. They'll be cautious. They speak English. You'll be able to understand what they say. Obey them."

We rode on, but I could see no one. Black murmured to us quietly. "There's one on our left, perhaps twenty yards out. Another on the right, I believe." We rode slowly now, the sounds of our horses and the creaking of the wagon the only sounds in the wet forest. And then they appeared as Jason said they would.

Three hooded figures stepped out from behind trees, two with bows, the third with only a sword at his side. I did not look behind, but guessed that at least as many were closing in from the rear. They varied in size and shape, as men would. The one with the sword threw back his hood, and for the first time I saw a live beastman.

Drawings had given me an idea of the creatures—hair forming a pelt covering all parts of their body except the palms of their hands and the soles of their feet. But the renderings I had seen also showed them half naked and gave them long canines—almost fangs—revealed in an evil grin below a piglike nose, and above which the eyes glinted snakelike with malice. However, the beastmen we saw were well covered by their dull green uniforms, and the face of this beastman was set in a puzzled frown. His teeth and nose were no different than any man's. His eyes too were like ours, and revealed no malice.

We halted and the beastman glanced at each of us in turn, meeting our gaze before finally looking at Jason. "We are not well met, Healer. You have no permission to bring others when you visit.'' His voice was that of a man, although the accent was different—softer and more abrupt at the same time.

Jason met the gaze of the beastman. ''My apologies, Watcher. You are—Sergeant Peterson, if memory serves me? There was no time to warn you. I was in the west of the kingdom when asked to accompany these men, and none of your spies were at hand to inform. Permission would have taken many days.''

''Who are these?'' the beastman sergeant asked warily.

''Representatives of King Reuel of Kenesee to parlay with your High Council, Sergeant Peterson. They are all high men of Kenesee, come at great risk for great need. Grave matters must be discussed. It will be dark before we reach your company post. Shouldn't we start now?''

The beastman sighed. ''Damn it, Healer, why do you have to come on my watch? Anyone in the back of the wagon?''

''No. Just we four.''

''Weapons?''

''We carry swords and knives.''

''All right. Dismount and give your weapons to me. Schmitt, Miller, tie their hands. Now, get them into the back of the wagon. You too, Healer. Miller, get in the back with them. Blindfold them. Schmitt! You drive the thing. Warn them, Healer. Any trouble, and we'll slit their throats.''

There was no need for Jason to restate the warning. I believed them already. We crowded into the wagon box. Murdock and Jason sat on the bed with the beastman while Black and I took the narrow floor. The beastman Miller tied the blindfolds on fiercely. I grimaced. ''Too tight?'' he mocked. ''Too bad.''

''Keep quiet, Miller. Make sure they keep their mouths shut, too.''

The door slammed shut and we sat in darkness listening to ourselves breathe. A voice commanded ''Forward'' and the wagon groaned into movement. My back was against the handle of a drawer. I shifted to avoid the knob, and something crashed against my head.

''Move again and I'll split it open next time,'' the beastman said hopefully.

I felt Black tensing next to me, and then heard a crack as his head gained the honors. The pain from my blow intensified, burned, and then after long minutes subsided to a dull, throbbing ache. I did not move again, nor did Black, nor any of us. Only the sound of creaking wood and horse hoofs and muted voices entertained us on the long hours that we traveled blindly into our unknown fate.

This was not quite the reception I had hoped for. Now we rode with our hands bound behind us, at the mercy of a fierce enemy. Things were not going so well. I had too much time to think, and that did not help my spirits any. I felt very weary. In spite of my fear, or perhaps because of it, I fell asleep.

The stubby end of something jabbed into my stomach, rousing me. "Come on, wake up. Move out." Still blindfolded and bound, I was thrust through the door, missed the step of the wagon, and fell to the ground. Behind me, the others stumbled out.

A rough, angry voice greeted us. "Get them into the cells. One each. No food, no water."

"Captain, the Healer too?" asked the voice of Sergeant Peterson.

"Yes, the Healer too," said the voice of the captain. "And then I'll see you in my quarters."

The healer spoke. "I have done nothing to merit such treatment, nor have these men. We come in good faith. We want—"

"I've been told what you want," the captain said coldly. "I'll soon see how much good faith your emissaries have—and you, too, for that matter."

A gag was stuffed in my mouth and secured with a rope around my head. I was led forward through a doorway which I bumped roughly with one shoulder, and my boots thumped on wooden floors. A guard pushed me down onto what I imagined was a bed, tied my legs together, and linked them to my wrists behind my back. Steps moved away, a door slammed, and the bolt shot home.

I tried to rest. But then, from far away and yet too, too close, there was the first scream. I took renewed interest in my bonds. More screams came, and went on for what seemed a very long time before stopping.

And then my cell door opened.

Hands grabbed me, removed the rope around my ankles, and then had to carry me anyway because my legs were numb. I felt and heard my toes drag over wood, across a doorjamb, and then leave trails in the dirt. Over wood again, and I was put upon my feet. The guards held me up. My gag and blindfold were removed, and I stood before the captain of the beastmen, the badge of rank on his shoulders the same as that in our army. My hands were unbound and my clothes removed, the guards frowning in displeasure at the wetness of my pants. But what else could they expect after hours without relief? They tossed them onto a long, narrow table set against the wall. There were other clothes piled on the table. Murdock's clothes.

They discovered the knife at my back and removed it while the captain whistled in appreciation. "Such a well-armed emissary," he mocked, enjoying the moment. He took the knife and unsheathed it. "Well made. And very sharp."

The beastman captain was sitting at his desk in front of me, a lamp burning in either corner. A fire crackled merrily on the hearth. The two guards bound me into a wooden chair and then took position by the door behind me. I was naked. For the first time I noticed that a strange smell permeated the room.

"I am Captain Mendel of the Border Watch. And you are Mr. Arnold Brant, or so the Healer says. Are you ready, Mr. Brant? Do you feel very brave, or would you like to talk?"

Of course I was willing to talk. Women, diplomacy, the military secrets of Kenesee. I was willing to tell him anything he wanted to know. I opened my mouth and a croak came out of my parched throat.

"Nothing to say? Too bad . . ."

A guard took a poker from the fireplace. Its tip had been resting in the glowing embers.

"You're shivering," observed the captain. "Cold, no doubt. We'll warm you up."

I figured out what the smell in the air was. Burnt flesh. Some men prefer stoicism under adversity. I found out it helps to scream. The guardsman removed the poker from my armpit and put it back into the fire.

"Anything to say?" smiled the captain, his hands folded contentedly on the desk before him.

I could only gasp for breath and try to live with the frightful ache from my side.

He went to the narrow table and began sifting through the stack of clothes which had been piled there. He found the leather envelope and opened it. "And what is this? Another note from your King, just like your friend had. And the King's signature! Such a nice forgery." He tore the paper in two. "Now, Mr. Brant. Who are you?"

"You have . . . my name," I croaked.

He raised an eyebrow and the guard picked up the poker.

"Uhh . . . what would . . . you like to know?"

The guard applied the poker and I passed out.

It would be nice to say I awoke in my cell, but such was not the case. Water was thrown in my face, and an invigorating slap across the cheeks made me open my eyes. I was in the same chair facing my tormentor. The nightmare had not ended. I must have been hallucinating, for the captain was taking on all the characteristics I had noted in drawings of the beastmen. Even his fangs were growing larger.

"No one gets off that easily, my boy. You must be thirsty." A bucket of water was placed on the floor before me.

"I'm . . . willing to talk. What do you want to know?"

"There's plenty of time for that. First, a drink."

My bonds to the chair were loosened, hands pushed down my head and stuck it deep within the bucket. I held my breath, but they held me longer. The captain's entertainment continued in one variation or another for a long time, fire and water apparently being his favorites. It was not a noble thought, but some small part of me prayed that he would seek variety and pick Jason or Black for his fun.

At last I sprawled limp in the chair, choking, half drowned, various burns dotting my armpits and sides, while Mendel stood over me, my knife in his hand. He trailed the point gently over my genitals, along my belly and chest, up to my face. Then he slashed downward, the blade cutting my cheek open from ear to chin. For one brief moment it didn't hurt, and I felt relief. At least I still had my eyes and my manhood. Then I felt regret, for my face was spoiled. And finally, the pain started. It was not so bad. The burns still hurt worse, but I screamed anyway. No use disappointing him.

Besides, I never did enjoy seeing my own blood.

"Mendel!"

The voice came from behind me. I heard the two guards snap to attention and turned my head to see. In the doorway stood another beastman, tall and powerfully built, his face fierce and menacing. Another angry beastman. Just what I needed. I slid off the chair and flopped onto the floor.

"Saluting is still regulation," the beastman in the doorway said. "Or have you decided it doesn't apply to you?"

Captain Mendel reluctantly touched his forehead.

"Now," said the newcomer, "what are you doing?"

"We captured some hairless ones," said the captain. "I was questioning them. Normal procedures—Major."

The newcomer took a breath, held it, and then dismissed the guards and slammed the door behind them. "Normal procedures," the major said scornfully. "I talked to Sergeant Peterson. These may not be thieves, you fool. Your friends on the Council may not want to help you if the hairless ones are who they say."

I managed to lift my head. Blood had trickled into my mouth and I spat it out.

The major looked at me. "Who is he?"

"He says he's Arnold Brant," the captain replied without interest.

I tried to talk, coughed, spat again, and finally gasped an answer. "I am Prince Arn of the House of Brant . . . and second heir . . . to the throne of Kenesee."

The major looked down at my naked groin, saw the birthmark, and rolled his eyes heavenward. "Aughh. The lost son of Reuel. That breaks it. What have you done to him?"

There was a bit of doubt in the captain's manner. The reprimand and my claim were perhaps having their effect. "Nothing serious. A few burns. A cut. He may have a scar."

The major came low and studied the wounds. "If these are who they say, King Reuel will just love this. His son's face slashed open. Have you done anything to the Healer?"

"No, Major," he said defensively.

"Good. Get him in here. And the others?"

"Just the magician. At least, that's what he says he is. We did about the same to him."

"And who might he be? The King's High Wizard?"

"No. He claims to be the leader. Says he's Murdock, an emissary."

The major sighed. "Wonderful. Just wonderful. Get the Healer."

* * *

Jason came in looking doubtfully at the beastmen, and then he saw me. He turned angrily to our captors. "Well, Major Kren, had enough fun for one night, or am I to be next?" He came to me and examined the wounds. "I need my medical kit."

Kren nodded and a guard went out for it. The major began to pace up and down. "Sorry, Jason. I wasn't here. Is this really Prince Arn?"

"Yes. And a lovely scar he'll have, too," he confirmed, still furious. "The King will be most pleased, I'm sure."

"Murdock," I gasped. "He may need help."

"All right. There's nothing here I can do that won't wait. Kren, let me see the magician. Get the boy into bed and keep him warm. And I'll want hot water and clean linen." I hadn't intended for Jason to leave me, but just to know that Murdock would need him too. Next time I would keep my mouth shut.

The two guards came back in at the major's call. "Help him back to his room." They untied me and began to haul me up, touching my burnt skin. I howled.

The major yelled. "Gently, you idiots."

I let them take me.

Sleep is a wonderful restorative. Unfortunately, you never get it when you need it. After the beastmen left me in my room, I lay breathing heavily and was allowed to fully savor the pain. My sides were burned, my cheek slashed, and with each movement the pain went from a sharp throb to a blazing lance.

After a while Jason and Black entered. The healer applied salve to my burns, cleaned the knife wound, and stitched it closed.

"How is Murdock?" I asked, wincing.

The healer tied the last stitch and cut the thread. "He'll live, although he started going into shock on me. Mostly burns. Our host had more time with him, you see, and he isn't a spring chicken anymore."

"Are there many like that one—the Captain?"

"Some. Perhaps too many. Why? You think only the beastmen use such methods? As for the Captain, at least he has a motive. He lost his father and brother during the King's little visit to the Beastwood ten years ago."

The healer gave me a powder and insisted I drink an entire pitcher of water. The medicine worked up to a point, but a steady ache still throbbed with each pulse of blood—easily enough to keep me awake. Jason left, and I listened to Black pacing up and down beside me, lost in thought. Perhaps I dozed, but I don't think so. It was a very long night.

The next morning they gave us hard rolls and butter—which I could barely chew, given my wound—and then the beastmen brought us out into the center of a clearing surrounded by a half dozen large cabins. The wagon and our horses stood ready in the center. I guessed at the cabin where I had been tortured the night before, and felt very little inclination to see the inside by daylight.

Two beastmen emerged from it, and I recognized the major and the captain.

They brought out Murdock on a stretcher—a smile turning to a grimace as they moved him. "Well, my friends, here we are again," he stated with a weak smile. "I fear all of my journeys in the Beastwood will be conducted in the back of the Healer's wagon."

His face had a gray pallor to it. He noticed our looks. "Have no fear. I'm fated to die of old age, a withered old man too feeble to chase the ladies. But how are you, Arn? Up and about. That's good." He was placed in the wagon. Jason saw that he was settled comfortably, then climbed aboard the driver's seat.

The major came up to us. "Your pardon, Prince Arn and Colonel Black. They said you were both fit to ride. Blindfolded, it will have to be. I have no choice in that matter. But you won't be tied if I have your word not to escape or attempt to see your path."

I looked at Black, who nodded. "Agreed."

"Good." They brought up the blindfolds and covered our eyes. Black mounted, his saddle creaking as leather stretched. But when I extended an arm to my horse's saddle horn it would go no more than halfway up. The pain in my armpit was too great.

"Reach, Arn," Jason ordered. "Stretch the skin, or it will heal tight."

My hand went up again, higher, three-quarters of the way,

and then I cried out. On the third try I grasped the horn and held on to keep from collapsing. Hands grasped and lifted me into the saddle. "Steady, lad," whispered the voice of the major, very close, as I fought a wave of dizziness and struggled to stay in the saddle. I steadied.

"Good enough," cried the healer. "You'll be all right."

Others mounted around us, and at last we set off. The sun was full out, and I felt its warmth on my right cheek, the good one, and realized we must be heading north. I was strangely comforted to know I had accomplished this tiny bit of reasoning.

"We're traveling north," I whispered to Black, who rode beside me.

"Northwest," he grunted back softly. He was correct, of course.

"The path takes many turns," said the major from behind us, amused.

"Where are we going?" I asked.

He spurred up next to us. It must have been a real road to ride with three horses abreast. The beastmen were accomplished, and I wondered how much force would really be necessary to conquer them. Perhaps more than any thought.

"Travel is not too difficult for you, Prince Arn?"

"Painful, Major . . . but not too difficult."

"I do regret what happened," he stated. There was a ring of honesty in his voice, and a note of embarrassment.

"Our purpose remains the same," I assured him.

A light wind rustled the treetops and we rode on.

Our travel through the Beastwood was rapid, yet the days passed slowly. Each morning and afternoon we were in saddle without being able to see a thing, so that we could only listen to the noises of our passage. Sometimes we could hear the gobble of wild turkeys in the trees. Once there was the howling of wolves. But of inhabitants we heard not a sound, though at times I thought I heard a faint mooing, as if a cow were shut up in a barn. If indeed we were passing through areas in which the beastmen lived, then their civil discipline was excellent, for besides our escort we heard neither man, nor woman, nor child of the beastmen.

In the evenings we were taken inside buildings still blind-folded, put together, and allowed to see only when we were safely within a shuttered room. There is little military infor-mation to be gained from a ceiling, floor, and four walls. On these matters Jason had no comment. Nothing of our location, nor where we stopped at night, nor aught else of the beastmen would the healer speak, though he knew the ways and traveled with open eyes.

After the second day Murdock was up and about, moving a good bit slower than he usually did, favoring the side of his wound and moving his arms carefully. But the pallor was gone from his face, and he was able to sit next to Jason during the trip. Like me, he exercised carefully, stretching his burns. He had a remarkable constitution for his age.

We arrived—somewhere—at last, in time to be led into another building, placed in a room, and finally left alone. The blindfolds came off yet again. I had gained a great deal of sympathy for the blind in the last three days.

Our previous quarters had been bare rooms. This was far different. The chamber was of polished oak, big enough for four beds, a round table, padded chairs, drawers, a chest, and a washstand with two basins. The beds were large, with soft flannel sheets and firm pillows. Thick woolen blankets were laid on top and tucked in at the corners.

A large fireplace held crackling logs and a pot of hot cider. The windows had glass panes larger than I had ever seen be-fore, but some covering had been put over the outside to pre-vent our seeing. A doorway led into a bath chamber with a shower bath and water from metal pipes that led into the ceil-ing. Our chambers at the castle in Kingsport seemed rough and crude beside this room. A beastman collected our clothes and gave us bed clothes for sleeping. I threw myself onto a bed and let its comfort envelop me. I had found heaven.

The next morning a knock on the door woke us and beast-men brought in our garments. The clothes were clean, our boots polished. Trays of food were served by a polite beastman who greeted us with a courteous ''Good morning'' and cleaned up afterwards. We ate slowly, and then waited pa-tiently for the summons. Possibilities and options were discussed, but all was speculation before the event.

And then a beastman knocked, stepped in, and spoke.

"The Council orders your appearance now."

Our waiting was over.

6

The Beastmen

We did not have far to go. Escorted by a dozen guards, we went down a flight of stairs, through a corridor, and into a meeting hall. The room was more austere than our guest quarters, but still comfortable. Windows set high in the walls let in a gray light but provided no view, while a fireplace offered warmth. Behind a long table five beastmen waited impassively, studying us. The center figure was large; not fat, not tall, but solid, with the bearing of a soldier. All five had pelts that were graying to one degree or another, the central figure more so than the rest.

We advanced and stood behind four chairs facing the Council. Jason was on the far left, then Murdock, myself, and Black on my right.

The healer gave the slightest bow and commenced his introduction.

"Councilmen, I am Jason Kendall, better known as Jason the Healer. I believe you all know of me, and most of you I have met before. I have kept my word and revealed nothing of the Beastwood to outsiders. Only a handful in Kenesee know that I am able to enter and leave your lands, and the reason for that privilege. At the request of King Reuel of Kenesee, I have brought emissaries to speak to you. This is Wizard Desjardins Murdock, by some called the 'Magnificent.'"

At this, there were smirks by some of the beastmen.

"He is an important magician of his realm and appointed High Emissary by the King in this matter. Next is Prince Arn of Kenesee, second son of King Reuel, the same who was lost as an infant and found as a boy. Last is Colonel Black, lately a member of the King's Royal Guards and now with the Army of Kenesee. He is a man of wisdom and ability. I thank you for your trust in allowing us to come before you today."

The center beastman gestured to the chairs. After we had been seated, he leaned forward and folded his hands upon the table. He introduced each of the other councilmen before getting to himself. "I am Sokol, Senior Councilman of the Beastmen. Yes, that is what we call ourselves. Beastmen. You have given us the name in fear and scorn, and we have made it a title of honor. I would say welcome, but such remains to be seen." He looked at me, and I imagined he was examining the bandage covering the right side of my face. "We have heard that your coming was marred by a lack of civility. This is an embarrassment to us. You have our regrets for this, and I assure you it was not our will. Rather, let us blame the enmity that has long existed between our peoples. We will hear you, and ponder any message you may bring from your King."

Murdock nodded in respect. One might never know he had been bedridden just a few days before. "We shall pass on your sentiment to our King when we return, and add our own gratitude for the hospitality that has since been shown us."

Very nicely worded, I thought—especially the part about returning. Let them know it would be profitable to send us back in one piece regardless of the results. Murdock's talents went beyond magic. Certainly, I felt his good will and wisdom spread through me as he talked. Murdock's charm spell was working normally, but his effect went beyond that. His voice resonated with a dignity I had not heard before. And his words were skillfully chosen, his speech flowing like verse. Murdock The Magnificent? It could well be. We looked at our companion with new respect.

"Our message," he continued, "is one we bring with sadness. Various lands have made alliance and threaten us with war. We fear that Spring, at the latest, will bring invasion and battle. Kenesee is united, and our army grows stronger than ever before.

"Yet the combination of our enemies is great, and we too may need allies. Virginia, Arkan, Texan, Mexico, and the Isles have all made claims against us. Some of these nations are far from your borders, and you may wonder why this conflict concerns the Beastwood. Yet, I am sure you have heard of the attitudes of the Texans towards other peoples. They are slavers. If their army bordered your forest, what action might they take against your people? This is why you must consider the effects of an Alliance victory.

"The history of strife between the Beastwood and Kenesee is unfortunate, and blame is too great to credit to either nation alone. Ignorance, more than ill will, is at the root. We would have such enmity put to rest. Perhaps, if you deem it proper, open commerce might benefit both our lands. But that lies in the future. For now, we ask for an alliance between the Kingdom and the Beastwood. With us together, our enemies would have little hope of success."

The beastmen eyed each other with a variety of expressions.

The senior councilman leaned back in his chair and stroked the pelt on his chin. It was like a man stroking his beard. "Your proposal is one we thought you might make. But still, it sounds strange to our ears. Why should we aid you? Few of us would weep to hear of hairless slaughtering hairless. You would have us weaken ourselves, sacrifice our finest men, so that your King may retain his throne."

Murdock shook his head. "The kingdom has made mistakes in the past, and doubtless will make mistakes in the future. No nation is infallible, nor any man. But slowly we learn. Those of the Alliance threaten not just Kenesee but the Beastwood as well. Should we be defeated, do you think their armies will stop at your borders? Their desire to conquer would be strengthened with success, and they will plunge into your forest to remove the last threat to their dominance.

"Your army has shown its strength and skill, but can you defeat three, four, or five battle-hardened armies that have already tasted victory? Even if you fend them off—of which there is little hope, for their numbers would overwhelm you— could it be done without seeing much of your land laid waste? It has been fifty years since the last slave was freed in Kenesee, and no man may own another there now. The Texans embrace slavery. Our people would be made slaves. That is the best your people might expect at their hands.''

The senior councilman hesitated. The beastman to his right—whose pelt was almost as gray as the senior's—spoke up bitterly. ''And what would have been our fate if your invasion had succeeded ten years ago? Peace? Friendship? Freedom? The freedom of death, I think. You wait until you are threatened, and suddenly worry about our fate. Where were you before?''

Murdock bowed his head, and then lifted it slowly. ''We cannot undo the past. Yet we learned that the Beastwood is not inhabited by scattered tribes plundering villages, but an honorable and prosperous people scorned and blamed and maligned unjustly. The question is one of survival—yours as well as ours. If this is not enough, I have also this pledge from our King. For your aid, we will recognize the sovereignty of the Beastwood. Never again will an army of Kenesee cross its borders, unless it be requested in time of need. Any citizen of Kenesee entering your realm will know that he falls also under your law. By treaty and by word, the King will pledge his honor to this.''

The overweight councilman on the end sneered. ''Honor among the hairless. There's something new under the sun.''

The senior lifted a hand for silence. He looked at me. ''You would guarantee such an alliance?''

I swallowed. It did not seem the time for a humorous quip. Nor a lie. ''The King has taken great risk . . . in sending us here. I would not have come, had I a choice. I do not want to stay here. But I am here. And I will stay . . . if necessary.''

The senior seemed to accept it, regrets and all.

He looked at Black. ''And you, Colonel Black. You fought us.''

Black stared back. ''Yes, sir.''

''It is said that a Sergeant Black of the Royal Guards helped frustrate my plans for the destruction of the Kenesee Army.''

''King Reuel saved the Army of Kenesee,'' Black replied simply.

The beastman nodded. ''Do you hate us?''

''One.''

''That I can understand. What about the rest of us?''

''No.''

''Why not?'' Sokol leaned forward again, waiting.

Black's answer was calm and unhurried. "I am a soldier. I fight my King's enemies. Your soldiers fought well, if without mercy. But they have not given me reason to hate them."

The senior nodded. "A soldier's answer. So perhaps we are not enemies." He shifted his attention to Jason. "Well, Healer, what do you say?"

Jason shrugged. "I have brought them. That is my part in it."

"They are your kind. Can your King be trusted?"

Jason stood up and strode to the fire. His back was to both the council and us. "All men are my kind. And I have no King." He turned around. "But I know these men, and I know Reuel. They speak the truth as they know it."

"We will note your statement. Are there any questions from the Council?"

Another councilman wearing spectacles nodded. "Were we to agree to this alliance, what aid would you expect of us?"

Murdock looked at Black, who took his cue and answered. "Only you know the size of your army. But ten thousand men would not be too many."

Most of the councilmen greeted this figure with equanimity. The fat one on the end seemed about to have a fit of apoplexy. "Why, to provide that number we would have to strip—"

"Enough!" interrupted the senior, giving the councilman a hard stare that made him look down at his hands. Then the senior turned his attention back to us. "We will discuss the matter and call you for our decision."

We were dismissed.

Guards escorted us back to our room, and when the door shut Murdock fell into a chair and sighed deeply. "Now we shall see."

Black sat down. "Your argument was well given, wizard."

Murdock shook his head. "All of you did well. You replied truthfully to the questions, John, and I think the Senior Councilman respected your words. He was a soldier. Perhaps that will help us."

A beastman guard knocked. "The Council would like to speak to the Healer."

Jason rose heavily, and for the first time I saw that he was older than Murdock, and feeling the years that weighed on him. He gave us a shrug and left.

Black lit his pipe. "What do you think?" he asked the wizard.

"Surely," I offered, "they have to see the danger too."

"They do," said Murdock. "And they see other dangers as well. We are asking them to bet the long odds. If the kingdom wins alone, they are no worse off than before. If we lose, the Alliance may be content and leave them alone. If they join us and we lose, their participation may only increase the wrath of the Alliance. If their army marches out to aid us, Kenesee might triumph while their own army is destroyed. What looks simple to us is very difficult for them."

"Then there is no hope," I concluded.

"There's always hope. Forlorn, perhaps, but it had to be tried." He laid down with a groan, closed his eyes, and did not stir. Quickly, his breathing became regular and deep.

It was an hour later that Jason rejoined us. Murdock's bed creaked and he rose up on one arm, grimacing as the skin was stretched too far.

"They wanted to know more about your mission," the healer answered to our unasked question. "So I told them what I knew."

"Did it make any difference?" Murdock asked hopefully.

Jason threw up a hand in a gesture of uncertainty. "It was hard to tell what they thought. They admired your performance, wizard. They were impressed that Arn had come. And Sokol likes Colonel Black—soldier to soldier. But what they think of your proposal, I don't know." And so the waiting went on.

The glow of light coming through the painted-over windows faded away with the hours. It was perhaps dusk when the door opened again and a beastman stood beckoning us to our final visit with the council.

We sat in the same chairs as before. The faces of the council members were impassive and gave no clue to their decision. Perhaps the time they had taken was a good sign. A slow decision meant they had given serious attention to our request, and perhaps even that some of them supported it. Then again, perhaps they'd had a long lunch and afternoon nap.

The senior was courteous in his formality. "We regret having kept you waiting so long. It was not without cause."

He paused briefly, studied some papers before him, and then resumed. "Your request for an alliance and aid to combat your enemies has been considered. We have talked much on this matter, and the healer had much to say in your favor. He did not hesitate to say what he thinks to the Council. We have never had cause to doubt his word, nor do we now. Yet you, long our enemy, ask us to fight beside you against those we have never seen. You ask us to strip our borders and leave them undefended to send our army far from the Beastwood, where luck or treachery could destroy it. You ask us to become involved in your wars when all we have ever wanted was to be left alone under the leaves of our forest."

He stared at us dispassionately. "The risk is too great."

Black shifted ever so slightly in his chair. His eyes panned the room, as if he were estimating distances and odds. And that was typical John Black. All he had to do was overcome the councilmen, kill the guards outside, find horses, elude the entire beastman army and escort us out of the Beastwood. No problem.

The senior noticed him, then continued. "When you return to your King—" He paused and met Black's eyes, while Murdock seemed to give the slightest sigh of relief. "—tell him that we do not agree to an alliance with Kenesee. Not now. But tell him also that we ally with no nation. He need fear no attack from this quarter. Nor will we take advantage of any situation which leaves you weak against us. I say again that we wish sovereignty over no lands outside our borders. We hold our forest inviolate and will destroy any who enter. Do you understand?"

The wizard bowed his head in response. "We do. The King will be saddened at your decision, but he will also understand the grave concerns which had to be weighed. Your pledge of neutrality is respected and welcome. I hope it bodes well for the future of our two people."

The senior nodded. "Perhaps it is time for the barriers to come down between us. Commerce might begin after this— this 'situation'—is resolved. For that purpose we will send an emissary back with you, if you agree." The senior gestured, and a guard left the room. "He will return with you to discuss areas of mutual profit."

"And to observe the course of events," Murdock added with a knowing smile.

"Yes. That too. We would like to get him back alive, please. Also, he will be permitted to send occasional dispatches to us. We have, ahh, friends who can accomplish this, and such matters can be easily arranged. That is the offer and the conditions."

The beastmen could deliver messages across the length of Kenesee? Interesting.

Murdock pondered the request. He looked at me and then at Black, and after a moment he nodded. We knew little of the Beastwood, but the beastmen already knew much about us. We had little to lose and much to gain. "Who is this emissary?" asked Murdock cautiously.

"An officer of our border watch. I believe you know Major Kren." The senior gestured and we turned to look. Standing inside the doorway was my rescuer from torture. He did not look happy.

Murdock smiled. "A military man to discuss diplomacy and trade. Well, so be it. Your emissary, Major Kren, may accompany us. Hopefully his reports will please you."

"There is one final condition," said the senior. "He must be allowed to return whenever he feels his mission is concluded, or for any temporary visit he feels necessary."

"I believe all conditions will be acceptable to the King. If not, the Major will be escorted safely back to your border. I can assure you of that much at least."

"Done. If you are not too weary, you will leave tomorrow morning. All your belongings and weapons will be returned to you at the border."

And that was the end of our meeting with the council.

We came out from the Beastwood without incident, the beastmen fading away in the undergrowth and leaving only Kren to accompany us. Apparently our tormentor, Captain Mendel, did have friends in high places. He remained with his company, while Kren lost his command. Kren had not been pleased about leaving his Border Watch battalion. But as he told us, the scent of adventure was too exhilarating to stay in low spirits. He did as much about his appearance as he could, putting on a winter hat that covered not only his head and neck, but had a flap that went around his mouth and jaw so that only his nose and eyes peeped out. He did not use the flap yet, but pulled up his hood until it extended far over his face and cast it in shadow.

He looked around for approval. "Will this do?"

Murdock nodded. "Unless we have a warm day. It serves very well, Major."

We arrived at the small town of Benton without incident. To our surprise, the Fourth Squad of the royal guards was camped beside the road outside the town, while children from the houses and even several adults stood fascinated, watching the guardsmen go about such unusual tasks as darning their socks and washing their faces.

Corporal Jenkins came out to the road and greeted us with a casual salute and a relieved grin while the rest of the guards hurriedly fell into formation. "Glad you made it back, gentlemen. The King sent us out three weeks ago to stand ready in case you needed us. More important, a courier is waiting at the inn with a message. There's trouble to the south, rumors of Easterner troop movements. Prince Robert is going further east along the coast road to Mooresville to guard the border."

Murdock frowned. "So. It begins. Well, we'll know soon enough. Let's get a room and see this courier."

The messenger was a bright-faced boy named Eric from the House of Brant—a second cousin. He recognized me and smiled broadly before presenting the mail pouch to Murdock. A look of relief crossed his face as he handed it over.

"Well done, Eric."

He beamed. "Yes, sir. Happy to be of service." He bowed his way out, caught his thumb in the door frame with a yelp, and finally managed to shut the door behind him.

Murdock suppressed his laughter until the boy was safely out of hearing. "He'll be a fine young man—if he doesn't destroy himself. Well, these bear the royal seal. Let's see what the King has to say."

Kren stood up. "I presume you would like me to wait outside."

Murdock looked up from the pouch in his hand, and considered the beastman carefully. "Well, I suppose this is where we must start. Trust, and all that. If Prince Arn has no objection, I will ask you to remain.''

I could see what the wizard was trying to accomplish. If the major's reports to the Beastwood were to make any difference, he had to be on our side. Distrust would not endear us to him.

I looked around. Jason and Black both nodded, so I did too. "I agree."

Very tricky, this matter of diplomacy.

"Thank you," said Kren, sincerely. He pulled back his hood and unbuttoned the chin strap of his cap. "I think I'll be very tired of this disguise before long."

We pulled chairs from the table and arranged them around the hearth, where the fire was just starting to take hold of the split wood. Murdock broke the seal, unfolded two sheets of fine paper, and began to read.

> *From: Reuel Brant, King of Kenesee*
> *The King's Castle, Kingsport*
> *November 10th, 2652*
>
> *To: Desjardins Murdock, Wizard and Emissary*
> *Extraordinary*
> *Arnold Brant, Prince of Kenesee*
> *Jason Kendall, Healer*
> *and/or John Black, Temporary Colonel,*
> *Army of Kenesee*

Assuming you have returned to Kenesee and will receive this letter without undue delay or difficulty, greetings, and my joyful thanks upon the completion of your mission and your safe return.

I trust your journey was not too unpleasant. While I held little hope of your success, I still feel it important that the effort was made. Who knows, your tidings may be such as to surprise us all and give greater promise in the hard months ahead. In any case, please send a report of your mission immediately. It is essential that we know the results as we make our plans and respond to enemy movements.

The Alliance already threatens us with feints. These may be to force us to mobilize early, or throw us off guard and dull our response when the real campaign begins in the spring. Or, they may be the opening moves of a fall or winter offensive. We do not yet know which is the case.

We have reports that the Easterners have made troop movements along the coast road towards our border. Robert is at Greenville and will advance to Mooresville to watch the coast road. The King's Call was issued to the cavalry regiments from Greenville, Knox, and Loren. They should soon be joining Robert.

I remain at Kingsport. Ships of the Isles were seen off our coast three days ago. Our enemies are not such fools as to show themselves before they are ready, and so I take this threat as a feint. Our fleet is patrolling the coast, but so far the enemy has not been seen again.

My worry is not for the south yet, but for our eastern border. Graven informs me that he is uneasy about the Rift Gates. I can tell you no more. Duke Santini at Knox is being informed and will ride out there as soon as he can. But he is far from the valley and has many other duties. Therefore, I entrust you with a new mission. Journey in haste to the Rift Gates and ensure that all is well. If trouble is found, you must respond with all the energy and skill you have to meet any threat. The Gates must be kept secure. Otherwise, an army could debouch at any time, devastate the northern counties, and march south into Robert's rear.

You understand our concerns. Now act immediately upon this information, and let us hope nothing more is involved than a wearisome detour of inspection before your return to Kingsport. KEEP ME INFORMED.

I entrust command of this new mission to Prince Arn. I know you will all give him your loyalty and obedience. Jason Kendall, my thanks to you for your help. You are not required to partake in this new task, although I hope you will follow and keep yourself ready for need.

My blessings upon you all.

> *Signed, Reuel Brant,*
> *King of Kenesee*
> *By the hand of Frederick Taylor*
> *Recorder, King's Castle*

No one spoke for a moment. I was not happy. Besides not returning to Kingsport, besides facing another potentially dangerous mission, the king had found an opportunity to test my powers of command. Such opportunities I could do without.

Kren broke the silence. "Most interesting. I look forward to meeting your King."

"Oh, yes," Murdock agreed, relieved. "Well, I suppose we must get you to Kingsport somehow. Perhaps you might accompany the messenger."

The beastman hesitated. "Umm—I'd rather go with you instead. A brief delay should not matter and, quite honestly, I'd feel safer with you than with the boy."

"But I'm sure a sheriff or two might be found to guard you. You'd be quite well protected," suggested Murdock.

"And so I would have said of you before I found you under the kind attention of Captain Mendel. Now, I'm not so sure."

"You have a point. What do you think, Arn?"

"If you think it's best."

"So be it. I'll write up a report tonight, and Eric can leave with it tomorrow—if that's all right with you, Arn? Would you like to read it first?"

"No—" Then I remembered my duty. If I was going to be responsible for things, I at least wanted to know what was happening. "I mean yes. Let me read it."

"Good decision," Murdock affirmed. "And with that, my responsibility will be finished. And yours is just begun, I'm afraid. What do we do now?"

Indeed, what to do now. The Rift Gates were an important part of the kingdom's defenses, overlooking the rift itself and guarding against any invasion from the northeast. The rift was reached by a peaceful valley of meadows and fields sheltered north and south by slopes covered with trees. Through the narrowing valley ran a paved road, the remains of an Old World highway. The road led to a wall of battlements and towers which had been built on the edge of the rift and stretched from one side of the valley to the other, dominating the passage. A gate of two wooden portals allowed trade between northern Kenesee and Virginia, and lent the entire work of stone its name: Rift Gates.

The rift itself was right below the wall, an immense chasm formed during the Cataclysm. It was a hundred feet wide, three hundred deep in spots, and stretched almost two hundred miles as it cut north and south through the mountains, forming a natural boundary between Virginia and Kenesee. It was about a hundred feet deep before the Rift Gates. The eastern side of the rift had crumbled at that point, forming a steep causeway across the chasm. A road leading up to the portals allowed for light trade in peaceful times. The occasional traveler used the Gates for easy passage, although heavily laden wagons had a difficult time with the steepness of the causeway. In two hundred years the Rift Gates had never fallen to enemy attack. Then again, they had never been attacked.

"Any suggestions?" I asked. At least I had learned how to ask for advice. A small virtue—or perhaps not so small.

Black cleaned out his pipe. "I think we should rest here tonight, Arn. We only have a few hours of daylight, and it might be best to make some plans. Maps would be helpful. Jenkins should have several. I'll get them."

"Yes. Thank you. Jason, will you come with us?"

"No, I don't think so. We're out of the Beastwood now, and you don't need me for this mission. There are many villages still waiting for a healer to visit. I may see you again as there is need."

"We haven't yet thanked you for your help."

"No matter," the healer grumbled. "I'm as responsible for this mess as any and—well, let's hope it's all for the best."

Responsible? His words puzzled me, but I did not pursue the matter further. I had enough to worry about. We ordered beer and waited until Black returned. The wizard obtained pen and ink and a tidy pile of paper, then sat staring in distaste. "I hate writing reports. I don't suppose any of you would care to do it instead? Ah well, I thought not."

Black strode back in with a soft leather case, and soon spread a large-scale map of northern Kenesee on the table. We brought our chairs to the table and sat down.

Black measured out spans on the map. "Without Jason's wagon, we can make Loren in ten days by horseback, at most. We have the Sixth Infantry Regiment headquartered there, and any message from the valley will have to pass through Loren. From the town it's only one day's ride to the valley, or two if the Sixth Regiment marches with us. Arn, if you're in agreement, I recommend we leave at dawn."

Jason saw us off the next morning, his awning extended as he set up his little office for the day. We thanked him while he boiled a pot of water and laid out instruments. He took the thanks as a matter of course. "I guess it worked out as well as could be expected. Take care of yourselves. If there's war, I'll be there."

We rode with Eric until we reached Knox, and then he waved farewell as he took the southwest road toward Redbank on the way to Kingsport. He carried Murdock's report in his saddlebag. At Knox we stopped for lunch with Duke Santini, explaining our recent journey and the new mission we had been handed. My bandage was off, and the duke was quite solicitous about the healing slash mark. Murdock had removed the stitches the day before, and had given me cause to practice my screaming again.

But it was when Kren removed his cap that the nobleman found something to really take his interest. "A beastman!" exclaimed the duke. "Imagine that. A beastman in my castle." Eventually, we got him past our recent trip and to the business at hand. The duke had not noted the urgency of the king's message to him. He had been prepared to send a small party to the Rift Gates for an inspection, but our assignment seemed to emphasize that the king took the threat most seriously. He promised to march with his household troops within twenty-four hours. If there was nothing to it, then the men would have had a good training march. If trouble waited, he would be ready to respond. We left him to his preparations and took the east gate out of town.

We had been in the saddle for long days when we arrived after midnight at the barred gates of Loren, the last major town before the Rift Gates. A horn sounded from the wall, and a head peered over, framed in the moonlight.

"Who goes there?" the gate watch leader called out.

Corporal Jenkins cupped a hand to his mouth. "Prince Arn of Kenesee."

We were put up at the town hall while the guards stayed at the inn next door. Mayor Jones joined us in a meeting room where we were given a hurriedly prepared but welcome supper of hot soup and bread. The mayor was a bookish man, which did not prevent him from serving as the colonel of the Sixth

Infantry Regiment. Quite a decent leader, supposedly, in spite of his looks, and one of the stalwart company commanders of the Beastwood Campaign. He accepted our explanation of Major Kren's presence with less wonder than the duke had, but still gave the beastman furtive glances throughout the meal. This didn't prevent him from voicing his immediate interest.

"Prince Arn, may I ask why you're here?"

"Of course. The King has some concern for the eastern border."

"Mayor, has there been any word from the Rift Gates?" Black asked directly.

"The Gates?" Mayor Jones repeated, tearing his eyes away from Kren. "No, nothing from the Gates or the valley. Everything's been quiet. Is something wrong?"

"We're here to find out," Black replied. "Has anything been reported amiss the last few days? Anything at all?"

The mayor thought a moment. "No. Nothing."

"Well, thank goodness for that," Murdock expressed for us all. Maybe we could get a decent night's sleep.

We had almost completed the meal when the door opened and the gate watch leader entered, hat in hand. He was out of breath, as if he'd run all the way from the town gates. "Sorry to bother you gentlemen. But there's someone else just showed up and is waiting outside the town. Says he's from the garrison at the Rift Gates—"

The man paused for breath, swallowed, and then grimly concluded his message.

"They're under attack."

7

Valley March

The man from the Rift Gates was disheveled and dirty when he came into the room, his dark face drawn with fatigue. On his brown army uniform he wore the "vigilant sword" patch of the Gate Keepers, the permanent garrison of the Rift Gates. His eyes widened when he saw us, though Kren had already hastily covered up.

"This is the Prince," the mayor indicated to him.

He looked impressed. "Nasty scar, there. You're Prince Robert?"

"No. I'm the other one. Now, what's happened?"

He started to sway. Black pushed him into a chair and stuck a mug in his hands. Presently, he began to tell his tale. "I'm Carl Ash, Private, Third Squad, First Company of the Gate Keepers. Four or five days ago Wizard Leroy got worried and said things weren't right. Then he got bedridden with pains in his head. Said the Easterners—those damn Virginians—were doing it. Their wizards, that is—"

Murdock banged his fist on the table. "That means they've slipped a few magicians close to the Gates. Leroy might have detected their presence, but would think them no danger to the Gates. At least, until they put up static. Then they could blanket him so that he couldn't detect the approach of military units. The headaches would be a typical side effect."

Private Ash looked none too happy about being interrupted, but listened quietly and once sure that Murdock had finished, continued his tale. He and a comrade had been on night patrol in the valley and were returning to the Gates when they noticed the woods were alive with soldiers carrying ladders and ropes. At great risk to themselves, they raised a cry to the sentries upon the battlements of the Gates, and the garrison was aroused just in time to meet the surprise attack. The first rush of the enemy actually put a few of them upon the battlements, but the garrison managed to push them off and turn back the first assault. After that, Ash and his comrade had to flee for their lives, and the other soldier fell to a Virginian arrow.

"I walked a ways until I came to a farmhouse," Ash continued. "I told the people to hide in the woods, took their plow horse from the barn, and rode all day until I got to Pulaski and warned the town. The men of the town were going to assemble their company and march for the valley. The captain said I should get a new horse and ride on to Loren to tell my story. And now I'm here."

"How many enemy were at the wall, Ash?" Black asked carefully.

The man considered. "Three, maybe four hundred that I saw, though more were coming out of the woods when I ran. I don't know. Oh, I forgot. I was almost taken by a party of a dozen or so, just a few miles further on. They were watching the road. I cut across a field and had to jump a stream. Never done that before, let me tell you."

Black pondered the information. "They didn't want anyone spreading the word. A good plan. Could have worked."

"They didn't plan on *me,*" Ash said proudly.

Murdock patted him on the shoulder. "The kingdom owes you a debt of gratitude."

Black nodded. "How long have you been a private?"

"Two years."

Black looked at me. Oh. "Well done," I said. "The King shall hear of your exploit . . . Corporal."

The man smiled in tired satisfaction.

Black paced up and down, his hands clasped behind his back. "The rift side of the Gates. Could they have launched a surprise attack from there too?"

"No," the new corporal said without hesitation. "We watch the rift carefully, and keep the trees and brush cut. No force could have snuck up without being seen. I think they counted on carrying the Gates by surprise from the valley. Since that failed, I bet they're moving up a force to the rift right now to try again. From both sides, this time.''

Black nodded reluctantly. ''I'm afraid you're probably right.'' He stopped pacing and stared at the fire a moment, then turned back to us. ''Arn, I recommend we call up the Sixth Regiment immediately. Mayor, how long will it take the regiment to assemble?''

''How long? Three days if we send out couriers now to the outlying companies.''

''Three days? That's too long. How many companies can be ready to march by dawn?''

We looked at each other. The mayor considered the question. ''The three companies of the town could be ready then,'' he answered.

''Then at dawn we march—'' Black stopped himself and looked at me. ''At least, that is my suggestion, Prince Arn. Time is critical. The garrison can't hold an attack from both sides.'' Black spoke with finality, and I accepted his judgment. If he hadn't been there, I probably would have waited for the entire regiment to assemble. But he was right. It was essential to reach the Gates.

I stood up. ''Mayor Jones.''

''Yes, sir?''

''Follow Colonel Black's advice.''

''But—yes, sir.'' He hurried out.

Kren had been silent up to this point. Now he spoke. ''You risk defeat in detail by marching before the regiment is together. They may have more men than you.''

''I've considered that,'' Black replied. ''But if they came over the mountains they can't have cavalry, and we have the guards. That's our edge. If they have only three or four hundred men, we can succeed.''

''And if they have more?''

''As you said,'' Black answered. ''We risk much, whatever we do.''

''But what about the regimental magician with the Easterners in the valley?'' I asked. ''Wouldn't he detect our unit as we approached?''

Black shook his head. ''Not if our own wizard lives up to his reputation. Murdock, can you neutralize their magician?''

Murdock grinned modestly. "Well, you know how I hate to brag—"

"We do?" asked Kren.

"—but I should be able to blanket a regimental wizard without too much problem."

"Ahhh," said the beastman. "Humility is such a rare virtue."

Shortly thereafter we could hear the town criers shouting the alert, their voices fading as they made their way down the streets of the town. Then a bell rang, a deep bong that came fatefully, signaling the end of the quiet night, the end of the peace, and the beginning of a new red dawn. Another bell rang, and another, and then all the church bells were ringing a call to war.

The beastman grinned. "Well, is this enough excitement for you, Wizard?"

"Quite enough," Murdock replied. "I like my adventures punctuated by rest at friendly inns. Unfortunately, such respite has been a bit short of late. And you, emissary? Sorry to delay the elegant court life of Kingsport?"

The beastman thought about it. "I think your party is more exciting right now. My only regret is that my battalion isn't here. You'd find it very useful."

"Doubtless," said Murdock. "But since we're freed of the heavy responsibilities of command, will you join me in drinking to the future? Nothing like a healing wound to develop a thirst. Which reminds me. Arn, time for ointment."

We stood on the stone porch of the town hall, watching as men in ones and twos scrambled in from the streets feeding the square, joining into little clusters abuzz with questions. Lamps and lanterns hung upon poles and doorways. By their light we could see more men come in, and more. The regimental flag and the three guidons of the companies appeared, and the men formed anew around the officer next to each. In one street a supply wagon with a team of four drew up, and then others behind it.

A glow from beyond the town wall betrayed sunrise. It was growing light by the time all were assembled. The night was cold, and the men's breath frosted in the chill air. They were arranged now in ordered ranks in the middle of the square, while dozens of women and children clustered around the edges of the formations. The men's uniforms were standard for the army's companies of foot. Over their coats they wore leather armor, while their heads were protected by leather helmets reinforced with metal plates. Over the armor the soldiers wore a brown tunic with a dark red regimental stripe that slashed across the chest from shoulder to waist. Each had a pack and bedroll. One company was armed with bows and carried large quivers of arrows, while the other two were armed with spear and shield. All carried a short sword at their side.

They watched us with curiosity. Word must have gotten out, for even in the shadowy corner in which he stood, the mysterious figure of Kren attracted their attention.

Mayor Jones, now in his role as colonel of the regiment, called the three companies to attention, introduced Black and me, and explained the situation quickly. He reached his conclusion. "And so, you march out now. I will be staying here to await the assembly of the other companies, and we will march to your aid as soon as possible. In my stead you have the honor of being commanded by a member of the Royal Family, Prince Arn of Kenesee, who has come to lead us in our fight and will now speak to you. Hooray for Prince Arn!"

The troops took up the hurrah without enthusiasm, and I couldn't blame them. Sleeping peacefully in your bed one minute and marching off to war the next does not promote good humor.

I stepped forward reluctantly and stood alone, hundreds watching me and waiting. I hadn't thought the mayor would ask me to speak. After one or two embarrassing episodes in my boyhood, the king had arranged that ceremonies not require my giving voice. This had worked well in most cases, except where enthusiastic hosts forgot themselves and invited me to speak.

Professor Wagner had once commented upon the problem. "Hmm. You know, Prince Arn, there was once a king with your affliction. Old World Europe. France."

"Really?" I asked with sudden interest. "What happened to him, Professor?"

"He was beheaded."

"I see. Good to know."

I still could not give a speech to hundreds of people, and found myself staring at the companies of the Sixth Regiment with a sinking feeling. The men began muttering as I glanced around. Murdock and Black looked at each other, then Black stepped up next to me and beckoned for silence.

"Men of the Sixth! I am Colonel John Black, advisor to Prince Arn and late of the Royal Guards." Some eyebrows went up in the ranks. Apparently the name of John Black was not unfamiliar to them. A goodly portion of the companies, especially the officers and noncoms, were still composed of Beastwood veterans. Their experienced leadership would be one of our advantages in the conflict ahead.

"Prince Arn," Black continued, his voice ringing out with authority, "has recently taken a wound in service of the kingdom, as you can all see!"

The wound was still a livid slash. There were murmurs from the ranks. One of the wittier men used a stage whisper, "Hooray for Prince Scar," and several of his companions laughed. But he had spoken too loudly. Black stepped to the edge of the porch, pointed at the man, and the laughter stopped immediately. All went silent.

Black's voice carried across the square. "Prince Scar! That's a good name. Prince Scar it is! Prince Scar will lead us. But since his wound has not yet healed, he has asked me to speak for him. Your regiment has been called to its colors. Even now your comrades are assembling. But, as your regimental commander has told you, we cannot wait. The enemy is in the valley.

"No, the Gates have NOT fallen. They still hold, but probably face enemy both in front and behind. They need our aid. The Sixth will come after us, but we must march now—three companies of the finest infantry in Kenesee. On each of you rests the well-being of our land, and the safety of your homes. Our task is not an easy one. With God's help, we will win through to the Gates.

"And now, Prince Arn—Prince Scar—will lead us in a minute of silent prayer."

All right, I could handle this. I fell to one knee, and the entire square knelt with bowed heads. I prayed the Easterners had left the valley so we wouldn't have to fight. I prayed

Robert would come north and take over this mission for me. I prayed I would never be asked to make a speech again.

Black rose first. "And now, prepare to march!" It had been the shortest minute of prayer in history.

I stepped off the porch and mounted. Black, Murdock, Kren, and Corporal Ash joined me. An order was given, and the guards mounted too. Forward. At a walk we headed toward the east gate. Behind us came the infantry companies, followed by wagons hurriedly loaded with foodstuffs and equipment. We marched through town with a clatter, the townspeople breaking into cheers as we got moving. I looked behind to study the progress of the long, snaking column of men as it wove through the streets, spears moving like the bristles of a caterpillar flowing onward, ever onward, as a hundred million men had marched into history before us.

The head of the column cleared the town gates. Next to me Black rode confidently, ever watchful, peering ahead at field and wood and hill. He gave a command to Corporal Jenkins, and several guardsmen spurred ahead to serve as distant outriders.

"Prince Arn, may I recommend we put out security?"

The woods were light and open fields bordered the road outside of town.

"Already?" I asked.

"Better not take chances. And it will get the men used to such measures."

I pulled off the road, let the guards pass, and reined in beside the captain of the light company. He was an unassuming man in his thirties, looking as if he should be holding needle and thread in a tailor shop rather than leading a company of archers. I found out later he actually was a tailor. He greeted me expectantly. "Prince Arn."

"Colonel Black told me your name is Daniels. Is that so? Good. Put out . . . security for the column."

His tone was respectful. "Yes, sir." Orders were barked without hesitation, and units went into motion. A squad of ten men began jogging forward to take position three hundred yards ahead of the column, which would still be far behind the mounted outriders. Another squad pulled off to the left, a

third to the right, and a fourth stepped off to let the column
pass so it could take a position at the rear.

I resumed my place in the front of the column. Black
watched the progress of the flankers with interest. "Did you
give Captain Daniels any instructions, Prince Arn?"

"Just the orders. Why?"

"Very efficiently done. His men are well trained. If you
find need, he might be trusted with more responsibility."

After an hour we called a halt for ten minutes. Men
shrugged off their packs, drank water from a stream, and went
to the roadside to relieve themselves. Already we had left
Loren far behind, and it was hidden by the hills and trees.
Black and I trotted back along the road to inspect the column.

The archer company was in good form. The first company
of spearmen on the road, under the command of a Captain
Carter, was also in good shape. The next company was less
so. A few stragglers were catching up as we approached. The
commander was a big man by the name of Shaw. His beard
was thick and black, and he spoke in a booming voice which
seemed to be ever dissatisfied and demeaning.

"They have stragglers," Black whispered to me.

"You have stragglers," I told the captain.

The information was less than welcome. "Yes, sir. I've got
my fair share of weaklings. But I can't be everywhere. They
drop off the end of the column. Don't worry, sir. I'll give
them what for." Shaw set off, met the first of the stragglers,
and cuffed the man on the side of the head. Then he shouted
at the others, who began to close the gap at a run. Shaw returned. "That'll take care of it, sir."

"I hope so."

"How many men do you have, Captain?" Black asked.

Shaw looked up at Black resentfully, glanced at me, and
held back what he wanted to say. "Well, now, I don't really
know, exactly. Not all showed up at muster. Staying home and
playing sick, as always. So . . . sixty or seventy, I'd guess."

Black fixed him with a stare. "The other two companies
are at full strength. Why isn't yours? Find out how many men
you have, Captain."

When I didn't deny Black's order, the man turned and
walked back to his men sullenly. "You're going to have trou-

ble with that one," Black stated. "And don't depend on his men till they've been tested."

I pondered his words. "A bad bunch?"

He shook his head. "There are no bad companies. Only bad captains."

We pressed forward throughout the day under standard march routine, pausing only for a ten-minute break each hour and for meals as prescribed in the manual of arms. We couldn't push too hard. The men were reservists, not hardened campaigners, and we didn't want to weaken ourselves through straggling. Black seemed to have an innate sense of exactly how much the men could take. In the evening we camped before dark in order to give the men a chance to settle in and get their fires going. It was cold, and we lay close together as near to the fires as we could. I had Murdock's foot in my face.

The next morning was uneventful, except for our march through the crossroads town of Pulaski. It was a small town of several hundred souls, but had already grown beyond its original palisade. Plowed fields with stands of bundled corn stalks surrounded much of the town. The townspeople revealed that its infantry company had indeed responded to Corporal Ash's warning, and bravely marched east towards the Gates. What had become of the company, no one knew.

We had almost reached the entrance to the valley of the Rift Gates when a guardsman outrider came galloping back down the road to us. "Sir, a man and woman have been found. They have information about the Easterners."

Black and I spurred forward, followed automatically by my little "royal party" of Murdock, Kren, Ash, and the guards. We found the couple near a clump of trees next to the road, watched by several of the archer scouts. The man was big, at least six and a half feet tall, and well-muscled everywhere. In contrast, the woman was almost as small as he was huge. She sat on a tree stump and her coat could not hide the fact that she was heavy with child. She was a pretty girl, in her own way, with innocent features and a shy gaze that was both hopeful and fearful at the same time. A tired horse was tethered nearby.

The sergeant of the archers gestured at the couple. "These people report there are a score of Easterners only two miles ahead, sir. Most likely a road guard. A large force is hidden a mile beyond them, perhaps four or five hundred men camped in a woods on either side of the road.''

We looked at the couple. The man removed his cap out of politeness rather than awe. He was not in the least intimidated. Kren had forgotten to cover himself with his hood, but the man took it calmly. ''A beastman. I've never seen a beastman before.''

''Who are you?'' Black asked.

''My name is Montego. This is my wife, Carlotta. We live in the valley, not far from the village of Prescott, several miles from the Gates. The sergeant said you'd be coming. You must be Black. Is this Prince Arn? He doesn't look like the drawings in the journals.''

''I've been ill,'' I said.

''What do you do?'' Black asked Montego.

''I'm a farmer.''

''You've seen the enemy?''

''We've seen the Easterners. There's a party up the road, and more in the Stanley Wood a mile beyond. I've already told your men this. You might be interested in knowing that another unit of Kenesee infantry marched into the valley a day or two ago and was ambushed. The survivors fled into the mountains to the north.''

''You saw it?'' Black asked.

''No, but a neighbor did. Then the Virginians came and burnt his house down. We could see the smoke over the trees. That's when I took to the woods with Carlotta.''

Black was thoughtful. ''Is there any way to get around the Easteners without being seen?''

''Well, there is the mountain trail.''

''A trail?'' Black asked, his voice betraying his interest. ''Where? How far does it lead?''

The man pointed off to the mountains on the south side of the valley. ''It begins there, climbs halfway up the mountainside, and then goes almost to the Gates before coming back down to the valley floor. I use it when I go trapping. The trail is hidden in summer foliage, but the trees are bare now. Only short stretches are masked by evergreens.''

''Will the trail take a horse?'' Black asked.

''If someone leads the animal, yes.''

Black's lips curved into the hint of a smile. He looked at the sky. The afternoon was already darkening. Gray clouds continued to lower and promised snow soon. "We can follow the trail and bypass the blocking force," Black pointed out to me. "If it snows and visibility goes down, we can win through to the Gates before we have to fight. Once inside the walls, we should have adequate strength to hold until the Sixth Regiment fights its way through."

I scanned the mountains ahead doubtfully. "You really think it will work?" I could think of many reasons it would not.

He shrugged. "Have we any choice?"

The farmer cleared his throat. "Gentlemen, we'll be going now. My wife hasn't been well, and I'd like to get her to shelter."

Black surveyed the mountain. "I'm sorry. You'll have to come with us as a guide."

The man's features hardened. "A guide? There's no need. The trail is well marked. My wife is due soon. I can't leave her."

Black shook his head with finality. "If it snows, we could lose our way. You'll have to come."

Montego looked from one of us to another. I think he was considering resistance, then thought better of it. I'm sure one or two squads would have been enough to subdue him. Montego studied Black. "You'll provide a guard to see her to safety?"

"No," Black answered. "We'll need every man."

"Then I cannot go with you."

"You must."

"I will not. She can't travel alone. They may find her."

Murdock raised a finger. "Ummm, John, may I speak to Montego alone for a moment?" He took the man aside, although not out of my earshot. He was his charming self. "Montego, is Carlotta able to travel?"

He nodded sadly. "She can travel, though I suspect the baby will be coming any day now. But that's not what worries me. You see, her head hasn't been right these last few months. She has—ahh—delusions. Visions. She thinks she's been anointed by God to deliver a prophet to the world. She's not thinking straight, and I'm afraid to leave her alone. Do you see, Mr. Murdock?''

"Yes, I do. Let me talk to Colonel Black and Prince Arn.''

Black was pacing up and down as Murdock returned. "Do you have any alternatives?'' the colonel asked.

"She could come with us, too,'' Murdock offered quietly.

"No,'' her husband objected. "No,'' said Black.

"What other choice is there?'' Murdock asked, looking at the two men. Black studied the mountainside, and then shrugged in acceptance, but Montego stood unmoving, doubt in his eyes.

The girl sighed and stood up. She barely came up to her husband's chest. "Montego, perhaps it is to be. I will come with you. Trust in God.''

"I do. It's these idiots I'm worried about.''

She turned large brown cow eyes upon her husband. "Please, we must hurry.''

He opened his mouth twice to speak but no words came out, and at last he threw up his arms in surrender. "All right. Colonel Black, Prince Arn, is there a healer with you?''

"No,'' I responded, thinking quickly. "But we do have a wizard. I'm sure he has, uh, experience in these matters.''

"Thank you, Arn,'' Murdock said in exasperation. "Yes, I admit, I have delivered once or twice. But—''

The column had almost caught up to us by the time we mounted. Our guide put his wife sidesaddle on the horse and led the mount by its reins. A light, powdery snow began to drift down as we turned from the main road east onto a cart path and marched southwards behind a woods which masked us from the enemy. The path led forward and up to the side of the mountain where the trail began. The trail was only man-wide and skirted fallen trees and rocky outcroppings while slowly and surely climbing upward and eastward, leading farther along the length of the valley. A squad of archers went ahead, followed by our party, the guards, and the infantry companies. Those with horses dismounted and led them on foot, while lances and spears had to be carried over the shoulder with the weapons angled backward sharply so they could pass beneath the overhanging tree limbs.

Only the woman remained on her mount, bent low, her

hands clutching the saddle horn. The narrow path forced us into a long, single file, and as the trail rose we could look back and see the men in company formations below, waiting to feed their ranks onto the trail, while behind them our three wagons turned around and began making their way back to Pulaski to wait for the regiment.

Were there enemy in ambush above us, they would have had little trouble springing down and casting us from the mountainside. Murdock's words were somewhat reassuring. "There are enemy in the valley, but I don't detect any force nearby. Lots of static, though. It's hard to be sure."

There was no wind, and the snow drifted down gently. In fact, it was quite peaceful, and the silence of the mountains was somehow comforting. But the snowfall increased, visibility shrank, and soon we could see no farther than a hundred yards ahead. I looked back again, and the end of the column was lost in gray. The snow began to collect on the ground, and soon the mountainside and valley floor were covered with a white blanket that deadened all sound. Thus protected from the watchful eyes and ears below, we made our way eastward, passing above the Virginian blocking force on the valley floor, and coming ever nearer to the Rift Gates.

We followed the trail far into the night, and had made good progress when the woman began to cry out. Kren lifted her down, and behind us the entire column came to a halt. Voices rose among the infantry until I sent a command back to keep quiet. Black and Montego had been forward with the point. Now they returned, and Carlotta held onto her husband. "He's coming, Montego. I have to lay down." She closed her eyes, gritted her teeth, and moaned.

It was a bad place to stop. At this point on the trail the mountain fell off steeply below us and rose sharply above, with no spot other than the trail itself suitable to recline. Montego caught Murdock with a you-got-me-into-this look. "Your turn, wizard," he stated ominously.

Black peered at the woman and shook his head. "We have to keep moving."

Carlotta sat, and then stretched out in the trampled snow of the trail.

"You can't do that here," Black objected.

Murdock chuckled to himself. "She's already done it, John."

"But she's blocking the path. We can't get around her."

"I would be most interested," Kren stated solemnly, "to read how your historians chronicle this auspicious moment."

Murdock groaned as he knelt down beside the woman. "Once more the Wizard Murdock gives his all. So be it. We need blankets. A dozen should do. I have a clean knife, but I may need needle and thread." He reached his hands under the woman's coat as Montego looked on in concern. "Don't worry, my new friend. I did this once before—though a few years have passed since, I'm afraid. I'll take good care of her. His hand continued probing. "Humph. Matters are rather far along. We'll need those things, John."

We lifted the woman, spread a half dozen blankets beneath her, and piled more on top. Kren held out the ends of a blanket to Black. "Here, hold this." They spread their arms and the blanket formed a roof over Murdock and the woman.

Black tapped Montego with a foot. "How far to the Gates?"

"Perhaps two miles."

Black looked at the sky thoughtfully. "I made a mistake. We shouldn't have brought the woman."

"Look on the bright side," said Kren. "If our little adventure fails, you've found a new profession. As a tent post."

Black peered ahead, frustrated by the gray that enveloped us. "Perhaps that's all I'm good for, after all."

"Oh, come man," Kren countered. "This isn't the time for self-pity. Things could be worse. You could be a woman giving birth on a mountain trail with only a scruffy old man for a midwife."

"I heard that," said Murdock from beneath the blanket. "I am not old."

8

Fight to the Wall

For an hour we sat in the stillness, three hundred men spread out upon a trail halfway up a mountainside, the snow falling prettily and collecting in white drifts upon our shoulders. "Excellent camouflage," said Kren.

And then a baby cried. Far off and above, as if in answer, some great beast roared.

"Saber-tooth," Montego whispered. "There's one that roams the mountains."

Kren grinned. "A Kenesee dollar says its a girl."

Murdock's head popped out from beneath the blanket. "I'll take that bet." He disappeared beneath the blanket again.

"A good omen," Kren told Black. "You said you'd need every man, and now you have another."

Murdock stood up and allowed them to fold the blanket they had been holding. Montego knelt beside Carlotta, staring at the well-wrapped bundle placed in his arms. Murdock rolled several wet blankets into a ball, wedged them into a crack in the stone, and covered them with snow. "Well, John, I think we can move in a few minutes. Knew you'd be happy to hear that."

Black nodded. "The woman is well?"

"Both are doing fine. I didn't have to do much more than watch. Amazing creatures, women. I told her of our peril, and not a peep did she make. Sound can travel far in the mountains, even with the snow. Most men would have been squealing like pigs. Heh, Arn?"

"Speak for yourself, midwife."

237

Presently Carlotta sat up, and attempted to stand. She was pale and too weak to succeed. Kren picked up the woman in his arms. "Don't worry," he told Montego. "I'll take care of her for you." He would carry her the rest of the way.

Montego nodded, handed the baby to Murdock, and went with Black to join the scouts waiting ahead. The delay over, the column started moving again, our breath forming clouds of steam. The night had long been full upon us, but the snow seemed to glow, lighting our way. Without it, we could not have gone forward on the path, for the clouds blocked out the moon.

The snow stopped falling and visibility began to increase, showing the path as it curved around the mountain ahead. We could dimly see our scouting party going around a crag of rock, and then a scout came scrambling back along the trail to our column. The fire of an Easterner watch post had been seen, perhaps a mile ahead and lower on the mountainside. The trail was already angling downwards towards the valley.

Black made his way back, gave an order to Corporal Jenkins, and then explained our role to us. "Wait here for twenty minutes and then come forward slowly. If all is well, I'll send a man back. If you hear a shout, come quickly, for it means they've gotten away and we'll have to fight our way through to the Gates."

Reins were passed to others, and then Corporal Jenkins and five royal guards followed Black forward on foot. The guardsmen carried little but their horse bows and knives. The minutes were counted off in silence, then Murdock gave me the sign. I gestured and the column began to snake forward. We made our way carefully, and eventually rounded the crag which had blocked our view. From here the trail began to descend more steeply. The going was slow on the snow-covered rocks. Fir trees closed in thickly overhead, and the men had to be careful lest the points of their lances and spears tangle in the branches.

Suddenly a shadow loomed ahead and I almost yelled out in surprise and fear. The figure spoke softly, and I recognized the voice of Corporal Jenkins. "All's well, sir. The enemy watch post is just ahead, over there. You can see it now." A hundred yards ahead a campfire flickered through the trees.

"Any casualties?"

He smiled with satisfaction, "No, sir. Just the enemy. We

caught them all around the fire. It was quick work.''

We reached the watch post. The fire was set in a small, level clearing next to the trail, still perhaps fifty or sixty feet above the floor of the valley. Through the trees, the fires of the enemy encampment, perhaps five hundred yards away, could be seen twinkling through the gray skies. Even as we watched, the clouds began to break above us.

Sprawled on the ground around the watch fire were the bodies of five men dressed in the dark blue coats of the Virginian Army, each sporting arrows from chest or back. Blood had seeped over the snow, marking it a dark crimson. Not a pretty sight for the men to see, but it couldn't be helped. I heard the baby begin to cry behind me, and then its voice was muffled as a blanket or hood was laid over it.

We continued on, following the trail until it reached the level floor of the valley. We were still surrounded by fir trees, and thus well hidden from the sight of the enemy. Jenkins followed footsteps through the snow and led us towards the edge of the woods. Ahead waited Black and Montego, flanked by watchful guardsmen and archers on either side.

''With any luck,'' Black whispered, ''this may just work.''

The sky was clearing rapidly now, and the moonlight shone down upon the snow, lighting up the scene in a brilliant silhouette of black and white. Less than two hundred yards ahead lay the wall of the Rift Gates, dark and massive before us. The wall was thirty feet thick, twenty feet high on the side of the valley, and large enough to house its garrison. The two leaves of the gate, made of square beams of oak reinforced with metal studs and bolts, were securely closed now. Two great towers bulged forward, flanking the portal. On the far ends of the wall, similar towers defied the cliffs around the narrow pass and prevented anyone from accessing the wall from those heights. The entire edifice was an imposing darkness against the snow except for several watch fires that glowed from the battlements.

To our left, out of bow range of the wall, dozens of fires burned brightly on both sides of the road leading to the Gates. A few enemy sentries moved around the camp, but many figures lay in clusters around each fire. There were no tents, and only a handful of captured plow horses tethered to a line by one of the fires. The sleepers numbered in the hundreds, perhaps the greater part of a regiment.

The Virginians were certainly bold, risking a unit in this way. Such a force coming across the mountains would have had a most difficult trek, and they would have had to come bereft of horses or supplies. Once here, they would be cut off, with only the rations in their backpacks to sustain them. They had to take the Gates, or retreat back across the mountains.

Murdock and Kren joined us, the beastman setting down the woman while Murdock held the swaddled bundle. Montego took the bundle from Murdock while others led forward their horses. The beastman took in the scene in a long glance. "Such a sight. What I couldn't do with my battalion."

Black pointed at the wooden gates set into the wall. "That is our goal now." He sent a runner back to get the company commanders.

Kren silently pounded his fist into the palm of his hand. "We've got complete surprise. Have you thought of attacking?"

Black nodded. "If the enemy troops were reserves, I would. But we checked the uniform patches at the outpost on the trail. We're facing the Virginian First Regiment."

"That's one of their three regular units," Kren grumbled. "Their best troops."

Amazingly well informed, these beastmen.

"They'll recover quickly," Black responded to Kren. "And they outnumber us. If the first charge didn't break them, then they'd have us. No, we have to get inside the walls and defend the Gates. That's our purpose, and we can't be tempted away from it."

Kren shrugged. "You're probably right. Still, it is a pity. . . ."

The company commanders came up then, all three showing the tension in their faces. Black pointed out the scene and explained the plan. "We're going to skirt their camp, reach the wall, and then march along it to the gates there. We'll form up here in the woods so we don't get strung out. Have the men drop their packs and blanket rolls. The guards will march out first, face to the left in line, and charge if necessary to delay the Easterner deployment. Captain Daniels, your archers should move out at the same time and form a skirmish line on either side of the guards. Advance if the guards charge. Just keep the Easterners busy, and don't get too far out. Form your men here in a tight column. Captain Carter will march just behind the archers and Captain Shaw will follow. Form your spearmen companies into columns of two. March out sharply, but *don't run*. Panic will destroy us. Keep your formations intact marching along the screen formed by the archer company. If the worst happens, facing to the flank will put you in line of battle.

"When we get there, halt in front of the gates and pivot your open flanks back to the walls. There's a sally port in one door of the gates. When the sally port is open we'll feed the men in by squads. Have the men drop their spears before they go through. We can rearm from the garrison stores later. Remember, the garrison will be supporting us with bow fire and bolt shooters if the enemy charges. When we get under the walls the guards will dismount and join us as a reserve.

"It's essential you maintain your formations. Do you understand what you have to do? Good. And for God's sake make sure everyone is silent. One noise and we can lose it all."

The captains left. My stomach had been gently simmering throughout the night. Now it began to bubble merrily.

Jenkins and the guards closed up, each leading his horse and keeping his lance clear of the trees. They mounted and waited, the breath of men and horses frosting in the cold night air. Occasionally a horse would snort, or brush up against a tree. We couldn't remain here too long before some sound would give us away.

Behind, men of the infantry companies filed through the woods and formed up tightly. Black looked at our little party. "Wizard Murdock and Corporal Ash, I want you to lead the way. Walk or trot directly for the wall, but don't gallop until the alarm goes up in the enemy camp. Let the garrison know who we are and tell them to get that sally port opened. If they've blocked it properly inside, it'll take them time to do it. I doubt that you'll be interfered with. Arn and Kren, stay behind me and out of danger."

Off to the side of the trail Montego held the reins of his horse in one hand and his son in the other. Carlotta sat upon the animal, weary and painfully uncomfortable.

"What about them?" asked the wizard.

Montego had been listening. "My job is done. I'll take the trail out of the valley."

Kren shook his head. "They'll not treat you kindly if they find you. I doubt if you'll have the same luck going back once they're alerted. Besides, your wife doesn't look like she can take much more. You'd better come along."

Black agreed. "Follow the last company when it leaves the woods. Pass behind them if they stop for any reason. You should be safe. But don't get in anyone's way. Can the woman ride this short distance? Good. Hold onto those reins tightly, Montego. The horse will want to follow the other mounts when they go."

"I can help Montego," Kren added.

Montego seemed about to speak, but looked at his wife, and perhaps realized he had little choice now.

Captain Daniels came up. "The assembly is done, sir. Everything is ready."

Black gave a final look around, ensuring that his orders had been carried out. He looked at me. His face was unchanged, but his eyes were bright, as if a fire had been lit behind them. It was like the time before the bandit attack on the way to the Beastwood. "Well, then. It's time." We mounted our horses. He raised his hand and swung it forward.

The packed column began to move, the only sounds being the excited breathing of men, the snorts of horses, and the crunch of boots and hooves upon the snow. Every eye focused on the enemy camp as we emerged from the woods. For a blessed moment or two, there was no reaction. Murdock and Ash trotted ahead, making their way peacefully towards the wall. The rest of us on horseback marched double file, our horses at the walk. Perhaps no one had seen us yet. More likely, we were noticed but the sentries hesitated, trying to determine if we were friend or foe. Black's plan was working splendidly so far. But such luck cannot last forever.

A shout went up from the camp, and then another.

Fifty yards from the woods the guards halted and faced the enemy, forming a short battle line. Black and I took position next to them. More shouts came from the enemy. Behind us, the archer company jogged towards the wall, squads of ten peeling off on either side of us into a loose formation of skirmishers. From the woods, Captain Carter's company of spearmen marched out in a column of twos.

Black studied the enemy camp. "They're responding too quickly," he said.

We could see men getting up, pulling on helmets, and picking up weapons. There seemed to be more of them than I had thought, but I knew their numbers had not changed, but simply their aspect. Sleeping men are less fearsome.

Carter's spearmen were a third of the way to the wall, and small clusters of enemy soldiers were already trying to head them off. Our skirmishers took them under fire and halted their advance.

I could see Murdock and Corporal Ash's horses prancing beneath the wall, and I could hear them shouting. Heads peeped over the battlements, trying to sort out what was happening. Time was the essential element. We needed time for the companies to reach the Gates, and time for the garrison to open the sally port.

"The guards will have to charge," said Black. "Arn, you stay here with the infantry."

Some orders are a pleasure to obey.

"Corporal Jenkins!" Black called out.

"Yes, sir," said Corporal Jenkins, his irreverent grin replaced by a grim earnestness that was no less eager. "Now, sir? Very good. Fourth Squad, FORWARD."

As one, the guards began to move at the walk, Black advancing in line with them.

Unfortunately, my own mare started forward with Black's. My mistrust of horses was proven once again. I pulled firmly on the reins. The bit was in its teeth. We had advanced only a few yards when the second command came.

"Fourth Squad, TROT" ordered Jenkins, and the pace quickened.

Black shot a look at me. "Go back, Arn."

I jerked the reins again. "I'm trying!"

The horses sent out plumes of frost as they exhaled, and the snow sprayed from beneath their hooves.

"Fourth Squad, PREPARE TO CHARGE."

The guards' lances fell from the vertical position to the horizontal. Black pulled out his sword and held it aloft. Jenkins leaned forward in his saddle.

"Fourth Squad, CHARGE!"

Knee to knee, the guardsmen broke into a gallop and surged towards the enemy. And regretfully, so did I, promising to donate my horse to a butcher shop when this was all over.

Forward we rode, closing rapidly with the campfires of the enemy. The Easterners had begun forming a ragged line before the fires, but as we drew near the enemy scrambled left and right to avoid the course of our charge. We thundered through and past, catching a few unfortunates in our deadly path. Yet our advance was not uncontested. Already arrows began to whiz about us from every direction, and on the flanks men came to hurl javelins or swing weapons as we passed.

Well beyond the enemy position we drew to a halt, wheeled about, and stood. Before us, the enemy line was reforming, trying to fill the hole we had created; but the Easterners were uncertain which way to face. Beyond them, our archers were firing arrows into the enemy. Behind our archers marched the two companies of spearmen, the head of the column now closing upon the wall.

Gaining approval from Black, Corporal Jenkins gave the word, and we advanced at the gallop. Black pointed his sword forward, turned to shout something to me, and then his horse swerved sideways, stumbled, and went down, an arrow sticking out of its foreleg. Black was thrown clear and rolled in the snow.

My horse skidded to a stop to avoid Black's, neighed in fright at the smell of blood, danced around, and then galloped off in a large circle trying to avoid the terrible figures approaching. Unaware of our demise, the squad of guards thundered ahead in their charge, throwing the enemy line into confusion again.

Black rose, sword in hand. He parried a swordsman, stabbed, swung, and a man went down. Another man jabbed a spear at him. Black grabbed it, stepped close, and thrust his sword in at the waist. The man screamed and fell, blood gushing from his wound.

My horse bucked as an axman swung his weapon, the head of it swishing through the air as it passed near my head. I jabbed with my sword and caught the Virginian in the shoulder as we pranced back and away. Another drew back his ax to swing, slipped on the snow, and fell on his bottom. I gave the fool horse a savage jerk on the reins, managed to turn the animal in the direction of the gate, and dug my heels into its sides. The horse lunged forward at the gallop only a moment before the enemy closed in.

Incredibly, without benefit of armor or shield, Black still defied the Easterners. Four or five of them were sprawled around him in the snow while he exchanged sword strokes with yet another. The Easterner went down.

Now, the stories say that I planned all that I did, that I risked myself to save John Black. In fact, I could barely control my horse. I was thinking of only one thing, and that was getting back to the wall. It was his good fortune to be in my path.

As I galloped past, Black stuck out his arm. I stretched out my hand, he caught it, and swung up behind me. Heavily now, the horse galloped towards the gap in the enemy line that the guards had punched through. With arrows zipping around us we rode through the center of the hole, past our own archers, and drew up next to the guards, who had been preparing to charge back in to save us. Such an effort would have doomed them, but that is their duty, after all. They had already lost two men to the Easterners.

So many things were going on that I barely heard the cheering from the battlements where our exploit had been watched by the garrison. Black's plan seemed to have worked so far. Surprise had been complete, we had taken advantage of the confusion in the Eastern camp, and we had delayed their deployment. But they were good troops. Now their archers were in position in front of their line, which had filled in the gap and was taking on an ominous solidity up and down its length. None of us would come back from a third charge.

Carter's company of spearmen was quite close to the wall now, marching in steady ranks. But Shaw's company following behind had shrunk to twenty or thirty men. The remainder, seeing themselves on the end of the column and furthest from the gate, had lost all discipline and discovered a more fluid formation. They clustered in a panicky mass and moved like a dark cloud on the snow, scrambling, some with weapons and some without, overtaking their steadily marching comrades from the other company and bounding directly for the gates.

One devoted friend had picked up his limping companion and was now carrying him piggyback. The human steed was rewarded with whacks to his head and neck, as if he were a race horse whipped towards the finish line. Apparently the encouragement was working, because he was at the head of the pack, running in great strides that barely touched the surface of the snow. Amazing what friendship will do.

The men holding their formation reached the wall, marched along its length to the towers bordering the portals, and halted. The column faced left and the flanks swung back to the base of the towers, forming a box around the gates, shields up and spears bristling outward in anticipation as the enemy drew closer. Within the box, the panicked men of Shaw's company had crammed against the wooden doors, pounding on the gate while Kren and Montego stood to one side, protecting the farmer's family from the mob of men.

It was to this situation that we came as Black and I fell back with the guards and the archer company. Discarding their lances, Jenkins and the guards dismounted, drove their horses away, and passed through the ranks of disciplined spearmen. Then they tried to push through the mob around the gates, but with little success. Kren shook his head at the pileup. He beckoned to Montego, and the two waded in. Each time their hands made contact, a man seemed to become weightless, finding himself flying through the air with limited time to ponder his imminent contact with the ground. Most avoided serious injury by landing on their heads.

A more obstinate soldier resisted this lesson in flying, and instead thrashed his arms at Kren. The beastman's hood fell back, his cap was ripped off, and his grinning head revealed in all its splendor. The man's eyes grew round, he screamed, and then found himself launched into the air. Kren regained his cap and continued his labor. The guards were quick to pick up the discarded heroes, stick spears back into their hands, and forcibly place them into line behind the stalwarts. In this way, the gates were gradually cleared.

Meanwhile, the enemy began to advance. Our archers still stayed outside the box and fired at will. From the battlements an occasional ballista bolt coursed into the ground, and even a rock or two from the catapults bounced about, though these were of little value, given the angle against a moving target. Far more deadly was the steady stream of arrows from above that found the enemy line as it moved into range.

However, the enemy were not the only ones taking punishment. The Easterners seemed to have at least as many archers as we had, deployed before their line launching well-placed volleys. Many arrows were falling behind our line into the milling mass of heroes that the guards were working upon. An occasional scream, and a man would come out clutching an arm or leg. Other times, a man shuddered and was still. To one side Carlotta still huddled protectively over the bundle in her arms, while Murdock had taken over Montego's role of protector. Murdock watched the flight of the arrows closely.

Upon the wall two helmeted heads peered down at us.

"Open the sally port!" I shouted.

"We're removing the blocks now," one called back. "Is that you, Prince Arn?"

"Open the damn *port*!"

"That's him," said the other.

Then my attention was distracted, for the enemy line charged. Daniels's archers retreated before them and through our ranks into the rear of the box.

The Easterners struck the right part of the line first, their men rushing in, flinging their javelins and swinging sword or ax. Our spearmen took the impact. Black strode up and down the line, shouting encouragement, giving orders, and urging the men to hold their places. Wisely, the spearmen kept their shields together and stabbed forward with their weapons. The rest of the enemy line swung forward to contact our left, but without the impetus of the charge that had marked the first point of impact. Yells and screams came from every quarter.

The Virginians were very good. They fought fiercely and well, with a cold determination to break the line. Yet, with nowhere to go, our troops now held as desperately, and many fought quite skillfully. Still, it would have gone badly for us had it not been for the support of the archers upon the towers and battlements. The rain of arrows from above was disconcertingly accurate, and shields could not protect the Easterners from arrows and spears at the same time.

Ultimately, it was this unremitting archery fire that told. On our right, where they had endured the worst, the enemy gave back and moved out of range. Slowly, like a bandage being torn away from a wound, the rest of the enemy line broke contact and fell back to regroup.

I looked behind me and shouted to Black. The sally port in the gate finally creaked open. Captain Daniels and his archers went through first with orders to get up to the battlements, then Shaw's men began discarding their spears by squad and filing in, the box shrinking to maintain a continuous line.

Kren stood beside me, and we watched the enemy reform. "It's going to be close," he said. "Very close."

Black looked at us without comment, then commanded loudly enough for all to hear. "Every two men, pick up one of the wounded and carry him through. We leave none behind."

There was a cheer from those in the line, and it was answered by those on the wall. The enemy paused, doubtful, wondering what good news—or evil tidings—we celebrated.

There were perhaps sixty men still outside the wall, most from Carter's brave company of spearmen and the royal guards. The wounded were all taken up, but Murdock and Kren stood with me, and behind us the woman and her husband waited.

"Your turn," said Black. "Quickly. Get inside all of you, and make sure the passage is kept clear. Keep everyone moving."

Murdock took the baby. "Let's go," Kren shouted, he and Montego supporting Carlotta. We went through the small door into an arched tunnel ten feet wide. At the opposite end of the tunnel were the barred and barricaded gates of the rift side. The far gate was reinforced with stone blocks wedged and propped by timbers, and the portcullis had been lowered. Around the sally port on the valley side, similar blocks of stone and timber had been hastily thrown to each corner. In the tunnel, wounded lay in clumps or were held erect by their comrades, who waited in confusion. Several men of the garrison stood near the stairs, and they directed our men upwards as quickly as they could. Kren stationed himself near the stairs.

"Clear the door," I ordered, and the men stepped farther back.

They were only just in time, for suddenly through the port came a continuous stream of men at the run, their weapons and shields discarded for speed. Kren was shouting in a commanding voice. "Clear the way. Keep going and clear the way." He was yanking the slow ones into the corners of the tunnel as they entered.

"Crowd into the back. All the way to the back," one of the garrison shouted. The small area filled quickly, so that men were pressed against each other and the wounded trampled underfoot. I tried moving but my leg contacted something and teeth bit into my boot. "Move your damn leg, you moron," came a muffled voice.

Men continued to flow in, and I wondered how many more there could be. And then the royal guards came through, the last of whom was Jenkins. Were the enemy upon them? Where was Black?

In answer to my thought he leaped through the port, slammed it shut, and threw the bolt. Immediately after there came the sound of blows against wood and faint yells. The door bar was dropped into place.

Black leaned against the inner gate, breathing heavily. He beckoned to the garrison members. "Seal it up."

Kren's voice seemed to boom amidst the crush of men. "Plenty of time. You had at least two seconds."

Then the laughter started, rolling up and down the crowded tunnel, a laughter of relief, a release of fear and excitement. I felt my legs weaken and I started to shake, the press of men all that kept me from sinking to my knees. It wouldn't do for a prince to collapse in front of the men. My stomach gurgled, and only its empty condition saved me from further embarrassment.

The laughter petered out, and then we could hear the groans of those upon whom we stood. The baby was crying.

Black took off his hat and wiped his forehead. "All right. Up the stairs, everyone. Be careful of the wounded. That's it. They'll sort you out upstairs."

The press thinned, and I could move forward to join them by the gate. The garrison men were carefully sealing up the sally port with stone blocks and timbers. After they were done, they would lower the inner portcullis. I could see now why it had taken so long to open the gates.

Kren patted Black on the shoulder. "Well done. Prince Arn,

it seems your military commander is also a hero. So we have two heroes amongst us.''

I leaned against the wall. My legs were still trembling. ''And who . . . is the other?'' I asked shakily. ''We'll need him.''

Kren chuckled. ''Why, it's you, of course. That was a valiant rescue. Quite incredible.''

I nodded and slid down to the floor. Yes. Quite incredible. I was too tired to lie. ''My horse bolted. I couldn't control it.''

He smirked knowingly. ''If you say so, Arn. The bravest often say such.''

I had recovered my legs by the time the last of the men were climbing the steps, and noticed that I was not the only one wobbling on my feet. Montego knelt over a wounded soldier, unbuttoning a tunic. His wife Carlotta sat tiredly against a wall. Murdock stood near her, still holding the crying baby.

''These men need help,'' Montego declared. ''Where is the garrison healer?''

As if in response to the words, a black-robed priest carrying a healer's satchel came down the steps. The priest looked around and shook his head. His hair was streaked with gray, his face long and gaunt, the cheeks marked by a stubble of whiskers. His clothes were dirty. ''I'll need help,'' the healer priest stated. ''These will have to stay here till we can move them up.'' He sent a runner for help and set about aiding the wounded.

The baby cried, and he heard it at last above the groans of men. Carlotta's face was white in the torch light. ''What's wrong with her?'' he asked.

Montego answered. ''My wife just gave birth, Father. We came with the Prince.''

The priest scrambled over a body and peered into her eyes while feeling her pulse. ''Take her up to the next floor. My room is on the left. Put her there. Cover her with blankets and give her something to drink.''

Montego scooped up his wife without effort and carried her up the steps. Murdock followed, cradling the baby in his arms.

A man came to attention before us, and saluted. ''Prince

Arn, I am Major Franz, Commander of the Garrison.'' He shook hands with a look of relief. "Welcome. God, I'm glad you've come. Now we have a chance. I'd held little hope before, but now . . . now we can do something. That was a brilliant effort.''

Black listened without comment. "Major, may I recommend we go to the wall for an inspection before we rest." He looked at Franz, evaluating him.

The major realized the meaning of the glance, and his face set. He drew himself erect, not sure why this man in merchant clothing gave orders disguised as suggestions.

I cleared my throat. "Uhh, Major Franz, this is Colonel Black, my advisor, late a member of the royal guard. It was his leadership that brought us here successfully. Any orders from Colonel Black . . . will be obeyed as if they were my own.'' I said the last firmly, or as firmly as I could in a quaking voice. This was no time for misunderstanding.

The major was taken aback. He looked at us both. "I see. My pardon, Prince Arn. A very fine effort, Colonel Black.''

"May we have that inspection tour now, Major?" Black asked evenly. "I'm afraid we're all quite tired. Fatigue is our enemy as much as the Easterners.''

"Naturally, sir. As you wish." He hesitated. "But I'm afraid you'll have little rest this morning. The enemy has assembled an army outside the Gates on the rift. They have a siege tower, and their preparations are almost complete. I expect an attack at dawn.''

9

The Rift Gates

The major continued to explain the situation as we climbed the steps to the battlements. "We considered a sortie against their tower, but it was too risky. The catapults have been tried, but the trajectory won't work. They're almost done constructing it, so I expect an attack at dawn from both sides. But perhaps your coming will delay their plans."

Murdock rejoined us at the second level and caught the end of the exchange. He sighed. "Well, dear Prince, the pace never slows for you, does it? A second battle in as many hours. Even the mighty Murdock needs a rest now and then, you know."

We emerged onto the top of the wall, ablaze now with torches and lamps and fires burning in braziers. A euphoria seemed to have gripped the men of our three companies, and it spread to the garrison. A cheer went up when I emerged from the stairwell. To my surprise, even the royal guards cheered freely. Corporal Jenkins shouted out, "Hurrah for Scar," and the refrain was taken up by our infantry companies, and then by the garrison, though they could not yet have known the reason for my new nickname.

Black emerged behind me. The cheers redoubled and weapons were pounded on the stones and wood in unison. And for the first time we heard the refrain that sounded from the battlements and went forth to the ears of the Easterners on both sides of the gates. "John Black," the men began to chant. "John Black. JOHN BLACK. JOHN BLACK."

And from that stone face, as if the granite of his jaws was finally cracking open, a smile broke out in full glory. He gripped my hand and held up our arms in a salute to the men. "All my life I've waited to hear the cheers of men after battle," he spoke in my ear. The smile faded at last, and his face was set back into its craggy features as he faced the task still before us. He went to the wall and looked out into the rift while the cheers continued. Then he stood upon an elevated cornerstone.

"Keepers of the Gate, we have come to aid you."

Cheers from the Sixth Regiment.

"You have fought well here under Major Franz. You have done your duty, and you have held the Gates!"

Cheers from the Gate Keepers.

"But now, the Easterners may attack very soon in a desperate effort. They must attack now, or else be too late, for our friends are coming to sweep the valley of our enemy!"

Thunderous cheers from all.

"To help you, we have come: a Prince of the Kingdom, a squad of royal guards, and three companies of the Sixth Regiment. We have won through." More cheers. "You have fought the enemy, and shown the Easterners what they must face. We will have little rest. Get what you can, and be ready at a moment to take positions. Remember! You fight beneath the eyes of a Prince, a Prince to whom we pledge our lives. Be worthy of him."

Could the enemy hear his words? Perhaps he wanted them to know.

I was struck by the power of his voice. Black and King Reuel both had the ability to inspire their listeners. The king filled each with his own enthusiasm and feeling, lifting spirits and instilling hope. He inspired men with a belief in his cause. John Black's aura was less emotional, yet generated just as much confidence, a quiet surety of success. John Black inspired men with a belief in themselves. I found comfort in his words.

"Company commanders, assemble here," Black ordered in conclusion.

Quietly, Captain Shaw was relieved of his company and made an aide, while his executive officer was promoted to command. It was not done unkindly, Colonel Black first stating to all assembled that more aides were needed for a decent headquarters staff. I almost felt sorry for Shaw at that moment, seeing the miserable look of shame and humiliation on his face. But I remembered how he had cuffed the stragglers and blamed them for his lack of control, and my sympathy vanished. Inability is one thing; denying responsibility is another.

With the company commanders following, we conducted our tour. The garrison was well prepared, catapults and ballistae in order, extra weapons in readiness, stocks of arrows near at hand. Only in men had the gate keepers been wanting, their original garrison of two hundred thinned by a tenth in fighting off the surprise assault that Corporal Ash had told us about. The remainder were split watching both the rift and the valley, whereas the garrison had been intended only to hold one side of the wall. Now their number had been doubled by our arrival.

Major Franz gestured out over the battlements to the rift. "There they are, gentlemen. The Army of Virginia."

Below us, in the first light of dawn, could be seen hundreds of men clinging to the steep slopes of the rift, waiting to advance to the five-foot-wide ledge of flat ground that lay between the wall and the chasm. Lines of archers four and five deep extended the length of the wall on the far side of the rift, and behind them, ready to advance, were companies of men with swords and shields. On the slope of road leading up through the rift to the Gates, a great tower on wheels had been built. The top of the tower was an enclosed platform that included a drawbridge ready to be lowered when the tower had reached the walls. Behind the tower, two great, hairy mammoths were harnessed to the structure, though just a bit of their protected flanks was visible.

This was an innovation. Mammoths were known to range the northlands above the Ohio. The nomadic tribes of the Northern Forests hunted the beasts on occasion for meat, but that was all. The use of animals for war was not prohibited by the Codes, but no nation had bothered to harness the beasts before. Without them to push the tower uphill, we had little to fear. With them, the situation was changed.

"So that's how they intend to move it up the slope," Black sighed, looking at the mammoths. "I'd wondered."

"Can they succeed?" I asked.

Franz nodded. "If they ever gain a foothold, they can overwhelm us."

Black gestured at the tower. "How are you prepared to counter that?"

"We have wooden beams to wedge against the drawbridge so it can't be lowered. We have oil too, but they've covered the tower with wet animal skins."

Oil was permitted under the Codes, but could not be targeted against men. It had to be used against objects and structures such as the siege tower. If men were burnt in the process, that was one of the horrors which the Codes tried to regulate and limit.

Dispositions were made in anticipation of the assault. Strangely, we had the devil's own time waking our men. In just moments, many had fallen asleep where they sprawled. Apparently this is not an unknown reaction for troops in their first action. The wounded were barracked below, units were assigned to portions of the wall, and the men were fed. Then we waited. I strolled back and forth between the walls, watching the Easterners prepare their assault from two sides. When dawn came full, the enemy were ready.

By the light of day I could at last make out the uniforms of the Virginians. Their winter dress was not far different from our own. The Easterners' leather armor was stained dark blue. Their oblong shields were alike in shape but each regiment had its own color, and on the upper corner were numbers separated by a slash which represented company and regiment. Their helmets were of metal, with a metal crest running along the center from front to back. Overall, they looked as if they were serious. Very serious.

The enemy in the valley had also positioned themselves for assault. Archer units were deployed out of range along the length of the wall. In the gaps between units stood columns of men with scaling ladders. Behind them on the road marched perhaps another three hundred coming to reinforce the assault. Most likely, these were some of the troops that had been blocking the valley the day before. It would be a tougher fight on this side than had been expected. In the valley alone the enemy had twice our numbers.

From the center of the enemy host in the rift a long blast of a horn was heard. From their comrades in the valley a single horn answered, followed by more horns and drums from both forces. In the rift the archers responded. Arrows were nocked and bows drawn. And then the Easterners attacked.

Like a colony of ants to sugar, the infantry surged forward. Below the walls the Virginians swarmed up to the ledge, awkwardly manhandling long, clumsy ladders and carrying grappling hooks attached to strong ropes.

The tower shuddered and began to move, pushed up the road to the doors of the Gates by the immense strength of the two straining beasts. The creaking of its timbers and the animals' trumpeted protests were so loud as to be heard even above the roar of thousands of voices yelling defiance as they came.

Black looked at the mammoths, and then at Murdock.

The wizard shrugged, embarrassed. "Sorry, John, I've tried. There's too much static, too many men, too many emotions. The mammoths aren't affected one bit."

Black nodded in understanding, and then drew his sword. "Arn, I suggest you take position with the Sixth Regiment on the valley wall. The men are tired. They need the inspiration you can provide." The first volley of arrows came over the wall. "Murdock, go with him. Corporal Jenkins and the guards will follow you."

Murdock came close. "What do you think, John? Can we hold?"

"The toss of a coin," Black said softly so that none other could hear. "No better. But no worse." He grabbed my arm and squeezed it. "Go on, now. Jenkins, watch the Prince closely. Wizard, keep him well."

It was only a few paces across to the valley wall, and yet it was enough distance to separate us from our companions. We stepped across and looked down. The Virginian archers had advanced to firing positions and men were swarming up to the base of the wall.

"What happens to us if they succeed?" I thought aloud.

Murdock shrugged. "Us? Well, the men will be taken prisoners. Of course, it might be worse for you and me." He stopped, as if he realized he'd said too much.

"What do you mean by that?" I pinned him down.

He answered reluctantly. "In wartime, the Virginians have been known to send back pieces of important prisoners as persuasive diplomacy."

Ladders were propped against the walls as the first volley

of arrows came from the valley. Murdock watched the flight carefully. A man at the battlements collapsed, and another screamed in pain.

I thought about persuasive diplomacy. "Hold Firm!" I shouted. "HOLD FIRM!"

Our archers had already begun to fire into the masses below, ducking whenever volleys came their way. When one stepped back it meant the enemy was immediately below on a ladder, and a shielded spearman stepped forward to take his place and contest the position with the foe. Several archers had already stepped away.

Another volley of arrows came over with ill effect, several men reeling back, pierced by the missiles. One arrow struck my chest broadside. It had turned in flight, its point deflected. I looked at Murdock, who nodded with a hard smile on his face. My fondness for the wizard increased dramatically. The king had been right. They did have their uses.

"Here they come," yelled Murdock.

Two of the enemy climbed over the wall where spearmen had fallen, and cut down an archer who had just drawn his sword. More heads appeared on the ladder.

I pointed with my sword. "Jenkins! Charge!"

The guards rushed forward as more Virginians came over the wall to reinforce their fellows. The guards and Easterners met in a fierce clash, the sound of sword on sword ringing through the air, and through it could be heard the dull thunk of an ax as it buried itself deep in the breastbone of one unfortunate. A few men from the Sixth Regiment rushed up and entered the melee.

Two more Easterners came over the wall further down, saw us, and rushed forward. "Murdock!" I shouted, and he intercepted the first man. The other came for me. He was a big fellow, tall and wide and very confident about his business.

Why did I always get the big ones?

For the first time I faced a man at equal odds. He was fully armed and concentrating on doing me irreparable harm. I didn't like it. I didn't like it at all.

I went into a crouch, wishing I had a shield. The Easterner swung his ax at me. I sidestepped the blow and stabbed at his stomach. The sword went under his studded jerkin and sank into his stomach with a squish.

I braced and pulled the sword out. The man dropped his ax and clutched his belly.

"You've killed me," he murmured in astonishment.

I was astonished too. Finally, my years of training had paid off. "Yes," I said in wonderment. "I suppose I have. Sorry." I stuck him again, and he collapsed.

Another head peered over the wall. I swung down, my sword clanged on his helmet, and he disappeared. Murdock stood next to me, his previous opponent sitting on the stones, crying and holding his wrist, for his hand was gone. Murdock picked up a spear and thrust it into a man climbing onto the battlements. The Easterner grabbed the spear with a scream. Murdock let go and the man tumbled backwards and disappeared.

Up and down the length of the wall our men were thrusting, chopping, hacking, and shooting, but I couldn't see that any of the enemy still stood upon the battlements. The first rush, at least, had been contained.

Another volley of arrows clattered down.

Jenkins and the guards rejoined us, eyeing the work of Murdock and me with nods of approval. Where they had fought, the bodies of six blue-clad Easterners lay, along with two dressed in the black of the royal guards and three in the brown of the Sixth Regiment. All were dead, a testimony to the fierceness of the conflict. An archer stood over the bodies, resolutely manning the wall and firing carefully at targets below.

"We've held them," I told Murdock.

The wizard watched an incoming volley of arrows intently while ministering to the enemy soldier whose hand he had cut off. He wrapped a cord around the bleeding stump. "I hope so. How is John doing?"

I turned and watched the battle that had developed at our backs. The narrowness of the ledge on the rift side made it more difficult to mount ladders for assault. The garrison seemed to be holding fairly well along the length of the wall and in the towers. But between the two towers flanking the wooden gates the enemy siege tower had been pushed slowly uphill on the road until it stood directly in front of the portal itself and within ten feet of the wall. Its topmost level was almost as high as our towers. Upon it, enemy archers exchanged a vicious fire with our bowmen. The exchange of casualties appeared to be even, but heavy. The problem was that a continuous stream of enemy replacements waited to climb up and take the place of those who had fallen, while we had few such in reserve.

Major Franz had trained his men well. A wooden beam was quickly wedged against the upraised drawbridge and propped into place on the wall. It kept the bridge from lowering. Garrison members with pots of oil began to hurl the contents across the gap, where the oil sloshed over the wet hides protecting the exposed underside of the bridge.

"More oil!" I could hear Black order. "More oil!"

A grappling hook was lowered from the top of the siege tower and swung under the wedge beam. It caught. Men heaved, and the beam scraped upwards. Another heave, and the beam moved even more.

Franz gave a command, and a dozen fire arrows thunked into the underside of the bridge to lick at the oil. The enemy heaved again, the beam popped up and free, then tumbled to the ground. The bridge fell forward with a thud onto the wall of the Gates.

Freed at last, the blue-clad men packed into the bowels of the tower rushed forward with a yell, swords held high, shields before them. A volley of arrows from three directions met the enemy wave, and fully half the men on the bridge were hit and went down, some collapsing on the bridge, others tumbling off with arrows stuck in limbs, torso, or head. The volley barely slowed them, for those following nimbly leaped over their fallen comrades and rushed forward to the waiting fence of our spear points. Locking shields, they threw themselves onto the spears, pushing them down and away. A half dozen died on the spears, but the fence was disordered, and more of the enemy pressed forward, leaping down onto the wall and exchanging blows with the garrison.

Perhaps fifteen Easterners fought on the wall. The enemy had gained their toehold.

"Good God!" exclaimed Kren, standing with drawn sword next to Black. "I'm impressed. What do they feed them?"

Wisps of black smoke were beginning to rise from the underside of the drawbridge, but still the enemy pressed forward to reinforce those on the wall, ignoring a steady stream of men falling victim to the archers on our towers.

Men in front went down beneath sword and ax and spear, but always there was another to take the place of the fallen and continue the combat. Like the grim exchange played by the archers above, the losses on the wall were roughly equal on each side. But this arithmetic we could not sustain for long.

Whiffs of smoke now rose from either side of the drawbridge. Flames could be seen probing from beneath to lick at the edges.

"It's working," cried Kren. "The bridge is aflame underneath."

"But it will burn through too late," warned Black. "We've got to get some oil on its surface."

"I'll see what I can do," said Kren and hurried off as if he were a loyal member of our army. I didn't think this was quite what the beastman council had in mind.

The fighting had spread as the enemy fed more men onto the wall. But off to the left, a strange motion could be seen. A hooded figure clutched the rope handle of a wooden bucket with both hands. The bucket whirled around once, twice, and then, released, made a high arc up and over the drawbridge. Kren had thrown too far.

"Corporal Jenkins," commanded Black. He pointed to the enemy incursion.

Jenkins nodded. "Aye, John, we'll see to it."

With a shout Jenkins and the six remaining guardsmen charged forward into the melee, and the line of battle was pushed forward a few feet, shrinking the bridgehead. Then the impetus of the charge was lost, and the guards were absorbed into the fight. Another man, a short sword in each hand, threw himself upon the enemy in a suicidal lunge. He drove through the first rank, cutting down an Easterner, and then crippled a man in the second rank. A half dozen swords and javelins pierced him, and he went down behind the Easterners. They had been disrupted for a few moments when time was precious. Captain Shaw had found an end to his shame.

"The Easterners fight very well," commented Murdock philosophically.

Black nodded. "We're fighting their best troops."

"Look!" cried the magician.

Off to the left, Kren was whirling another bucket. It left his hands, floated in a gentle arc, and landed on the middle of the drawbridge, splashing most of its contents over its wooden timbers and the rest onto the legs of the enemy crossing.

"That will help," said Black with satisfaction. "That will help, indeed."

A few men doused with the oil leaped quickly away from the fires licking at the edges of the bridge. Tongues of flame reached the new fuel, and the fire spread across the top of the drawbridge. Men who had been rushing forward from the tower drew back, and the flow of enemy reinforcements stopped.

Another bucket flew threw the air, spilled half its oil onto the bridge, and then tumbled off the side. The flames leaped higher, throwing up a wall of heat and licking at ropes and bindings. Disheartened, the enemy atop the wall hesitated, then began to draw back, step by step, fighting as they went.

With a yell, our men pressed forward on all sides, the sight and sound of the high flames before them making clear their victory. From the rift, a horn sounded two long blasts, and then slowly the enemy siege tower drew away from the wall, its flaming bridge hanging free, and then as ropes burnt through, it swung down on its hinges to crash against the front of the tower, tear loose, and fall. Yet the Virginians were too late, for now the tower itself was aflame, fed by the buckets of oil poured over the structure during the struggle. The mammoths were unharnessed and retreated in terror. In a matter of minutes the tower was engulfed, burning fiercely from top to bottom.

In the rift the enemy scurried back down the slopes and out of range. The score of Easterners still alive on the wall retreated into a tight mass behind their shields.

"Do you yield?" Major Franz called out.

A voice came from the mass. "We claim the Rights of Prisoners."

Black nodded to Captain Franz.

"Granted," said Franz. "Drop your weapons." Reluctantly, swords, axes, and shields clattered to the stones. A great cheer went up all along the wall.

The anxious look on the Easterners' faces turned to wariness, then sadness, and finally awkward embarrassment. A man with officer's insignia stepped from their ranks and saluted. The Easterners were led off under guard to an empty storage room, while the officer was brought forward to stand before us. He saluted again. "Lieutenant Dunne, Executive Officer, First Company of the First Regiment of the Army of Virginia. At your service. Who have we had the privilege of fighting?"

Franz made the introductions.

The lieutenant's eyebrows went up. "A prince of the kingdom and the royal guards, too? No wonder, then. Well fought, sir. You have won the first round. My congratulations, and my thanks for accepting us as prisoners." He offered little else under questioning, and was finally led away to a cell below.

Another prisoner was more helpful. A member of the Virginian regiment in the valley, the soldier was wounded and captured upon the battlements after climbing up on an assault ladder during the last assault. He appreciated the hot mug of cider we gave him, and responded to questions he deemed harmless. Murdock mentioned that he had not been able to detect their regimental wizard anywhere.

"Oh, him. Crayton," he replied knowingly. "He broke his leg when we crossed the rift. Had to go back with some others who couldn't make it either. We didn't have any magician, otherwise you couldn't have caught us by surprise the way you did last night."

"Perhaps," Murdock said with a grin. "Perhaps."

We set about clearing up the wall. The aftermath of battle was not a pretty sight. Exclusive of the enemy, there were scores dead and easily as many seriously wounded laying about. Dozens more were afoot bearing minor wounds. Below the walls, in the valley and the rift, perhaps three to four times as many of the enemy were down.

Our archers held their fire while rescue parties removed the wounded and dragged back the bodies. Our own casualties were taken to chambers below, and soon we could hardly tell a battle had been fought—except for the blood splattered all about, and the screams of the wounded drifting up from below.

Kren joined us. We stared at him.

He looked sheepish. "Ummm, sometimes I get a little carried away."

Murdock laughed. "And so now we have yet another hero in the Battle of the Gates."

"Quite a good fight, wasn't it?" the beastman exclaimed, pleased. "But I won't be throwing any more buckets of oil for you soon, I'm afraid." He was holding his shoulder and from between his fingers protruded the stub of an arrow.

Murdock ran up to support him. "Emissaries are not supposed to fight battles, my friend."

Kren shrugged and accepted his support. "Ouch. Easy, Wizard. Would you deny me a little entertainment once in a while? Well, Prince Arn, if all your enemies fight like this, you have your work cut out for you." Murdock took the beastman below.

Franz circulated through the units and reported back to Black. We had taken twenty percent casualties beating off the assault. Black looked around grimly. "So. We're weaker by a fifth, after barely holding the first assault. Are you an engineer, Major Franz?"

"Yes, sir."

"How long do you think it will take them to build another tower?"

"A few hours if they have materials prepared. A few days if not."

Black stared into the west. "A few hours. I feared as much."

Captain Franz was more encouraging. "I don't think they have what they need. The tower took many wagons of timber, all of which had been precut and fitted. I didn't see any materials left over. There's time yet."

"Let's hope so," said Black.

I went below to rest, the major having been kind enough to offer me his quarters. The room was small and dark, with nary a window nor arrow slit to light it. The only furnishings were a bed, desk, and chair, while a clothes trunk apparently held all of the major's possessions. I kindled a fire while a private brought me a tray of food. He stared at me as if I had come from the moon.

"Thank you, Private." "You're welcome, sir," he said, still staring. "I don't need anything else." "Yes, sir." "You may go now." "Yes, sir." "The door is over there." "Oh. Yes. Sorry, sir." He bowed his way out, still staring.

It's not always easy being a prince.

The meal was a simple one, dried beef and moldy potatoes in stew, a hunk of day-old bread quite suitable for pounding nails, and a mug of water. It was delicious. I took off my boots and lay down on the bed. How long had it been since we'd slept? Had it really been two days? Strange that I wasn't tired. I watched the flames crackle, felt the warmth creep into my toes, and thought of buckets of burning oil.

"Wake up, Prince Arn." It was the private.

"Hmm? What?"

"You've slept almost round the clock. It's night. Father Chalecki, our Healer, asked that you come and speak to the wounded. He said it will do them good."

This was not the awakening I would have preferred, but there was nothing to do but go with the man. I splashed water on my face and followed him out, the guard outside the door taking position behind me. Including Corporal Jenkins, there were only four left of the original ten of Fourth Squad. I was using up royal guards at a fearsome rate. We went down a level and up a passageway, the sounds of anguish growing louder as we approached.

The wounded had all been placed in two barracks rooms. Down either side of the rooms ran a row of bunks filled with wounded, while more were placed on the floor between the beds. Arrow slits in the walls on either side gave light during the day and chill air at all times, and also meant that the wounded could look forward to having healthy archers clambering over them to reach the slits during attacks. The stench was bad going on worse. More unpleasant were the screams and groans. I had heard more terrible screams before—namely my own. But the number of voices contributing to the chorus was unnerving. My cries had been a single note. Here was a symphony.

Afterwards, I went up on the battlements for air. Two large fires were burning in the darkness. I looked over the rift wall and saw hundreds of tiny campfires below, each with its cluster of enemy gathered around against the cold. A stiff, steady wind was blowing. It was a good place to be, up on the wall. You could barely hear the wounded.

I was there only a moment before my guard stepped close. "Are you all right, sir?"

"Yes, I'm fine, Phillips." I breathed deeply of the wind.

"If you say so," he said doubtfully.

I decided to change the subject. "Anything happen during the day?"

"Yes, sir. Colonel Black and Major Franz are meeting now. I think Wizard Murdock and the beastman are with them. Trying to figure out what to do about that." He pointed at the enemy siege tower. No, not the blackened skeleton which was all that remained of their original tower. The new one that was under construction in the rift. It was partially visible, military engineers clambering over it as they worked, their torches flickering in the wind.

Murdock and Sergeant Jenkins approached. "There are more forces in the valley," said the wizard. "I've just told John."

"More forces? Theirs or ours?"

"I can't tell. The Easterners have magicians near the rift, and they're keeping up a constant static. Wizard Leroy is feeling better, but he's still blanketed. I was lucky to catch what I did."

Magic can be frustrating at times. "So, either we'll be rescued soon, or we're finished."

"That's about it, Arn."

It would be dramatic to say that there was a last vicious struggle for the Gates, and that we were rescued by the appearance of our relief just in the nick of time. But it didn't happen that way. There was no final assault, for our rescuers arrived just a few hours later. The Sixth Regiment and Duke Santini marched up the road, the Virginians formed up to meet them, we sent out our three companies of the Sixth, and the battle was joined. Outnumbered now, cut off, discouraged by the failure of the attack, and outflanked by Duke Santini's household guards, the Virginians retreated to the slopes and then broke, climbing up the mountainside to escape. We took over two hundred prisoners.

That was really the end of the Valley Campaign. The whole of the victorious Sixth Regiment filed onto the battlements, and the Easterners in the rift realized the siege had been lifted in the valley. Their attempt had failed. They pulled back across the rift but stayed for two days, waiting for some miracle to tumble down the stone walls of the Gates. Finally they dismantled their tower and marched away.

It had been a near thing, but the surprise stroke had failed. The luck of an early snowfall, a handful of brave men, and a soldier named John Black had foiled the first move of the Alliance.

But when would they strike next?

PART · THREE

THE
BURDEN
OF WAR

1

Winter Camp

The Virginians from the valley retreated over the mountains and, half-starved, eventually crossed the rift, thus clearing our northern border of the enemy. We were to find out later that Robert had met a thrust along the coast road by a superior force of Virginian cavalry, and had turned them back with an admirable campaign of maneuver. By January there was not an Easterner left on Kenesee soil.

Black, Murdock, and I held council before sending reports to the king, for promotions and plans had to be made. The fierce charge of the Sixth Regiment had cost Colonel Jones his life and crippled his second in command. Captain Daniels was promoted to lead the Sixth. The Fifth Regiment came marching in from Knox and, with mixed relief and regret, found that they had arrived too late for battle. We held them in the valley, and Black's rigorous training program started for both regiments.

Duke Santini rode back to Knox with the rest of his household, less one squad. Soon after, the beastman Kren was to accompany a messenger who carried my extensive report to the king, as well as reports from Black, Murdock, and Duke Santini. Kren and the messenger would be guarded the entire way by a full squad of the duke's household troops. The beastman emissary had decided that since all the fun was over, he had better be on his way. Kren no longer wore his hood and cap, unless it was for the cold, for his presence was no longer a secret. He still generated long stares and whispers, but all knew he had the king's protection. Suspicion and distrust were also greatly tempered by the reputation he had earned during the siege.

The day after the duke's departure we said farewell to the beastman. He stood with us outside the open portals of the Gates (on the valley side, that is), the messenger and the squad of household troops already mounted and waiting.

"Any words you would like me to convey?" Kren asked, shaking hands with each of us.

We had already given him several personal letters to carry. Mine was to Angela. It pays to let women think they're in your thoughts. Especially if it is true.

"Tell the women that Murdock the Magnificent will come when he may," Murdock stated soberly. "Until then, the poor creatures must make out as best they can."

Kren grinned. "I'll tell them. And you, Colonel Black. You haven't given me any letters. Is there no one to whom I can extend greeting?"

Black shrugged. "None in Kingsport. I have only one living relative."

Kren nodded sympathetically. "Well, then, I'm off, though I'd much prefer to stay here. I fear things will be a bit dull for awhile. Summon me if the Easterners return. I'll bring a cartload of oil."

Black nodded. "A few battalions of beastmen would be more welcome."

"I'll work on that," Kren said seriously.

And then they were away, trotting through the fresh snow down the valley road until they disappeared from sight beyond the trees.

The first weeks thereafter passed slowly for me, although I can't say I was not content—or as content as any man can be deprived of female companionship. A comfortable cabin was built for us in just a few days, and I settled into a busy routine of exercise, training, and setting a good example.

More than four weeks passed before a messenger finally came from Kingsport, bearing proclamations from the king. The proclamations were being distributed throughout the kingdom. The country was being put on a war footing to use the winter months to best effect. The King's Call was effective immediately, with all regiments and eligible men reporting for active duty. New regiments were formed. Not including the nobles and the royal guards, at full strength the field army would total twenty infantry regiments of a thousand men each, and fifteen cavalry regiments of five hundred men each. And still we feared the Alliance would outnumber us two to one.

The messenger also brought letters. The letters for me included one from the king and one from Angela. I opened Angela's first and followed the small, neat handwriting that filled a single sheet of paper.

December 21st, 2652

Dearest Arn,

The beastman carrying your letter arrived a few days ago and I've just discovered a messenger is leaving within the hour for the Rift Gates so I will have but a few moments to complete this note. I received your letter and was so relieved to hear you were all right that I immediately wrote to Megan telling her that you were well. She and her father were invited to Redbank for the holidays but will be back in January to continue her studies with the university though she does resent being the only woman in the class. I think I would like to go to the university after my year as server is over, but Megan says her father and Duke Gregory had to be very persuasive to get her admitted as a student and also that the professors do not take kindly to her presence, but still I would like to try. What do you think, Arn?

Megan and Paul Kendall? I've known of her love for years, ever since we were girls together. She didn't have to tell me because it was obvious to anyone with eyes and sometimes I wonder why men cannot see past their noses. I have never seen her happier since Mr. Kendall declared his love for her and she is waiting for him to return in the next month or two.

The beastman Major Kren is quite amazing and he has all the castle in a tither with everyone wanting to look at him and staring and while he has been quite good about it I'm sure he must be lonely for his own kind and I will try to make sure he is well taken care of, and no, not that well taken care of so don't worry. But some of the servers have stated they find him quite interesting in appearance and wonder if—well, never mind about that.

They are calling me for the messenger is ready to leave and I must finish this letter. I talk about everything else and not us when perhaps that is what you want to hear. I am sorry your return to the castle was so brief and that we missed a chance to be together, but each day I am waiting, hoping and praying for your return.

Angela

Angela. Sweet Angela. The letter left me with a physical ache for this young woman, and I won't even deny that such need was perhaps the most prominent aspect of our romance. It is hard untangling lust from a relationship when one is not yet twenty. Yet, I felt a certain contentment when she was near that I'd found with no other woman, and a lifting of my spirits in her presence no other person could accomplish, unless it be Murdock, with his unvarying cheerfulness and optimism. Strange how she affected me.

I picked up the other envelope and broke the royal seal. The letter was written in the king's own hand, not scribed:

December 20th, 2652
The King's Castle
Kingsport

My dear Arn,

Congratulations and thanks for your success! I cannot tell you the relief your mission and victory bring. The neutrality of the Beastwood is promised. The Rift Gates have been held. Our eastern border is now secure. Well done!

We were saddened to hear of the Virginian assault, for our fears have come true and the slight hope for peace is gone. Robert, too, has met an enemy thrust, turning back their horsemen at Mooresville. These were but opening moves for position, yet enough to know that it is open war between the Alliance and Kenesee. At least, all doubt is now gone, and there is still time to prepare. As well conceived as their first move was, I suspect they will eventually regret spurring us so early.

Your emissary, the beastman Kren, is making quite an impression on the court. The women are both repelled and fascinated, while the men have been taken by his hearty and forthright manner. He has been reticent about his own exploits at the Gates that you reported, and I have said little about this in public to avoid embarrassing his leaders. I wonder what his own people will think of his actions.

I gather that he is very favorably disposed towards us, or at least, towards his recent companions in battle. Every evening he has been forced to retell at length the story of the Gates. You and Colonel Black are quite the heroes now. You did not mention in your report that you alone slew fifteen enemy with a broken sword. Still, the truth is glorious enough, and again I say it. Well done.

Colonel Black has proven himself to be quite an important piece on the board. He has done all that I expected, and more. I regret losing his services with the guards, yet his talents are for greater things. I had made him a temporary colonel for your mission to the Beastwood. Now I appoint him permanent colonel in the Army of Kenesee. I do not give him command of any regiment, for I feel he will be of more value at your side.

Enclosed are colonel's insignia for you to award to our ex-sergeant now. I have also enclosed a general's stars. Tuck them away for a while. Use your judgment about when to use them. Yes, under this national emergency, I grant you (and Robert) power to command and rule wherever you go. You will be subject only to my will. (Read the proclamations, Arn.) You now have the power of life and death over men. You can make and ruin as you see fit. Use this authority wisely.

Elsewhere, all is quiet. Robert is at Mooresville with his cavalry. The Virginian forces on the coast road seem content to watch now. One of our ships chased down and boarded a scouting vessel of the Texan navy off our coast. But that is all that we know. Graven says there is no immediate threat anywhere. Kendall is still gone, *and no word has been received from him.*

I agree with Black in regard to the strategy of our enemies. Given the winter storms at sea, the Alliance will wait for the spring. The Rift Gates are now secure, and we need have little worry about an attack from there as long as we keep the Gates well garrisoned.

I suppose that is all for now. My son, I cannot tell you how your report filled my heart with pride. Robert was born for the lance and the sword, and that he will continue to play a valiant part in the coming struggle is without doubt. I know that you were made for things other than war, and that the cruelty endured during your early years left scars inside you far worse than any that can be seen. Many have questioned your courage and truthfulness since the Rite of Manhood. Yet ever have I loved you, and known that blood would run true. Your bravery and nobility are now beyond doubt. Hold yourself safe for the struggle ahead.

I will call you back to Kingsport in a month or two, and we will discuss our strategy for the campaign. During those weeks, Colonel Black and Wizard Murdock will manage without you somehow, I am sure.

Your proud father,
Reuel

I folded the letter, placed it in a leather envelope, and tucked it carefully within my breast pocket.

Poor Reuel. He too believed the lie. Or did he? I did not deserve acclaim, yet would have to endure it. There was some advantage to the situation. Perhaps it would serve me well in the future. Yes. Respect without responsibility. A small castle, well-protected by loyal guards in some pleasant spot of the country, safe from the intrigues of court and kingdom. A warm fire in every room, Angela running the household, a cellar filled with food and drink. Then life would be complete. Perhaps Murdock and Black might join me to provide company. It was a pleasant thought.

There was a knock on the door. The head of my private popped around the door. "Pardon, sir. Got to collect the slops bucket."

I sighed. "All right, take it away. Be careful! Don't spill it." A thought suddenly occurred to me. "By the way, do you wash your hands before serving food?"

He looked puzzled. "Wash?"

Good servants. The castle would definitely need good servants.

The next day I pinned the colonel's insignia on Black's new uniform in a simple ceremony in my cabin, and then others were promoted as well. As a proud colonel, Franz left the Rift Gates to command a new regiment at Wickliffe. Corporal Jenkins became a sergeant and took over the Fourth Squad permanently. The promotion was just in time, as the reserve guards arrived, swelling the squad of ten (before casualties) to a squadron of fifty. The bravery and ability of the men were beyond question, but some were wearing a few more pounds then they should. Sergeant Jenkins whipped his men into shape under the watchful eye of Black, who demanded much from his old unit.

Colonel Black was kept busy running the training of the two regiments and seeing to the inclusion of the new recruits who streamed in, numerous enough to replace all our losses and form three extra companies for the Sixth Regiment. With Murdock's guidance, I took care of the few civil matters that arose, such as an incident of corruption by the owner of a weapons forge and a guild steward at Loren that brought me and the wizard to that town. I addressed the problem in a way which I felt was both fair and practical. I hung the two villains in the town square. This, with my treatment of the bandits outside the Beastwood, would earn me a new name to go with that of Prince Scar. Now, they also called me The Hanging Prince.

We were preparing to leave Loren when I again saw the familiar squat figure with the two eagle feathers sticking in her round felt hat. She wore a long, stained sheepskin coat to protect her from the elements, but across her back was the familiar bedroll and sack. She waddled up through the February snow and stared at me. Her black hair was run through with a few streaks of gray, yet her face was unchanged, the seams and wrinkles the same as I remembered from over a decade before. And her odor had not improved any over the years.

"Hello, Mary."

She reached out a hand, but paused as my guards made ready to lunge forward. I gestured. Half-drawn swords were returned to their sheaths and the guards backed to a respectful distance, still ready to leap to my defense. Jenkins stared at Mary with suspicion. Where had this seedy woman come from? Her finger touched my face and gently traced the new scar that cut across my cheek and jaw.

She grunted and let her hand fall. "Prince Scar."

Murdock cleared his throat. "I don't believe we've been introduced."

Mary eyed him with disdain. "I can feel you prying into my mind. Not getting very far, are you? Your charm won't work on me. I have no interest in you, Wizard Murdock. Nor any wizard."

Murdock cocked an eyebrow. "Well, I can certainly understand that. We are a rather disreputable bunch. Pity though. One doesn't often meet a sorceress."

"No help to you and your School of Magic. Men only. Humph. Idiots only."

Time to go. "Well, Mary, it's been nice seeing you. Have a safe—"

"We must talk." She gestured at Murdock in a wave of dismissal. "Not him."

"Of course," Murdock bowed, and stepped away a polite distance.

What do you say to a soothsayer? Go away? Leave me alone? Take a bath?

One thing did come to mind. "Are you following me?"

She shook her head. "I go where the visions lead. Sometimes you are in the visions. More often now."

It was nice to have women dream about me, but this wasn't quite what I had in mind. "Visions? What visions?"

"My end draws near."

So that's what she had seen. "Goodness, Mary. I'm sorry to hear that."

"You should be. It's your doing."

"Oh." I had learned to respect those with premonitions. Graven had been right about the Rift Gates. And Mary had

certainly been right about me. No wonder she was upset about
her latest dreams. Still, how could I be responsible?

"What happens to me doesn't matter," she continued. "But
many others will die with me. Innocent people."

"Regrettable. Well, Mary, it really has been a delight talking with you again—"

"I see two futures for you. Terrible visions. In one, you
grow old in a dungeon, cold and miserable, alone and forgotten in your cell, and you stare into the darkness with empty
sockets."

She let me think about that one for a while. Mary did know
how to strike a chord. "What? What?" I stammered. "How
can—"

"In the other, you have your victory. But it will cost you
your soul. Your very soul. You cannot be both a great man
and a good man."

No danger there. I was certainly not great, nor ever would
be. But then, the alternative wasn't very likely, either. I opened
my mouth to reply, but Mary had already turned and was
walking away with heavy steps.

"Good-bye Mary!" I called. Hopefully, it was for the last
time. But in this I was to be disappointed.

"Until spring!" she called back with surety, and then waddled off.

Dungeons? Eye sockets? And just when I was starting to
sleep well again.

"Who was that?" Murdock asked immediately.

"My personal fortune-teller," I said regretfully. "She likes
to pop up occasionally and scare me to death."

"She has precognition? That's the rarest of gifts. Perhaps
she could help us."

"She won't," I said. "She comes and goes as she will.
Forget her."

He watched her disappear around a corner. "Did she say
anything this time?"

I shook my head. "No, nothing," I told him.

Nothing I wanted to hear.

2

Preparing for War

With April came the long-awaited order from Kingsport.

We were to march out April 10, pick up the new Sixteenth Infantry Regiment at Loren, and continue on to Nash. There, the regiments from Wickliffe and Louisville would join my command, and we would await the king's next order. Robert would also move on the tenth, withdrawing his cavalry from the border to Greenville, where he could upset the enemy's timetable but not be cut off. He would eventually take command of the forces assembling at Knox. The remainder of the army would take position at Redbank.

Black and Murdock considered the sheet of formal orders with calm interest. Black read the document and looked far away, as if trying to peer through the mountains. "I'd have liked another month to train, but we're as ready as any. The Fifth is a fine regiment, and the Sixth is even better."

The two regiments *were* excellent, thanks to Black. "And now," I said reluctantly, "to battle."

We set off at dawn on the tenth of April with the Gate Keepers giving us a silent salute. We marched with the squadron of royal guards at the head of the column, followed by the two infantry regiments and trailed by dozens of wagons carrying supplies and equipment. Behind us we left over three hundred men garrisoning the Rift Gates. Spies and scouts found no enemy near the rift, and Murdock agreed that he could detect no enemy presence.

The weather had been wet but mild, melting the snow from the mountaintops weeks before and bringing out the first growth of leaf upon bushes and trees. Though rains began as we set out, the old crete road was not muddy. We marched steadily up the valley, the brown, grassy meadows newly turned a spring green. I looked at the peaks around me for one last time and thought of our trek along the mountain slope four months before. I knew where to look and still could not pick out the mountain trail we had used.

"I can't see it either," Murdock agreed. "Without our guide, we would never have known it was there."

"Oh, yes," I remembered. "The guide and his wife. How are they doing?"

Montego had been subject to the King's Call, but objected to war. Any war. He had prepared to refuse service, which should have earned him an execution. Black and Murdock would not let me hang him, saying he had already done enough. Instead, I gave the man a signed exemption from service. A rare document, indeed.

The wizard pointed up the road. "Their farmhouse is just ahead a ways. You'll be able to see for yourself." He grew mellow. "The baby is a charming little fellow, and they're doing well. The woman is a wonderful cook."

As the troops began to march by the family's cabin, two figures emerged and waited beside the road, the woman carrying the child in her arms. Montego waved to us. "Thank you, Prince Arn," he said, gesturing at the newly rebuilt home. "Your men were most helpful."

I nodded in acknowledgment. The woman smiled shyly at the party, but seemed not to notice the many glances from the troops who continued marching on behind us.

One of the soldiers whispered. "It's been a long time since we've had any of that."

His comrade spoke in a tone of exasperation. "Mel, you've never had any of that. All you've ever had are sheep and cows."

"That's not true. What about the ducks?"

Oblivious to looks and comments, the woman lifted the baby, who watched with wide eyes as the column passed, and then began to giggle and laugh.

Murdock waved at the baby. "Gentlemen, we are being laughed at."

"Speak for yourself, Wizard," said Black. "Perhaps he knows something we don't."

Carlotta took the baby's hand and waved it. "He is giving you God's Blessing!" she announced over and over to each company in turn. Montego rolled his eyes upward and shrugged helplessly. The baby smiled at the troops and gave Murdock a bubbly laugh. But he had only a look of serious contemplation for me.

Carlotta waved me forward, and spoke softly. "We have named the baby after the man who has most entered our hearts."

I was touched, I must admit. I had never had a baby named after me.

"What do you call him?" I asked. Would it be Arn, Arnold, or Brant?

She smiled prettily. "Murdock."

I left the column later that morning, forging ahead, for the orders bid me to come to Kingsport for a last strategy meeting with Robert and the king. I rode with only Phillips and Reynolds, since three riders could use fresh mounts from the various messenger depots established for the war along the major roads. In this way we made excellent speed.

So it was that late on a rainy afternoon one week later, tired and sore, we clattered over the drawbridge and into the courtyard of the king's castle. The watchman at the north gate had trumpeted the return of royalty, the castle trumpeter had repeated the call, and thus the yard was rapidly filling as barracks and house emptied to greet the returning prince. It was a far cry from my departure in secrecy months before.

The king greeted me with open arms, then examined my scarred cheek with a grim look. "Arn! Arn, my son. I can sleep well again, at last, with you and Robert here. You've recovered from your wounds? No ill effects? Good. Good."

Robert assessed the facial damage, and me, while shaking my hand. "You have done well, I understand."

I shrugged. No use trying to fool Robert. "Colonel Black and Wizard Murdock guided me."

"So it is said."

"And that's the truth of it. But you turned back a thrust

along the coast. Quite brilliantly, against superior numbers of cavalry.''

It was Robert's turn to shrug. ''The Virginians were conducting more of a cavalry raid than anything else, though they might have brought up infantry if they'd met success. Still, I did rather enjoy it.''

There were individual greetings to a dozen others, then we made our way towards the entrance of the house. To one side I saw a cloaked figure standing silent. I restrained myself, and merely nodded. From beneath her hood Angela watched, a sly smile beckoning to me. And then I was swept into the castle to wash quickly before the dinner bell rang.

In my room I greeted Walter and Marta. Walter was stoking a fire into being while Marta ensured there was hot water in the pitcher and fresh towels on the dresser. ''I hope you don't mind our freshening things for you,'' said Marta. ''Mr. Lorich gave us your key to do so, otherwise we don't come in.'' She bustled out to get fresh linens for the bed.

Walter built up a fire. ''There you are, Prince Arn. I'll check it after dinner and add some more wood.'' He came close to whisper. ''I've missed our occasional drink together. Marta's on her Bible again, so it's the devil if I have a drop. Maybe later, eh?''

At evening meal worries about the coming war were set aside by my return. Robert and I sat on either side of the king, with the select invited to join us at his table. Around us sat Sir Meredith, Graven, Megan, beastman Kren, and Professor Wagner, along with others at the farthest ends. I had already invited Apprentice Lorich to join us—one of his rare opportunities to sit at the king's table—and he took a seat beside Graven a few moments later, almost knocking over a mug in his excitement.

Graven sighed.

Lorich seemed not to notice as he gazed my way in admiration. ''Oh, sir, you *did* come back!''

''That *was* my intention, Wizard Lorich.''

Prayers were given, and then we began to eat. Or rather, the others began to eat, for I was forced to give my version of events on the road north, the attack of the bandits, and our mission into the Beastwood. In all this, I omitted mention only of the torture, indicating merely that an enraged beastman had slashed my cheek. Little would be gained by spreading the truth of the encounter. Amidst the exclamations, comments, and questions I stuffed food into my mouth. When they were ready for more, I concluded with the journey to Loren, the valley march, the fight to reach the Rift Gates, and finally our defense of its walls. There was more excited talk, and I took the opportunity to refill my plate and lead the topic away from my adventures. "And now, what's happened here while I was gone?"

Lorich broke into an eager smile. "Oh, Prince Arn, I've learned so much since you left. About running the kingdom and the importance of the High Wizard and the castle and all the people who live here. Many have been very nice to me. Angela has become such a good friend. I didn't know women could be so smart."

Megan gave him a look, but somehow he avoided keeling over dead.

"And Corporal Jenkins taught me how to ride before he left. Every Saturday we'd go to the parade ground and practice. And then afterwards we'd come back, and he'd get some money and we'd go into town and—"

Graven's eyes had opened wide. "Lorich!"

"Uhhh, yes, master?"

"Eat your dessert."

The boy cast us a reluctant glance and lowered his head.

"I have received a letter from Paul," Megan offered.

The king nodded. "It came in early March with a dispatch he sent me, confirming his earlier report from January. His information was valuable. Most valuable."

"Let us pray Mr. Kendall's information is accurate," Graven added.

Megan seemed about to respond to the high wizard, thought better of it, and instead addressed me. "Paul was here in January for a few weeks, and then went off again. He wouldn't tell me where, and the letter gave no clue." She shifted her attention. "King Reuel, can't you tell us where he might be?"

The king shook his head. "I have an idea, but do you really want me to endanger him by sharing it?"

Her smile faded. "No. I suppose not."

Robert watched her. "I'm sure he's fine. No cause for

worry. Arn, did you know that Mr. Kendall and Megan are promised? He has beaten us both, and we didn't even know he was in the game.''

Robert didn't seem too disturbed by the news. And yet— was he just a bit too casual, a bit too unperturbed? Had it been more than a game for Robert, or was it just that he found it hard to lose?

Megan smiled. ''Although Arn wasn't really playing the game any more, I suspect.''

''Poor Prince Robert,'' said Kren. ''Yet, there may be one or two women in the kingdom willing to consider him.''

The king rose. ''I need to meet with my advisors and Robert, if they're finished? Good. And we'll give Arn time with his friends. Tomorrow is soon enough for him to join us at council.'' Sir Meredith and Graven followed the king and Robert out of the hall, leaving us to a moment of silence.

The servers started removing the platters. I almost stopped them, and then thought better of it. The night wasn't over yet, and physical exertion is not good on a full stomach. I settled on a mug of cider to wash it all down.

Kren studied me. ''You know, Lady Megan, I do believe that scar does something for Arn. What do you think?''

''Some women might like that sort of thing. But as for me . . .''

''Well,'' Kren continued, ''he was never very handsome to begin with—''

Huh?

''—so anything might be an improvement. What do you say, Mr. Lorich?''

The boy nodded. ''Definitely.''

Definitely? Definitely what?

Megan stared pensively. ''Then again, it does add a certain character. He needed character.''

For this, I could have stayed with Murdock.

There was a sweet voice behind me. ''Hello, Lady Megan. Major Kren. Mr. Lorich.'' The voice grew soft. ''Hello, Prince Arn.''

I had caught glimpses of Angela serving one table or another, but had been too busy to let my eyes feast as well as my stomach. Now I turned, and she stood not a foot away. I gulped and understood how Lorich had felt upon first seeing her. *Arrgk grrrg.*

Her lips were parted, and her eyes bored into mine. "I can bring the fruit basket. Would you like some fruit, Prince Arn?"

Soured apples, spoiled pears, rotten peaches. Yes. Yes. Anything.

"No, thank you," Kren broke in cheerily. "We're quite set here, aren't we?" Megan and Lorich nodded at the beastman. "There, you see. Thank you, Angela."

"Yes, sir," she said meekly at the dismissal, gave me a long backward glance, and disappeared into the kitchen. I looked after her in disappointment.

Megan smirked. "We're all glad you're back, Arn. It's so good to spend an evening with you again. We want to hear more of your adventures."

"Uhh, I'm a bit tired. The ride and all . . ."

"Nonsense," Kren corrected. "You're in the prime of youth. A few hundred miles on horseback is nothing to you."

"No, really—"

"We've missed you," Megan pouted. "Don't deny us. Do you have your pipe? Get it. I want to see how you look smoking, and you can tell us more about your adventures."

With a sigh I trudged back up to my room, mumbling dark thoughts about friends who will not spare the weary traveler. I opened the door—and standing there was Angela, holding my pipe and tobacco. Her auburn hair fell to her shoulders in a cascade, and the skirt of her dress swirled ever so gently as she turned to face me. Her eyes narrowed.

My voice almost failed, but at last I found it. "Uhh—" I began, and then she was in my arms. It had been a long time.

A few hours later we lay together, Angela snuggled quite comfortably against me, the faint chiming of the hall clock marking the hour. She lifted her head. "I need to go back to my room now."

"You do?"

She slipped out of bed and began dressing. "Otherwise my roommates will talk. We must observe the proprieties."

The proprieties. I had the same respect for them as I had for tradition. Inconvenient and often hypocritical, if not dangerous. But if Angela wanted to observe the proprieties, then I would not object. I watched her brush her hair. "Do you think they're still waiting for me in the dining hall?" She laughed and folded herself into my arms, her fingers stroking my cheek and, inevitably, finding the wound.

"Oh, poor Arn."

"Does my scar bother you?"

She lifted her head to look. "No."

I turned to profile. "Don't you think it adds a bit of character?"

"Ummmm . . ."

I gave her a swat on a soft area. "Disrespectful wench. Answer my question."

"Ask a question I can answer."

"Do you really want to attend the university?"

"Either that, or find some young man to marry and have a family."

I pictured a half dozen little Arns running around screaming "Papa," and a cold sweat appeared on my forehead. "I'll talk to Professor Wagner."

Morning meal was a decent affair, with boiled eggs, sausages, biscuits, and jellies eaten with a mug of fresh coffee. The coffee beans from the far southlands were carried by traders of the Isles, so we could expect little more of that commodity, and in fact the castle held the last to be had in Kingsport. I enjoyed as much as I could of it before the king rose and we followed him to the council chamber.

Since the last time I'd seen it, the room had become even more crowded with maps and stacks of books. On the table was another map of the kingdom carefully tacked down upon a board. Small leaded figures of infantry and cavalry were deployed on it to mirror our forthcoming campaign. There were also a few figures to represent personalities. I picked one up. "Which one am I?" I asked, and Graven pointed to the one I held. I placed it down carefully.

As King Reuel explained, we were going to follow the traditional defensive strategy for Kenesee. To that end, the regiments were moving towards the center of Kenesee, deploying in the triangle formed by Nash, Knox, and Redbank. From these points, the forces could unite in only a few days at any one of the three towns and strike the enemy a blow. A classic, if conservative, strategy.

King Reuel's one variation from the traditional deployment was Robert's position at Greenville on the coast road midway between Kingsport and the border. From Greenville, Robert could threaten and delay the Virginian advance. It might appear very risky at first glance—and it was—but the Allies' concentration of five different armies into one force involved timetables, and slowing the Virginians would throw their schedule off, perhaps providing opportunity to strike a blow. And with the Rift Gates secure, the north road from Greenville left him a safe route of withdrawal to Knox.

Following the king's explanation, Robert and I were given numerous details and situation reports. Graven, Sir Meredith, and Bishop Thomas each delivered summaries of various war preparations. Perhaps all this was normal for a council of war. Still, the council meeting puzzled me, for everything could easily have been given to us in written reports, and I wouldn't have had to ride two hundred miles through rain and storm. Afterwards I shared this observation with Robert.

He looked at me in wonder. "You still don't understand? Father called us back because he wanted to see us again before the campaign starts. He wanted us with him one last time, just in case."

How was I supposed to know?

Robert had that look again. Disappointment. "Since you'd shown so much courage at the Rift Gates, I thought perhaps you'd have changed in other ways, too. But you haven't, have you? Still the same old Arn." He walked away shaking his head, and I heard the words he muttered. "Poor father."

I stayed at the castle for almost a week, meeting with the council, attending formal and social occasions with the king and court, sitting next to the king at meals, enjoying a few hours of intimacy each night with Angela, and sleeping soundly and well in my own bed. Just before Robert and I were to leave, King Reuel came to my room, watched me stuff a last few items into my saddle bags, then gestured to a chair. I sat while he paced slowly around the room.

"I've seen Robert. He's all ready. You have everything you need, Arn?"

"Yes, sir."

"And you understand what you're to do? Hold yourself in readiness at Nash until you get orders?"

"Yes, sir. The orders were perfectly clear. I've taken notes and will share them with Colonel Black and Wizard Murdock when I meet them at Nash."

"Good. Well done." He stepped to the arrow slit and peered out, his arms folded across his chest, one hand stroking his beard. "You've seemed quite happy—well, happy is not the word. Content, rather. Yes, you've seemed quite content during your visit. Have you been?"

Of course I was content. No one was trying to kill me. "Yes, sir," I answered.

"I'm pleased. Very pleased. You know, I probably didn't have to call you and Robert back to Kingsport, but I did want to see you again. Both of you."

"It was our pleasure being back," I assured him.

"There was one thing I wanted to ask you about. . . ."

"Yes, sir?"

"This server. Angela."

"Oh."

"She's not beautiful in the classic sense," he ruminated, "but quite attractive in her own way."

"Yes," I agreed. "Quite attractive."

"She possesses a wonderful smile and great personal warmth."

"Yes," I nodded.

"You're not trifling with her, are you? It's wrong to trifle with women. It's not fair." He grew thoughtful. "Terrible things can happen. Terrible things . . ."

"No, sir. I'm not trifling."

"Good. How serious are you about her?"

"Serious?" I responded, looking bemused. Was I serious about her? I didn't know. "She does have her charms, I must admit. And I do enjoy her company. But 'serious' might be too strong a word."

He looked at me with lifted brows. "Too strong a word. I see. Well, I just wanted to say that she seems like a fine young woman. I've talked to Sir Meredith about her. She comes from a hardworking family of modest means, though their lack of wealth must be credited to honesty and generosity rather than any lack of ability. Her father is not the most imposing of men, and yet Sir Meredith considers him one of the best mayors Lexington has had. As do I.''

"She would be pleased to know that," I agreed.

"She already does. I've told her." He clasped his hands behind his back. "I just wanted to remind you that should this develop into anything . . . serious . . . that marrying commoners is not unusual among Kenesee royalty. Certainly, I would have no objection. And—well, enough said. Come here, my boy."

I stood, and his arms went around me in his bearish hug, and for the moment I considered clasping him back. But before I could decide, he had broken off, wiped his eyes, and smiled. "Well now. It's time for you and Robert to depart. You've said good-bye to Angela and your other friends? Good. No use delaying, then. Take your saddle bags. Have everything? Then, you're off."

Completed good-byes or not, the courtyard again was filled with well-wishers. Robert and I shook hands solemnly and mounted, our guards taking position behind us. We rode out together, but while I took the road to the north, he took the road to the east. Before we lost sight of each other, he lifted an arm and gave a single wave. I waved in return, but the corner of a building came between, and whether he saw my response, I did not know.

A week later I rode into Nash, tired after more days in the saddle in a windswept rain but pleased to have arrived at last, and looking forward to resting in comfortable quarters. Infantry and cavalry were encamped about the town, but Black and Murdock had not yet arrived with the regiments from the Rift Gates. At the town hall I found that the three regiments from Louisville were those I had seen encamped, but that the Wickliffe regiments had not appeared, nor was there any word from them. A message had been received from Black, who would be arriving with our men the following day. Quite good timing on my part. I slept well that night.

Black's word was good. By early afternoon the three regiments of infantry from Loren and the Rift Gates marched in and set up camp next to the other regiments. Black and Murdock hurried forward to the town hall to greet me, followed by Sergeant Jenkins and his squadron of guards. We all hid our relief at finding each other well, and immediately settled in to update ourselves on the last fortnight.

Black was quick to turn the conversation to current matters. I informed him of all King Reuel had told me concerning the strategy of the campaign, and that I'd found two infantry regiments and a cavalry regiment from Louisville awaiting us here but that the three regiments from Wickliffe had not arrived. I assumed they were simply late in marching, but Black was concerned.

"It's an easy march to Nash from Wickliffe," he said, "and we know of no reason for delay. Murdock, anything?"

"No, John, nothing positive at this distance. But I'm running into a lot of static from the west. I don't know why. Could it signal a move by the Alliance?"

Black pondered this piece of information and studied the map. "We could march northwest to the Wickliffe-Louisville road to secure the crossroads and aid the Wickliffe force if it's in trouble. To do so, however, pulls us out of position at Nash and more than doubles the length of our march should the King need us. That could lead to disaster. At the same time, the loss of three regiments would be a serious blow to the strength of Kenesee."

He stood over a map and mused aloud. "Something isn't right. The regiments have been assembled at Wickliffe for over a month. All should have their orders by now. Why doesn't Duke Trudeau bring them to Nash?"

I tossed in my penny's worth. "Ahem. Duke Trudeau is not a very efficient administrator. Perhaps that has some bearing on the matter." I disliked mentioning the poor duke's incompetence, which was even worse than Duke Santini's. He was a bumbler who could not make up his mind, and always put off decisions. The king had to ensure that Trudeau had good administrators to compensate. Yet for all his faults he was a kindly man who meant well, and had always treated me with welcome and respect.

Black listened, lit his pipe, and puffed upon it in silence, staring at the map as if the answer would suddenly appear in magic letters. Finally, he shrugged. "Whatever the reason, we won't win by playing it safe. I think we have to take the risk and go after them. Arn, I'll take full responsibility for anything that might happen, and put it in writing. But blame will still fall on you if it doesn't work."

That's the problem with war. You get blamed for everything. But I knew better than to ignore a suggestion by Black. I took a deep breath. "All right. Let's go."

We broke camp at dawn, and the column, grown twice as long with five regiments of infantry and one of cavalry, stretched out behind us as we set off. I suppose it could be a heady feeling to lead almost six thousand men to war—for those who enjoy such things. I was simply aware that upon us depended the lives of all those men, and I thanked God that Black was there to handle it. I didn't need any additional cases of indigestion.

Five days of steady marching brought our six regiments to the town of Curtis, where the Wickliffe-Louisville road crossed the Nash road. The Louisville infantry regiments that joined us at Nash suffered straggling from men who hadn't trained under a taskmaster as rigorous as John Black. Still, they would have to learn.

Curtis was a lowlands town surrounded by gentle watercourses that flooded every ten years or so. The floods sent the inhabitants to their roofs but deposited silt that made the soil excellent for crops. The community numbered over a thousand, including the many farms that clustered around and came under its authority. The inhabitants were both happy to see us and fearful too of what it meant. No fools, these country folk.

Reports had come in from watch posts that large Arkan patrols had been seen on the far bank of the Ohio. Hearing this information, Black recommended that he secure the crossroads with the regiments and that Murdock and I take the guards and ride to Wickliffe.

"Be cautious when you arrive. Things may not be as they seem."

Murdock bit his lip. "Treachery, John?"

Black hesitated. "I can't say. I know little of Duke Trudeau. I could be unjustly accusing him. Perhaps a mistake has been made. Or the messenger bearing the King's order did not get through. That's what you'll have to find out."

I didn't like the idea of going ahead without Black at my side, but I had to admit it was necessary. Our regiments could be trapped on the road to Wickliffe, caught between the river and swamp if the Arkans crossed the river and reached the crossroads. Curtis had to be held. At the same time, I was the only recognized authority above Duke Trudeau who could order the Wickliffe regiments to move. If it came to that.

Black gave one last bit of advice before we left. "Wherever the regiments are, get them back here. March hard, and don't waste a minute."

We took Black's advice and made good progress. The land was relatively flat, the road well-maintained in spite of Duke Trudeau's management, and the land peaceful, if overly wet. Further south, after we had marched across bridges spanning the Cumberland and Kenesee Rivers, the swamps closed in on both sides. A winged creature that might have been a pterodactyl flew overhead, but of other dinosaurs we saw none. Scores of hooves clopping on the crete warned most of the monsters that the roadway was not a good place to be, and watery undergrowth was never far off for the creatures to hide in.

The sky was gray and a cold drizzle fell periodically throughout our ride, but we pushed hard, and the miles fell behind us. The only event of note was on the morning of the second day, when our two scouts rode back hard towards us, closely pursued by a half dozen riders on speedy mounts. When our column of guards came into view the riders slid to a stop, reversed direction, and disappeared up a side road.

Sergeant Jenkins called the squadron to a halt, declining to pursue the horsemen, and reported to us. "They wore civilian clothes, sir. But somehow, I don't quite think they're civilians. Nor citizens of Kenesee."

"Arkans?" I asked. "Why would they attack our scouts?"

Murdock looked down the road they had taken. "Maybe they didn't know our two men were scouts. Maybe they thought our men were messengers. If so—"

We ignored the riders, put the scouts back out, and continued on our way. By mid-afternoon we knew we were nearing Wickliffe, for the swamps there back off from the road and leave miles of firm ground on either side. We climbed the last gentle rise before the walled town and stopped. It lay before us with its gates open, flags and banners flying from its walls. Beyond, the spires of Duke Trudeau's castle could be seen, and the masts of merchant ships on the river docks peeked above the battlements. The Navy Keep overlooked empty docks, for the ships of the King's Navy normally berthed at Wickliffe were out to sea. All was as it should be.

And we had located the missing regiments.

In the fields outside the town scores of tents were set up in neat rows, and hundreds of horses were securely tethered in long, straight lines. Flags and banners of companies and regiments flapped lazily. On the muddied fields the men of three regiments stood at random or huddled around campfires.

Murdock held up his arm and our column came to a halt.

"Something is wrong."

For once I was on top of things. "Yes. I noticed it too. The men are idle. That's not normal and—"

"No, no!" Murdock interrupted. "There are more men to the south. And very close. There was a lot of static and I couldn't separate the two forces. I thought they must be our regiments. But if our men are here—Arn, there's no time to lose."

We spurred forward and splashed our way into the center of the camp, where regimental banners flew above three command tents all nicely clustered together for convenience. The sentries at least knew their job, for word was given as we neared, and from each tent a colonel clambered out and sprang to attention. As one, they saluted. Some traditions were hard to break.

I reined in before them. "Do you know me, gentlemen?"

They nodded. One familiar face grinned at me. It was Franz, the former commander of the Rift Gates. "Welcome to Wickliffe, Prince Arn and Wizard Murdock."

We did not smile back, and his grin quickly faded and gave way to puzzlement.

I tried to keep my voice calm. "Why didn't you march to Nash . . . as ordered by the King?"

The three looked at each other in confusion. "We received no such order," said Franz. "We've been training here since winter. The Duke is in command, but he's given us no movement order from the King. His only order this week has been to rest the men and keep them in camp to prepare for any necessary marches."

Murdock and I looked at each other. Things were indeed

amiss. "I will see Duke Trudeau. Prepare your men to march immediately."

"The enemy is coming," Murdock warned them. "Probably Arkans."

"How far away?" asked Franz.

Murdock threw up his hands. "I don't know. Close. Very close. An hour at most. Probably less."

Mouths fell open. "No time for the tents," Franz advised the others. "Runners! Notify the Mayor and militia captains to sound the alarm. The enemy is approaching. They should prepare the town for siege."

And then the colonels all started spouting orders, and the previous inactivity was replaced by a flurry of men running back and forth. Bugles, horns, and drums all began to sound.

"Better send a message to John letting him know what we've found," Murdock reminded me. I made sure an aide had the message down correctly and was on his way back to the crossroads, safely escorted by a dozen men from the cavalry regiment.

We didn't have to seek Duke Trudeau, for he came to us, riding into camp with Wizard Garth. The duke was clearly relieved by our arrival, and wondered why he hadn't received any orders yet. Murdock explained how the King's Messengers must have been intercepted on the road by Arkan spies. Open mouths again greeted the news that the enemy was approaching. Wizard Garth was unaware of enemy movements, the static completely blanketing him. Both men hurried back to the castle to get the household guards, the duke noting that he'd had them assembled and ready for the last week.

The town's church bells began to ring above the pandemonium of the camp. Orders were shouted as men formed into ranks, horses whinnied as they were being saddled, and whips snapped as teams were hitched to wagons. A few command tents had been struck, but most of the others still stood in place. Colonel Franz came up. "Sir, my men are ready to march."

"Then put them on the road." I thought of something. "But not your wagons. All wagons will follow the infantry."

Murdock nodded approvingly. I would have to tell Black how well I had remembered his lessons. Franz gave the order, the last few men working on tents grabbed their weapons and fell into ranks, and the companies began filing onto the road in columns of four, heading northeast back towards the cross-roads. I breathed a sigh of relief. At least we were moving.

Murdock asked Franz about the regiments.

"Colonel Mendez has trained his infantry hard," said Franz. "I think they can be depended on in any situation. My regiment is a new one. Enthusiastic enough, but slow in maneuver."

"I'm sure they'll acquit themselves well," I told him.

"And the cavalry?" Murdock pursued. "How are they?"

Franz shrugged. "Colonel Smith's regiment is spirited, but tends to become uncontrollable in the charge. Even in training they seem to go wild. Recall is most difficult. I would recommend maneuvering them close before charging, and leaving them plenty of time to re-form."

The other colonels joined us. "Ready to march, sir," they reported. "We're light on supplies, but we should have enough food for two or three days."

"They're closing the gates," said Murdock. "Where's the Duke?"

We looked and saw the gates of the town swing shut, the last of the civilians from outside the walls scuttling in just before they closed. Militia began to appear on the battlements. And then the gates opened again, and the duke cantered out, followed by over fifty mounted men-at-arms.

I intercepted them and pointed up the hill. "Duke Trudeau, you will proceed to the head of the column and ensure that the road ahead is clear for the infantry." They galloped off.

"Well," I said, quite satisfied, "it looks as if we'll be getting away clean."

"I'm afraid not," said Franz. He pointed.

To the south, a horseman halted in the middle of the road, watching us.

He wore the gray uniform of the Arkan Army.

3

Calculated Risks

There are times when racing around waving arms and hat and sword makes sense, and times when it does not. My companions seemed to take the sight of the Arkan calmly, so I resisted the impulse to flap my arms and shout orders and act like an idiot. The leading infantry companies of Colonel Franz's regiment were already stepping off smartly, and the other regiments waited patiently for their turn. Still, it took time to feed two thousand infantry onto a road. What if more of the enemy should appear?

Colonel Franz tried to be helpful. "Our patrols ranged out ten miles this morning and saw no one. The enemy will have marched far today. Their horses and men will be tired."

"But not too tired, I'm afraid," Murdock added.

Some men might have been exhilarated by controlling the forces set in motion. I was overwhelmed. Black was not around to take the awesome responsibility, which weighed upon me as an unrelenting burden of fear and uncertainty. I took a deep breath and thought our problem out. What would Black do? And that gave me my answer. "Colonel Smith, move your cavalry regiment up there behind that crest north of town, so you can't be seen from here. Form a double line of battle . . . centered on the road, facing this way. Five companies in the first line, five in the second. Twenty yards between lines. Do you understand?"

He repeated it back to me. "Anything else, sir?"

"Use the fields if you have to, but don't block the road. The infantry is on it. I'll join you in a few minutes."

"Yes, sir. The Tenth Cavalry will do proud, you'll see." Smith was off, and soon the cavalry followed him in company columns across the plowed fields and pastures.

So far, so good. I leaned over and whispered to Murdock. "I wish I knew what I was doing."

"You're doing fine," he whispered back. "Just stop chewing your fingernails."

I put on my gloves. Then I took the gloves off. I took out my pipe, filled the bowl with trembling hands, and lit up. Then I put the gloves back on. It helped.

Two more Arkans rode up and joined the first one. Colonel Franz cast a careful eye over our companies, and then looked south at the Arkan horsemen, measuring distances. "I think we'll be able to get the men away. The wagons might be a different matter."

"I want the wagons," I declared. Black wouldn't lose the wagons.

"Don't get greedy, my boy," Murdock warned.

The first companies of Mendez's infantry regiment were also on the road now, marching towards the rise a quarter mile away. The cavalry regiment outpaced them in the fields to either side and soon gained the rise and disappeared behind it.

Several companies of infantry and all the wagons still waited to gain the road, but it was time for us to take a position where we could control events. We used a grassy strip beside the road and galloped two abreast alongside the marching column. Cheers broke out from the men as we passed.

We caught up to the head of the infantry column as it was cresting the rise, and while the foot soldiers continued marching forward we peeled off and took position just beside the road. The cavalry companies were still aligning themselves on the reverse slope. The maneuver was a bit slow, but according to my orders.

Colonel Smith rode up. "We'll be deployed soon, just as you commanded. But the men are not happy about leaving the town to the enemy."

"Understandable," said Murdock. "Let them know we can be bottled up inside the walls, which won't save the town; or we can return with an army to free our land. Which would they prefer?"

"I will let them know the options, sir."

I summoned Franz. The last company of his regiment had almost reached the crest, with the head of Mendez's regiment only twenty yards behind. But the very end of the column—supply wagons—was still inside the camp. It was one thing to move little figures about on a tabletop. It was quite another to move real armies.

To the south a small cluster of Arkan horsemen appeared. "First the outriders, now the scouts," said Murdock. "The main body will not be far behind."

The Arkan horsemen galloped forward down the road leading to the town.

Murdock leaned over to me. "Slow down on the pipe or you'll pass out. You look like a human chimney."

I watched the movements around us carefully, trying to analyze what needed to be done. "Colonel Franz, have your regiment double time for one-half mile. Standard march security." He saluted and made for the head of his regiment. I passed the same order on to Colonel Mendez.

Colonel Smith joined us. "The cavalry is ready, sir, and waiting for your orders."

A solid column of horsemen trotted into view to the south and followed the road towards town. The first enemy regiment. I pointed to it. "The enemy is coming. We must stop them. Prepare your first line . . . to counter charge when I give the order. ONLY your first line, colonel. Make sure the second line . . . knows that they are to stand. Tell every man."

"Yes, sir, I will. But the boys are a bit rash sometimes. They won't like waiting while their friends go in."

Murdock answered for me. "They'll get their turn. If they go in together, we could be finished." He understood what I was doing.

An idea struck me. "Sergeant Jenkins. Place the guards between those lines of cavalry. Maybe that will discourage the second line from going before they're ordered."

"I see. Yes, sir. We'll stop them."

Below us, the infantry companies had begun to jog at double time. Word had percolated down to them of the need for haste, and many were looking over their shoulders. The enemy scouts had reached the fields where the camp had been and turned up the road that led to our position. The end of our train of wagons was no more than two hundred yards in front of them. The enemy broke into a gallop.

"We're going to lose a dozen wagons, Arn," Murdock predicted.

I had made another error. If I'd left a few cavalry behind, they could have turned back the scouts.

"What's in the wagons?"

"Some have hay and grain sir," someone answered. "Others have foodstuffs. Many are empty. There was no time to pack the tents."

"So. Nothing essential."

"Nothing. Except the teamsters."

I nodded. My mistake. Their death.

As the scouts had done, the enemy column reached the campgrounds and turned up the road toward us at a gallop. In town, the church bells were all ringing the alert.

"Colonel Smith," I croaked dryly, and harumpfed. Murdock handed me a water skin, I sipped, and then tried again. "Upon my order, your first line will charge. ONLY your first line. And ONLY as far as those wagons. No farther. Every man must know that. Sound the recall then. Those five companies will assemble in line . . . two hundred yards behind us astride the road. Do you understand?"

He grinned happily. "Yes, sir. Charge the first line up to the wagons. On your orders. I'll tell the officers."

"Tell all your men in the first line," Murdock specified. "They can't see what's happening. They must know."

"Yes, sir." He rode up and down the line passing on the instructions.

The teamsters were lashing their teams forward, but a few of the loaded wagons were up front and the slope had its effect. The lead wagons were slowed, and those drivers further behind tried to pull off the road to go around. Wheels quickly sank into the wet plowed ground, teams crossed and tangled, and the desperate drivers leaped down to run.

The Arkan scouts were upon them. One teamster was caught in the back by a lance. Another was struck down by a saber. A third leaped beneath a wagon, and two horsemen thrust lances between the spokes of the wheels. I thought I heard the faintest of screams as the lance bit into him. More teamsters went down, and the rest fled up the hill, the Arkan scouts pursuing them with fervor. A dozen teamsters came running over the crest in a panic, followed by a score of confident Arkans.

The Arkan horses slid to a stop. Their riders looked at the five hundred horsemen waiting for them, and paused. No, perhaps not today. They wheeled about and fled down the slope.

Our cavalry let out a yell. "Not yet!" I screamed to Colonel Smith. "Hold them! HOLD THEM!" But it was too late. Seeing the enemy flee, the horsemen in the first line started forward of their own accord, and Colonel Smith gave way to the inevitable, raising his sword and leading them over the crest. With a shout of anticipation, the first line of Smith's cavalry rushed past on the left and right and swept down the slope.

The Arkan cavalry column had reached the jumble of wagons and horses at the bottom of the rise. They saw our cavalry descending upon them and tried their best against the surprise attack, counter-charging uphill in column. The two forces swirled together, Smith's line enfolded the column, and then the Arkans broke and fled in a clump, intermixed with a disorderly cloud of Kenesee cavalry. The mass of enemy and friends swept back to the jumble of wagons, and then beyond.

Our trumpets began to sound a frantic order of recall. Beyond the town, another Arkan cavalry regiment came into sight. "This is the moment," Murdock said, waving frantically. "If they keep going, they're lost."

Perhaps our cavalry had seen the enemy reinforcements. Perhaps they had a taste of real battle and were content. Or perhaps they simply remembered their orders. For whatever reason, the horsemen began to respond to the trumpets' repeated call and gradually, in ones and twos, the riders in the five companies came to a halt a hundred yards beyond the wagons and were content to see the enemy flee before them. Then they turned and came back.

I started to breathe again.

"Your order to attack was perfectly timed," Murdock complimented, trying to keep a straight face. "Congratulations. By the way, that was a charge you ordered, wasn't it?"

"Since you were standing right next to me, how could it have been anything else?"

"Quite right." He clapped me on the shoulder. "Now you know how battles are won."

A man trotted up from the second line of the cavalry regiment and saluted.

"Major Tuan, Executive Officer of the Tenth Cavalry Regiment, in command of the second line. Your orders, sir?"

I surveyed the line. Sergeant Jenkins had interpreted my orders one better. He had placed the horses of the guards head to tail, almost a solid wall of horseflesh blocking the second line from any hope of charging with the first. I signaled to the sergeant, who came up. "Move the guards behind the line as a reserve. Well done."

He saluted. "Yes, sir. And your attack was perfectly timed. Colonel Black couldn't have done it any better." He set the guards moving.

I turned back to the commander of the second line. "Major Tuan, when the guards are clear, advance your men to the crest and halt there. No charges except upon my orders."

Murdock scratched his chin. "Wouldn't it be better to keep them hidden?"

I considered. Could I be wrong again? No. When you're weak, make the enemy think you're strong. "I want to make them cautious. We're playing for time. They still won't be sure what else might be coming up to join us, and seeing these will give the Arkans pause."

He smiled. "Well, that does sound like John talking. Yes, you're right, as long as our horsemen don't get carried away and charge in response to a feint attack."

I hadn't thought of that.

The second line advanced to the top of the hill, saw the results below, and let out a cheer for their comrades streaming past us to the rear. Colonel Smith galloped by and I called out to him. "Good job. Tell your men."

He grinned, waved his saber above his head, and was gone.

A small number of wounded, some led or helped by friends, trickled past. Below, the enemy regrouped at the camp, where they were joined by the fresh column of horsemen. Behind them, a column of infantry appeared, and hurried up the road towards the town.

We watched the enemy below, but they made no move forward. Two hundred yards behind us, the first line of the Tenth Cavalry was reassembling, while the last wagon of the column passed their position.

Sergeant Jenkins came up. "They could still have us, couldn't they?"

Murdock nodded. "If they come full tilt in the next half hour, yes, there would be a good chance. After that, things will look better. Prince Arn has made them think twice."

We waited, growing in confidence with each passing minute. The enemy still made no move, though the Arkan infantry had now reached the far side of the town.

"Why do they just wait?" Major Tuan asked.

"They're afraid we might come down on them, sir," answered Sergeant Jenkins. "They think it might be a trap. Also, their men look tired. A forced march, most likely, to catch us by surprise. Clever."

The last of the wagons was now far ahead on the road. It was still only midafternoon, the sun still high in the sky.

I wiped my brow. It must have been a hot day, for I was dripping like a sponge, although no one else seemed to notice the heat. Major Tuan was instructed to leave one company behind to keep off the Arkan scouts, and to leapfrog his others behind Colonel Smith. The men were set in motion.

"Excuse me," I said to Murdock and dismounted. In a nearby growth of bushes I was loudly sick, and came back with wobbling knees. My horse looked very tall.

"Murdock?"

"Yes, Arn."

"Can you help me mount?"

He smiled kindly. "With pleasure, sir. With pleasure."

The Arkans did not pursue with any vigor. Their little trap had not worked, and their men had marched hard and fast to reach Wickliffe. They needed rest before pushing forward against unknown strength. Or at least, that was what we assumed when word came that they were following at their leisure. In actuality, they thought they still had us trapped. And with good reason.

I sent another messenger to Black with word of our near escape, and an estimate of enemy strength. Our scouts saw two thousand cavalry and at least four thousand infantry. Whether there were more, we didn't know.

That the enemy were leisurely did not mean we were. The responsibility of command weighed like an anchor upon my shoulders. I was constantly afraid of doing the wrong thing, or forgetting to do the right thing. I tried to think of everything Black and King Reuel had taught, and kept Murdock at my side constantly. He was silent for those measures he approved of, suggested those I had forgotten, and questioned those he doubted.

The good land around Wickliffe shrank as we marched north, the swamp coming close to the roadway on both sides, easing worries about the rear of our column. The bridges crossing the Kenesee and Cumberland Rivers likewise presented easily defensible positions but we had to keep marching. There was no thought of destroying the bridges, as destruction of unfortified structures was prohibited by the Codes. Very inconvenient. The need to reach the crossroads burned in my mind.

I put out as much security as possible, and kept the men marching into the evening and through the night, our way lit by lamps from the wagons and improvised torches. I was so preoccupied that when a large, shadowy beast stumbled out of the swamp towards the road, I galloped past the ranks of frightened men and reined to a stop in front of it, barely controlling my horse at the sight and scent of the giant lizard. In the dusk it had looked like one of the two-legged plant-eaters, and so I took it to be.

"BACK!" I yelled, grabbing my coat off and flapping it before the creature's eyes. "GO BACK!" I hadn't been this close to a dinosaur since the Rite of Manhood, and can only credit my irrational behavior to desperation and fatigue. In any case it worked, for with a roar of frustration the beast turned and lumbered back into the swamp. Jenkins galloped up with the guards and proceeded to lecture me on the difficulties of protecting royalty who throw themselves in the way of meat-eaters.

"A meat-eater?" I asked weakly.

"Why, yes sir. I saw the razor teeth clearly when it turned. But don't try pretending you didn't know what it was. We know your tricks by now, sir. Sir?"

Perhaps my audacity had puzzled the monster as much as it had puzzled me. Perhaps the beast had been frightened by the waving coat. Or perhaps it had sniffed an old acquaintance and remembered a bit of indigestion. Whatever the case, I was not about to pursue the matter further.

I let nothing delay our march northward, where I could turn this burden of command over to Black. It would take at least two marches for the infantry to reach the crossroads. The night provided one march, and the day would provide another. The dawn brought many grumbles from the ranks as I continued the pace throughout the morning and afternoon, pausing only for meals and the ten-minute rest each hour specified in the manual.

By evening we made camp and the men collapsed with exhaustion, most not even bothering to light campfires. Potential stragglers had been reminded that the Arkans would be coming up, and that kept their numbers down in spite of the pace we held. Many who had straggled came in during the night and got what rest they could. As tired as any, I still could not sleep. Through the darkness I wandered the encampment and looked at the snoring men who depended upon me to lead them to safety. It was not a good feeling.

At dawn we ate the last of the food in the wagons, and the column re-formed on the road under a clearing sky. It looked to be a beautiful day, and soon we would be rejoining Black at the crossroads. I felt almost good.

We had marched for several hours when a messenger galloped down the road past our scouts and up to the banner that marked my location near the head of the column. He had the look of a man who had ridden hard and was feeling it in all the worst places. His horse was ready to drop. An hour at the gallop is not fun.

"Colonel Black is in battle and requests your help, sir."

The colonels joined me at the side of the road while the column continued moving. The messenger took out a crude map. The drawing was in Black's hand.

The messenger left no doubts about the situation. "Arkan cavalry are pushing back our security and their main body is moving up for combat. Colonel Black estimates the number of Arkans he faces to be between eight and nine thousand. They came from the northwest, advancing from the Ohio towards the crossroads, as Colonel Black had feared. The colonel stated that he would take a position which would leave the

Arkans open to a surprise attack from the flank by your force.
The position is just north of Curtis.

"He sees great opportunity if you can arrive in time. There
is a dirt road which bypasses the town to the north and will
take you just west of his position. Your approach will be covered by a low, wood-covered ridge. He is leaving a strong
screening force there to prevent the Arkans from knowing of
your advance. His regimental wizards are attempting to blanket the enemy with static, but he recommends Wizard Murdock do the same. If you sweep down on the enemy's flank,
the Arkans can be destroyed."

"How long have you ridden?" asked Colonel Franz.

"Almost an hour. It will take your men three times that to
arrive and deploy. The Colonel estimated the Arkans would
need at least an hour to march up and prepare an attack, perhaps more. The enemy is cautious. The battle may not yet be
joined. I'm to lead you to the spot."

Franz looked at the map approvingly. "Prince Arn, have
you considered riding ahead with the Duke and the cavalry?
Those, at least, might prevent Black from being overwhelmed.
We'll follow as fast as we can."

It was a good suggestion. The messenger took a new mount
and then we set off at the trot. The pace was rapid, but not
such as to exhaust the horses before we might need them. As
it was, Duke Trudeau's household maintained good order, but
the cavalry regiment straggled out as some of the weaker animals fell behind.

A while later I listened carefully for a noise above the sound
of hooves and Murdock's chatter. "Do you hear anything?"

Murdock nodded his head. "Battle is joined. I can feel it.
God help them all."

We met the screening force of cavalry Black had put on
the ridge. He had used his entire cavalry regiment for the
purpose, and they had been successful. The sounds of battle
were clear now as we halted just below the crest, thousands
of voices lifting in battle lust and pride, the chant of
advancing lines, and the yell of determined defenders.
Dismounting, Murdock, Duke Trudeau, Sergeant Jenkins, the
messenger and I walked the last few steps to the top. Below,
the scene of battle was laid out before us like a tabletop
war game.

Jenkins and Murdock looked at each other. "Good Lord!" exclaimed the wizard. "What has John done?"

"He's put his neck into the noose this time, that's what." Jenkins cocky voice was only a whisper.

Indeed, it did look as if Black had led us to disaster. Ignoring the heights, he had deployed his regiments in the open meadows of a shallow valley. Facing northwest, his front was open ground. His flanks, drawn back almost at right angles from his center, rested on steep-banked but shallow streams, and at his rear was a narrow river with only a single bridge to serve him. The Arkans were deployed around him with strong forces to his front and flanks, and the bridge was blocked on the far bank by a regiment of infantry.

Black was surrounded.

The enemy's array was both formidable and correct. In front, a solid line of infantry ten-deep faced Black's regiments. On the Arkans' left and right, infantry and cavalry deployed along the streams and skirmished with Black's men. Behind his center, the enemy commander had two infantry and two cavalry regiments in reserve. Nowhere was the front actually engaged, though archers in front of the lines and along the stream exchanged fire. The Arkan commander might be slow and cautious, but his tactics were correct, taking advantage of the deadly box in which his opponent had placed himself. There was no place to retreat for Black. If any segment of his line failed, the entire force would be overwhelmed and taken whole.

Sergeant Jenkin's mood improved. "It's not as bad as it looks. John's got a strong position. The streams have a foot of water at least, and the river looks deep. Unless one of his units should break—but that won't happen with John frowning at them."

Trumpets sounded, there was a massive yell, and the center of the enemy line surged forward. On the far sides of the streams the enemy formed assault columns and charged into the water, casting their javelins on the run and drawing swords. Along the water courses the Kenesee troops held their positions atop the banks and struck down at the enemy. In the open center of the front, our troops counter-charged a few seconds before the enemy struck, and the two lines smashed into each other, long spear against long spear. We could hear the collision as an audible crunch. The lines held, but the weight of numbers gradually made bulges in our line as casualties and confusion dominated one spot or another.

Kenesee trumpets again sounded the familiar note of attack, and Black's second line charged forward to reinforce their comrades, flattening out the bulges and halting any further progress by the enemy. On the streams, the precise lines of the defenders met the disordered ranks of the enemy as they emerged from the watercourses, and pushed the Arkans back down the embankments. The seconds ticked away, stretching into minutes, and then a trumpet sounded and the enemy slowly broke off the engagement and backed away in good order to reorganize for another try.

Up and down the Kenesee ranks a chant started growing in volume and force. "John Black." One of their own was leading them. "JOHN BLACK." A commoner, a man of humble rank. "JOHN BLACK." A man who would give them victory. "John Black. JOHN BLACK. JOHN BLACK."

"That's my John," said Sergeant Jenkins, proudly. "The Arkans may kill them all, but his men won't break. Not while John is still on his feet."

The enemy trumpets blew, the lines charged, and the fight was renewed with the same results as the first time.

A third time they charged, and a third time they withdrew.

I looked back, and behind us the duke's household troops and our cavalry regiment stood waiting impatiently for orders. Beyond it, far away but marching fast, the infantry of the Tenth and Twentieth Regiments under Mendez and Franz could be seen.

"Thank God," said Murdock. "At last."

I was amazed. "I didn't think they could be here so quickly."

Sergeant Jenkins had his cockiness back. He looked at the sky. "We've been here two hours at least, sir."

Two hours, and still the Arkans did not realize another force was approaching the battlefield, their magicians blanketed by our own. Murdock, Garth, and the regimental wizards were doing all that could be asked.

Two figures detached themselves from the marching column and galloped ahead on the road, past the cavalry regiment below, and then up the slope to join us. The colonels reined up and saluted. "The regiments will be up in a few minutes," reported Franz. "But the men are tired. We've pushed them hard. Are we in time?"

I smiled as they took in the battle below. "No, it's not as bad as it looks." And before they could become too discouraged I noted the strength of Black's position and what he was doing. I gave them orders and they galloped off to rejoin their units. Murdock and Sergeant Jenkins were studying one regiment of enemy horsemen with large red plumes on their helmets.

I took off my gloves and got out my pipe. "They look determined, don't they?"

Jenkins snorted. "Damn mean, if you ask me, sir. Arkan Royal Guards, if I remember my manual."

Murdock frowned. "Think the Tenth Cavalry can handle them?"

Jenkins looked at Smith's cavalry and then his lips turned down in a sour expression. "Sorry, sir. Even with the Duke's Household leading, I'd have to bet two-to-one on the red plumes."

I lit the pipe. "Would your Fourth Squadron of Kenesee Royal Guards change the odds?"

A sly smile crept over his face. "Well, sir, that certainly sounds very nice. But Colonel Black told me that if I let you out of my sight he'd have a certain part of me for a new tobacco pouch. Now, if you *ordered* me to go forward, that'd be a different matter."

"Done."

"I need a promise, sir. That you'll stay up here clear of the fighting."

I fought the urge to smile.

"I mean it, sir. I won't have it said we let you come to harm."

"Sergeant Jenkins, you have my solemn oath that I won't leave this ridge—until there is no danger." At last, an oath to my liking. "Now, I suggest you move the guards into position."

Finally satisfied, he left five men with me and led the rest away through the trees.

Marching steadily, the regiments had finally reached us. Breathing heavily, the infantry deployed to the left and began to ascend the slope, while directly behind us the cavalry as-

sumed battle column on the road. They all advanced to a point
perhaps ten paces below the crest, halted, dressed ranks, and
waited.

From the valley we could hear the enemy trumpets sound
the charge and combat below was resumed a fourth time. I
climbed to the crest and looked down. The Arkans had reinforced their right, adding pressure to Black's left flank, but
putting even more of their force into jeopardy. Their backs
were to us as they went into the attack.

Our men were breathing easier with a few minutes' rest.
The colonels watched me. I gave the sign, the royal standard
rose and waved, and the colonels gave their command. Over
the crest went the long line of infantry. Beside them Duke
Trudeau led the cavalry column forward. The men were silent,
but not grim. Then they saw the backs of the enemy, and
smiled as they advanced through the trees. I smiled too. This
was my kind of fighting.

The advancing line became hard to see in the spring growth
of leaves and underbrush, even for those who knew where to
look. They were undiscovered almost until they emerged from
the woods at the bottom of the slope and advanced upon the
enemy rear and flank with a yell. Black saw the Kenesee regiments and sounded the advance also. His units surged across
the stream, pinning the enemy down until my regiments
slammed into their rear. The Arkans responded promptly, but
their dispositions left little recourse. The entire right of the
enemy line disintegrated, hordes of men running to escape the
trap and disordering the center of the line and their reserves.
Then the Arkan center was hit in the flank too, and came apart.

The Arkan cavalry tried to face the new threat, but such a
move with a thousand horsemen takes time and space. Our
cavalry had reached the valley floor and were charging toward
the red-plumed enemy. The first company of the red plumes
had completed their turn and counter-charged the duke. Lances
forward, the opposing columns crashed into each other in a
jumble, and more companies thundered into each other and
completed the confusion.

Sergeant Jenkins and the guards emerged from the woods
on the right and swung into the flank of the red plumes, rolling
them up. Admitting defeat at last, the enemy turned and fled.
The other reserve cavalry regiment saw their own guards

routed and gave up the effort. They withdrew in a disorderly mass, all organization lost. The rest of the army followed them, hurried along by Duke Trudeau and our cavalry, who were in their glory.

Thousands had thrown down their arms and were being taken prisoner, shepherded into a dejected-looking mass in the center of the battlefield.

I smiled at Murdock. "Well, sorcerer, I think we may safely go down now."

He laughed and clapped his hands. "Yes, your oath is fulfilled. A difficult one it was, Arn, but your control was admirable. Let's find John and congratulate him."

We met the royal guards at the bottom of the slope preparing to come up to find me. They cheered when I arrived. Sergeant Jenkins was wearing a red-plumed helmet. "What do you think, sir? Goes well with our uniforms, no?"

I nodded. "Yes. But I don't think the King will see it that way. Tradition, you know."

He sighed regretfully and dropped it to the ground. "Oh, well. Probably looks terrible when it gets wet, anyway."

We rode up and dismounted, joining Black on the ground as he addressed the colonels. "Cavalry regiments, keep threatening any formed units and pin them down. I want to force battle on them. Infantry regiments, get your men marching on the road. We're going to get their entire force before the day is out."

The colonels saluted with enthusiasm and got their units moving.

Murdock put on a fierce scowl. "John. Can't we leave you alone for a minute without your getting into trouble? I suppose not." His scowl dissolved into a grin. "But a neater victory has not been seen this century. Well fought, Colonel Black. Well won."

The architect of our victory was calm, but under his serious face the elation shone through like a beacon. "You're both well? No wounds? No burns? Good. Good. Now I can rest content. Arn, the victory is yours. You waited until the precise moment. I'm pleased."

He hesitated a moment, then stepped forward and swept us both into his arms.

So this was victory. Not bad. Not bad at all.

4

Funeral Pyre

On the battlefield alone we took almost three thousand healthy prisoners, plus hundreds with serious wounds. Hundreds of Arkans lay dead, many cut down from behind as they tried to flee. Against this, Kenesee had suffered less than two hundred dead and three hundred seriously wounded.

Black brought the remainder of the Arkan force to bay a few miles further north. Their command, once numerically superior, could now field an organized force only half the size of ours. The Kenesee regiments formed up opposite the Arkans, facing them across an open field in the late afternoon.

Black, Murdock, and Sergeant Jenkins accompanied me to midfield under the white flag attached to the sergeant's lance. Soon a half-dozen horsemen emerged from the enemy ranks and rode to meet us. In the forefront was an old man in chain mail, his gray hair topped by an ornate crown embossed with gems, his helmet held against his side. With him rode a dignified officer with a star on either shoulder, a pair of nobles in mail, and two red-plumed guardsmen. One of the guardsmen flew a white flag from his lance.

They drew up in a line and were silent, their faces grim. I bowed from the saddle. "I am Arn Brant . . . Prince of Kenesee. This is Colonel John Black and Wizard Desjardins Murdock."

The old man with the crown nodded to each of us in turn, and ventured a sad smile to me. "I recognize you, though you have grown to manhood now, Prince Arn. Or should I call you Prince Scar? Do you remember me? I visited Kingsport on a diplomatic mission seven or eight years ago. I am Peter Herrick, King of Arkan.''

"I remember you well," I lied. "I regret . . . we meet under such circumstances.''

He introduced the others with him before asking the inevitable question. "You come to offer terms?''

"We do.''

He held himself erect, but age and fatigue were heavy upon him. "Name your terms.''

I nodded to Black, who stated the conditions from memory. "The surrender of all the forces of Arkan upon Kenesee soil, including those that were encountered at Wickliffe. The immediate surrender of your men's weapons and armor, except for officers and nobles. The surrender of all towns, villages, and territories of Kenesee seized or occupied by your forces. The release of all citizens of Kenesee, military or civilian, under your control. And the return of all treasures, possessions, and weapons seized by your forces. In exchange, we offer the Rights of Prisoners. The oath of a year and a day for yourself and for all your nobles, officers, and men. Your cavalry must give up their horses. The animals will be returned to you at the border, except for the mounts of your Royal Guards and household troops of the nobility. We will provide immediate escort back to your kingdom. We ask nothing more. We have never asked for anything except the friendship of our neighbors and peace between us.''

The officer with the stars grunted in surprise. "Your terms are generous.''

Murdock and Black had insisted there be no ransom. There was still a war on. We needed to eliminate Arkan quickly.

"They are generous," the king agreed. "But I cannot guarantee the surrender of forces elsewhere in Kenesee. They are under Baron Ziminski. He is a proud man, and won't surrender to you.''

Black spoke up. "The terms apply only if all forces are surrendered. You will accompany our army to enforce their obedience. If they refuse, we will destroy them.''

The king looked at the two glum nobles with him, and got their reluctant nods. "All right. Agreed.''

I bowed again. He wheeled his horse, and then paused.

"Prince Arn.''

"Yes, sir?"

"Tell King Reuel I'm sorry. My heart was never in this war, and I came reluctantly. I wish him well." And then he set off slowly for his lines.

Murdock looked after him. "I almost feel sorry for him."

"Every king regrets his defeat," Black retorted. "Keep your pity for the men who died from his foolishness."

The surrender that evening went without problem. Lit by torches and campfires, the Arkans gave up their mounts, piled their weapons and armor, took the oath of a year and a day, and bedded down glumly. The next morning they marched off north the way they had come, escorted by a watchful regiment of Kenesee cavalry.

Then, accompanied by King Herrick, his general, and a few of his guards, our forces turned at the crossroads and headed back to meet the Arkans coming along the Wickliffe road. The Arkan leaders were a small, demoralized party in our midst. A soft drizzle fell on us, and Jenkins had been right. The red plumes really did look terrible when wet. King Herrick had resigned himself to fate, his depression giving way to sadness and anger that he expressed freely.

"Surprise. Speed. These were the keys to victory, or so they told me. And I agreed. Aye, I agreed. Wars are won by such. But what of the enemy? I cautioned them. What of concentration? Might not King Reuel use his central position to strike each of our probing fingers in turn? Shouldn't we mass our force and strike as one irresistible fist? My counsel was not heeded. They dissipate their strength with trickery and end up tricking themselves."

That was encouraging to hear.

"I did not want this war," he continued. "King Reuel and I have had our differences, Prince Arn. But he is reasonable. A man of honor. The same cannot be said of all my allies. I don't understand why we're fighting this war. I am sorry I let them persuade me in this venture. The other four nations were united before their delegates came to me. They made veiled threats, and I feared their might. I was afraid of the price if I refused. So I agreed. In spite of my advisors, I agreed. I would not listen."

Murdock listened with interest. "All your advisors were against this war?"

"No," King Herrick admitted. "Opinion was divided."

"You have an advisor from Pacifica," Murdock noted. "How did he feel?"

"Mikofsky? Yes, he was my advisor. But how he would have voted, I don't know. Died of a sudden fever just after the delegates arrived. Worst luck. He was always a sensible man. He might have made the difference and convinced me otherwise."

Ill luck indeed. If it was luck.

Murdock was quick to respond. "Perhaps Arkan might now be persuaded to make alliance with Kenesee. Together with us—you might yet enjoy victory."

The old man shook his head wearily. "I have taken an oath to the Alliance. My surrender does not negate my word. So it must be."

And so it was. Later that morning we encountered the Arkan force that had almost trapped us at Wickliffe. They hurriedly deployed across the road, surprised at our unexpected advance upon them. Black arranged our own units into a battle line, and then our party went forward under a flag of truce. The commander of the Arkan force, Baron Ziminski, met us at midfield, his dark face turning darker still when he saw his king. King Herrick explained the situation and then gave the baron a direct order.

For a moment I thought we would have to fight. But with tears in his eyes, the baron rode back to his regiments. There was some commotion by unbeaten men questioning why they had to surrender, but at last the weapons were stacked, cavalry dismounted, and long lines formed before the dozens of our officers administering the oath of a year and a day.

By late afternoon these Arkans too were marching north under the watch of our other cavalry regiment. We sent messengers to notify King Reuel of our victory and the elimination of the Arkan nation from the campaign. Camp was established, and the men built large fires that night. Those of Black's original regiments sang and danced around the fires in celebration, while the Wickliffe regiments, still exhausted, quickly fell asleep.

* * *

A farmhouse was a welcome haven after the exertions of the day, the mother and children taken in by a neighbor for the night and thrilled that their home had been chosen as our shelter. Her husband was with the Twentieth Regiment. The house was a sturdily built three-room cabin. For all its outward solidity, the inside was well tended and softened with domestic touches. Everything was clean and neat, furnished simply but with a few items that showed the farmer was successful in his trade. One bedroom held a large, comfortable bed, a crucifix hanging above it on a wall. Three small bunks and a chest of drawers filled the other bedroom. The main room was as large as the other two, and held a table and chairs, cupboard, and chest of shelves. Cooking instruments were hung over the fireplace, which now held a small fire kindled by Sergeant Jenkins. The house even smelled nice, the scent of vanilla lingering in the air.

I was pleased simply that it was warm and dry. Too much had happened in the last few days. I slumped into a chair across from Murdock and Black, and stared at my hands. They were dirty, and they trembled. My eyes ached, and my head buzzed. I had slept little in the last three days. I wanted nothing more than food and rest.

Outside, the men finished the last verse of ''Camping Tonight'' and started ''Lorena.'' There were many other songs new and old that the men sang, but the army seemed enamored with the songs of the civil war that had once been fought on the American continent. The old tunes seemed appropriate, somehow, though there were problems with the words. What was a bonnie blue flag, for example? The men didn't let such matters bother them, and sang the rousing marches with gusto, and the ballads with a tearful eye.

I paid scant attention.

Black stared at the ceiling, and slowly his mouth turned upwards at the corners. It spread into a smile. There was a chuckle, then a full laugh filled the room. All came to a stop around him. We would have done the same had we seen St. Peter appear before us.

The wizard rubbed his chin. ''This is a day for the chronicles to note. John, either you finally got that joke I told yesterday, or else you're laughing at the girth of my backside.''

Black shook his head, gasping, and wiped his eyes. "Both are cause of humor, sorcerer. But no. Listen."

We did, and heard a new tune. The song came from hundreds of voices around the campfires outside.

> *We march by day, we march by night,*
> *And at the end, we have to fight.*
> *Our packs are full, our feet are sore.*
> *But if we have to march some more,*
> *In lowland fields or mountain pass,*
> *We'll grab their nose and kick their ass.*

Murdock smiled. "Well, not all battle songs get into the history books, fortunately. But the men are in good spirits, and well they should. If the King and Robert are doing as well, the war will soon be over."

"We've been lucky," Black responded cautiously, the shadow of a smile still lingering on his face. "If the enemy at Wickliffe had been commanded by a more aggressive leader, their pursuit of you would not have been so leisurely. He might have pressed more closely. You couldn't have launched your attack. And we'd be the ones marching off as prisoners."

"We made our own luck," countered Murdock. "The victory goes to you, and Arn."

"Yes, Arn has done well, and so has Murdock the Magnificent. My hat is off to both of you. One member of the Alliance has been eliminated. Now there are only four."

Only four. We didn't need any reminder that our quick success could still come to naught in the weeks ahead.

Murdock frowned. "John, may I ask you something?"

"Will it matter if I say no?" Black filled his pipe and tossed his pouch to me. We lit up and he folded himself comfortably into his chair.

"Do we have a chance to win now?" Murdock asked.

"A chance? There's always a chance. I think we can win, especially from some of the things King Herrick said. And the odds are better now, aren't they? But it will take skill, and luck, and some mistakes by the enemy." Black fell silent for a moment as he puffed slowly before the fireplace. He watched the smoke swirl, and then his eyes roamed about the room.

There were curtains over the windows and a tablecloth of bright colors. Oil lamps rested on the mantel, where a short row of books had been carefully placed. A sewing box sat next to a padded chair before the fire. Another box in one corner held wooden toys.

Black scanned the titles of books, nodded approvingly, and then sat back down.

"It would be nice to have a house like this. A family . . ."

"Home and hearth are not for us," the wizard remarked gently. "Those are the choices we make. That's the price we pay."

"I've paid the price," Black responded. "But I was never allowed to choose."

The wisp of a smile returned. "You know," he mused softly, as if not quite aware that he was speaking aloud, "it's not often a man can rest content. Not often . . ."

Murdock eyed Black over his drink. The wizard's face was thoughtful, and perhaps a bit sad. But for once he had nothing to say, and whether his sadness was for himself or the colonel, I could not tell.

I slept like a rock that night, as did most of the men. The sleep did not answer all my needs. Only Angela could do that. But the anxiety I'd felt for the last three days was gone, and I could actually see without squinting through tired eyes. I would have turned over for another few hours' rest, but Murdock pulled the blankets off.

"Don't forget. We must be up before John for once."

The rain had stopped, the clouds had broken at last, and the sun promised the first of what were to be many warm and pleasant days. Murdock and I found one urgent matter after another to delay Colonel Black in the cabin that morning, so it was some minutes after sunrise that he finally emerged. The regiments were assembled and facing center when Black, unsuspecting, stepped out to begin the day. The colonels were lined up before him. He looked at them all drawn up at attention, and stopped, for once baffled by events he could not explain.

Murdock and I stepped out on either side of Black, removed the eagles from his shoulders, and replaced them with stars. Murdock made a short speech announcing that by the authority vested in Prince Arn, Colonel Black was hereby promoted to General, with all the privileges and responsibilities, blah blah blah. The sober face did not change, but Black coughed and took a moment before noting to the men that they would do anything to avoid a dawn march. The ranks burst into laughter. General Black thanked us all and told the men that under the leadership of Prince Arn, he looked forward to going into battle with them again. That was enough. The men broke into cheers and began chanting his name again. They even gave three cheers for me.

The brief ceremony over, we marched towards the sun. We would soon be back at Nash, and if the war had not been lost because of our march westward, all would be well.

The pace was steady, the men buoyed by the successes of the past few days. Even the men of the new regiments kept formation. They had tasted victory, and hungered for more. We camped early, made sure all received a hot meal, and bedded down.

With the men tired, we marched for six days before arriving at Nash to the cheers of the people, the front page of the local journal proclaiming our victory over the Arkans. Our messenger to the king had shared his tidings on the way, and that was good. People's grim resolve had been replaced by a resolute optimism. Of course we would be victorious.

Our own fears had been for naught, and the gamble had paid off. Murdock gave a noticeable sigh of relief when we found that no movement orders from the king had yet arrived. The decision had been the right one, and our initiative had not resulted in any disaster. There were rumors of an advance by the Easterners and landings by the Islanders, but nothing definite was known.

The men set up camp and we settled in to wait for some word. We let the men sleep late the next morning, and it was a quiet day of badly needed rest for the footsore infantry and tired horses. It was late the following day that orders finally came. The messenger was Eric, the same clumsy and unsure second cousin whom we had met outside the Beastwood. Only now he looked like an overgrown gutter rat, uniform caked with mud and face coated with dirt, his eyes heavy with fatigue. He was limping badly on his left leg. Perhaps he was just too tired to be self-conscious, for his clumsiness and shy

diffidence seemed to be gone. He wearily handed me two
sealed papers without a word, and gratefully drank the mug
of beer Jenkins gave him.

One of the papers was a formal document ordering me to
march the regiments to Redbank and join the king there. I
passed it on to Murdock, who read it aloud. The other was a
letter to me from the king, but in the script of a castle scribe.
I read the letter through quickly, and then handed it to Murdock. The letter was written before our struggle at the Crossroads. The information was badly out of date, for the situation
had changed. We had already defeated the Arkans. Still, it
gave us insight into King Reuel's intentions, and his orders
for us. The king's intentions and orders were still valid, Arkans or no. Murdock cleared his throat before reading the letter
to our companions.

May 13th, 2653
The King's Castle
Kingsport

Dear Arn,

*I must be brief. The Virginians have been advancing
along the coast road since April 24th. The Islanders and
Mexicans have landed on the east coast and joined the
Easterners. Their united force marches upon Kingsport,
and will soon be here. Operating out of Greenville according to plan, Robert's cavalry sparred with the enemy until he was forced to withdraw northwards. I trust
by the time you read this he will be at, or near, Knox.*

*Elsewhere, there have been raids on coastal villages
by Texan ships, and these have been cruel. Villages have
been burnt, the old and weak slaughtered, and the rest
carried away into slavery. These are but feints to con-
fuse us and scatter our forces. Graven is concerned for
both the southwest coast and the western border. But so
far we have no reports of any Texan landing of ground
forces, nor word of the Arkans, though it must be assumed they are about to strike from the west, if they have
not already done so.*

If the enemy advances tomorrow, I will withdraw from

Kingsport towards Redbank, delaying them as I can. Robert and you must join me there with all your men as soon as you are able. Together we will strike a blow before the Texans and Arkans link up with their allies. At least, this is my plan. With God's Grace and the courage of our men, we will drive them from Kenesee.

I must go now. God speed.

Reuel

*By the hand of Frederick Taylor
Recorder, King's Castle*

Black looked at the messenger. "The documents are dated May thirteenth. Today is the nineteenth. You should have been here before this."

Eric wiped his forehead with the back of his hand. "Yes, Col—uh, General. I left the morning of the fourteenth. I made good time until I found the bridge crossing the Kenesee River near Redbank washed out with the rains. I searched for a ford or ferry, but there were none. I ended up swimming my horse across. My horse was swept away by the current, but I grabbed a trailing branch and hauled myself onto the bank far downstream. My leg was injured and I lost a lot of time."

"Well done, my boy," Murdock congratulated him. "A brave ride. Not all the heroes of this war will be from the battlefield."

Black nodded intently. "Agreed, it was well done. But the bridge, Eric. Are they trying to repair it? Were any engineers around?"

The messenger frowned. "No. No one. It had just occurred. The river is swollen and fast. I doubt that they could have made much progress anyway. But that was days ago, and I'm no engineer."

Black summoned us around the map. "We don't know if this weather will hold. It may rain again, or it could even be raining now in the mountains that feed the Kenesee River. We could reach the river in three days of forced marching, but might find ourselves isolated on the north bank of the Kenesee, unable to cross. Or, we could march for Knox and then turn south for Redbank. That will double our march. Knox is where

Robert will be. With the Nash road bridge uncertain, the King will fall back towards Knox, if he must.''

Murdock estimated the distance roundabout. ''That's a good ten-day march, John.''

''We'll do it in eight,'' Black stated. ''Arn?''

I tucked the letter away with the others at my breast and nodded glumly. I was developing saddle sores.

Many of the messengers looked a bit worn, but we sent off several of the most rested to take word of our plans to King Reuel and Robert. We followed at dawn, and continued marching past nightfall. A long march. We did the same the next day, the tedium relieved only by meals and hourly breaks. Discipline was good, and we had suffered just moderate straggling when we finally reached Knox late on the fifth day.

The regiments that had assembled at Knox were gone, leaving empty fields and the blackened remains of campfires scattered across the greens. The militia commander of Knox rode out to meet us and passed on documents which confirmed what he said. ''Our field regiments were summoned to join the King at Redbank. They left a week ago, and should be with him by now. Prince Robert came through four days ago with cavalry on his way to join the King. More we do not know.''

Black pondered the news. ''Hopefully, the King will refuse battle until we arrive. We'll send a messenger to let him know we're coming, but we can't march farther today.''

The weather was mild, the ground dry, and the hour late, so the tents were left folded. Fires were built with wood left at the encampment, a meal was eaten, and the men wrapped their blankets around themselves and lay down around the fires in tired clumps. Soon a sea of huddled forms covered the ground, unmoving, too tired to even stir in their sleep. But not too tired to snore. The gasps, snorts, buzzes, and whistles of seven thousand sleeping males drowned out the night sounds, and could the women of Kenesee have heard, they might have sworn off men forever.

Yet I didn't sleep well that night, and woke several times. And each time I saw Black seated next to the fire, his pipe in hand, puffing slowly and staring off south, in the direction of the king.

We were moving at dawn, marching southwest on the Redbank road, and watching from afar the slight plume of smoke put out by Kelley's Inferno. The day promised to be sunny and bright, but the smoke from the Inferno seemed dark and some of the men took it as an ill omen. Black heard their mutters and told the men his pipe would billow dark smoke too, if he filled it with cow droppings. The troops liked this; the story made its way down the ranks and, with the sunlight, dispelled the gloom. Soon the men were singing, and Black seemed satisfied.

In the afternoon our outriders returned, their horses lathered with sweat. From a distant hill they had seen the parked wagon trains and tent banners of the Army of Kenesee. In response we rode ahead to determine the situation. We came first to the wagons bearing the seal of the medical service, and unfortunately they seemed to be at work. Murdock pointed to a clearing nearby. In it was a familiar boxlike wagon painted green and red, and still boldly proclaiming JASON THE HEALER on its sides.

"He said he would come when there was need," Murdock reminded us.

Supply wagons, tethered teams of horses, and tents dotted fields and clearings on both sides of the road, marking the rear of the army. We rode on until we came to one meadow crowded with men and horses. Squadrons of the royal guards were deployed around the meadow, and at its center was a large, unlit pyre upon which lay a still form.

Pyres were used only for members of the royal family.

Shadows lengthened upon the ground in the hour before dusk. Familiar faces greeted us in silence as we rode up. Kendall, Bishop Thomas, Sir Meredith, High Wizard Graven, Apprentice Lorich, the beastman Kren, Sergeant Major Nakasone, Professor Wagner, Doctor Amani, nobles, and the colonels of the army looked on in mute grief.

King Reuel was dead.

The crowd stood a respectful distance from the pyre, leaving Robert alone near the body lain upon the wood. I walked up and stood next to him, staring down at the still figure and realizing it would never move again. And yet I did not see the form as it was, but rather lost sight of it in the memory of a thousand moments. King Reuel upon his horse, accepting the cheers of the crowd with a beaming smile for all. King Reuel in the throne room listening to a case, his brow beetled in concentration, considering those before him and questioning with the wisdom of a Solomon. King Reuel throwing Robert over one shoulder and me over the other, and then dancing around the terrace with the two boy princes hanging face down behind him while he laughed and sang a ditty. King Reuel sprawled back into his chair in the council room, legs thrust out before him, giving Robert and me another listen-and-learn session. King Reuel throwing his arms around me in a bear hug of greeting.

A numbness crept over me, and I felt . . . nothing.

I sighed and looked at Robert. One quiet tear and then another coursed down his cheeks. For a moment I thought he wasn't aware of my presence. Then he spoke softly. "Father decided this was a good place to give battle since you would be arriving soon. He fought off the enemy cavalry with ours this morning. A lance pierced his heart."

I nodded.

He turned and looked at me. "Don't you have any tears for the King? Oh, that's right. You don't cry, do you? Father said you bottled up all the tears. But I was never sure. I think perhaps you have no tears to hide."

There was little I could say. "I'm sorry."

Bishop Thomas came forward, and then the others. The bishop intoned a final prayer, while torches were put in our hands. We thrust them into the pile, and the oil-soaked wood smoked, kindled, and began to burn. The fire spread quickly, the crackling turned into a roar, and we stepped back as the pyre was engulfed in flames reaching high above our heads. The smoke wafted skyward in a thick, dark column that soared ever higher. Around us there was a massive sigh, and then the drums beat and the Army of Kenesee began to chant the King's Dirge.

The body was only a silhouette within the flames now, all features lost to the brightness of the fire. Reuel Brant, King of Kenesee, was no more. I felt for the leather envelope in my breast pocket. A few letters, mere words on paper. That's all that was left. . . .

"Arn! Arn, my boy, come back from the flames. You'll be singed. Come back and join us." Murdock pulled at my arm, and I let him lead me back to the group. All had backed away while I mused, the heat of the fire too intense. I joined them and stood in uncomfortable silence until the chant was over.

A despondent Graven spoke first, his voice hoarse with sorrow. "I'm sorry, there is no time for grief. We must move on to other things. We must. Prince Arn has joined us, so we are all together again at last. You have done well, Prince Arn. I had underestimated you. Your arrival has been anxiously awaited."

Was their disapproval in his last sentence?

"We came as we could," Black responded.

"Yes, we know," the wizard conceded. He looked at the stars on Black's uniform. "And it is General Black now, I see. Well earned, General. The defeat of the Arkans was unexpected good fortune. It greatly encouraged King Reuel—" He paused for a moment, regained his composure, and continued. "But now the army is assembled at last, and we must know what Prince Robert will do, or help him decide, as he wishes."

Robert's eyes were dry now, an air of authority about him. "And what do my advisors say?"

Graven ventured to answer first. "Prince Arn, how many regiments do you bring with you?"

I knew that answer easily enough. "Seven of infantry. Almost seven thousand men."

"All have been tested in combat," Black added, "and proven worthy. Two cavalry regiments escorted the Arkans to the border and have not yet rejoined us."

Graven nodded in satisfaction. "Then the assembly of the Army of Kenesee is almost complete. We may never be stronger. Of the Alliance, only the Texans have not been located. We have reports that they landed on the coast west of Kingsport, but the exact date is unknown. Since then we have had no information of Texan movements. Our scouts have been unable to penetrate the enemy's cavalry screen. It is doubtful our spies will get back to us in time, if they survive. Perhaps the Texans are still far south of here. If so, it gives us the opportunity to battle the other three nations before they arrive."

"And what is their strength?" Black inquired.

Professor Wagner took out a notebook and cleared his throat. "I have been keeping tally for the Council of Advisors as they provide me with updated information. The figures are imprecise, of course, being based upon full-strength units. The enemy may have experienced straggling. They may have dropped off forces to garrison key points. Also—''

Robert interrupted him. ''The numbers please, Professor Wagner.''

''The Islanders—''

''Just the totals, please.''

''Uhh, thirty-two thousand infantry and seven thousand cavalry. Not counting the Texans.''

''And against them,'' intoned Graven, ''we have twenty thousand infantry and over seven thousand cavalry on the field, including the Nobles unit and Royal Guards unit.''

The bishop ventured a question. ''I know quality can make a difference on the battlefield. Are there any differences between the troops?'' Not a bad question, considering the source.

Kendall spoke up. He was pale and thin, as if recovering from a long illness, and only then did I notice that the sleeve of his left arm hung empty at the elbow. His mission *had* been hazardous. ''In training and morale, our regiments should be able to hold their own against the enemy. We have the advantage of fighting on our own soil. The struggle will be to overcome their numbers.''

Robert thanked his advisors. ''Does anyone disagree with this assessment? Good. Then we are faced with determining a strategy.'' He waited for a response.

Murdock ventured a comment. ''There are only two courses. We can fight now, or fight later.''

Sir Meredith spoke, and the other nobles listened attentively. ''There is much to say for offering battle tomorrow. The position is not a bad one. Our force is united, and the enemy is not. Let's fight now.''

Nobles and a few colonels nodded in agreement with the straightforward logic.

Robert listened carefully, as if the burning pyre were a thousand miles away. ''Anyone else?''

Black stepped forward and looked around at the circle of men, then focused his attention upon my brother. ''Prince Robert, I have not had a chance to examine the position we hold. Perhaps it has strength. But I suspect that a set piece battle is to the enemy's advantage. A war of maneuver farther north might offer great possibilities. There would be opportunity not only to meet the enemy in open combat, but to deceive and destroy their army through surprise. Yes, surprise is possible, even with wizards to give warning. We did it at the Crossroads. I recommend withdrawal during the night to lure the enemy further north.''

Many of the colonels nodded in agreement. Several mentioned locations they thought might be better suited for battle. Others ruminated, weighing the two alternatives upon which so much depended.

Robert nodded thoughtfully. "I have considered this course already. There is much to say for withdrawal, especially when the suggestion comes from a general who has already helped defeat the Arkans.'' There was a chorus of agreement, and many smiles for Black. We waited for Robert to continue, not a few looking as if they expected him to give the order.

"However, there are other considerations. Who can guarantee that the Alliance will follow us north? General Black, can you? They may tarry here in the south, plundering our towns, taking control of roads and bridges, living off our food stores while we wait in the north. Eventually we would have to come south to give battle, and then we would face a united enemy.

"Yes, the Alliance will outnumber us tomorrow, but they will never be weaker. Every day increases the chances that the Texans will link up with them.

"And there is one final consideration. King Reuel fought for this position, and died for it. It has been paid for in blood. I have spoken to the men. They are ready to avenge their King, and will fight harder for this ground than any other. We have to take advantage of their resolve.

"Tomorrow we will take position and let the Alliance shatter themselves on the Kenesee shield wall. And when they have, we will attack and destroy their army. Tell your men. Tomorrow we fight!''

There were cheers, and the circle broke up into drifting groups of men, some pleased, some doubtful, some talking in low voices.

Black had fallen into worried silence.

"Is everything all right, John?'' Murdock asked.

He shook his head. "Just a feeling. I want to examine our

position before it gets too dark. Stay with Arn. I'll return soon."

Kendall, Lorich, and Kren caught up with us and extended their greetings. Lorich and Kren seemed unchanged and happy to see us again. Kendall noticed me staring at his arm.

He smiled sadly. "Such things happen. The whole story will have to wait for a quiet night before the fire. But I found out what I needed to. There was treachery involved, I'm afraid to say. You know that the six nations each have an advisor from Pacifica. For two hundred years these advisors have been loyal, devoted to the Codes, to the advancement of the nation which they serve, and to peace between the nations. There have been some of my countrymen who tired of their role, and retired to quieter lives. But never before have any betrayed the cause of peace and controlled progress. I'm afraid my countrymen in Virginia and Texan and the Isles plotted this war against Kenesee. The unification of the continent is in their plans. I fear they'll abolish the Codes, too, once they're victorious. And what tragedies might happen then, only God knows."

His face was troubled. "Even if we win," he mused, "not all can be undone. I fear what they have already started in their nations. The world may change, and change for the worse, in spite of what we do here."

Kren nodded. "Kendall and I have talked already. Murdock, the arguments you made to the Council in the Beastwood may be true. The Alliance plans to invade the Beastwood after Kenesee is conquered. The Virginians considered extermination to be the best future for my people, but the Texans feel that some should be spared. There is great hope we might provide a new source of stock for their slave trade."

"Ahh, yes," said Murdock. "A nation of kindness, Texan. And such fine businessmen."

"I have sent a report to the Council," Kren continued. "What they'll make of it, I don't know. There is no proof, and the emissary from the Alliance offered peace. If it were up to Councilman Sokol alone—but it is not."

Murdock held up his hands in sadness. "Well, we cannot control everything in life. And we already have enough tragedy to fill a tale."

And how much more would the morrow bring?

After a while Black rode back into the meadow, wove his way among the mourners, found us in the light of the pyre, and joined our tiny group. Kren fidgeted, waiting impatiently for Black to speak, and finally voiced his question. "Well, General Black, what do you think of the battlefield?"

Black was pulled out of some reverie. "What? Oh. Sorry, Major. The battlefield? Not bad. Not bad at all. It would be a good position against well-matched opponents," Black stated evenly. "High ground with clear fields of fire. Woods to anchor the ends of our line. But there is open ground for a flank maneuver around the position. Against a united Alliance . . ."

"What does Graven have to say?" asked Murdock.

"He doesn't know," Kendall replied. "His wizards confirm the enemy army is deployed south of us, but they can't tell the size of the force."

Black stared off in the direction of tomorrow's battlefield. "Have the wizards foretold anything about the morrow?"

"Premonitions?" Kendall clarified. "Nothing reliable, according to Graven. He himself foresees great bloodshed, but cannot foretell if our course is for good or ill. His wizards' predictions have been contradictory."

"Magic is an imperfect tool," Murdock added in sympathy. "And the Alliance wizards have been putting up a lot of static. Most of our magicians are blanketed, and feeling ill besides. Did I tell you about the headache I've had today? You wouldn't want to know, let me assure you."

Kendall swept his good arm at the potential battlefield that lay beyond a rise. "Yes, things might be difficult if the Texans arrive. But we don't know that for sure."

Murdock studied Black. "What do you think, John?"

Black shrugged. "I have a feeling . . . well, never mind. What I think doesn't matter. We fight here, to triumph or ruin." He looked weary. I'd never seen him weary before.

When all was said we focused upon the conflagration behind us. The dusk was banished in the glow of the burning pyre. Like many, we watched the flames and silently said good-bye.

5

The Battle of Yellow Fields

The morning shone red and gold, a beautiful spring dawn such as poets choose for their verse. Everywhere the new life of spring gave forth its chorus of color and sound. Crickets chirped in the grass, birds sang in the trees, and a gentle breeze rustled the leaves. White clouds danced in a blue sky, glorifying the budding green of the world below. Yellow flowers carpeted the meadows, bright in the sunshine. All was alive and aware, and gloried in the gift of life.

Idyllic, no? Well, we were soon to change that. We deployed that morning upon those meadows, columns of men and horses filing into position amidst the flowers and grasses, the creak of leather and the rasp of metal drowning out the buzzes and chirps of nature. Our men gazed upon the meadows, and even before it was fought the flowers gave name to the struggle. "Look at that!" one soldier stated. "Yellow fields. A battle in yellow fields." The Battle of Yellow Fields it was to be, though another soldier caught the tragedy in his response. "Well, they won't be yellow for long."

Our line of battle was formed just below the crest of a long, low rise, facing southwest. The slope leveled out across open meadows and small copses to the Army of the Alliance, which assembled for battle on another rise a half mile away. A woods at either end of the Kenesee battle line anchored our position. The Redbank-Knox road ran over the rise and bisected our battle line. Where it did, the rise sloped downward into a wide, gentle cut made for the road long ago.

Our infantry companies were stretched out from one woods to the other in ranks of spearmen five deep, archers deployed in front as skirmishers while each regiment held companies back in reserve. Some regiments could manage only a few companies in reserve, while other regiments were almost able to form a second line. Another half dozen infantry regiments waited in columns distributed along the reverse slope of the rise, our tactical reserves for each wing. Beyond the two woods, a few regiments of cavalry were posted on either flank. The rest of our horsemen formed a strategic force behind the center of the rise, ready for Sir Meredith to lead them in delivering the riposte.

Robert controlled the center of the line, as well as retaining overall command of the army. Duke Collins commanded the left wing while I had the right. The troops of my wing were most of those we had brought with us from the Battle of the Crossroads.

Kren and Kendall had rejoined the Royal Party, leaving Black and Murdock with me in the center of our regiments. Bishop Thomas had already made his way down the line, where the men knelt as he blessed them and asked God's protection from the vile invaders who had desecrated the soil of Kenesee.

"Our turn now," said Black. "Time to inspire the men."

"Do they need any more?" I asked. "They seem quite eager."

Murdock grinned. "Did we ever find out what they fed the Easterners?"

"After you, Prince Arn," Black gestured, and I spurred forward, a squad of guards dutifully following us while the rest of the squadron waited for our return. We rode up the line, stopping before each regiment. "Third Regiment from Knox," Black would call out. "Will you fight?"

"Aye."

"Will you fight for Prince Scar?"

"Aye!"

At that point I would raise my sword and wave it around over my head while they cheered. I really had grown quite good at sword waving.

"Will you fight for the King?"

"AYE!"

"Will you fight and will you win?"

"AYE, AYE, AYE!"

We rode back over the crest of the hill, and the Fifth and Sixth Regiments in reserve didn't even wait for our approach. These old stalwarts, trained by Black himself, began drumming spear against shield in a deep, powerful rhythm while a low growl burst from two thousand throats. Black rode up to the standard-bearer of each regiment in turn, grasped the flag, and waved it. The men redoubled the growl and the drumming quickened.

"Have you ever seen such men?" Black shouted at us proudly above the roar. They broke into a chant as we headed back up the rise.

"John Black. JOHN BLACK! JOHN BLACK!"

We resumed our place upon the crest of the ridge, and studied the deployment of the enemy. A solid front line, deeper than ours and backed up by a strong second line of reserves, stretched the length of our own front, with the flags of Virginia, Mexico, and the Isles visible as they stirred in the breeze.

"They outnumber us a bit," observed Murdock wryly.

"We're fighting to defend our own soil," Black mused. "That's an advantage. Pray it will be enough."

There was no time for more prayer, though, for three squadrons of elite cavalry trotted out from left, center, and right of the enemy lines, a white flag flying at the head of each. A hundred yards in front of their lines the squadrons halted, and only the small party leading each continued to midfield, where they joined and halted.

"Somehow," said Murdock, "I don't think they're offering to surrender." We waited until Robert started forward, and then rode to join him. Duke Collins came from the left flank and joined us as we reined up before the enemy contingent. Behind Robert waited Sir Meredith, Graven, Kendall, and Bishop Thomas. Next to them, Black, Murdock, and Duke Collins took position. I rode up beside Robert.

Before us, resplendent in their battle dress, the leaders of the Alliance sat erect and confident upon their horses. Governor Rodes of Virginia, Prime Minister Billy Bay of the Isles, and Patron Carlos Estevez of Mexico. Only General Jack Murphy, President of Texan, was absent. Behind them waited a handful of distinguished-looking men. Two were staring at a point behind me. I turned and saw Kendall returning their stare. He hailed them by lifting up the stump of his arm and giving them a cold grin. I think they were less than enthusiastic about seeing him.

One of them muttered to his companion, and I recognized the accent. Pacifican.

"He's alive. You said he was dead."

"It doesn't matter," the other murmured in the same accent. "The army is united now. They have no chance."

Their army united? No chance? If so, Robert had to be told. Unless . . . what if it was a trick to make us abandon our position? What if—

I waited, torn by doubt. What had Black taught us? A good decision is better than a bad decision, and a bad decision is better than indecision. Should I tell Robert? And what could he do about it if he did know? In the end, I did nothing.

Robert waited in silence. Governor Rodes, clearly the first among equals in the Alliance, studied us both. He looked at the crown upon Robert's head, and then held up a hand in greeting. "King Robert. Prince Arn. We have heard of the loss you suffered. May I extend my regrets at the death of King Reuel. His fate saddens us."

The governor paused, waiting for a response. There was none from Robert, and so he continued. "We are here to offer terms."

Robert maintained his silence.

The governor exchanged a glance with Billy Bay and Carlos Estevez, then forged on. "Rather than waste the lives of your men, we are willing to accept your surrender now. We offer the Rights of Prisoners, the oath of a year and a day to your men and officers, and immediate parole so that they may return to their farms and fields. We do not wish the people of Kenesee to starve next winter."

Silence.

The governor tried to hide a frown of irritation. "We also offer, and guarantee, the safety and freedom of all members of the Royal Family and of the Nobility. You may go back to your castles and continue to administer your kingdom. Our sole condition is that you enter into negotiations with us to resolve certain points of diplomatic dispute. Some loss of territory and other arrangements may be required. These are our terms.''

Robert looked at each of the leaders in turn, as if studying animals he was about to dissect. ''So. You ask our surrender, after which you would be willing to negotiate. Tell me, how would we negotiate? As equals at the table, or as vassals before their lord? And what would we negotiate? What 'loss of territory' would you ask? The same as your emissaries demanded in their arrogance last fall? What 'arrangements' would be required? The disbanding of our army? The last coin in our treasury? Our firstborn children for the slave pens of the Texans?

''You have waged an unjust and unnecessary war against our land. King Reuel and many others are dead because of your unholy alliance. And now I warn you of your doom. We foiled you at the Rift. We parried your strokes on the coast road. And we have defeated the Arkans—''

''We already know of that,'' Billy Bay interrupted. ''You aren't facing fools like King Herrick.''

''That remains to be seen,'' Robert stated coolly. ''Leave Kenesee now, and we will resume our cordial relations with you all, nation to nation. Stay, and you will be destroyed.''

Patron Estevez looked as if he regretted the entire matter. ''Brave words, King Robert, and to your honor. But have you considered the odds against you? Come, my boy, sit with us and talk reasonably. You have a long life ahead of you. Surely what we offer can't be so bad. Better to lose a little rather than lose everything. We all have to compromise.''

Robert did not bother to reply.

''So be it,'' Governor Rodes declared after a moment, and his satisfaction could not be hidden. ''This parlay is done. You've chosen your fate.''

They turned and rode back to their lines.

''Well done, my King,'' Graven stated with satisfaction. There was a chorus of agreement.

Sir Meredith voiced our hope. ''Texan was not represented. General Black, what do you think? Are the Texans here?''

Black looked at Graven, who shrugged. ''My wizards still don't know, nor can I tell. Every magician on the battlefield is generating static. Even if none were present, I could not tell you whether the enemy had twenty thousand on the field, or forty thousand. And if the enemy were hiding a force behind their hill, I would not know it even then. It is too close to their other forces.''

''Their cavalry screen has been quite effective,'' added Sir Meredith. ''Our scouts have not been able to locate them. Nor have any of the spies returned with positive information. Battles have been lost due to the fog of war. But the Texans would have deployed by now if they were here. They're not.''

I shook my head. ''No, Sir Meredith. I heard the Pacificans whispering. They say they are united.''

Robert nodded, as if my words only confirmed what he already knew. ''They are here, my friends,'' he said sadly. ''They are all here. Rodes was too confident. Graven mentioned their hill. Behind that hill the Texans wait. My apologies, General Black. I made the wrong choice.''

''Your reasons were valid, King Robert,'' Black said gently. ''If they are here, then all the greater our victory.''

''Did you hear that?'' Robert asked us, roused into a fierce determination. ''With such men, how can we lose?''

''Perhaps,'' Murdock answered calmly, ''by staying in midfield while the enemy launches their attack. May I suggest we return to our own lines before discussing battle strategy?''

We resumed our place on the crest. Now, some accounts of the battle say a strange silence fell over the army as it stood in place, waiting for the enemy to begin their offensive. But I remember no such silence. Put twenty-eight thousand men and eight thousand horses on a field in battle gear, and see how much quiet you get.

Black and I casually discussed the deployment of several companies, as if we were on the parade ground rather than the field of battle. Then he leaned towards me. ''It will start soon,'' he said softly so that none other than Murdock could hear. ''Are you ready?''

I shivered in the pleasant warmth of the morning. ''Yes.''

Nothing like a good battle to start off the day.

''I have a feeling about today,'' he spoke, hesitantly. Yesterday, I had seen him weary for the first time. Today, hesitant. ''If—well, if things should go ill—don't give up hope. There's usually a way, if you're willing to pay the price. Will you remember that?''

"Yes, John. I'll remember."

He seemed satisfied. "Good. We've done well together these last months. Whatever happens—"

Far off, horns blew and the enemy army stirred beneath its waving banners.

"Into the breach once again," said Murdock. He looked down at himself. "Let's try not to get wounded, shall we?"

The sun glinted off metal in the panorama of the enemy maneuver. The entire army of the Alliance was in motion, two heavy lines of infantry screened by archers slowly advancing upon us in front. Their left flank was covered by four or five cavalry regiments, while on their right a much larger force of horsemen had been assembled.

"Arn, Murdock, do you see?" Black pointed at the enemy's banners. "Opposite us are the Islanders. In the center and reserve are Virginian regiments, then the Mexicans in front of Duke Collins. That mass of cavalry on their right is Virginian and Mexican—"

He stopped as columns of infantry and cavalry began to top the far rise behind the enemy cavalry. They bore the banners of the Texans.

Murdock shaded his eyes with his palm. "Well, the King was right. The slavers are here."

My stomach did a flip-flop, and I swallowed hard.

The Alliance was united.

Murdock eyed the enemy advance. "Is it too late to withdraw?"

Black shrugged. "I'd hate to try."

The Virginian and Mexican cavalry swung wide to our left to circle the woods on Duke Collins's flank, the Texan infantry and cavalry marching dutifully behind with flags and banners flying in profusion.

On our side, a lone figure—Sir Meredith—spurred away from the royal party and back to his cavalry regiments. Trumpets blew their notes, and the Kenesee horses filed off to the left to meet the threat. The cavalry force which we had expected to use in a brilliant riposte was going to fend off the mass of enemy horsemen.

But Sir Meredith would now be facing infantry too. Messengers galloped from the king, and soon the infantry regiments on the reverse slope of the left and center turned and followed the cavalry, stripping those portions of the battle line of their reserves. Even the archer regiment, deployed behind the spearmen in the cut, formed into column and marched off. No orders came to us. My two regiments on the reverse slope now became the only reserve available to the army.

"Well done, Robert," Black murmured. "See, the King's not committing forces in dribs and drabs, but in enough strength to bring the flank attack to a halt. He's left us our reserves because our line is thinner here on the right. He's doing a fine job so far. He was just unlucky. Let's see what we can do to help him."

He beckoned to Colonel Daniels of the Sixth Regiment, who galloped up immediately. "March your regiment towards the cut. Stay out of sight on the reverse slope, but tell King Robert that the Sixth Regiment is available to him. Got that? Good. Get moving."

The gap closed between the armies. In front, the skirmishers came within bow range of each other, and the first arrows began to fly.

Colonel Daniels joined the royal party briefly to deliver his message. The figure of Robert waved an arm at us in appreciation. We waved back.

"Arn," Black stated in the same tone he had used in the classroom for so many years. "What is the enemy trying to do?"

That was easy enough. "They're going to pin down our front line while they outflank us on our left."

"Brilliant observation. Does that offer us any opportunities?"

I studied the enemy. Their two lines were approaching our front, and with our reserve regiments gone, they easily outnumbered us by two to one here. There was nothing else I could say. "Their second line is almost as strong as their first. If we marched out on the attack their cavalry would envelop our flanks. I don't see any opportunities."

Black nodded. "That's the problem."

Two hundred yards off, the enemy lines halted, waiting while their flanking force continued its march around the woods. Islanders faced most of my force, although the two regiments on the left of our wing opposed Virginians. The Easterners were a steady line of dark blue uniforms, varied shield colors marking the different regiments, daunting in their steadiness. Their three regular regiments, armed with javelins and swords, were in reserve behind the center. But the rest of their forces carried the long spear, like ours.

The Islanders were no less formidable. Their dark faces were painted for war. They were active, gesturing with ax and shield even as they stood in place and began their battle song, a long slow chant that gradually grew in volume and speed, ending with a pounding rhythm and blood-stirring force just prior to a charge. Their shields were black, and above their white-clad ranks flew flags of red and yellow.

We noted where the battle line halted.

"The enemy commander is competent," Black noted. "Too bad."

"Governor Rodes of Virginia," said Murdock, "is an accomplished man and a formidable opponent."

"Then let's hope his allies are not."

We had lost sight of the flanking force as it went behind the woods, but now, to the left and rear we could hear trumpets blowing and the thunder of hooves in the charge. Battle had been joined. As if in answer, more horns blew to our front, and before us the enemy line started forward, advancing ponderously towards our spearmen. The archers fell back through friendly ranks as the opposing lines closed.

With a shout the Islanders and their allies rolled across the meadow and up the rise to crash upon our spears and shields. Roused to a fever pitch, the Islanders fought with a fierce energy, and the front line began to undulate slowly, like a snake, as men struck and jabbed and pushed and shoved. Where a coil arched too far back, reserve companies were committed to straighten out the front. But the line didn't break, and our steadiness eventually told. The Islanders fell back a hundred feet to regroup.

To our left rear, a haze of dust now showed where the cavalry was engaged in a frantic swirl of charge and countercharge as they maneuvered for advantage. The haze was much further into our flank than I would have liked, but did not move deeper for the moment. Apparently Sir Meredith was holding his own.

In front the enemy charged again, the line of the Alliance rolling up against ours, melding the two into one. The enemy charge was less fierce this time, but just as determined. The Islanders threw themselves upon our spears, trying to drive between the tips with their shields in order to use their axes effectively. Sometimes they were skewered. Sometimes a stroke fell upon a Kenesee shield. And sometimes an ax cut deeply into one of our men. The infantry jabbed and chopped at each other for long minutes, defiant shouts from thousands punctuated by the screams of scores. A trickle of wounded stumbled and crawled from the ranks, ignored by those still fighting.

Near the far right, adjacent to the woods, our line bent backward from the assault, and the Islanders threw in a reserve regiment. The line began to sag dangerously under the pressure. Black had to commit the Fifth Regiment to equalize the struggle.

Only the Sixth remained, the last reserve of the army.

For long minutes the contest went on, and then the enemy fell back a hundred yards and our line dressed ranks, the men breathing hard, their arms becoming heavy with the fatigue of combat. And now the advantage of numbers made itself felt. Horns blew and drums beat from the enemy rear. The second line of the Alliance strode through the ranks of their first and took position to the front, fresh and eager troops waiting to assault our tired ones.

"That was well-timed," Murdock commented upon the maneuver. "Now it becomes difficult."

"That's not our only problem," warned Black. "Look."

On the far rise behind the enemy line, a dozen great mammoths bearing war towers came into view. Following the road, the mammoths clumped down the rise and towards our position in a double line, lanes opening up in the enemy ranks for them to pass through. The armored beasts were aimed directly for the low cut in the middle of our position. The first of the mammoths cleared the enemy front. Trumpets, horns, and drums sounded, and the Alliance came forward in one massive attack.

Black grabbed Murdock's arm. "The mammoths. Can you do anything this time?"

Murdock shook his head. "I've already tried. It's like the Gates. There are too many men, too many emotions, too much static."

"All right, then," Black said grimly. "We'll do it the hard way."

Robert had been right about the men. They took the death of the king as a personal affront, a wrong to be made right. They were filled with a terrible resolve—not enthusiasm, not impetuosity, but a firm determination to hold what King Reuel had died for. The stalwart qualities of Kenesee infantry were never clearer than on that day. From one end of the battle line to the other, the fresh enemy threw themselves upon us with eager confidence. Yet though the front bent and twisted as men surged against each other, up and down the line our men fought without wavering, holding their foes and frustrating every effort to fight through. No man could break our line.

No man.

Only in one place did our infantry waver, and that was amongst the unlucky regiment posted in the cut. The mere sight of the great beasts approaching made the men take an involuntary step backward. I could understand their fear. The mammoths came closer, wicked tusks waiting to skewer the men, armored skirts to brush them flat, great round feet to crush them into the earth. Could anything stop them? Robert had seen the point of danger and spurred forward, royal party and guards following. He made the difference, for the men shook off their doubts, grounded the butts of their spears into the earth as if to receive cavalry, and took the first impact of the great beasts.

Black nodded approvingly. "Well done, Robert. Now, hold."

But that was not so easily accomplished. Spears splintered and broke, men went down, and the beasts plowed through the ranks. In the towers upon the mammoths were javelin men, archers, and pike men, thrusting and shooting downward in relative safety. These alone would have made the hairy beasts formidable. But between each came a company of Easterners, ready to take advantage of any disorder. In seconds the damage was done, the mammoths striding through the regiment, the enemy infantry swarming forward behind them. The regiment collapsed, infantry fleeing up the cut, followed by a stream of Easterner columns. Only around Robert did the line hold, the tide of Virginian blue flowing around until his position formed a shrinking island of brown and black uniforms.

Black spurred off towards the Sixth Regiment with the rest of us on his heels. Colonel Daniels was already deploying his troops for a counterattack when we reached him.

"You know what to do," Black told him.

Daniels looked at the challenge. "Yes, sir. I'll try. But we're only one regiment."

Murdock yelled. "Look. The King is in danger."

A mammoth was seeking to stride across Robert's little island. Most of the guards had dismounted, their horses almost out of control in terror of the mammoths. Yet Robert still rode his, forcing the animal closer to the beast. His sword held high, he was trying to close so that he could thrust it into the eye of the shaggy head. But at last the horse would take no more, attempted to back up, and went down instead, the mammoth advancing over them.

"The King is down," Murdock called out.

"Dismount," Black ordered us all. "The horses can't take the beasts." He turned to Daniels. "Charge. Now."

The Easterners were no fools. From the cut they had seen the Sixth Regiment deploying, and two regiments had turned to face us. Behind this shield wall still more Easterner troops followed the mammoths up the cut, thrusting deeper into the rear of the army.

Into the maelstrom we went, my squadron of guards a tight square around me as we charged in line with the Sixth Regiment. We endured the volley of thrown javelins from the enemy and then crashed into the Easterners with a fearsome impact, driving down upon them and pushing them back. Perhaps, had our opponents been of lesser quality, we might have shattered them with that charge, closed the break, and cut off the enemy in our rear. Perhaps. But we faced our old friends from the Rift Gates, the First and Second Virginian Infantry, two of the best formations in the Alliance. They gave ground but continued fighting, refusing to rout. The cut became a slaughterhouse, both sides gripped by a killing fever, and both superbly trained to fulfill their bloodlust.

Black led us forward, foot by foot, towards the shifting crush of men deployed around the King's standard. And now our attention focused not upon the battlefield as a whole, but simply upon the men facing us, individuals now, cutting and stabbing in a frenzy as they gave way or died. A man thrust his sword at Black, missed, and lost his life as punishment. Another was skewered by Jenkins. We pushed forward.

An arrow zipped by and bounced off a shield. Beside me, Murdock's face dripped with sweat, his eyes darting in every direction as he watched for threats. I was going to thank him when a sword swished past my head, and I was preoccupied with the need to stay alive. The sword swished again, and I cut deeply into the wielder's arm. The sword and its owner disappeared into the chaos of battle.

We were close now, no more than two or three ranks separating us from the King's circle. Spears jabbed forward, swords thrust and cut, men screamed and went down, only to be trod underfoot. But the fierceness of our charge could not be denied, and suddenly we were through to the island. On all sides the fighting raged, but in the small span of a few yards there was a pocket of room, an open space like that in the eye of a great storm, paid for by the surrounding wall of royal guards and Kenesee infantry. In that space, a solid floor of dead and wounded covered the grass of the hillside, bodies of men and horses draped over and across each other, the few trampled flowers still visible stained red.

Robert lay upon the ground, his eyes closed, his face pale. Graven and Lorich crouched beside, holding a shield over him, eyes watching for arrows. Graven looked up and saw us, desperation in his eyes. "The beast trampled him. I couldn't turn it."

Murdock reached down and lifted the high wizard to his feet.

"We have to move the King," said Black. Four guards picked Robert up and slowly carried him through the ranks, the royal party following behind.

The clamor of battle roared around us. The Easterners had extended their front, and our forward impetus had finally been stopped, the weight of two crack Virginian regiments proving too much even for the Sixth. We had only half-closed the break in our line, and the enemy continued to pour through.

Just as the king's party had been enveloped, a far vaster pocket was being formed around the left and center of our line. The greater part of the army would soon be surrounded, and there were no reserves left to prevent it.

"We can't do any more," Black shouted at Murdock and

me as an arrow buried itself in the ground at our feet. "We'll have to fall back."

He stood for a moment then, sword in hand, tall and proud, the sweep of his gaze taking in the chaos around him. I recognized that gaze. I had seen it in the Beastwood, and under the Rift Gates, and at the Crossroads. The practical man, calmly aware of the realities, was still the undaunted warrior. He yet watched and hoped for the unseen opportunity by which he could make companies do the work of regiments, reverse the tide, and turn defeat into victory.

Black beckoned to Daniels. An arrow turned sideways in midair, and bounced off my chest. Another whizzed by at the same moment, entered above Black's collarbone, and buried itself deep in his chest. He frowned, dropped his sword, and staggered onto me.

I sat down, unbelieving, with him in my arms.

Murdock sank to my side. Black looked up at us.

"I'm sorry, my friend," the wizard moaned.

Black lifted his hand as if to touch my face, but his arm had not the strength. He coughed and tried to speak, but no words came from him. Only blood came, pouring from his mouth in a crimson stream, and I held him while he drowned in it. The light faded from his eyes, and then he stared unseeing.

I looked up. "He's . . . gone."

Murdock, Daniels, and Jenkins were clustered around us. "So he is," the wizard said gently, a tear trickling down one cheek and mingling with the sweat that dripped off his brow. "But we have to go. They're pushing us back, my boy. Put him down. That's it. Here's my arm. Take it. Now stand up, Arn. Up."

There were moments left before we would be cut off.

Jenkins grabbed a corporal whose mouth had fallen open in surprise and horror. "General Black!" the corporal cried out.

"Yes," shouted Murdock. "Can you carry him?"

The man was big, and the fight had given him a strength found only in battle. He dropped his shield and spear, scooped his arms under Black, and heaved the body up. "I've got him!" he yelled, and then a sword stabbed into his belly and he went down heavily. An Easterner stepped over the bodies, with more of his comrades right behind.

Murdock clutched my arm and dragged me backward. "We have to leave him. There's no one left in control of the battle. We've got to get the army out." I nodded, almost numb, and we fell back through our men as they slowly gave ground before the resurgent enemy. We clambered back uphill to our horses. At the crest we turned, and the battle was laid out below in all it grim truth, unreal yet real, unbelievable yet happening. Our wing was still intact, still fighting, still firmly holding the Islanders in place, although in truth they were the ones holding us in place. Pressed by superior numbers, the Sixth Regiment on our left flank fell back slowly, giving up the ground they had covered, widening the gap through which the Virginian regiments still marched.

Had these units turned towards us, my command would have been flanked and overwhelmed. But the enemy was wiser, with a greater prize than just routing my wing. The breakthrough regiments marched towards their right, into the left rear of our army, in order to link up with the Texans and complete the envelopment of our center and left.

With Robert down I now commanded the entire army. Yet I was cut off from the greater part of that force, and unable to signal them of their danger. My trumpeter sounded the retreat for our own wing, and either the individual regiments of the center and left wings heard it, or Duke Collins had become aware of the danger, for the threatened regiments began to back step their way up the hill. While falling back, the infantry fought resolutely, many unaware of the doom they faced. Even those who knew continued to resist, the regiments nearest the cut bending back, stretching, yet still maintaining a battle line against superior enemy numbers.

It was only when the jaws had almost closed behind that the center and left collapsed, some regiments going into square and forming islands of resistance, others dissolving as commanders realized the danger and ordered flight. And that is when the slaughter began.

Our cavalry, fighting a costly and futile effort to prevent the trap from closing, could not stand before the mammoths. Half the enemy forced our horsemen back, while the remainder wheeled in and completed the encircling ring.

I looked at Murdock in despair. "What can we do?"

"Nothing. Nothing but save our wing."

Several colonels rushed to me to confirm the order they had heard the trumpets blow. They looked at the blood on my tunic.

"Where is General Black?" asked one.

A weariness fell upon me. "Black is—is dead. Pull back your regiments. We have to regain the road so we can retreat."

"But the army," objected another, with more courage then sense. "We must save them."

Murdock came to my rescue. "We'll be lucky to get away ourselves. We've got to break contact. Carry out your orders. Quickly."

They looked shocked, but saluted and hurried back to their regiments.

Certainly, the infantry commanders deserved credit for the job they did during our withdrawal. The movement could easily have become a rout, but they backed us off without giving the Islanders and Easterners any openings. Likewise, the cavalry leaders did a masterful job fending off enemy attempts to outflank us. But in truth, we got away because the Alliance let us go.

We were theirs for the taking, but they were single-minded in their objective, mesmerized by the destruction of the units in the pocket. Much of our cavalry was able to avoid the encirclement, and they joined us, freezing the Islanders in place with threatened charges so that our infantry could break contact and withdraw. We marched backwards in line, step by step, till we were down the reverse slope of the hill and a quarter mile beyond, almost amidst the camp tents of the army, from which teamsters were already fleeing with their wagons down the road. Facing about in turn, the regiments streamed off, while close by we heard and saw our comrades still fighting, and the screams of our fellows being cut down.

We marched away and left them to die.

6

The Plan

"Why haven't they followed?"

Graven posed the question that night to the colonels that remained of the Army of Kenesee, a mere dozen left of the original thirty-five. Majors and captains commanded the rest of the regiments that had survived. They stood around the campfire—dusty, disheveled, and not a few wearing bandages on head or limb—watching flames devour the wood. Beyond flickered a thousand smaller fires, men sprawled about them in the sleep of exhaustion, others restless with nightmares. Dawn would awaken them soon enough.

We had marched away from Yellow Fields, continued on throughout the afternoon, passed Knox in the darkness, and heard the bells of its churches sounding the alert. We kept going and paused only when we knew the Alliance was not pursuing. Yet. On the road, wagons—that fraction lucky enough to escape—trundled northward still, many loaded with wounded. One went by that reflected the light of a fire, although its driver was in shadowed darkness. It seemed to be painted red and green, and had scroll-like yellow lettering on the side. It was a comfort to know that at least some friends had gotten away.

Sir Meredith, his arm in a bloodied sling, gave answer to Graven's question. "Why haven't they followed? Why should they? They can have us at their leisure now. Our scouts say the enemy were preparing to sleep on the battlefield."

A colonel seemed fearful of asking the question. "Our men. Were they really all slaughtered?"

344

"The Alliance took a few thousand prisoners at the end," Sir Meredith answered. "Certainly less than half those in the pocket. None were offered the Rights of Prisoners. Many fought to the last. Many who tried to surrender were cut down."

The circle was quiet. They were beaten. Defeated men in a defeated army, without hope.

"What do we do now?" asked Colonel Daniels.

"We must surrender," answered another colonel.

Sir Meredith scoffed. "Would you trust them to accept your surrender?"

"What else can we do?" asked the colonel.

Colonel Franz shook his head. "NO. No surrender. Not to men who carry off our people to their slave pens." The beastman Kren gave a nod to the colonel.

"Then what can we do?" asked another.

Silence descended again.

"We are still the Army of Kenesee," Murdock reminded them. "What strength do we have left?"

"My regiment numbers seven hundred," said Colonel Franz.

"I have eight hundred in the Sixth," Colonel Daniels followed.

"Almost seven hundred," said another.

Murdock held up a hand. "All told, what do we have?"

Professor Wagner added the figures on a piece of paper. "Seven infantry regiments and various companies escaped from the field. Five thousand men, at most. And over three thousand horsemen, including what's left of the Guards and Nobles. More may have escaped into the countryside, but not many, I fear."

A cavalry colonel grunted in disbelief. "Almost twenty thousand lost? Today they outnumbered us two for one, and destroyed us. Now they outnumber us five times over and more. What can we do? Nothing. We prolong the inevitable."

"How is the King?" asked Kendall.

Eyes shifted to the nearby cabin where royal guards stood sentry.

Graven shrugged. "King Robert lives. But his wound is serious."

Sir Meredith looked at me, his face troubled. "Excuse me,

Prince Arn, but it must be asked, no matter how painful." He turned to Graven. "High Wizard, tell us. Will the King live?"

Graven folded his hands, the mottled colors of the skin visible even in the firelight. "I don't know. Probably not."

The group stirred.

"The King is wounded and General Black is dead," another added. "Who else have we lost?"

I stared at the fire. So many pieces swept from the board. King Reuel dead. John Black dead. Robert dying. Two-thirds of the army destroyed. Was there any choice but surrender? Would it not be better to end the conflict now, before more died? I could flee to Louisville, take disguise, and disappear. Perhaps catch a ship down to the coast, even head into Arkan. They wouldn't think to look for me in their own lands. Or I might even risk the long and dangerous voyage to Europe. The kingdom would be no worse off, and I would be safe from the dungeons of the Alliance. Yes, I could do that.

"Duke Collins was encircled with the army," Bishop Thomas stated. "He could have escaped, but he would not leave his men. His household was decimated with the Nobles unit."

Most of the nobility were casualties, trapped in the pocket or fallen in the vain attempt to hold it open. Besides Duke Collins, Duke Santini and his household were gone, and most members of the House of Brant as well. In command of the cavalry, Sir Meredith had escaped, but he had lost most of his household that had ridden with the Nobles unit. A dozen other names were mentioned. Only Duke Trudeau and Sir Meredith were still with us as leaders of their houses.

"I think that is all," said Professor Wagner.

"Is that not enough?" asked Graven. "The King is dying. The nobility are decimated. The finest men of Kenesee are dead."

"Don't despair," said Kendall. "There's still hope."

"Hope?" Graven asked bitterly. "Hope in what? Do you have a plan to defeat the Alliance?"

Others began to mumble their own doubts to each other.

"No," Kendall admitted. "Mine have all come to naught. I have no more plans."

Graven nodded with a smirk. "You learn too late."

Kendall stiffened. "And who advised the King to fight? Who—"

I was tired and frightened and had no patience with their bickering.

"ENOUGH!" I said, and even I was surprised at the tone in my voice. It brooked no argument. The babble stopped, and all eyes turned to me for the first time that evening. I met their glance. "We need rest. We'll continue our retreat at dawn. Good night."

Some looked at me doubtfully. But those who wanted to speak thought better of it. The commanders drifted away to their regiments, then the advisors, until only Murdock and I remained at the fire. And so I found my voice at last, even as the day of defeat ended on a final bitter note of argument and backbiting. I took command of a broken army in a kingdom that soon would be no more.

Just my luck.

Before dawn we rose, ate what there was, and then formed the regiments. The column started north, infantry leading, cavalry behind to fend off any pursuit by the enemy. Outriders went before us to the towns so that food awaited us at noon, and then we marched again, a growing column as old men, women, and children stumbled along beside us in the fields, abandoning their homes when they heard the slavers were coming their way. Many were bereaved, wailing as they heard news that their men had been caught in the disaster of Yellow Fields.

A few days later we crossed the bridge over the Cumberland River at the town of London and made camp there. The bridge could be held easily, and the enemy would have to find passage up or down stream before they could engage. It would give us time to rest and reorganize, and still retreat without difficulty if the enemy advanced.

We had received reports that the enemy cavalry was following at a leisurely pace, still savoring the sweetness of their victory, secure in their knowledge that the war had been won, even if not the last battle.

We had lost most of the tents and equipment in the camp at Yellow Fields. In the woods around London the army set up a camp which consisted mainly of blankets thrown upon the ground around the campfires. The weather was warm and dry, so no one suffered unduly from the elements. A company

tent had been found and provided while the staff arranged
better quarters for me. I sat in it with Murdock, away from
the eyes of the men for the first time that day.

"Thank God our enemies aren't pressing us," said Murdock. "They act as if the war were over."

"Isn't it?" I responded glumly.

"Perhaps," Murdock responded. "But we mustn't let the
men know that." He reached into his saddle bags. "Arn, I
have some things for you from John. Maybe one day we can
put them in the royal museum in Kingsport. With his guard's
uniform, it would make a nice display."

He handed them over carefully.

Black's pipe and tobacco pouch. I held them in my hand,
and then thrust them deep into a pocket. "Thank you."

"John gave them to me that morning. Said I should give
them to you. He knew, Arn. His only worry was for you."

"We needed him."

"I know. I'm sorry," Murdock apologized bleakly. "There
were too many arrows. He told me to keep you safe. I couldn't
cover you both. . . ."

"No wizard could have done more," I admitted.

Murdock paused, staring at me, a frown of uncertainty upon
his face as if making up his mind. Then he spoke. "There's
something else I can tell you now. A secret long kept by John.
A matter of the heart. Your mother, Nancy Brown. King Reuel
was not her only lover."

I puzzled over his words, until the full meaning burst upon
me with a painful glare. "Is it true?" I asked. "You mean
John was—"

"John shared this with no one but me. Arn, you look like
your mother, rather than either John Black or King Reuel. John
was convinced that you were his son. I think the odds are
about even on that, assuming that Nancy Brown didn't bed
anyone else. We'll probably never know which of the two is
your father."

I shook my head in disbelief. "He never told me."

"John and Nancy were in love at the time," continued Murdock, "though they kept it a secret within the castle—no mean
feat in itself. Then Nancy Brown caught the eye of King
Reuel. Nancy's reasons for the tryst are uncertain. The aura

of royalty, a wandering eye, some favor, intimidation—there's no way of knowing. John was not the most expressive of men, and perhaps she just wanted someone who showed feeling. In any case, the castle knew of Reuel and Nancy. And John heard, of course. He loved her, and forgave her, and loved her to his last day. Perhaps that is a measure of the man.

"He thought at first that you were Reuel's son, and that caused some hard feelings that he buried deep and shared with none before me. But as you grew, John came to feel that you were his own. And that is just as well, whatever the truth of the matter. Still, it was hard for him, watching another man raise the boy he thought was his son. He could not show it, but he loved you as King Reuel loved you."

And now King Reuel and John Black were both gone.

Gone.

I shivered. My head was pounding, and my hands were trembling again. "I can't do this, Murdock. I'm frightened, and I don't know what to do. What will happen to the army? What will happen to me?"

"There's still time to decide that," Murdock consoled me. "For now, continue to provide the example. Be silent if you must, but be strong. You are the last member of the royal family able to lead, and everyone looks to you. You're not just Arnold Brant; you're the symbol of Kenesee. Whether you feel hope or not, we must think you do."

I laid my head on the cot, exhausted, and escaped into sleep.

The next morning the sound of a rider came to us as he galloped up to the tent. He passed security with the guards and entered. "Prince Arn. High Wizard Graven summons you to join him at the bedside of the King."

I glowered at him as if I was angry. I was. "A High Wizard does not summon a Prince of the realm."

The messenger reddened in embarrassment, but stood his ground. "My apologies, sir. The ill-chosen words are mine. The High Wizard respectfully requested that you join him at the King's bedside. He feels it is urgent."

"Where are they?" asked Murdock.

"A mile north, outside a small village. I can take you there."

It might have been easier to seek a more comfortable room

for Robert in the town, but we didn't want him too close if a battle should start. His wagon could get trapped too easily, and having the king captured was not the way to raise the morale of the army. We trotted north after the messenger and soon were at a village that consisted of not more than a dozen homes and barns. Before one house a detachment of the guard stood watch, coming to attention as we rode up. Sergeant Major Nakasone was among them, his head bandaged where he had suffered a blow from a Texan horseman. The battle had been a hard one for the royal guard. Robert's squadron had been decimated in the cut, and the rest of the guards had lost half their number trying to prevent the enemy pocket.

Bishop Thomas was seated on a bunk outside the simple cabin, reading scripture. His head lifted wearily, but a slight smile and a wave greeted us. Graven, Lorich, and Dr. Amani came out of the house and joined the bishop.

I nodded at Graven. "You asked that I come?"

"The King asked for you. Don't overtax him. He's weak."

Graven followed me in and closed the door behind us, keeping the others out. The shutters were open, but Graven closed those too, so that the tiny room darkened except for a fire in the hearth. Covered by wool blankets, his face pale and drawn, his eyes yellowed, the king watched as I approached his bed and sat down.

"Hello, Robert."

His breathing was labored. He grinned, and it was more a mocking leer of death than a smile of life. The change was shocking. "Hello, Arn."

"You're doing well, I hear."

"No," he gasped. "I'm doing poorly. You will be King after all."

I shook my head and looked away. "I don't want to be King."

On the mantel over the fireplace was a framed woodcut print of King Reuel, and beside it a vase of fresh cut wildflowers. Robert's bed was turned so that he could look at the mantel as he rested.

He swallowed and gestured at the woodcut. "Father made me swear to take care of you." He began to cough and his face was seared by pain.

Graven came forward. "Robert, you must rest now. Please."

Robert waved his hand for silence. He wheezed as he spoke. "High Wizard, an oath. Swear to serve Arn . . . as you served me and my father."

"My King, you—"

Robert lifted his head from the pillow. "Swear it by God. It is your duty. I trust I may speak of duty—now that I have shed blood and health and youth for the kingdom?"

The words brought tears to the high wizard. "I swear. By God, I swear I will do whatever you ask."

Robert's head sank back onto the pillow and he breathed easier. He gestured weakly. "Leave us, Graven. I wish to talk to Arn."

The high wizard wanted to speak, but he bit his lip and went out.

Robert watched the door close behind the magician, and then with pauses to catch his breath, delivered his speech. "Graven has, on occasion, done terrible things," he said, musingly. "He has hurt you, and others. The High Wizard sees enemies where there are none, just as you see slights where there are none. Graven imagines you are under Kendall's sway, just as he thinks I am under his. He has tried to drive a wedge between us, and perhaps he has succeeded. Do you know, Arn, that when we were boys he implied that you were somehow responsible for the Queen's death? And that you were deficient for your role as Prince?"

These were hardly revelations. "On the second, he is not far wrong," I admitted.

"I have long stopped listening to Graven on such matters," he continued. "In my head, I knew they were falsehoods. But in my heart, they were not so easily dismissed. I let them fester there too long, when I knew better. It was dishonorable."

Nice of him to admit it. Nothing like the deathbed to bring out the confessor in all of us.

"There is something else, Arn. Not all the evil of the kingdom can be laid at Graven's door. When you are king, watch Kendall closely. I cannot deny that he has served the kingdom well. But Kendall's loyalties are not to Kenesee. Remember Professor Jameson, and the others who infringed upon the Codes? There is a mystery here, and it is time to solve it. This war is being fought for more than just conquest and gain. The roles of the Pacificans are greater than they would have us believe. Not Kendall, perhaps, but the others. Did you see them at the parlay before battle? This war is being fought because of the Codes. The world is changing, Arn. The Codes may have to change, too.''

Kendall had voiced the same concern about the Codes. Perhaps they were right. But I had other things to worry about at the moment. I came out of my thoughts and found Robert staring at me amusedly.

Robert put on his death grin again. "It's so hard to know what you are thinking and feeling. So silent and watchful, so cool and reserved to all. Father was very tolerant. When he hugged you and you didn't hug back, it hurt him. Did you know that? 'Don't worry,' he would tell me. 'This is Arn's way to survive.' Do you know what he told Murdock before you left on your mission to the Beastwood? He said you were like a bottle, and kept your feelings corked up. One day they would overflow. But I wonder. Love, happiness, sorrow. Do you feel any of these, Arn? Do you know? Or do you lie to yourself?''

"Do you expect an answer?''

"Perhaps not." He coughed, and his face contorted in a spasm of pain. "I must remember not to cough. Ah, well. It won't matter soon. I know you will carry on. Your courage has met every challenge, and that is enough. The kingdom is yours, if I have not lost it for you already.''

"Enough of such talk," I said.

"We shouldn't have fought there. John Black was right and I was wrong, and we are both dead men now. Lord, I'm tired.'' He gasped a feeble laugh and closed his eyes. "It was good to have a brother," he murmured, and then his breathing slowed into a troubled rhythm of sleep.

I sat at his bedside for a while with my head in my hands, and then left. Before opening the door I took a deep breath and squared my shoulders in the bearing of a prince. The royal party waited uneasily outside, uncertain whether to stay with Robert or begin following me.

I strode up to them. "The King is unable to perform his duties. The royal party will follow me until he is well. Dr.

Amani, you stay with the King. Do you know Jason the Healer?''

"Jason Kendall? Of course. Pacifica is ahead of us in surgical technique and pharmaceuticals. What they've shared with us has been most beneficial. But I haven't seen him for years.''

"Could he do anything for the King?''

Dr. Amani turned thoughtful. "I don't know. The pelvis is shattered and organs damaged. Jason might have some answers. But who knows where he is?''

"I saw his wagon. Jason is with the army. Find him.''

My headquarters had been moved into London and established at an inn. We ended up there at the end of the day. During the hours in public I adopted the proper pose of determined confidence and strength of will for low and high alike. In the room I shared with Murdock I could drop the pretense. I put my head into my hands with a groan, the weariness rolling in like a tide. So distressed was our situation that I had not even thought of women for—well, for several hours. I wanted only to lie down and go to sleep.

Sergeant Jenkins knocked on the door, stuck his head in, and told me that two men from the ranks requested permission to see me. I glanced at Murdock with a sigh, and nodded to Jenkins. General Black always had a policy of seeing any soldier who wanted to talk to him. But God help the man if it was something that could have been solved by his unit commanders.

I straightened in my seat, adjusted my uniform, and assumed an aura of confidence and purpose. A great actor I would never be. But I tried.

The two men were shown in, and as appropriate I remained seated while they stood before me. Both seemed resolute, but cautious and unfamiliar with the royal presence. One of the men was a sergeant, short and heavy, perhaps forty. The other was a corporal, tall and strongly built, in his late twenties. I watched them and waited in silence.

Jenkins took up a position behind them.

The younger of the two spoke. "Excuse us, sir. We don't mean to bother you. I'm Carver Lee of the Twentieth Infantry from Wickliffe, and this is John McGregor from the Sixth

Regiment. The boys have asked us to talk to you a bit."

I leaned back and folded my arms across my chest. "I'm listening."

They eyed Murdock and Sergeant Jenkins, exchanged glances with each other, and then the older shrugged and spoke. "I'm sorry, sir, but the men said to talk to you alone. No others, if you please."

"Oh, is that right?" Jenkins challenged.

The two men looked behind them resentfully, but kept their tongues.

I considered the situation. The army's position was bleak, but there were no adverse feelings towards me, as far as I knew. At least, not yet. There was probably little chance of violence. And morale had to be maintained—what there was of it.

"All right, we'll talk alone." I signaled, and my companions left the room, Murdock nodding in agreement at my decision, Jenkins looking back reluctantly. "We'll be right outside if you need us, sir," he said, eyeing our visitors suspiciously as he closed the door.

I gestured towards chairs, and the men sat. "Now, Sergeant. If this is entirely satisfactory . . . ?"

He fixed his eyes firmly on me, his words crisp and to the point. "Yes, thank you, sir. The men don't want to be thought disrespectful, or afraid, or anything like that. That's why they wanted us to talk to you alone. But they are wondering how long this will go on, and for what purpose. Our homes may not be overrun yet, but they will be at the rate we're going. The men would like to be with their families to protect them."

"I see. And how much protection will you be in your homes when a Texan patrol breaks down your door?"

The older man nodded. "You're right, sir. But the men don't see it that way. They think it'll be worse in the end if we continue to fight now that the army's been destroyed."

What could I say? I stalled for time by taking out my pipe. "Sergeant, is that a pipe stem sticking out of your pocket? Do you have any tobacco in—"

"Yes, sir," he said, promptly pulling out a pouch.

"Please join me."

"After you, sir."

The corporal looked at us in distaste.

"It's a filthy, disgusting habit," the sergeant eulogized. "Want to try it?"

The corporal declined the offer.

I filled my pipe bowl and soon the two of us were puffing vigorously while the corporal shifted impatiently on the stool. I was much better at it now. I blew a smoke ring.

The sergeant smiled sadly. "For a moment, sir, you looked a bit like General Black sitting back and smoking his pipe when he was thinking."

"Did I? Well. Thank you, Sergeant. Back to the matter at hand. What would the men like me to do?"

The two looked at each other. "Sir?"

"What solutions do you recommend? We could surrender. I'm sure the Texans would welcome us most warmly. Or, we could disband the army. Of course, getting home with Easterner patrols roaming the roads might be a bit difficult. I'm not sure how they would deal with those they catch . . . considering the slaughter at Yellow Fields. Do you like either of these choices?"

The sergeant puffed his pipe in amusement while the young firebrand searched for words. "The men don't want that, sir, they just . . ."

"They just what?"

"They just don't know how we can win, and can't see fighting another battle if we're going to lose anyway."

"We're not going to lose the next battle," I said, slowly and confidently.

Such is leadership. The ability to lie convincingly. I was quite proud of myself.

The sergeant took the pipe out of his mouth. "Uh, no disrespect meant, sir, but how are we going to do that?"

"By winning, of course."

"Oh. Any particular tactics you have in mind, sir? The odds are a little steep."

My mind raced. "Surprise," I said pleasantly.

"Yes, sir. They sure will be surprised. So will we."

I grinned with him, and then grew serious. "I can't tell you yet what the plan is. I ask you to trust me as you trusted General Black. There is hope. We can win."

The sergeant looked at me, wanting to believe. "Can we?"

"General Black thought we could. It's his plan."

The corporal took notice. "General Black's?"

I leaned towards them, as if sharing a secret. "He saw what was happening, and told me what to do before he died. It's his plan. If the men remain firm, we'll have the victory. If the men don't have faith in this—then we might as well surrender today."

The sergeant's eyes brightened. "The General had a plan. Well, that does put a different color on it. The men will want to hear that." The sergeant gave the corporal an I-told-you-so look. "Satisfied?"

The corporal nodded. "As long as there's a reason for what we do. That's all we wanted to know."

The sergeant tapped him on the shoulder as a signal to go. "We thank you for your time, sir, and we'll pass the word." They saluted, and were about to go out.

I raised a hand and stopped them for a last moment. "Tell the men . . . not to give up hope."

The sergeant nodded. "Yes, sir. We will." And then they went out.

"You heard?" I asked Murdock as he came back.

"I would never think of putting my ear to the door and listening in on a private discussion. My boy, maybe you can refresh me on that plan. I'm so absent-minded I forgot all about it."

I blew smoke at him. He sat down heavily. The banter which had sustained us so well in past adversity seemed somehow empty. The shock had still not worn off, and it showed now in Murdock's worried brows.

"What are we going to do?" he asked, and the question was more to himself than to me. "I've racked my skull searching for solutions. In another day the Alliance will be here and force us north. Five days of retreating and we'll be at Lexington. What then?"

"I don't know."

"Surprise, you told them. Not a bad idea. That was John's specialty. So we surprise the enemy and rout half of their army. Then the other half kills us."

"Yes," I admitted. "That is a problem."

"I wonder what John would have done if he were here.

Even he never faced the odds we do.''

I sipped at my wine. Good wine from Lexington. I needed to get drunk.

What would Black have done? What ridiculous, completely unrealistic plan would he come up with to transform defeat into victory? And then, unbidden, an idea began to form in my head. I puffed more fiercely. "Murdock, remember the puzzles Black told us? When is an army not an army?"

"When they're sleeping."

"And when are they most vulnerable?" I asked, thinking quickly.

"After victory."

"And when—"

"I see. I see," Murdock said. "But can it be done?"

"What choice do we have?"

We sat quietly, thinking out the details, and then began to share our ideas. Within an hour or two the basics took shape. The royal advisors were called and informed of the plan. Maps were brought out and positions described. They greeted the plan with less than wild enthusiasm.

"That's it," I concluded. "Any questions?"

Sir Meredith was reluctant. "This is a desperate venture. And my town will pay the price."

Bishop Thomas grimaced. "I find some of the arrangements reprehensible."

"Consider the alternatives," Murdock addressed the bishop. "What will happen to our people if we lose?"

"That is true," the bishop admitted. "Still, I don't feel good about this. I must in conscience advise against it."

Graven looked up from the map. "The Bishop raises a key point. The use of civilians violates the Codes. The laws were made to protect noncombatants."

"The townspeople will be enrolled in the militia," I countered.

Kendall shook his head. "I am in agreement with High Wizard Graven on this. The use of the townspeople runs counter to the spirit of the Codes."

Murdock glanced at each in turn, and then spoke, his tone full of sympathetic understanding while his words clarified the issue with cool rationality. "We agree with you. But a decision must be made. We have a choice. Bend the Codes this one time, in order to preserve them. Or follow them blindly to defeat, and watch the Alliance abolish the Codes entirely."

No one spoke.

I got tired of waiting. "Kendall? Graven? You two are the firmest defenders of the Codes. Do you object?"

They looked at each other for a long moment, and then shook their heads.

I was satisfied. "Then we'll proceed with the plan as it is. Begin thinking of all we need to do to make this work. Dismissed."

Preparations went forward for the rest of the night.

I called for the beastman Kren, and a few minutes later he stepped in, greeting Murdock and me warmly, if none too cheerily. "Well, just like old times, almost. I'm sorry Black isn't here. I liked him."

There was little time to waste. "Major Kren, you remember what Mr. Kendall told you about the Alliance and their plans for the Beastwood. Extermination or slavery. Do you believe him?"

Kren pulled up a chair. "I do. And I've already sent a message to the Council to that effect."

"Can we expect any help from your people?"

Kren shifted uncomfortably. "I knew you'd ask that. You won't like my answer. They'll say no. Senior Councilman Sokol was the only man to vote for an alliance with Kenesee. The rest want to stay neutral. And now that your army has been destroyed. . . ."

Murdock smiled. A real smile. "We have a plan."

Kren took the news well. "Oh. Isn't that nice."

Again we went to the maps and explained the plan in full, the beastman stroking the pelt on his cheeks as he listened. His cynicism gave way to appreciation.

"Interesting. The key lies in deception. If the enemy becomes suspicious, then it won't work. And much could go wrong in any case. You know that, don't you?"

"Never thought of it. Now, will you help?"

"I'll do what I can. But I'm not optimistic."

We sent him off, and he rode out of camp the next morning, escorted by a dozen guards ordered to see him safely to the

Beastwood. They had been given the sturdiest and fastest mounts we had.

Then Graven and Kendall took a squadron of cavalry and followed Kren on the road northward. They were going to Lexington to prepare the way.

A half dozen volunteers from the ranks were brought forward and Murdock told them their role. "Your task is to pose as stragglers or deserters and allow yourselves to be captured by the Alliance. Hopefully, they'll be interested in information and accept your surrender instead of killing you."

Brave men. They didn't flinch when told the nature of their mission.

"Tell the enemy that the last remnant of the Army of Kenesee is melting away, the men discouraged, tired, and disappointed in the leadership of Prince Scar. Tell them the army is without hope."

Unfortunately, this could easily have been the reality. I shook the hand of each and sent them on their way.

Murdock paced up and down, animated for the first time since the battle. "The men will have a purpose now, something to put their hope in."

"There is so much to go wrong," I said glumly, and drank some wine. We were drinking a lot of wine lately. "What do you think our odds are?"

"Quite respectable. Quite respectable, indeed."

"The odds, Murdock. What are they?"

He smiled brightly. "If preparations work out right? Oh, one in ten, maybe. Arn, don't choke."

7

The Battle of Lexington

The enemy approached leisurely and made a crossing up-stream. We then continued our withdrawal, and the Alliance seemed to agree that there was no need for haste. The inevitable would come, sooner or later. So it was a full five days before we came into sight of Lexington, the men renewed by hope in the secret plan of General Black.

Lexington was well known to me. It was a pretty town of more than five thousand nestled along the western side of a shallow valley twisting north and south between a line of steep hills. To the east, the hills were wooded. To the west, they were covered with vineyards. The town wall was made of white crete from the Old World, its roofs made of red tile. Above the wall rose the turrets and battlements of the castle of Duke Sims. I had stood on those battlements with the old duke and Robert and Megan, waiting for our army to march back from the Beastwood.

On the hillsides above the town, vineyards were planted almost to the shadow of the stone wall. Their fruit provided the main commerce of Lexington, for within the town were wineries with giant casks waiting to be tapped, while in cellars thousands of bottles and kegs nestled in racks, aging contentedly.

At the base of the hill, entrenchments were being dug on either side of the town by several thousand militia brought in from across the northern counties. From a distance these units did not look too bad. They dressed properly in their uniforms, snatched up their weapons, and came to attention as we passed. But a closer look revealed that there were too many gray-haired men and too many boys of fourteen in their ranks, eagerly or reluctantly preparing for their first and last chance at glory.

Most of our infantry and wagons kept marching up the road northward and into the hills beyond, where they disappeared from sight. But the Fifth and Sixth Regiments filed into the entrenchments on the north side of the town, while the militia units took position to the south.

The gates of the town were closed, as ordered. The number of refugees with the army had grown into the thousands, and these were sent along the west road towards Louisville with bread, cheese, and sausage. There were even pitchers of milk for the children and infants. Once these refugees were on their way, the children and elderly of Lexington were ordered to follow.

I had met Mayor Kauffman before, and knew of him from his daughter, Angela. He may have had hopes that his daughter might snare one of the nobility, but he certainly didn't know that Angela and I had established a relationship. What he might have thought of it had he known, I was never to learn. The man, a helpful sort with bushy eyebrows, hesitated when he received his orders. "Yes, Prince Arn, I see. The young and the old must leave. The men we have left are all enrolled in the Lexington defense companies and have their assigned places on the wall. They will do their part, I'm sure. But Prince Arn—ahh—what about the women of the town? Many of them are widows now. Wouldn't it be better to let them go with their children?"

Murdock gave me a sorrowful look. We had discussed this matter before. I paused only a moment before speaking. "The women will stay. They'll be auxiliaries to the town defense, and assist the men."

The mayor's expression went from surprise to confusion. "I see. But this will place them in some danger. And the women have not been organized. They—"

"I'm sure you'll be able . . . to use them effectively," I responded, stiffly giving him a pat on the back. It was meant to be encouraging, something I had seen others do to good effect, and I'd used it on the wounded. But I had never done it before to a man still on his feet. Still, it seemed to have some effect.

Or perhaps it was just my next words. "Make sure the orders are obeyed. Tell the women that their children will be taken care of, and are safer away."

The south gate was opened, and soon enough the old and the young—many of them protesting—streamed from the town and followed the other refugees west. With the royal advisors I watched them from beside the gates, studying the progress of our preparations. Last from the gate was Gregory Sims, leading the elderly servants of his household on their way. Gesturing with his cane, the ancient Duke Sims limped up to our party in a huff.

"Arn! Arn, you young whippersnapper—"

Jenkins looked puzzled. "Whippersnapper?"

The duke continued without a pause. "Is this your doing? Why are you fighting here? This is no place for a battle. Look at those entrenchments. Bah. Find an open field and beat them proper. And what's this about the women? You can't keep the women here. You know that."

Sir Meredith held up his hand. "Father. That's enough. Get along now. Take care of the others. They're depending on you."

The duke turned on his son. "Don't think I can't figure out what you're planning. To do this to your own daughter."

"Megan?" whispered Sir Meredith.

"She's here?" Kendall asked.

They both turned pale.

"Of course she's here, you fools. Where did you think she was supposed to go?"

"She was supposed to stay in Kingsport," Kendall complained ruefully.

"The Alliance left its siege equipment far behind," Sir Meredith argued. "They're after our army, not the towns. She would have been safe in Kingsport."

"Safe or not, she's here," Duke Sims repeated. "And what are you going to do about it?"

Kendall and Sir Meredith looked at each other, and then at me.

Poor Megan. Poor Kendall. Poor Sir Meredith.

"You agreed to the plan," I reminded them calmly. "No exceptions."

Duke Sims frowned at us. "So. You're just going to leave

Megan up there with her friend to wait for the enemy to—''

"Her friend?" I interrupted.

"Yes. That dark-haired girl. The Mayor's daughter. Angela."

"Angela is here?"

"Where else would she be?" the Duke asked, exasperated. "Does that make a difference?"

Angela was in Lexington. Warm, kind, beautiful Angela. Well, well, well. How stalwart I had been in deciding the fate of the town. How courageous in maintaining the order for Megan. How brave by enforcing fairness for all, regardless of rank.

And now I was put to the lie.

The others watched me expectantly, hope upon the faces of Sir Meredith and Kendall, and others too. The column of young and old was passing into the distance. I looked up and saw the flag of Kenesee above the gates, fluttering in the breeze. The warm day had suddenly turned cold.

The others still stared at me. I looked at each of them in turn.

"No exceptions."

Duke Sims threw up his hands, and there were tears in his eyes. "Bah. It's not proper. It's dishonorable. Dishonorable." And with that he stalked off and led his little band away.

Later I called Sergeant Jenkins over where none could hear. "Megan and Angela will be expecting me to come see them tonight. Send a messenger with my respects, and tell them the situation prevents me from visiting them."

"Aye, sir," he said promptly.

I grabbed his arm as he started off. "And if they come around to see me, or the other advisors—''

"Yes, sir?"

"Keep them away."

Preparations went on throughout the day. Roads and paths leading up into the hills were blocked and rendered impassable to cavalry. Hidden trails for infantry were cleared through the vineyards and carefully pointed out to the men. The army's pay chests were taken into town upon a pair of wagons and left in the town square, securely guarded by a squad of infantry from the Sixth Regiment. Other small units of the Sixth took position at the gates of the town reinforcing the Lexington units on the wall, and also at the gate of Castle Sims.

In late afternoon I rode through town on a final inspection and stopped in the town square to check the infantry guarding the treasury. Besides these troops, there were few people in the square. Some women had come for water, and the infantry watched them with appreciation. I waved my followers back, dismounted, and walked over to the fountain.

The women there eyed me with a mixture of caution and respect, then edged away. One stout figure was seated on the edge of the fountain, basking in the sun. She wore a loose skirt, colorful shirt, and a wide-brimmed felt hat with two eagle feathers pulled low over her forehead.

Crazy Mary did not seem surprised at our meeting.

"Why is it," I said, "when I see you I get a bad feeling?"

She snorted. "Humph. Because I bring you the truth."

"How about some good news for once?"

"No good news to bring. Not for Prince Scar."

"Thanks for the encouragement."

"I'm not here to joke with you," she said in a flat tone. "Does Robert still live?"

I nodded. "Yes. They think he's getting better."

Mary sighed, and for a moment her wrinkles softened into a look of troubled sadness. "I did not foresee that. I saw you with the crown. Well, perhaps that does not matter since you are still in command. The decisions are yours, whether you wear a crown or not."

"Has the time come?"

She nodded. "Tomorrow. I do God's will."

"How do you know that it isn't His Will that you live?"

She paused. "I don't. But what about you? What does He want you to do?"

I splashed some water from the fountain on my face. "That's what I'm trying to figure out. I'm doing what I have to."

She took out a piece of bread and sausage and began to eat. "Many will die."

"Many have already died."

She spoke between chews. "Yes. But those were not your fault."

I wondered why I had bothered talking to her. "What will happen tomorrow?"

She gestured around her. "Look. What do you see?"

The square was paved in bricks, with several large elms and maples providing shade to stone benches. The buildings were whitewashed, the shutters painted and decorated with designs, and flowers bloomed in all the window boxes. It really was a pretty town, perhaps the nicest in Kenesee.

"This is my favorite place. This will all be gone tomorrow," she stated bluntly. For the first time that I could remember, her voice became soft, pleading. "The women. Those old men and boys in the trenches. Let them go."

Let them go. Just like that. Let them go. I considered her request. A last chance to change my mind? An angel to guide my path, or a devil to lead me astray? Not my will, Lord. . . . And if the Alliance won, what of those women and children then? What of Kren's people, the beastmen? What would become of us all?

"Mary, I need them."

The grumble was back in her voice. "Humph. Why?"

"Otherwise, they'll end up in the slave pens."

"Maybe. Maybe not."

"Tell me I won't need them for victory."

She snorted again. "I can't do that. Whatever happens, there is a price to pay."

"Someone else told me that recently."

"You're getting good advice. Good-bye, Prince Arn. I will pray for you."

I had been dismissed. Again.

I shook my head, mounted, and left her there at the fountain eating her bread.

The night was quiet, the morning a fine one. The men slept till after sunrise and had a good breakfast, after which they made final improvements to their entrenchments and prepared their weapons. It was precisely at noon, while the town hall clock chimed, that the first outriders of the Alliance came within sight of the walls. They viewed the entrenchments and reported back to their leaders. By one o'clock, scouts were skirmishing on the road. By the time the clock chimed two, the Alliance cavalry began to arrive, banners flying arrogantly.

Sir Meredith's horsemen enjoyed several spirited and bloody clashes before allowing the enemy to drive them off to the north.

I watched all this from the walls, and then went down to the town hall where the others waited. The meeting room was long and narrow, with the flags of Kenesee and Lexington at either end. Murals depicting great moments in the history of the city were painted along both side walls. Most of these had to do with destruction and rebuilding. Through open windows we could see birds perched in the trees of the town square and hear them twittering their little songs, while a cool breeze made the room pleasant. All rose as I entered, but I gestured them back into their seats and sat down at the head of the table.

"The enemy cavalry have appeared," I informed them, which set off murmurs around the table. "Our time is short. Murdock, if you please."

A nod to the wizard and he began to summarize the situation. "Our plan has gone well so far. All the troops are in place, and unit officers have gone over the terrain since yesterday. Preparations in the town and entrenchments are complete. The treasury is in place, the wine distributed and stocked, and—and those necessary retained for duty in the town. All others are gone. Everything has been done that can be done. Now, we can only wait for the enemy to conform to our plans."

He nodded back to me.

"Murdock is wrong," I said, and he looked up in surprise. "There is one more thing we can do. The Alliance must be fooled . . . into thinking their victory complete. They must have a prize, a great prize, to reassure them."

Those at the table looked at each other.

The next words were difficult, but I forced them out. "I will stay behind in the town . . . and allow myself to be captured when it falls."

Objections burst out from around the table. "No!" "It's too dangerous." "You must not." "Never."

High Wizard Graven stood and put up a mottled hand for silence. I could imagine what he would say. *Regrettable, but necessary. And after all, Arn is a prince, not a king. We will always remember the sacrifice he has made.* Oh, yes. And they would listen to his logic, and accept it. And I would stay in the town as I had planned.

Finally, he spoke. "Prince Arn is correct. A great prize would help confirm the completeness of their victory." He paused and stared down the length of the table at me. "But without the King here, it is neither appropriate nor necessary for our leader to remove himself from command during the critical hours ahead. Prince Arn must remain with us. However, another servant of the Kingdom might accomplish the task proposed. The servant must be recognized both by reputation and by face to the leaders of the Alliance. Therefore, I will remain in the town, and I will be the prize."

Graven ignored the voices of protest. "Prince Arn, do you see the wisdom of this?"

I hesitated long before answering.

"Yes, I do." He was right. I couldn't leave while Robert was still bedridden, unable to command. Arnold Brant, pitiful excuse for a leader, was expendable. Prince Scar of Kenesee, symbol of hope and victory, was not. Perhaps I knew that all along, and was just hoping another would offer himself in my place. Still, I had been ready to stay.

Perhaps that counts for something.

The table fell quiet except for a whispering voice. "Master Graven, you can't do this."

The high wizard looked down at Apprentice Lorich. "I must."

"Then I'll stay with you."

"No. You'll be needed in battle, helping to guard Prince Arn and using the talents God has given you. Remember, obedience. Never fear, all will be right in the end."

I rapped knuckles on the table. "The matter is decided. The gratitude of the King and the Kingdom are yours, High Wizard. Reward will follow the battle. And my thanks to all of you. Now, Murdock will accompany me to my command post . . . and the rest of you will leave the city and go to the assembly point. Use the north gate, and God be with us all."

Murdock stayed seated beside me. The room emptied except for Graven and Lorich, who talked together quietly in a corner.

"Mr. Lorich," I said sternly.

"Yes, Prince Arn?"

"It is time for you to go."

"Sorry. Yes, sir." He looked up at the wizard shyly. "Don't do anything foolish, Master. Don't get them mad."

Graven snorted. "So. Now my Apprentice gives me advice, does he? Do you think me a fool? All right. I won't turn them into frogs. Satisfied? Now go on, boy. It's time for you to get safely out of the city. And keep yourself whole. My boots will need polishing."

Graven watched him as he limped out of the room, and then he spoke to us. "He is a good Apprentice, and will be a powerful Wizard. Already, he surpasses me in raw strength. Take care of him. Nurture him." He was silent, and then took a deep breath before giving a last instruction to Murdock. "Remember to keep up the static today, my friend. Every wizard must do so." He bowed to me. "And now, Prince Arn, if you will allow me a few moments with my old friend Murdock. . . ."

I went out and saw Lorich safely off with the rest of the party. A member or two were sent off at short intervals to avoid the attention a larger group might attract from the enemy scouts, and soon all were gone. I waited on horseback with Jenkins and the guards until Murdock came out.

"Thank you for waiting, sir. Sorry to be so long," he apologized.

"Anything I should know?" I asked.

"Nothing right now, at least," he said sadly. "Well, let's be off, and God have mercy on Lexington."

We took the north gate out of town, circled by the wall road, and came to my command post. It was located a few dozen yards above the entrenchments on the hills, just to the east and north of the town where a spur of rock jutted out and permitted a clear view of all our forces.

By three o'clock the Alliance infantry could be seen as they marched into view and began to deploy before us. Even though we were prepared for it, the sight of the enemy was depressing. There were just so many of them. They formed up in deep masses that piled three and even four times our number on each yard of front, and yet still they came up, extending both flanks until they overlapped ours. Islanders, Easterners, Mexicans, and Texans, they took position in line from left to right respectively, standards marking the position of each ruler. Held in reserve were the mammoths, eight of them standing on the road, war towers on their backs, waiting to be used. There had been a dozen at Yellow Fields, so apparently we had managed to destroy a few of the beasts after all. But even those remaining would never be needed, and everyone knew it. The Islanders faced us confidently, yelling and cursing and pounding shields. Even the stoic Easterners were yelling in anticipation.

"Now?"

"I think so," Murdock agreed.

"Distribute the cases and bottles in the entrenchments," I ordered. "And tell the men that they will be searched, and any man found with a bottle will be hanged."

This threat—from me—carried weight.

Messengers fanned out across the hill to each regiment, and the carefully located stocks in the entrenchments were opened. Not too obvious, of course, but in places where they could be plausibly explained and easily found.

"Any message from Major Kren?" I asked, knowing better.

"Nothing from the Beastwood," Murdock confirmed. He smiled encouragingly. "You don't look so good."

"I know." I leaned over discreetly and was sick.

"This is becoming quite the tradition," Murdock observed, moving upwind. "Feel better?"

"Not really."

"You look better. Not as green." He passed me a water jug. "Well, this is the big one, isn't it? You've thought of what happens if we lose, haven't you?"

I took a sip of water, swished it around in my mouth, and spat. "There will be no more battles. Then I won't have to be sick again."

"They've cut the west road to Louisville," he continued cheerily. "So we'll have to head for the Northern Forests."

"Where we can starve or be roasted by the tribesmen," I observed with appropriate detachment. "We could seek refuge with the beastmen."

"Until the Alliance attacks the Beastwood. Or we could take ship down the river."

"I've already thought of that."

"Strange," he mused. "We checked them at the Rift Gates, at Wickliffe, and at the Crossroads. Robert frustrated them along the Coast Road. And then the Battle of Yellow Fields.

Did our efforts merely set us up for defeat? Is that what God plans?''

I thought about it in order to take my mind off my stomach. What could we have done differently? Were the decisions we had made actually wrong? Had we been fools, congratulating ourselves while each step brought us closer to disaster? I shook my head to clear it. Such matters had to be left to the philosophers. Professor Wagner and his colleagues could discuss it in the quiet hours over a good beer and invariably come up with the solution. But today I had to face the problem in truth, and we would get no second chance. Today there was no time for the might-have-beens. The game had to be played out, for good or ill.

''The odds always were against us,'' I responded. ''We took advantage of every mistake they made. They just didn't make enough.''

''You're right,'' Murdock admitted. ''Maybe one day we can sit down and mull it over before the fire.'' He was silent a moment. ''I hope.''

Five o'clock had already come when the Alliance completed their deployment and came out to parlay. Four parties emerged from the enemy ranks and rode to midfield. All the familiar faces were there. Governor Rodes, Prime Minister Billy Bay, Patron Carlos Estevez, and their advisors, Pacifican and otherwise. A newcomer was General Jack Murphy, President of Texan. There are some men who look treacherous, but are not. And there are others who look quite respectable, and are snakes. Jack Murphy looked exactly like what he was. He was a crude, ill-spoken murderer who had lied and cheated his way to power in Texan. No more despicable ruler was to be found. We might have gotten along well except for the circumstances.

I met them at midfield with only Murdock and Jenkins. The Alliance party outnumbered us four to one, and if so inclined could have ended it right there. But there was no need to dirty their hands with further treachery. As all knew, we had no chance anyway.

Like Robert I waited, but this time they were silent too. Perhaps the opposite tact would be more effective. I took a deep breath. ''Have you come . . . to surrender?''

They broke into laughter. Governor Rodes was so taken by my statement that tears actually rolled down his cheek. After the roaring had subsided, he took out a kerchief and wiped his eyes. "Ahh, Prince Arn. That's the best I've heard all week. 'Have you come to surrender?' I must remember that."

He put away the kerchief. "No, my young prince, we have not come to surrender. But we have come to offer terms. Again. Your brother scorned us the last time. Now his army lies buried to the south, and he is sorely wounded, so we hear. Or has he died?"

I could hear Sergeant Jenkins squeezing his fisted gauntlets so hard that the leather creaked. I wondered what shade of red his face looked like at the moment. A nice, vivid crimson, perhaps.

"No," I responded. "King Robert lives."

"Ahh," the governor exclaimed. "But crippled for life, if the rumors are true. I regret that. I do. Death would be better. But he has none to blame but himself. We offered very generous terms. Now, we come to offer the same to you."

I paused for just a moment, thinking. "The very same?"

"Exactly," Governor Rodes stated firmly.

I hesitated. The same terms. I could still return to the castle and live a quiet life. A battle need not be fought. Men need not die. Life could go on as it had, and I could leave politics to others. For a moment I was tempted. Sorely tempted. Murdock looked sideways at me, and I gave him a glance. He responded with the slightest shake of his head. No.

Could we trust Jack Murphy? Could we even trust Governor Rodes? How many of our people would find their way into the Texan slave pens? Would I one day find a regiment in the courtyard, waiting to escort me to the dungeons in New Richmond? These men had power. They did not have to worry about terms and promises. They did not have to worry about honor. For them, the sanctity of the Codes was broken. The Codes had become a convenience, to be used or not as they chose.

I squared my shoulders. "The terms are . . . unacceptable."

Governor Rodes became exasperated. "Come now, Prince Arn. You're trying my patience. I—we were content to fight King Robert and resolve the issue by force of arms. We have done so. We have won our victory. We have enough military glory. More will just be unnecessary bloodshed."

He waited for a reply, and I gave it to him.

"Withdraw from Kenesee . . . or you will be destroyed."

Patron Estevez gestured for attention. "Prince Arn. We've heard of your exploits. We know you have fought valiantly and well, you and all your men. But consider your losses. King Reuel, dead. General Black, dead. King Robert, terribly wounded. Your nobility, shattered. A score of Kenesee regiments destroyed. Please. Reconsider."

"Aye," Prime Minister Billy Bay smirked. "And from prisoners we know what your troops think. They know they can't win. They're deserting more and more every day. Your army is melting away."

I felt Sergeant Jenkins stirring behind me. Yet I knew that what Billy Bay said could easily have been the truth. I was glad I'd lied to the troops.

"I warn you," I retorted shakily. "You are doomed."

"You warn us?" General Jack Murphy said mockingly, his voice scratchy and coarse. "You can't even hide your fear. Is this the great Prince Scar we've heard about? Is this the man who defeated the Arkans? Or maybe it was John Black who did the thinking and the fighting while you sucked your thumb? Are you afraid of going back to the gutter? We'll send you somewhere far worse than that when all this is done. We'll pluck your eyes out and throw you in the dungeon till you're old and gray."

Maybe we wouldn't have gotten along so well after all.

Governor Rodes cast a sharp glance of reprimand that silenced Jack Murphy, then turned back to me. "Our colleague enjoys his colorful threats, but bear him no mind. Still, the day is passing. One more chance, Prince Arn."

Now was the time for silence. I kept my mouth closed.

Governor Rodes shrugged. "So be it. But I warn you now. We will seek you out. You will not escape. Beware." And with that threat they wheeled away, leaving us to return to our own lines.

"I think they were trying to intimidate you," Murdock observed.

"They succeeded," I confirmed. Jack Murphy's words had horrified me.

Jenkins began to curse under his breath. I looked at him and discovered that he had given 'beet red' a new meaning. "Seek us out, will they? Well, we'll see about that."

"How did I do?" I asked as we rode back.

"Not bad," Murdock said. "You didn't reveal anything, and they revealed much. They believed the prisoners and think our army is falling apart. They're over-confident. And their terms for peace are lies. You could have done much worse."

"I thought you did a fine job, sir," Jenkins congratulated me as he calmed down. "That was quite a piece of acting. You had them thinking you were scared. Why, for a moment even I thought you might really accept their terms. Then I realized how you were playing them along."

"Thank you, Sergeant."

"Think nothing of it, sir."

I frowned at Murdock. "Don't say anything."

"Beautiful weather we're having," he replied innocently.

We had not even regained our command post when the signal to attack rose from the enemy lines. There was to be no subtlety in their tactics. The entire mass of infantry started forward at the walk, and then into double-time. Like an incoming tide the enemy rushed up to the entrenchments. The battle lines joined first on the far right where the hill with the militia thrust forward at the Alliance. For a moment the militia held, an incredible act of defiance against an enemy superior in both skill and numbers. From behind their embankments and stakes the old men and boys thrust wildly at the enemy, holding them back with a desperate fury. And then the pressure grew too great, and the enemy troops swarmed over the entrenchments.

I gave a signal and trumpets blew the retreat. Beneath us, the men of the Fifth and Sixth Regiments left their positions at the call, fleeing up the hillside towards us even before the enemy made contact. They were the lucky ones, retiring before there was anyone to cut them down from behind. The militia were not so fortunate. The enemy pursued the running conscripts up the steep side of the hill, catching many of them in the back. It was too far to see the details, fortunately.

The squads of the Sixth Regiment on the town walls followed their orders well. As soon as the militia broke, a white flag was hung over the battlements and the town gates swung open. If lucky, the squads might make it out by the west gate before the enemy encircled the town.

Sergeant Jenkins cleared his throat. "Time to go, sir."

"Murdock, everything is in place?"

"Yes, Arn. It's too late to do any more now."

The first of our men fled by us.

"We really must go," Jenkins repeated.

And so we did. From the top of the hill we saw the entrenchments and hillside swarming with the enemy. We quickly made our way down the reverse slope into another valley, and then up and over the hill on the far side. Safely hidden behind that second hill, the other regiments of the army waited in neat ranks. The men of the Fifth and Sixth reassembled next to them, while the survivors of the militia threw themselves down behind the safety of our troops, exhausted. They were content to find haven, too relieved to question the presence of an organized force where they had expected none.

Murdock and I crouched low on the hilltop, hiding behind the staked vines and watching the hill we had fled from. The enemy had gained the far crest and stopped, waving their weapons and cheering in disorder. They did not pursue further.

So far, our plan had worked.

For the Alliance, the last battle had been won. Their enemy had stood to fight under the command of an ignorant prince too stupid to surrender. Accordingly, the last remnant of the Army of Kenesee had been shattered with great loss and put to flight, its discouraged troops fleeing the hopeless struggle in disarray. The panicked survivors could be hunted down and taken at leisure.

For now, there was a victory to enjoy. The war was over, and the first walled town had fallen. There was wine everywhere. And soon word spread of other booty. The town was actually inhabited. The populace of the smaller towns and villages throughout Kenesee had fled into the mountains when the Alliance had approached. But this town had women! And that was not all! The King's Treasury had been found! Chests full of coins, right in the town square, abandoned by guards running for their lives. Even the castle of the local duke had surrendered, opening its gates and hanging out a white flag. Yes, inside the walls of the town were treasures enough to satisfy the appetites of any man. Thousands rushed to get their share. Thousands of others ambled over to the gates with more dignity, preferring to do their pillaging in a more restrained fashion. Still others simply sat in the entrenchments and fields, opening the wine kegs and celebrating their victory.

By seven o'clock, many were on their way to the best drunk of their lives. At eight o'clock the looting was in full progress, and by nine the raping had begun. Discipline collapsed as the night went on. Drunk, the men ignored their officers, or were too often led by them, captains as ready to partake as the rest. Even the military staffs, the key officers and advisors and magicians, relaxed and enjoyed. Everyone knew that no enemy remained to give challenge. Here was plunder, here was treasure, here were the spoils which had been promised them when victory was achieved. Victory was theirs, and now they would take what they wanted.

The treasury was quickly dispersed among the first hundred who found their way there and furtively made off with the coins. Disappointed, others ransacked homes and shops, the soldiers draping themselves in civilian clothes of both sexes and carrying furniture out into the streets. The wiser found food and sat down at tables to eat. All had a bottle or keg near, and as the night wore on the search for women grew less furtive and more brazen. Most of the Lexington militia men had already surrendered on the walls and been led out of town, although a few had snuck back to defend their homes. Those that resisted were cut down. The men of the Alliance wandered the streets, entering each house to see what fun was to be had, seeking the third, fourth, fifth woman to rape that night, and waiting in line for the privilege.

From our hillside we listened to the clock of the town hall chiming the hours faintly as Lexington endured its night of horrors. It was after one when the first fire broke out, and an hour later a quarter of the town was alight, its glow visible to us from beyond the next hill.

"Who ordered that?" I asked severely.

"No one," Murdock responded. "It's their doing. I've seen it before. Nothing like a little burning to enliven a party. Everything is going exactly as planned, God forgive us."

"Is now the time?"

Murdock wore a pained expression. "Too soon. Sacking a town takes time."

The rioters left the heat of the town and staggered out into the countryside, taking the women and wine with them into the roads and fields. The drunken orgy went on.

The town clock did not chime four, for the town hall was ablaze with most of the rest of the town. I assembled the regimental commanders.

"I am told the enemy has no pickets. Is that correct?"

They nodded assent.

"Your regiments are ready?"

"Aye." "Yes, sir." "Now is the time."

"Now is the time," I agreed. "Remember, no drums, no horns, no trumpets. Move silently until the signal is given. Watch my standard for orders. Any questions? No? Then lead your men out."

In seven regimental columns our five thousand infantry climbed over the crest and down the hill, strode across the peaceful valley, then ascended the reverse slope of the hill upon which the battle had been fought. Our scouts had been sent forward to ambush sentries, but the information was correct. The Alliance had put out some cavalry pickets on their flanks down in the valley, but they were sleeping. Of infantry sentries, there were none.

The Army of the Alliance had no security.

Behind the crest we stopped, aligned front, and the regiments deployed into company columns. Already the flames of the town made a dull roar, punctuated by the yells and screams and curses of the revelers in the valley ahead.

On foot my party followed the infantry, then passed the columns as they dressed. We came to the crest and looked down, the night lit not only by the moon's white glow, but also by the red glow of the town. Down in the valley, thousands of tiny figures lay about in drunken sleep, while thousands of others roamed about, enjoying their victory. Behind them, dark lumps signified the sleeping mammoths, their war towers now unstrapped and resting on the ground nearby like so many fortified keeps. To either flank, the tethered forms of five thousand cavalry horses were two black shadows against the dark earth. And to the north, even now approaching at a slow walk from up the valley, the dark cloud of Sir Meredith's cavalry drifted closer and prepared itself for the signal.

I waved my arm. Behind me and safely below the crest, a torch was waved in the darkness. The companies started forward.

We stayed on the hilltop for a moment as the columns of infantry passed around us and down the hill through the paths we had readied for this moment. Already they ran into an occasional foe, and there was the briefest clash of weapons before the scream of the enemy dying. But here the destruction of Lexington worked in our favor. The roar of the flames helped cover these sounds, if any were paying attention, and there were many screams from those captured in the town who were now being put to various uses. At my signal we followed close behind the columns.

At the bottom of the hill the troops climbed into and over the entrenchment, halted, and the companies deployed from column into line. Torches were quickly lit, and within seconds every other man in the second rank held one aloft.

And still, miraculously, no alarm had been raised.

I looked at my trumpeter and nodded. Without hesitation he brought the instrument to his lips and blew. The notes carried forth, and were echoed by seven other trumpets up and down the line. And then we started forward.

Surprise was complete. Those who slept in our path, and those who were too drunk to run, died quickly. Clumps of enemy—soldiers mingled from many units—stood and fought for a few moments before going down, but dozens, then hundreds, and finally thousands were fleeing before us, their minds dulled with wine and crazed with fear. They were confused and alone amidst the thousands of their allies—strangers now as before—who fled beside them.

Some troopers of the cavalry regiments woke and tried to gain their horses. Our archers shot them down, while scouts cut the tethers and spooked the animals with torches so they bolted and galloped through the enemy camp in huge herds. The mammoths too were running, their masters nowhere near, and terrified by the torches poking at their eyes from out of the darkness. Into this confusion came Sir Meredith's cavalry, sweeping up the valley and through the enemy camp, cutting downs hundreds of men before them. Through the center of the enemy camp we advanced, driving across the valley and towards the forested slopes of the eastern hills.

And yet, for all our success, their numbers were too great. Well-disciplined companies of Easterners fought here. A regiment of Mexican guards stood there. A few companies of

Islanders resisted between. The enemy began to form a rough battle line before our charging troops, and our unopposed advance slowed. We continued to grind forward and inflict many casualties, but now we actually had to fight.

More of their soldiers fell into line and joined the battle. Our advance slowed to a crawl and then halted short of the wooded slopes on the opposite side of the valley. The sheer number of enemy who resisted proved enough opposition to stop our advance.

"Such a victory," said Murdock in wonder. "And still we're about to lose."

"Can't Sir Meredith do something?" someone asked in desperation.

"He's chasing half their army," Kendall noted. "It's the other half that's too much for us."

"All for nothing," another voice murmured. "It's all been for nothing."

"Shall we retreat?" asked Bishop Thomas.

"Where shall we retreat to?" Professor Wagner responded.

So, it had all been for naught. The planning, the prayers, the pretending in front of the men. Good, but not good enough. There was nothing left to do. The enemy would extend flanks, overlap us, and the Army of Kenesee would be done for good. I would attempt to run, and they would find me, and burn out my eyes and leave me to rot in a dungeon for thirty years.

I would not give them that pleasure.

Oh, well. It had been a short life, but the last ten years hadn't been too bad. And a quick end was certainly preferable to their plans for me. The horizon was brightening to the east, and I knew it was the last glow of dawn I would see. Soon it would all be over.

I raised my sword and pointed it at the enemy. "Sergeant Jenkins. One last time, if you please."

His features set. "Yes, sir. One last time. FOURTH SQUADRON!"

Around me, the royal guards readied their weapons and prepared to charge.

And then, from the woods behind the enemy line, there was the deep sound of a drum, and then more, all in unison, each boom hanging heavy in the air. For a moment the battle seemed to pause as both sides listened to the quickening beat of doom. The soldiers of the Alliance cast anxious glances behind them. A thick dark line of infantry, eight thousand at least, moved out of the woods, each sure step in cadence with the drums. They gave a massive shout and charged into the rear of the enemy.

"The beastmen!" shouted Murdock. "The beastmen have come!"

The Army of the Alliance dissolved.

And I fainted.

8

The Price of Victory

I opened my eyes and the spots faded to a circle of smiling faces that stared down at me in the torch light. There was Murdock and Lorich and Kendall and Wagner and Jenkins and the rest of the party. And with them were the faces of two beastmen, Major Kren and Senior Councilman Sokol.

Murdock shook his head in disapproval. "Another tradition you're starting, Arn?"

I looked in wonder at the beastmen. "You came."

They laughed and helped me to my feet.

Councilman Sokol nodded. "Yes, we did. The army has been assembled in the Beastwood for weeks and I'd been put in command again. We couldn't take any chances when the land is torn by war. Major Kren notified me of the disaster at Yellow Fields. And he told me what Mr. Kendall found out. Extermination or slavery."

"I'm glad," said Murdock, "the Council finally saw things clearly."

Councilman Sokol coughed. "Ahem. Well, you see, there wasn't time to gather the Council. I'm afraid I've violated the instructions they gave me to defend the borders. Kren told me about your plan. Quite a gamble, I must say.''

Kendall shook his head in amazement. ''And for you.''

''Well, yes it was. But we had no choice, now, did we? Not that the Council will see it that way. I'm afraid it will be time for me to retire now, in spite of the victory. I haven't slept well since your visit last fall, but I think that will no longer be a problem. This will be one for the history books, Wizard Murdock. I'm sorry your General Black isn't here to enjoy the victory.''

Victory. We had won. Then Black's name triggered a thought. ''The pursuit! We must organize a pursuit.''

''That's already been done,'' Murdock reassured me, pointing. Thousands of the Alliance had already surrendered to our men, but many more were fleeing in terror, our horsemen and infantry pursuing them in every direction and cutting them down as they ran.

''We'll need to take as many prisoners as we can for bargaining chips,'' Murdock continued. ''We want no citizen of Kenesee in the slave pens of the Texans. But I'm afraid there will be a good deal of slaughter, still. The men are in no mood for mercy.''

They had ample reason, as became clear when the sun rose above the hills and flooded the battlefield with pale light. We walked back towards the town, and the horrors of the night were revealed in full. In the fields we found what remained of the women of Lexington, moaning and weeping, their night of trial over. All had been ill used, a good number beaten, and a few score killed, the lucky ones quickly. There were a dozen of these just outside the town gates, and I tried not to see the bodies. In this, I failed.

Shocked and frightened by what they saw, Kendall and Sir Meredith wandered through the survivors, calling out.

''Megan! Megan, where are you?''

''Megan! We're here, Megan.''

And though some answered to the name, golden-haired Megan Sims was not to be found.

Within the walls a few buildings still burned, but much of the town was a smoking ruin, houses and shops reduced to burnt timbers and smoldering embers. The streets were covered with rubble, but a path could be made down the center of each, heat still radiating from stone and brick, the hot ash puffing up with each footstep. Scattered up and down the length of each street and alley were bodies, most half-buried in rubble, many swollen into blackened and charred corpses of which neither sex nor age could be determined.

The town square was barren, the town hall and all the buildings around it destroyed, with one last structure still burning. Even the grand trees in the square had not escaped, their now leafless skeletons blackened by the flames that had destroyed them. The emptied treasury wagons had been burnt too, and the ash covered the square as thickly as anywhere else. At the fountain several bodies lay, though whether killed by men or suffocated in the inferno we could not say. The fountain was still half-filled with water, brown from the ash and littered with burnt chips of wood.

And floating among the refuse was a round, wide-brimmed felt hat sporting two eagle feathers, stained with blood from brim to crown. Crazy Mary's vision had come true. My soothsayer would have no more bad news for me.

We went on, working our way slowly towards the Castle of Sims.

The castle was open, of course. The squad of infantry from the Sixth Regiment had done its job well, making sure the drawbridge was down and the gates standing wide. We had considered it important that the Alliance capture the place. Much of their leadership would want to see the first castle fallen to their might, and so would pass through all the temptations of the town to reach it. And it proved to them that our morale was completely broken, for not only were the town gates thrown open in surrender, but those left to guard the castle had fled rather than fight.

We went through the gates and into the courtyard. The castle seemed to have escaped the flames that had enveloped the town, although the ash had settled over everything here, too. Furniture and debris were scattered throughout. And there were bodies, of course. The bodies, fortunately or not, could be identified with little difficulty. A dozen dressed in Kenesee militia uniforms lay piled in one corner, perhaps a local unit captured in the streets, brought here under guard, and killed at some time during the night. A score of the enemy too were sprawled across the yard, and we found more inside, all cut down by our companies assigned to clear the town. Near the gate were the broken bodies of two serving girls.

"Look!" said Jenkins, pointing to the entrance of the main house.

Sprawled awkwardly across the steps, the thin corpse of a robed man rested, a javelin still thrust into his chest. Mottled hands clawed upward at the sky in one last denial of reality.

Murdock sighed. "Graven. Another friend gone. Lord, weigh his sacrifices and forgive his mistakes."

Lorich collapsed next to the corpse and took one of the hands in his own. He looked up at us, the tears already flowing. "The High Wizard was a great man, wasn't he?"

"Yes," I said, choosing my words carefully. "He was a great magician."

We went into the duke's house, and found where the main partying had gone on. Tapestries and paintings had been pulled down and torn, furniture overturned, art destroyed. The glass case Duke Gregory had kept his collection in was shattered, and most of the contents gone. But amidst the rubble were the remains of a wooden boat, broken in two.

It was in the duke's quarters that we found Megan and Angela, along with a half dozen other women in various bed chambers who had shared their fate. They were all alive, but just as battered as those survivors we had seen in the fields, if not more so. Bruises covered their bodies. Megan's arm was broken, and Angela had two cracked ribs as well as a cut on her head where she had been struck. It was unfair of me, I know, but I had hoped that their status, their location in the castle, might protect them, earning some measure of mercy from the soldiers of the Alliance. I had been wrong.

Broken. Everything was broken.

And I was responsible.

I was only dimly aware of Murdock calling all the aides and messengers and speaking softly to them. I heard the words, but they meant nothing to me. "Find the Colonels. Make sure those captured are all granted the Rights of Prisoners. Go. Quickly."

Kendall and Sir Meredith were with us, and they handled it

well, or as well as they might. Kendall even told me it was not my fault. It was nice of him to lie.

In the afternoon, both Beastwood and Kenesee units began to march back in. Some were tight-lipped and grim, some happy and joking, but all tired. Many came with droves of prisoners, and others brought carts and wagons filled with slain enemy. The victory had indeed been total. Hundreds, perhaps thousands, still hid in the hills and woods around us, desperately trying to make their way south or east. They would be collected over the next week or two. But almost twenty thousand prisoners had been counted already. The rest had paid with their lives for their rulers' folly.

We stayed another day, and buried our dead in long trenches in the valley. One short trench was also dug and the beastmen dead consigned to it. Over each a mound was raised, and banners left flying in respect. Other trenches were dug by the prisoners and the enemy dead piled in and buried.

Our only military disappointment was the failure to capture all the rulers of the Alliance. Patron Carlos Estevez of Mexico had surrendered right after the beastmen assault, his rank saving him from slaughter. Prime Minister Billy Bay of the Islands had fought his way clear of the beastmen, but fallen prey to our cavalry. His body was brought back for our inspection, and then buried in a separate grave near the trenches. I would have given him to the dogs, but the advisors felt it important to show respect. We still had many things to resolve with the Islanders, and with all our enemies. Additional cause for bitterness would not help. I tried to keep that in mind.

Governor Rodes of Virginia and General Jack Murphy had escaped with their parties, and cavalry patrols were sent out along the roads to search for them. The patrols brought in more prisoners, but these two could not be found. It was unlikely we could stop them from reaching the coast, and safety. Too late for the battle, our two cavalry regiments rejoined us after finally seeing the Arkans back across the Ohio River. We sent them forward with a few other regiments to sweep southwards and capture any of the enemy still left between Lexington and Kingsport.

Other than these units, the armies rested for a few days, and took care of the matters at hand.

Quite a trade sprang up between human and beastman in the two armies, perhaps as much an excuse for contact as a reason for it. After the first cautious hours, Sokol and I encouraged the familiarity. Fights between beastman and human did break out, but most of the troops had been sated with blood, and disputes were few. Tobacco, cloth, war trophies, and even coins of the realms became items for barter. Several of the more clever in both armies made small fortunes in the days we camped next to each other.

We went to see Robert, and I left the others outside while I talked with him. Jason the Healer and Dr. Amani were securing him to his cot so that he could be moved.

His face was no longer a death mask. "Arn. You've been busy."

"I'm sorry I couldn't come before. You look better."

"I'll live," he stated glumly.

"Jason did it," Dr. Amani added. "There's still much to learn from Pacifica."

Jason shrugged. "I couldn't have done it without the Royal Physician. And Robert has an amazing constitution. I've told him the worst, and the best. He'll always be crippled. But he may walk again, in a fashion, if all goes well. I'm just sorry I couldn't do more."

"Is he ready for duty?"

The two physicians exchanged glances. "Yes," they said together.

"Good. Thank you."

There was silence, and then they got the idea and left the two of us alone.

I started to pack the bowl of my pipe. "Robert, it's time for you to resume your duties."

He laughed. "Resume my duties? A bedridden cripple? A man who lost the battle of Yellow Fields? I think not."

"You may walk again."

"Perhaps," he said bitterly. "In a fashion."

I lit up. "We'll see. As for losing the battle, General Black told me you were just unlucky about the Texans. Your reasoning was sound. And he thought you fought the battle well."

Robert looked doubtful. "He did?"

"Oh, yes. 'Well done, Robert.' That's what he said. He

commended your use of the reserves, and how you tried to rally the men in the cut.''

"He was a fine leader,'' Robert sighed. "Like Father. The two were so different, and yet much alike. And now they're gone.''

"Yes, they are.''

"And you will lead,'' he countered.

I was in no mood for argument. "You're the King now.''

"I intend to resign.''

"And who'll take your place?'' I argued. "Don't look at me. I won't accept. I've done enough. God knows, I've done enough.''

He shook his head.

I plunged on. "You don't want it? All right, let's see, who would be next in line? So many were killed. Only some younger cousins are left in the House of Brant. Sir Meredith is the most popular, but not the most senior by rules of succession. His father, Duke Sims, is too old. So next in seniority would be—why, it's Duke Trudeau of Wickliffe. Now, I'll be the first to admit that Duke Trudeau is a good and gentle man. But as a King, he's as unfit as I, and you know it. Yes, the crown would go to Duke Trudeau, I do believe.''

He looked shocked. "You wouldn't let that happen!''

"Why not? If you can shirk your responsibilities, why can't I?''

He sputtered for a moment. "It's not proper.''

"Exactly,'' I agreed. "Enough foolishness. Get yourself ready to sign the treaty. I'm tired of doing your job while you take it easy.''

I stood up to go, and he put his hand upon my arm. Just a bit of his old strength had returned. "Arn. Do you think I'm fit? To govern?''

I covered his hand with my own. "Is there anyone in the kingdom with greater courage or honor?''

I came out and gestured to the royal party so that they clustered around me. "The King is ready to resume his duties.'' There was applause. "I return you to his service.'' More applause. "Thank you for your assistance during ... during these difficult days. You made victory possible.''

And to my surprise, they applauded again.

Robert was carried into the sunlight on his bed. He was weak and thin, but the color was back in his face, his faculties were intact, and he conducted himself like a king. The advisors and others clustered around him and extended their congratulations. He talked long with Sokol, then signed a treaty guaranteeing the borders of the Beastwood and requesting friendship and commerce. Sokol would have it in his pocket when he went back to the Council. Perhaps it would help.

I passed among the field hospitals that afternoon, Kenesee and Alliance wounded intermingled in tents. I made sure they were all sheltered and receiving the best care that could be provided, and assured them that all would be well. The enemy was due such care by the Rights of Prisoners. Lucky them.

Later I visited Megan and Angela, for the army would be heading south on the morrow, and Robert had ordered me to go with it as commander. Both women were still in bed, just beginning their recovery. Megan was sustained by her anger, taking grim satisfaction in each new tally of dead and wounded and prisoners suffered by the Alliance, and then inexplicably bursting into tears. I overheard when she asked Kendall the inevitable question.

Her face was battered and bruised, her lips swollen and cracked. "I have been—dishonored."

Kendall scoffed. "No one can dishonor another. One can only dishonor oneself."

She took hope from his words. "Do you still want me—like this?"

Kendall gave her a teary grin and held up the stump of his arm. "I was going to ask you the same thing."

Things seemed to go better for them after that.

As for Angela, she had lain half-conscious for several days from the head wound and drugs given her, and only on my last visit did she seem more aware of her surroundings. But she did not smile when I came to her, nor did the expression of sadness on her face change while I explained what had happened.

And the look was there in her eye. She did not ask the question as Megan had, but it remained hanging between us from the moment I sat at her bedside. Perhaps Kendall had the right idea about handling it.

"All that has happened here is my fault," I admitted. "The women of Lexington. The militia. Megan. You. My fault."

A bandage covered the side of her face, which was swollen and bruised. "I know," she said. "They told me."

"And your father."

"I heard."

"My fault too. Knowing all that . . . do you still want me?"

A smile appeared on her lips at last, and she grimaced at the pain of her effort. Her head moved on the pillow, a weak nod. All she could do. "Yes, Arn."

I kissed her gently on the cheek and bid her get well soon so she could return to the castle at Kingsport. I reminded her she still had two months as a king's server to complete. I think that made her happy, because she started to cry.

And that took care of that.

The next day the beastmen left us, marching off with Kenesee guides and scouts to smooth their journey. Major Kren joined us as we watched their passing. He would stay with the royal party at Lexington while the king recovered strength enough to travel. Kren would keep his duties as emissary, at least until a formal ambassador could be appointed.

He eyed the beastman army with satisfaction. "Thank God for Councilman Sokol. If any of the others had been in command, we'd still be sitting in the Beastwood, waiting for our turn. He didn't hesitate when I told him what the Alliance intended to do and what your plan was. We marched forty miles a day, you know. Murdock, you should have seen the expression on the faces of the villagers as we passed. In any case, it worked. That's all that counts. The threat is over."

"We owe you much," I admitted.

"Well, keep me in mind if you need a traveling companion. I've always wanted to see what lay beyond the next tree."

When the beastman army had cleared the road my party started south, the regiments of our army following smartly. Behind them the prisoners trudged along dejectedly, well guarded by cavalry and infantry. And so we left Lexington, its rape and battle over, and only the broken fragments of lives to be resumed, as they would have to be over all Kenesee—

and over all the Alliance, for that matter. We moved south at a relaxed pace, waking each dawn and moving after a leisurely breakfast. The weather was good, giving us beautiful days of warmth and sunshine. Further south, even Kelley's Inferno seemed benign, only a wisp of white smoke escaping from the cone and drifting innocently into the sky.

Our men were in high spirits when we started, but as we marched they became subdued, and after we passed Knox they were dour and moody. On one side of the road was a meadow, and in the meadow a charred and blackened spot where a king had rested one last time. The men began to sing the dirge as they passed, and I went and stood beside the spot for a long moment. I reached inside my pocket and touched the leather envelope that held his letters, but a numbness came over me, and at last I remounted and took a place in the long column. We approached the Yellow Fields reluctantly, and at that point the men marched in silence, some avoiding any glance at the fields, while others looked left and right, finding their positions and remembering that day all too well.

I rode to the crest with Murdock and the guards, and again halted. Much of the army passed by on the road below while I brooded, some regiments saluting, others showing respect with an informal wave of hands from the men in the ranks. The Sixth Regiment passed by without any gesture until Colonel Daniels's voice sang out his order. Their helmets came off, not for me, but were clutched to their chests respectfully as they entered the cut where their general had fallen.

The flowers were gone now, the green meadows decorated instead with abandoned and broken equipment. Shields, spears, swords, helmets, and all the other gear that is left after a great battle littered the field. Most of the dead had been collected. We found that burial trenches for each nationality of the Alliance had been lain out in the meadows while the Army of the Alliance basked in victory after Yellow Fields. Banners and standards flew above the freshly turned earth, and stones had been used to edge the burial sites. But only a raw mound of earth marked where the Kenesee dead had been rolled into a giant pit and covered over. The internment had been done with no disrespect, but with little care.

"Wait here," I ordered, and then dismounted and walked forward alone. I found the spot below the crest where General

Black had stood and directed our regiments, and then I walked down into the cut to the scene of our counterattack against the Alliance breakthrough. The prisoners were passing now on the road nearby, a continuous stream stretching back out of sight beyond the trees to the north. They watched me as they passed, and the knowledge of who I was went down the line in whispers. I thought I found the spot where Robert was wounded and Black fell, but I couldn't be sure exactly. Had it been on this side of the road, or the other side? The grass had been washed clean in a shower, and was growing green and long. I crossed the road and the column parted for me as I strode through.

I went around an enemy burial trench and out to the mound of earth covering the Kenesee dead. It came to my chest, an uneven pile of clods and clumps of soil and clay at which I stared for a long time. He was in there, somewhere. I reached deep into a pocket and felt his pipe and pouch, safe in their confines. I took the pipe out and opened the pouch, smelling the rich aroma of the blend he liked so much.

I thought of him long ago sitting in the Silver Spur, puffing away, writing in his notebook and raising an eyebrow at the ragged boy before him. I could hear him teaching us in the tower classroom, patiently drumming in the principles of war. I could see him standing straight and tall, his eyes sweeping the battlefield, the men chanting his name. And I remembered him clutching us to him after the victory of the Crossroads.

"John?" I called out softly. "Can you hear me? We did it, John."

But there was no answer.

He was gone, like so many others.

And then I thought of Reuel, and Robert, and Kieno and Angela and Megan and the women of Lexington and the Army of Kenesee and the gutter rats shivering in the alleys and cellars and doorways of the world.

I felt wetness on my cheeks.

A hand touched my shoulder and Murdock stood beside me. "So, the bottle overflows at last. It has to do that, or shatter."

I shook my head. "A gutter rat never cries."

He smiled gently. "I forgot. Here, use my kerchief. Wipe your eyes. Blow your nose. Good. All right now, that's better."

He was silent a moment. "You know," he said at last, "he's resting with his men. That's not a bad ending for a soldier. And I think he'd be pleased at how things turned out."

"Do you think so?"

"He'd be proud of you, Arn. You've done great things."

"Great things."

"Come, Arn, it's time to go. One day we'll come back and visit him. There will be grass growing here and trees planted and flower beds. And every year there'll be yellow fields again, and we can remember him then. We can remember them all."

I followed him back to the road, where Jenkins waited with our horses. Strange. The guardsman's cheeks were red, and streaked with tears.

"Everything all right, Jenkins?" I asked.

"Yes, sir."

"It almost looks like you've been . . ."

"Hay fever, sir. A royal guard never—"

I held up my hand and he fell silent.

I patted Jenkins on the shoulder and gave him my kerchief. "I know."

"Thank you, sir."

"It's time to go," Murdock reminded us.

We mounted and fell into column behind the prisoners. I looked back at the battlefield one last time, and then forward towards Kingsport.

There was much to do.